MAROC

DANIEL EASTERMAN

HarperCollins*Publishers*

HarperCollins*Publishers*
77–85 Fulham Palace Road,
Hammersmith, London W6 8JB

www.fireandwater.com

Published by HarperCollins*Publishers* 2002
1 3 5 7 9 8 6 4 2

A catalogue record for this book
is available from the British Library

ISBN 0 00 225862 5
ISBN 0 00 225864 1 (trade pbk)

Typeset in Sabon by Palimpsest Book Production Limited,
Polmont, Stirlingshire

Printed and bound in Great Britain by
Clays Ltd, St Ives plc

Daniel Easterman was born in Ireland in 1949. He is the author of 13 critically acclaimed novels.

To Beth: because you're worth it.
What's more, you're worth more than
the entire world.

Thanks to the very best of editors and most loyal of friends, Patricia Parkin.

Thanks to my dapper agent, Giles Gordon, for his many efforts. And, above all others, thanks to my shining and insightful wife, Beth.

The translation of the poem by Ali Mahmud Taha on page 264 is by the author.

In the City of Dreaming Spires

Prologue

Marrakech
November 1942

The interrogations had taken a long time, and neither Abd el-Krim nor the woman who had made him welcome looked the same by the time the beatings were done. It had been too late for her to destroy the papers he'd brought, to burn or swallow them, but she hadn't talked, hadn't given them a single name. Abd el-Krim had broken, and had given them every name he knew, but they were just the names of family and friends – what other names did he have to give them?

They marched them outside. In the windows of the houses opposite, curtains twitched and fell back. Two cars were waiting, each one with a Gestapo officer in the front seat. Abd el-Krim and the woman were thrown onto the rear seat of the first car, and the door slammed after them. The engine revved, and the car pulled away from the kerb at speed, followed by the second.

They drove for about half an hour. Abd el-Krim could say nothing, but he was certain he was to blame for what had happened. As he ran into the arms of his captors, he had caught sight of a face he was sure he recognized, the face of Mbarak, whom he had never known very well. He wanted to apologize to the woman, but his mouth had been so badly beaten, he could not form words.

The cars stopped on a narrow country road somewhere in the Atlas foothills, by the side of a small field. Suddenly, Abd el-Krim felt deadly sick. He bent down to throw up, but all he could manage was a dry, racking cough. The woman helped him to his feet.

'Don't be afraid,' she said.

'*Déshabillez-vous. Vous, madame, et le garçon. Venez, venez.*'

They undressed as ordered. Nakedness meant nothing out here. Just once Abd el-Krim looked round and saw the woman naked, and thought she was very beautiful, except that her face had been beaten to a pulp and her hands were bleeding.

They were marched beneath a stand of trees, and lined up together. It was almost evening, and a wind had sprung up from the mountains, chilling them. As they came to a halt, the woman did something Abd el-Krim would have considered unthinkable until that place and that moment. She reached out and took his hand in hers and held it tightly. He squeezed back, even though he still did not know her name, and she was a Christian, and she was naked.

'Stand straight!' the senior policeman ordered.

Abd el-Krim looked up and saw four other policemen holding guns in their hands, pointed at him and the woman. Would they kill him for a small packet? For his ignorance?

He was dead before the sound of the first gunshot reached his ears. The woman was pulled to the ground, her hand still clutching his, and she thought she'd been hit. She waited for the pain from the bulletholes, but it didn't come; and she waited for death, thinking it might come before the pain reached her, then thought that she was dead already, but still aware of her surroundings.

Someone grabbed her by the wrist, and someone else tore her hand from Abd el-Krim's. One of the men in Gestapo uniform pulled her to her feet.

'You,' he snapped. 'Get dressed. You're coming with us.'

'You may as well shoot me here,' she said, stubbornly. 'There's nothing you can do that will make me talk.'

'By the time we've finished with you,' he said, 'you'll do anything to be allowed to talk.'

1

Oxford
March 2002

Somehow, Nicholas thought, sunshine had become a thing of the past. He looked out of the window onto Broad Street and wondered why spring was proving so coy this year again. Of course, wondering was pointless: they all knew what it was, it was global warming. Global warming, by a great irony, was taking away the sunshine, abolishing the seasons, substituting rain for warm summer afternoons and sleet for midwinter snow, and causing plants to flower at improper times. All so needless, all so preventable.

'I think we should commission a book on global warming. What do you think?' He continued looking down into the street, where students, not yet in the frenzy of exams, strolled in and out of Blackwell's, or headed off to start a lifetime of unsatisfactory springs. He saw a startlingly pretty girl pass, heading for Parks Road. Two young men followed close behind her. His heart jammed until she had gone by.

'It's been done,' Tim bellowed from the next room.

'Yes, I know, but . . .'

Nicholas turned and walked to the doorway that separated them.

'I was thinking of a series,' he said. 'Small books. Hundred, hundred and fifty pages each. Just little manuals, you see.'

'All on global bloody warming?'

'Yes, but regionally based. "Global Warming and East Anglia", "The Effect of Global Warming on Scotland". You get my drift.'

'I think I do.'

'We could get good regional sales. People want to know if it's safe to build a house on a spare piece of land, how their environment will change. They'd sell in spadefuls.'

Tim stood up. He'd been fine-tuning the wording on the new Ben Foley contract. Foley was Déjà Vu's star, an author they'd been building steadily from day one, whose sales were beginning to attract interest from the shops. He was young, good looking, trendy, and he got good reviews; it was just a matter of time before he broke through into the big time, taking Déjà Vu with him. Provided he stayed loyal to the publishing house that had found and nurtured him.

Tim had set up Déjà Vu two years earlier with severance money from his firm of architects, when they'd been bought up by a huge American enterprise and forced to make half their staff redundant. He'd always wanted to run a publishing house, and at forty-five it had seemed too good an opportunity to pass by.

His brother Nicholas had joined him one year later, when he'd taken early retirement from the police force, from

Special Branch, to be precise. Nick had been a Special Branch Commander, one of the Branch's experts on terrorism – Irish, Islamic, right wing.

Three years before that, Nick's French wife Nathalie had left him, and he'd started to find work difficult. So many of the incidents he was called to were enough to darken anyone's day. Previously, he'd led a second life with Nathalie, a life totally separate from the one he led at work. They'd gone to operas and concerts, there'd been time for plays and French cinema (she loved Roemer with a passion, he liked to keep his knowledge of the language fresh). Without her to take him in hand, he'd let an enormous workload build up over him until he could no longer breathe.

When he suddenly offered his resignation and said what he was planning to do, there'd been a lot of sharply intaken breaths at Special Branch headquarters. His former colleagues had been shocked, not just because he'd decided to cut short a career that might have taken him to the very top, but also because he'd joined a publishing outfit, of all things.

Publishers, like newspapers, were old enemies, and none of Nicholas's former colleagues was easy with the thought that one of their number, ripe with so many hellish memories, should have turned up in one of the few places where cans of worms were held in high esteem.

For his part, Nicholas had not even thought of using Déjà Vu as a vehicle for airing his discontents. None of his colleagues, now making haste to hide files and bury evidence, need have lost a moment's sleep. Nicholas wasn't a rat, and even if, on cold reflection, he knew he could bargain his way to a decent six-figure sum from a mainstream publisher, he also knew it just wasn't him.

In any case, he knew as well as anyone the sort of hassle he could expect if he did wash some dirty socks in the presence of Jeremy Paxman and the *Newsnight* audience. They'd do everything they could to break him. They'd plant false evidence, they'd have him arrested as a paedophile, they'd crucify him on the nearest tree. Above all, there'd be a trial at the Old Bailey, one that would break him even if he won the day. He preferred to stay where he was.

'Not everybody believes in global warming, you know. I don't think you have to. I don't think it's compulsory. But you may be on to something. Let's see if we can find some pliable young meteorologist from the university, someone willing to take fifty pounds as an advance and present us with the first six titles in less than a year.'

Tim looked at his wrist.

'By the way, Nick, that was Peter on the phone just now. He's in town, and he says he'd like to have lunch with both of us.'

'Is something up?'

Peter was Nicholas's son, a journalist of twenty-five, unmarried, globetrotting, more often than not in a jam of some sort.

Tim shrugged.

'Hard to tell. But, yes, I think he sounded . . . not quite himself. I said we'd see him in the Old Parsonage in half an hour. You free?'

'I, ah . . . yes.' Nicholas frowned. 'I was hoping I could read through young Foley's contract, once you've finished going through the clauses that need fine-tuning. Look, let's just leave it till after lunch, then maybe we can both cast an eye over everything before it goes to his agent. You are planning to stay on this afternoon aren't you?'

'Very likely. Unless something comes up with Peter, of course. He did sound a little . . .'

'Anxious?'

When Nathalie had walked out four years ago, Nick had been expected to shoulder all the burdens of being a parent to grown-up children. Peter had been twenty-one, and Nick's daughter, Marie-Josephine, just eighteen and starting a degree course at Edinburgh. It had been a factor in his leaving the police force.

'No, more flat. He sounded down.'

'That's not good.' There had been episodes of depression in Peter's past; nothing serious, but he'd always been coaxed through them by his mother. When Nathalie had gone, Peter had needed fresh treatment, and Nick had found himself in the front line when the drugs weren't working perfectly, or when a fresh psychological blow came along to knock the boy off his balance. Nick had not begrudged the hours spent listening to his son's fears and anxieties. They had brought him much closer to Peter than he had been since his son was growing up.

Nick sighed. 'I take it this has something to do with the new girlfriend.'

'Who, Daisy? They've been together a year or so now, haven't they? I thought she was a nice girl. Very pretty, and far brainier than the young man himself, if you don't mind my saying so.' Tim had two sons, neither of them the high-flyers he'd once hoped they would be.

'No, not at all,' said Nick. 'That's what I think too, as a

10

matter of fact. Smart girl. Pete's bright, but he's not in her league.'

'She's got the right disposition, though, don't you think? Sunny.'

'You mean she can handle his down times?'

Tim nodded.

'I got the impression she loved him like crazy, and could do a lot of listening.'

Nick smiled at his brother. 'You're right. We'll get her to write a book about it in a few years' time.'

Nick and Tim had once quarrelled, but now, working together, they found little occasion to argue. Nicholas had known Tim on and off all his life. There were only three years between them. They'd been close as boys, had fallen out badly when Tim was twenty-one and Nick eighteen, over the same seventeen-year-old girl, but had picked up the pieces in their thirties and continued much as before since then. Nicholas knew exactly what his brother meant.

'You don't think he could have news of Nathalie?' Nick asked. 'It's not impossible, is it? Actually, it must be that: it's his birthday in a week or so. Nathalie would never let it go past without getting in touch.'

Even after all this time, Nick had no clear idea why Nathalie had left him. He guessed at this or that, but there'd been no note, no definite reason. He was sure she still contacted Peter, and Marie-Josephine, their daughter. Most of the time Nick thought it was because he'd been a policeman, and negligent of her.

'Does she get in touch?' asked Tim. 'With Peter, I mean. He would never tell me. He's still very loyal to her.'

'She contacts him now and then, I think. He never says

anything to me about it, if she does. Marie-Josephine gets all the postcards. Pete never was Nathalie's favourite.'

'Wasn't he?' Tim seemed bemused. He'd never been good with children, and blamed his own boys' lack of success on his having been so busy while they were growing up. 'I thought she treated him perfectly well when he was a little boy. He was delightful, and she used to speak with him so prettily in French.'

'It wasn't that she didn't love him, just that she came to prefer Marie-Josephine.'

Nicholas felt the anger and hurt coming into his voice, against his will, felt emotions rise that he had long fought to suppress or eradicate. He went on.

'Pete was very badly hurt by what she did. I honestly think he found it harder to cope than I did when she walked out. He had to see a doctor, I know that. Just don't pass it on; it's confidential. Pete never forgave her. I doubt if she'd be in touch with him now if it wasn't for his birthday.'

'I never knew he took it so badly, Nick.' Tim was sympathetic. He too found it hard to understand why his sister-in-law had taken it into her head to get up early one morning, leave the house, and never return. 'When it happened, I was more concerned about you, to tell the truth. Maybe you didn't see a medicine man, but you were badly affected. You'd never have taken early retirement if it hadn't been for old Nat running off.'

'Less of the "old Nat".'

Nathalie had been the seventeen-year-old they'd had the falling-out over. Taller than most girls her age, she'd been slim, green eyed, vivacious, and French: the most beautiful creature either of the brothers had set eyes on until then.

12

She'd been in Oxford on a year-long study exchange, and had been staying with neighbours of theirs.

She came from a wealthy family in Reims and was perfecting her English, not with any aim of getting into university or pursuing a career, but in order to be polished enough to bring out in society. At seventeen, she'd been a lot more mature than the average thirty-year-old, and if passion had not seduced her to a life in England, she'd have gone back to Reims to make a good marriage to some wealthy bachelor with a small château in the Loire and a villa in the hills above Nice. The middle classes of Oxford never recovered from having her in their midst.

Nicholas, although three years younger than Tim, had won her heart by means both fair and foul. Of the two brothers, he had always been the more confident, and so it had turned out in wooing Nathalie.

It had been to Nick's benefit that Tim, although better looking, more intelligent and older, had been forced back to university, to his lengthy course in architecture, within months of the brothers meeting the object of their affections.

Nicholas, still working for his A levels, had used guile to further his chances. He had hidden letters from Tim to Nathalie and, when asked to pass on messages, had failed to do so. He'd asked her out, she'd found him dashing, he'd dared to kiss her on their third date, she'd responded with an eager tongue. It was all decided, then, in an autumn and winter of love and brotherly deceit.

By the time Tim returned for the Christmas vacation, Nathalie was out of his reach for ever. At first, not understanding this, he had continued to court her until, one day in the long interstice between Boxing Day and the New Year, she had told him everything.

Nicholas, less intellectual than his wounded and unforgiving brother, had headed for police college. On the day of his graduation, he and Nathalie had married in a quiet ceremony in Oxford Town Hall.

A year or so after that, Tim built his first commission, a block of ten postgraduate flats for Wadham College. Two days later, still heady with his passion for bricks and glass and mortar, he fell madly in love with a secretary in the college bursar's office. They married soon afterwards, and were still married.

Nick had married Nathalie in a haze of passion, a haze that had never really left him. Now, so many years later, he was still in love with her. Her unannounced departure had left him numb, and her refusal to communicate with him churned up feelings he'd rather not have known existed. Yet he loved her and would have her back if she ever decided to return.

'I think it's time we made tracks,' said Tim. 'I'll leave Foley here. He won't mind.' He put his head round the door of his office. 'Jenny, will you please remember to ring that blasted software company, and tell them if they don't have our copy of the new version of InDesign on my desk tomorrow morning, the order's cancelled. Thank you, Jenny. Have a nice lunch.'

'I'm just going to pop to the loo,' said Nick.

With the door closed behind him, he ran the cold tap and splashed some water onto his face. He fumbled for the towel and dried himself. As he put the towel back on its rail, he looked up at his reflection in the mirror. For the first time, he saw himself as he really was, a man of sorrow and guilt. Sorrow for having lost the only woman he'd ever loved, and guilt for having taken so little care of her.

He made up his mind to find her, wherever she was, and to bring her back to continue their interrupted life.

2

'This arrived with the morning post.'

Peter Budgeon pushed a battered-looking envelope across the table, to where his father and uncle were sitting. The envelope had been opened, and in one corner there peeped out the edge of some light pink paper, on which a deliberate hand had written in heavy black ink. A faint odour of perfume rose from inside.

Tim bent down and drew back again.

'Lalique,' he said. 'It's sold in the most beautiful bottles. I bought some for Sinéad for her last birthday. Cost me a bloody fortune.'

Sinéad was Tim's Irish wife, his compensation for the lost Nathalie, an award-winning poet and lyricist, beautiful as winter sun, and as cold. She attended launch parties, soignée and poised, a Yeatsian figure with dim emerald eyes and clothes of silk, on the hunt for gauche young authors to whom she would give lessons on her long slim body at weekends after Mass. Tim put up with her, and for the most part adored her, though he thought of his brother's missing spouse more often than his own, and with more spirit, and with unfailing erotic intent.

Nicholas glanced at the handwriting on the envelope. The letter had been sent from France, but the postmark was blurred and illegible.

'It's your mother's handwriting,' he said.

'There's no doubt of that,' said Peter. He looked round at his fellow diners, heard their animated conversations, and wondered if coming here for lunch had been such a good idea. They needed privacy, if what he thought was true.

'Never knew her to use this perfume, though. Or write on pink paper. It seems such an affectation.'

'Read the letter, Father. We can discuss the niceties afterwards.'

Nicholas bent to the task in hand.

'Dear Peter,' the letter began.

I should be writing this in French, but I know how you think that's terribly bourgeois, so I won't. I suppose I ought to be writing to your father, offering some kind of explanation for my conduct, but I won't do that either. I feel no sense of obligation towards anyone, least of all my husband or my children. I love you all, of course I do, but love was never enough somehow, and domesticity came near to killing me.

Darling, you'll find out when you're a lot older that there often comes a time when it doesn't really matter any more. Going on, I mean, trying to be of some use, or some significance. Whatever ambitions you may once have had bid farewell and sneak away overnight, much as I did. And hopes and dreams, you can't imagine what traitors they are. And you start to wonder to yourself, what's the point of hanging around, waiting for a place in some dreary old folk's home in Bournemouth or Wigan?

17

And the years ahead don't seem much of a consolation any more; it's not as though they're preferable to death.

Marie-Josephine tells me you have a nice new girlfriend. I hope this one lasts a few years at least. You shouldn't marry, it's not clever at your age. I married your father when I was much too young, and however happy we were, I could never lose that sense of having forfeited my youth. He was just a policeman, after all. I hadn't sacrificed myself to a genius, a painter or a composer or a great singer, as I'd once planned. At first, that's all right, you make a virtue of it, and the sex is great, then there's the minor thrill of being married to the Mob, as it were. But the sex gets routine, he's with the Mob more than he's with you, and you can't tell anyone because not even your children are supposed to know he's with Cosa Nostra.

You and Marie-Josephine were a wonderful distraction for a while, as children are. MJ was fey and winsome, as lovely a daughter as a spoiled creature like myself might have been blessed with. People used to say she got her pale looks from me, and when she was small, she was biddable and weak, mine to fashion as I wished. You were always your own person, and I never won your affections as I did Marie-Josephine's.

What did it matter in the end, anyhow? You didn't stay children for long, you'd both left me even before you left home. I'd enjoyed being a mummy while it lasted, reading bedtime stories in my funny accent, baking birthday cakes, cramming stockings with presents, trimming the Christmas tree. I always enjoyed your English Christmas much more than my French Noël. Then you grew up and told me there was no Santa Claus, no old man in a white beard tramping through the snow with a sack on his back. My world fell apart when you told me that.

18

Your father saw none of this; he had his work and his security of the realm to see to. I used to offer myself to him in bed, like a bawd, like a French *putain*. You never knew what went on behind our bedroom door. He had time for it at first; wasn't I supple? I had a gift for satisfying men in bed. But the IRA, and Hizbollah, and the National Front, men who had never seen me arch my back, soon started to come to bed with us. I'd see them as if they were really there, row upon row, just standing watching, their pigs' eyes on him, not me.

In the end, I just left. Was there another man? Perhaps, perhaps not, it really doesn't matter now. I'm altered anyway, alone or in company. I can't come back, I know that with absolute certainty. Perhaps, if my mother hadn't died, if they hadn't sent me that box, if I hadn't opened it ... Well, we'd all like to go back and undo things, wouldn't we? Untie the strings, or tie them up again. Bind up old wounds, suture the past, lay sticking plasters on every inch of cut and bruised flesh. I'm sorry, I wish we could be a family again, but it's the one thing I can't do. I don't have enough sticking tape.

Another thing I can't do is face that old people's home in Wigan. Or Nice or Deauville for that matter. Old girls like I'd become, leaning on their zimmer frames, melancholy and in search of death. Well, Peter, I'm melancholy enough, and I've been in search of death for as long as I can remember. Death as repair or death as oblivion, I really couldn't care less. It's the peace I'm after. The afternoon nap in the conservatory, the moment on the beach when the waves stand still and fall no more.

By the time you receive this letter ... No, I won't complete that banal sentence. It's just that I hate springing surprises. The truth is, I've set no timetable for myself, I have no date, no precise hour or season. But I won't write again. Show this to whomever you like, I'm past caring, or will be. Apologize to Marie-Josephine; I think she believed she had the strength to bring me back. None of you has that strength. *Sois courageux, sois fort, sois gentil.*

Ta Maman

Nicholas let the letter fall to the table, on a spot where red wine had stained the cloth. He seemed frozen, as though Nathalie had written a witch's spell for him to read, all unsuspecting. She'd seemed a witch to him from the very start, tenacious, self-willed, seductive, possessed of all the powers of enchantment and guile. This letter topped all that. It was as if she'd stepped off a roof somewhere beyond the sea, and he'd caught a glimpse where he stood, while watching the horizon, straining his eyes for her.

Tim took the letter.

'May I?' he asked. He addressed his request to Peter: the letter had been addressed to him, after all.

'Yes, of course. By all means. I'd value your opinion.'

Nicholas looked up.

'Have you told Marie-Josephine about this?'

Marie-Josephine was in her final year studying history of art at Edinburgh. She'd been very close to her mother. Nathalie had sent her postcards from towns with blurred postmarks: melancholy sunsets, unidentifiable ruins, the interiors of tiny churches filled with candle wax and small flickering flames.

Peter shook his head.

'I don't think we should say anything to her until we know what's going on,' he said.

'Isn't it obvious what's going on?'

'You mean, she's gone and done it? She's topped herself?'

Nicholas looked at his son reprovingly; but earlier battles had convinced him there was nothing to be gained by criticizing Pete's use of language.

'As a matter of fact,' he said, 'I don't think we should assume anything of the sort. Notes like this get written every day, and in most cases the writer's alive and well somewhere, frightened to come out and admit to their embarrassment. It's what these notes are for, to frighten a husband or wife, to persuade everyone who reads them that they need to be taken seriously, that life is a burden to them.'

'A cry for help, in other words.'

Nicholas shrugged.

'Sometimes, I'm sure. Other times, I don't know. They're more like a punishment: "You treated me badly. This is what you deserve."'

'Did we treat her badly?'

'She seems to think so. Or she thinks I did, at least.'

Tim looked up.

'I don't think it matters who upset her,' he said. 'Nick's right. People write these to get attention, or they write them and chicken out. There's no need to rush to conclusions. She's probably alive. But if she is threatening suicide, then it's imperative we get to her. I take it neither of you has any idea where she could be?'

They shook their heads simultaneously.

'She mentions Nice and – what's the other one?'

'Deauville,' said Peter. 'One's in the south of France, the

other in the far north. She could be in either one, she could be in the next town along . . . she might not be in France at all.'

'Nick, this is your territory. If this were a police investigation, what would you do?'

'Grind my teeth. Missing person jobs are among the hardest. If somebody doesn't want to be found . . .'

'But she sent this letter. Why don't we assume it *is* some sort of cry for help, that she wants us to find her? There must be somewhere we can turn.'

'I'll ring Marie-Josephine.' Peter was suddenly sure it was the right thing after all.

He took his mobile down to the little foyer, and sat on the sofa to make the call. It took several rings before she answered.

'MJ? It's Pete. Listen, have you heard from Mother?'

'What, you mean a phone call?'

'No, a letter or something.'

'Not for a couple of weeks. Have you heard from her?'

'I'm in Oxford, MJ. With Dad and Uncle Tim. I had a letter this morning. I think you'd better take the first train down.'

3

Deauville

She was in Deauville. That was all Marie-Josephine knew. The postcards she'd been sent contained few clues. Some were clearly from the south, but the more recent ones had shown hints of northern skies, and one had shown a glimpse of Les Planches, the decked shopping strip that skirted the beach in Deauville.

'She forgets that I spent a summer in Deauville,' said Marie-Josephine. 'With my obnoxious pen friend Lucette. We were both ten. I was small for my age, and she was rather large, and she spent the entire summer knocking me down. She was odious, and her parents were just as bad. When I was on my own, which was precious seldom, I used to walk down Les Planches and look in the shops, wishing I was anywhere but Deauville.'

'Might she have gone there . . . ?' Peter's voice died away in his throat.

'For revenge?'

'No, of course not. In all likelihood, Lucette Hautekeur's long married and blessed with ugly children. But, mother . . . to meet someone, perhaps, to . . .'

23

'She wasn't seeing anyone, I'm certain of that.'

'Father . . .' Marie-Josephine took his arm tentatively, then let it fall. 'In her letter . . .'

'Yes, I know, she says "perhaps, perhaps not". I can't make anything of that.'

'Was there anyone in Deauville?' asked Tim. 'I don't mean another man, not necessarily. But an old friend, perhaps. A friend of the family, her family.'

Nathalie's family had been commerçants *in Reims. The Le Tourneaus had acted as middlemen to the great champagne houses for several generations, exporting their produce to an ever-widening range of countries. Their shop in Reims was small, disguising vast chalk cellars in which they stored bottles bearing the labels of Krug, Mumm, Canard-Duchêne, Gosset, Hamm, and numerous others. Nathalie's father, Gérard, had been a younger son. In the autumn of 1936, thinking to expand the family's fortunes and his own, he had married Béatrice Bombois, who had trained as a grape-grower and wine-producer in neighbouring Epernay.*

The newly-weds went straight from the altar to a wedding breakfast based around the consumption of half the champagne in Reims. Not quite as sober as good manners required, nor half as drunk as they might have been, given the circumstances, they made their way to the railway station, where they boarded the Paris train.

In Paris, a taxi took them straight to the boulevard des Capucines, to the agence *of the travel company P.-O.-Midi, where their tickets were waiting for them. They had ordered a pair of* billets directs simples, *one-way tickets that would*

24

take them via Bordeaux and across Spain, all the way to their final destination of Fès. The journey would take them exactly fifty-five hours, something unheard of, Gérard said more than once, not so many years ago. He'd been out before, and he knew the ropes.

They lunched late at the Tour d'Argent, as planned. The patron, André Terrail, was an old friend of the Le Tourneau family, from whom he bought all his champagne. He gave them the best table on the newly opened sixth-floor terrace. Béatrice, who had never been to Paris before, was treated to the best view of Notre Dame in the city. The heart of Paris lay at her feet, while some of its finest food made its way to her hungry stomach. At three o'clock, the bells of Sainte Anne, Sainte Geneviève and Sainte Clothilde heralded her ortolans sur canapé, and when they struck the half hour, a plate of homard à la parisienne was gently placed in front of her.

Before the happy couple left, M. Terrail appeared again, this time carrying a large shiny black box, which he presented to Mme Le Tourneau, with a knowing look in the direction of her loving husband. Béatrice would open this box later on the train and find that it contained a long black dress with gold embroidery from the suddenly fashionable atelier of Elsa Schiaparelli. Years later, she would discover from Schiaparelli herself that the dress had been designed with the help of Jean Cocteau. It would pass from Béatrice to her daughter Nathalie, and from Nathalie, in the past few days, it had now come down to Marie-Josephine, whom, by some sleight of destiny, it fitted perfectly, as it had fitted her mother and grandmother before her.

Having eaten what they thought might well prove to be

their last really civilized meal, the young couple – he was thirty-five, she twenty – they did some last-minute shopping, adding several kilos to their already generous first-class baggage allowance. Some hours later, they turned up at the quai d'Orsay railway station and boarded the Sud-Express train, which would take them to Bordeaux overnight.

Once inside their private compartment, the blinds closed, the light soft against the mahogany panelling, they undressed, all thumbs and averted glances. As the train began to pull away from the platform, so they started to make love for the first time. For the rest of her married life, Nathalie's mother would always associate the vigorous poundings of sexual intercourse with the thrustings of a well-oiled railway locomotive as it hurtled through the night.

The next day they changed at Madrid, into the wagons-lits of Spanish Railways. Another tedious journey brought them to Algeciras, where they caught the ferry for Tangier. Disembarking several hours later after a rough crossing, they fell into the pell-mell that was Morocco. Mesmerized by the sights and sounds that assaulted them as they descended the gangplank, they struggled to keep clear heads for the remaining leg of their journey. Once their suitcases had safely cleared customs – and they had brought a lot of luggage – they found a barouche to spin them to the railway station.

Here, they ate in a convenient little café that served French food and wine. They lingered over the wine knowingly, and with a sense of anticipation. For had they not given up everything to take up residence in a small farm they had bought near Meknès, where they planned to grow grapes and produce wine à la mode Française? They were not *the first colons to see an opening in a market that grew and sold alcoholic beverages in a Muslim country, but they hoped to be the first to produce champagne-quality sparkling wine – if they could only find a region suitable for growing the Pinot Noir, Meunier and Chardonnay grapes on which the enterprise depended. With their luggage, they had brought boxes of seedling vines, ready to be planted in Moroccan soil.*

At a table on their left sat a group of Germans, distinguishable by their language and the arrogance with which they treated everyone.

'Should we be worried by them, darling?' asked Mme Le Tourneau, sipping her oversweet mint tea through brightly painted lips.

Her husband shrugged. After all, he'd been out before. He could be blasé if he chose.

'I shouldn't think so,' he said, frowning at something. He'd asked for a coffee, but it tasted bitter, and he did not trust the milk. 'They'd be up against the French empire. They'd be cut off if they tried to make any moves in Africa. Relax, dear. Let them enjoy their day in the sun. And, by the way, just for me, would you mind very much using a less ... vibrant lipstick? I think scarlet is rather vulgar, don't you?'

'No,' said Nicholas. 'No one she ever told me about.'

'All the same, we have to consider a lover,' said Pete. 'There's always the question of her mother.'

'Like mother, like daughter, is that what you mean?' Nicholas was growing irritated.

'I'm sorry, Dad, but ... it bears consideration.'

'Look, there's no point in speculating.' Tim hated to see his brother so self-deceived. 'Whatever her reasons for leaving, whatever took her to Deauville, we have to find her and bring her back if we can.'

'If she wants to come.' Marie-Josephine, who had no lover, but wished one would appear sooner rather than later, disliked what her mother had done, but found herself defending her from this phalanx of male relatives and their easy assumption of female guilt.

'I'll go,' said Nicholas. 'Out of all of us, I think it's best I go.'

'I'd rather you didn't, Dad. You'll only intimidate her, make her feel guilty. Let me go. She trusts me.' Marie-Josephine felt as though she'd argued with her father since birth. She'd been her mother's choice, almost too predictably, and, like her mother, she'd chosen the arts as a profession. Her father's police work, and his personal devotion to it, left her cold and sometimes indignant.

'It's better I go first, love. If she's in Deauville, I can find her. Quickly.'

He meant, *before she does herself harm*; but they all knew, it was what they all feared.

'And if you do find her? Shouldn't I be there to talk to her?'

He shook his head.

'I'd rather be alone. But if I find her, I'll ring you right away. Stay in Oxford and be ready to come.'

'I'll come with you as far as Le Havre. I'll wait there.'

He reflected.

'Yes, very well. That's not a bad idea.'

*   *   *

28

They took the earliest available flight from London City airport, an Air France twin-prop that left at 7.55 and arrived in Le Havre at 8.45. The flight went by in near silence. They sat together, listening to the tight thrumming of the engines, growing unsettled as the turbulence rose in intensity. Marie-Josephine had never been a good flyer.

'Hold my hand, Dad. I can't stand all this bumping and banging about. Why on earth do they take off in weather like this?'

'It suits their schedule. But we're safe enough.'

He took her hand and squeezed it, and somehow it seemed good to do so after so much time. Holding her hand brought back memories of Marie-Josephine as a little girl. What had come between them? he wondered. His work? Or something more basic, something that separates fathers from daughters all their lives?

'She's dead, isn't she?' she asked. The plane lurched upwards, seemingly out of control, and she clutched his hand even more tightly.

He never had a chance to answer. An announcement, made first in French then English, told them it was time to prepare for the descent. Marie-Josephine closed her eyes, and they went down out of the storm together without speaking again.

Deauville still clung to the last of its winter sleep. A grey sky wrapped it from above, and a curtain of icy rain hung between the long beach and the sea. Drab waves, their edges ragged, swept in from the Channel and fell spent on the granite-coloured sand. Seagulls, driven by hunger, squawked and railed, rising and dropping on sudden currents, diving on anything that moved. Nicholas walked along the shore, on a straight line between the casino and the sea. He saw a rider, his head bent down low across his horse's mane, make his way across the sand, leaving a trail of hoofmarks that the waves would soon erase.

It was time to begin his search. He walked up into the town and set off to find the *commissariat de police*. The streets, with their timbered shops and houses, were almost deserted. If there were tourists, they were indoors somewhere, hiding from what they had come to see. The festival-goers and the neat boys come for the polo had yet to arrive.

At the desk he asked for Inspector Vanier. He had not been idle: a phone call to old friends at the Préfecture de Paris had dug up Vanier's name. He should be helpful, they said. He's worked in Deauville all his life, they said. Nicholas had not thought this much of a recommendation, but he reasoned – as, perhaps, they had reasoned – that even a dull cop who knew his territory would be a lot more useful than a bright spark who'd been here less than a month.

Vanier was neither dull nor a bright spark. Nicholas knew the type very well: a policeman who got his results by effort rather than inspiration, impatient of younger or sharper men, zealous for the law, but at times all too willing to bend the rules to suit an investigation. He'd be a family man, with all that meant of amiability and dullness. In a place like Deauville, with its luxurious casino, its grand hotels, its equestrian events and two film festivals, he'd have felt out of place all his life.

They spoke in French. Vanier's English was at best medio-cre, picked up from tourists or film buffs.

'The message I received . . . it said something about your wife. She is missing?'

Nicholas showed him the postcard. The Frenchman con-firmed the picture was of Deauville's Les Planches.

'Quite a popular card,' he said. 'They started selling this one last season. Unfortunately, you can also find it in Trouville or Honfleur. Perhaps even in Le Havre. It need not have been bought or posted in Deauville.'

'Let's assume it was. I'd prefer not to have to go from door to door the length and breadth of the town. I imagine you have an awful lot of hotels and *pensions*. Let me be honest with you. I'm worried she may try to take her life. There may not be so much time for a proper investigation.'

'That's the only sort of investigation I know, monsieur. To be thorough. To knock on all the doors if necessary.'

'Do you have anyone . . . ?'

Vanier shook his head.

'I have no men to spare, if that's what you're asking. The Asian Film Festival will start in a few days, and I'm worried there may be an attempt to ship drugs into Deauville for the event. You're on your own, monsieur, unless you can afford to hire some private detectives.'

'Do you have a record of hotel and *pension* guests?'

There was a long delay. Vanier wore a grey moustache that drooped on either side of his mouth, lending him a hangdog look.

'You would not have the right to see such a record,' he said. 'I am right in thinking that this is not an official visit?'

'Not official, no, but I hoped you would do a favour, help another policeman to solve a personal problem.'

'Ex-policeman. So I'm informed.'

'My friends who asked for this favour are still on the force.'

'Ah, yes. Special Branch. One hears of you. But, you know, she may not want to be found. I'm sure that she does not, otherwise she would write to you with her address; you would not need to be here.'

'I have to be here because she may be planning to kill herself. Or she may have done so already. That's why I need your help. To prevent a tragedy, if possible.'

'Very well, I will see what I can do. Come back here in an hour. I will see what I can arrange for you.'

Vanier's printout showed a rich tally of names. Deauville's visitors were here, even if they were invisible on the streets and beach. He could not find her name anywhere among them. First, he looked under Budgeon, then under Le Tourneau, her maiden name. Finally, he began to skim through the list, keeping an eye out for anything that rang a bell, and there she was, barely concealed, on the third page: N. Bombois, staying at the Pension Lutèce on rue Honfleur. Bombois had been her mother's maiden name. She hadn't been trying too hard to hide herself away.

The guesthouse owner nodded in recognition. She was a spry eighty-year-old, far from ready for the *hospice de vieillards* two blocks away. Yes, Madame Bombois had stayed with her for about two weeks, from the day of her arrival in Deauville.

'Isn't she with you now?'

A regretful shake of the pampered grey locks.

'Three days ago, monsieur. She left here three days ago. I have a record. I keep a record in my book.'

Nathalie had been there, all right. He recognized her signature, or the handwriting, at least.

'Do you know where she went?'

'Anything I know is confidential, monsieur. I'd ask you to respect that. I may be old, but I don't blabber.'

'Madame, I am her husband. *Vous comprenez ça?*'

'You are Monsieur Bombois?'

'Strictly speaking, no. My name is Budgeon. Monsieur Bombois was her mother's father. She was Le Tourneau when I married her.'

'How do I know any of this is true? If you are indeed her husband, and you are looking for her, I imagine she won't want to be found.'

'I am her husband. I can prove it, if you like. I am also a policeman. With your permission, I'd like to ring Inspector Vanier at the *commissariat*. I'd like him to speak to you; I'd like him to explain.'

He was sure now that Nathalie had stayed in Deauville. Where she had been before that remained unknown. On leaving Oxford, she'd emptied her bank account. Nicholas had not known exactly how much there'd been in it, but he had an idea that it was more than enough for a single woman to live on if she moved invisibly from seaside town to seaside town, off-season, and without gambling or amusement of any kind. He also knew that she had money from her family, a trust fund or something that had been accruing interest in an account with the Crédit Lyonnais and its amiable lion.

Until now, it had not occurred to Nicholas that Nathalie might have been frustrated by her bourgeois existence. She had, after all, been born to something else. What use were the best clothes, Miu Miu shoes, a dressing table stacked with the finest perfumes and the most expensive creams, if you had nowhere to flaunt it all? Few of her Oxford friends and neighbours would have known Armani from Marks and Spencer.

Thought of this way, she seemed a superficial woman, but in fact she'd been quick witted, a fluent linguist, and very well informed of business affairs. She might well have run her own business, an English branch of the family enterprise, perhaps, or an expensive clothing shop. With her looks, her charm and her accent, she was already a legend among the wealthier parts of Oxford society, and finding a clientele for jewellery or perfume or old rope would have been the easiest thing in the world for her.

Yet she waited and waited, procrastinated and procrastinated, until Marie-Josephine's eighteenth birthday brought her face to face with reality. Instead of taking this as her opportunity, she had bolted. Only to turn up at last at Madame Cornilleau's *pension*.

Madame Cornilleau thought she'd rented a small apartment in one of the newly built *immeubles* on the Tourville road. Vanier lent Nick a phone and a desk, and he spent the next half hour speaking to almost every letting agency in Deauville. None of them had heard of a Madame or Mademoiselle Bombois, until he reached one of the smallest inserts, for the Agence Aristide. Yes, he knew a Madame Bombois. No, he couldn't hand out personal information about his clients. No, not even to ex-policemen. His name was Aristide Sadoun, and he had made his way in the world by being a tough cookie.

'It's all right,' said Vanier, although he sounded weary of Madame Bombois and her husband. 'I'll speak to him. He'll co-operate.'

'What's he done?'

'Unpaid speeding and parking fines. Quite a lot of them, actually. I'm glad you brought him to my attention. Give me ten minutes.'

The town, made inhospitable earlier by the rain and wind, now wore a bedraggled and wasted look, as though the inclement weather had simply washed it out. It seemed to be waiting for someone: not daytrippers, not American movie stars, not pale men and women in limousines, just plump tourists with a little money and a few years to spend. The black-and-white timbered shops and houses reminded Nicholas of Leominster, where he had spent time as a boy, and at moments he felt himself disoriented.

He gave Vanier fifteen minutes. When he rang back, the Frenchman had an address, and directions on how to get there. Nicholas felt his courage fail him. In his career, he'd gone up against hard criminals and terrorists bent on murder. But now, faced with the simple prospect of confronting his wife in some low-cost seaside apartment, he wanted to hold back.

It was a three-storey apartment block clad in black marble and set back from the road. In time, cypresses and larches would grow up and camouflage it completely. For now, it felt raw and unnecessary. It seemed an inappropriate place for Nathalie, who had always had taste and a sense of refinement.

Nobody answered his ring, or his knocking. She could be anywhere, he thought: shopping at Les Planches, leaning on some stranger's arm in the casino, watching a film in some ill-heated, empty cinema. Or here, behind the door. He'd anticipated this, and brought out his old lock-picking kit. He hadn't used it in years, but none of his former skill had deserted him. A minute later, he was inside.

Afterwards, he told himself that nothing could have been changed. Not if he'd gone back three or four days, to when she was still alive. Not if he'd gone back to the days before her abrupt departure from Oxford. Not if he'd gone back ten years and more, to the time she'd had her sad affair with a professor of Arabic whom she'd met at a Festschrift celebration in St John's. Not if he'd gone back to the days just after they were married, still in love, still entranced by physical passion. Such things are endless, he thought. You can work your way back inside the womb and never set things right. He'd loved her. Why hadn't that been enough? Why hadn't that prevented the tragedy that had greeted him on opening her apartment door?

He could not tell at first how she had died. Two things grabbed his attention: her body, sprawled in the middle of the living room, half-naked, face down, and very white; and hundreds of sheets of paper, cards and photographs strewn over the floor and the few items of furniture that stood on it.

He could not be sure it was Nathalie at first. His first thought was that he'd stumbled on a different woman, the victim of a different life. But when he knelt down and moved her face, distorted by the uneven flow of blood to the left side, a simple glance told him the truth.

He bent his head and kissed her on the lips, and she tasted of death, and when he got to his feet again, there was an odour of death in the room, a slight hint of early decay. He wondered where she'd found the poison, then remembered that she could have walked in anywhere, looking like a million francs and a world away from suicide. Someone like Nathalie, whose every gesture spelled success, could have found a way. As he lifted his head, he reflected that she could have gone into almost any pharmacy and said, 'I want poison to kill my husband with,' and they'd have wrapped it up and given it to her with a smile.

This was not the time to give way to grief, he reasoned. He knew he'd have to ring Vanier straight away, give him the bad news, then leave the scene. It was not a crime scene, as far as Nicholas could tell, but Vanier would want to establish that for himself.

A sixth sense, born out of years investigating serious crime, told him to examine the papers. He noticed a black metal box sitting near the gas fire, from which he guessed the papers had been taken. On the lid of the box was a dark green printed label that read, *Vetea Bihin et Raymond Bihin, Notaires Assoc.* Beneath the names were three addresses: *18 r Varennes sur Allier 08270 Saulces Monclin, 50 av Gambetta 08300 Rethel*, and *21 r Thiers 08600 Givet.*

He could see right away that most of the papers were legal documents of some sort, although, as far as he could tell, none bore the name Bihin & Bihin. He could not imagine why a firm of solicitors in some obscure part of the French countryside should have been in contact with

Nathalie, much less why they should have sent her a tin box full of legal documents. Could the papers be connected in some way with her suicide?

He gathered them all, pausing from time to time to read a line or a paragraph, but by the end he was no nearer making sense of them. Almost all of them were old, dating back to the 1930s and 1940s. Several were concerned with legal matters in Morocco, and of these a majority had been prepared under the Vichy regime. He found a jellygraph newsletter produced by a unit of the French Resistance, an English passport in the name Alice Dennison, some photographs showing mostly young people, a few dancing or enjoying themselves at a beach – Deauville? he wondered – others holding rifles or pistols and looking grim. But there was simply too much of it for him to make any real sense from it.

When all the papers were back in the box, he pushed the lid down firmly and locked it with a key that Nathalie had left next to it. He'd noticed that the apartment next door was still empty: there was a large red sign in the window reading *à louer*. A few minutes with his lock-picking tools, and he had found a hiding place for the tin just behind the hot-water tank.

He went back to Nathalie's apartment. She was still there, still dead. He went to the bedroom and found a sheet to cover her with. It was not very professional, he knew, but he could not bear to see her so white and done with life. It made him feel partly dead, this death of hers, because her life had been so much a part of his living.

There was a telephone, installed before she moved in, he supposed.

'Inspector Vanier?' he asked. 'This is Nicholas Budgeon. I need to report my wife's death. It looks as if she committed suicide. I think you should come over now.'

He put down the phone and hesitated briefly before picking it up again. The number was in his wallet. He dialled and was answered almost right away.

'I'd like to speak to Mlle Marie-Josephine Budgeon, please. She's staying in room 212.'

4

Oxford

> God, Lover of Souls,
> you hold dear what you have made
> and spare all things, for they are yours.
> Look gently on your servant Nathalie,
> and by the blood of the cross
> forgive her sins and failings . . .

The prayer, intoned diligently, but with more than a hint of disapproval by the priest indoors, was worn away here, among old graves and withered flowers. A pall of wretched weather had come across the Channel with Nathalie's body, and lay now, very English in its stillness and greyness, over Wolverton Cemetery. The graveyard lay a short distance from the centre of Oxford, a pretty place whose low graves were overhung by rows of graceful trees.

They buried her three rows away from Tolkien, creator of Middle Earth, among the Catholics, the perverse Mary worshippers, who lay waiting for Judgement Day, to be refused entry to a Protestant heaven. Nicholas wondered about that. He was not much of a believer, but he had vaguely looked forward to an afterlife in which she figured. Now, he could not even imagine a ghost of her. She would not appear across the gravestones, she would not walk silently past his bed that night. And he realized he had in part buried her years ago, when she'd left him, or before that even, in one of their moments of coldness, and now, he thought, he was free of her, and she of him.

The priest was an old man, white haired, thin necked, a Jesuit or something of that sort, Nicholas guessed. His name was Chabert or Joubert, Nicholas had already forgotten: a Frenchman sent to England to care for French students at the university. The white hair was cut short, leaving the old man's undefended pate looking like a brush. Nicholas had heard he drank. He supposed Nathalie had told him this at some time, among all the gossip she used to relate. She seemed to know everyone's secrets, except, perhaps, her own.

She'd been a believer, she'd visited the old priest to confess her sins and chat about God, in that cloying, intimate way believers do, like erotomaniacs whispering together about the true orgasm. Every Sunday she'd attended Mass in the Catholic church, and she'd come home smiling, and never breathed a word about it to Nicholas or her children. It had been her private experience, a step along her driveway to the infinite.

The children had never gone; there had been an agreement between her and Nicholas that they remain secular. She'd found them once, imitating the singsong of the Mass, the silver vessels replaced by cups and bowls, an old black sheet round Peter's shoulders in impersonation of a cassock, his eyes lost behind their lids, his pale hands decked with rings he'd taken from her jewellery box. She'd lost her temper, almost the only time it had happened. There'd been tears, a period of estrangement, then a making-up with hugs and kisses all round. Much like the real thing, if you thought about it, Nicholas had observed at the time. A wry enough observation, he thought now, his gaze moving away from the grave and back again; but none the worse for that.

He'd contacted her relatives in Reims straight away, even before the reality of her death had sunk into his own consciousness. They were still there, of course, still stocking their cellars with the best vintage champagne, wine they could sell in the next generation for hundreds of times the original price. He'd met them all at one time or another, a mixed bag who had never really welcomed him. In their book, a policeman, however senior in rank, was still rough trade. There were dozens of them, uncles, aunts, brothers and sisters, and now Nathalie's nieces and nephews, coming of age. Practically all of them belonged in some way to the family business, although Maison Le Tourneau had only a dozen serving on the Board at any one time. Very few Le Tourneaus ever seemed to have the imagination or drive to seek any other form of employment.

He had telephoned Reims even before Nathalie's body had been taken to the morgue. He'd asked to speak with Thierry, her eldest brother and company Chairman. He and Nicholas had never really got on as brothers-in-law should. They'd never actually quarrelled, but they had spent a few rather frosty Christmases together. Nicholas, however, was fond of Thierry's wife, Thérèse, and it was she who had come to the phone. They'd talked briefly, and he'd sensed genuine sadness on her part.

The chief thing had been to get the family on his side. No one could afford a scandal, however minor. Telephone calls were made, there was a discreet meeting between Thierry and the *coroner principal* of Reims, after which another phone call, equally full of discretion, was made from Reims to Le Havre, where the inquest on Nathalie was to be carried out. Later, a few lucky men and women would receive Christmas gifts of incredibly expensive champagne. For the moment, all that mattered was that Nathalie's death was recorded as being due to misadventure. Accidental poisoning served to camouflage the thing.

It had satisfied the good old Jesuit, without whose consent Nathalie's remains would never have been given a Christian burial. Nicholas watched him, wrinkled hands clutching a black prayer book, dressed in funeral attire, intoning the rite of committal in a voice devoid of emotion. He was a priest, not a bereavement counsellor, and whatever consolation he offered was ultimately meaningless to Nicholas.

In sure and certain hope of the resurrection to eternal life through our Lord Jesus Christ . . .

Rain fell, sure and silent in its drive towards the open gash in the ground. The priest's voice wavered.

We commend to Almighty God our sister Nathalie . . .

No one looked at anyone else. Everyone found something on which to rest his or her gaze, out of embarrassment or pain or grief. Nicholas could not take his eyes off the offending grave.

and we commit her body to the ground:

43

He wanted to cry suddenly, but tears would not come. He stood watching mutely as the earth took her.

earth to earth, ashes to ashes, dust to dust.

The priest brushed the damp soil from his hands. In the grave, the coffin shifted. The raw earth smelled like death itself.

Nicholas invited everyone home. The family house in Summertown was a short distance away. The long funeral cars, glistening even in rain, conveyed them all to the door. Inside, a firm of caterers, supplemented by French patisseries from Maison Blanc, had set up tables for a buffet. Somewhere, a hi-fi was playing *chansons*, all chosen to lift the spirits of the mourners. Relieved to be indoors and dry and presented with such a rich array of sweetmeats, they began to relax. Conversations opened up, people were introduced to relatives they'd only heard of before, and in a corner of the main room a romance began between Thierry's shy and pretty daughter Amélie and Tim's younger son Mark, who was still studying for a degree in architecture at London University. A problem for another generation.

There were Budgeons there as well, of course, come to back up Nicholas in his time of need. Sinéad was there too, ready at Nicholas's elbow for whatever intimacies he might choose to utter, revelations, indiscretions. Funerals, she knew, were a perfect moment for such *faux pas*, and since she had never liked Nathalie (knowing her for her husband's lost love), she had resolved to mourn her well, and to tell tales of her when the time was ripe.

Throughout all this coming and going, this incessant chatter and munching of canapés, Nathalie's portrait, a black-and-white photograph by Sieff, stood on the living room mantelpiece, a black ribbon across its top left corner. No one who passed it could fail to be reminded of why they were here, and in consequence, a wide space had opened between it and the nearest visitor.

Sinéad went off suddenly in search of her husband, whom she suspected, as always, of flirting with whichever nubile young thing might have caught his gaze (when, if the truth were known, he had never held a flame for anyone but Nathalie, and had never contemplated an affair, unless out of anger at Sinéad's suspicious nature). Marie-Josephine was upstairs in her bedroom in floods of tears, being comforted by her cousin Janice, a plain girl from Leeds who had recently qualified to teach the Alexander Technique, and quite fancied herself as a listening ear.

Nicholas was standing with his gaze focused on his dead wife's photograph when he felt someone slip beside him.

'*Comme elle était belle ce-temps-là.*' Thierry's approbation was quite genuine. He had always envied his little sister for the quality of her good looks. At the age of sixteen, she had posed naked for him, while he experimented with his new Leica and toyed with thoughts of a career outside the narrow confines of Reims and the family business. He still had the photographs in a box in his study at home, and even now he'd look at them from time to time, just to admire her soft skin and silken hair, or so he told himself. He looked at the photograph on the mantel, at the black ribbon cutting across it, and resolved to get rid of the last evidence of his youthful folly.

'I thought so,' Nicholas replied. 'I still think so. She was also very kind and loving and loyal when he took that.

45

Twenty years ago now. It seems like forever. But let's not start brooding. Tell me how things are with you. You and the Widow.'

'I'm sorry?' It sounded like an accusation of infidelity. He could not guess what his brother-in-law meant.

'The Widow. It's Victorian slang for champagne. I thought you'd know that, what with all your expertise. The Boy's another one. You'll really have to brush up, if you want to expand into England seriously.'

'We already have plenty of outlets in this country, as I'm sure you know.'

'I was joking, Thierry. Anything to lighten the mood in here. I'm sorry. How are you, really?'

'Good enough. The business is healthy. My family are well. No, that's not quite true. My brother Lionel, the one with the moustache, in the next room – his doctor has declared him, what do you say? *Diabétique?*'

'Diabetic.'

'Yes. But not with insulin. If he eats well, he can live a normal life. Still, it is not good news for him.'

'I'm sorry to hear that. The charms of middle age.'

'Yes. Illness, and attending funerals. Nicholas, excuse me, but we must talk.'

'Now? Can't it wait till later?'

'Later? Yes, of course. I'm sorry, but you have a lot to attend to. Listen, I plan to spend a few days in London. Thérèse and I will stay at the Basil Street Hotel. I have business with several of my outlets there, and one or two who want to buy from us. May I come back after I finish, before we go back to Reims?'

'Of course. I've no plans to leave. There'll be a lot to

do round here. I have to . . . I have to see to Nathalie's things.'

'*Écoutes*. Thérèse will see to that. There's very little to keep her in London.'

'It's OK, I . . .'

'No, no. She will insist when I tell her. You won't stop her. She was very fond of Nathalie.'

'More than yourself?'

Thierry shrugged.

'Nathalie was my sister. Perhaps we had differences, but I loved her for all that.'

'Glad to hear it. Look, I . . .'

Thierry took Nicholas's arm in a firm grip.

'Nicholas, there is one thing. Perhaps I can ask it now, to save time later. When you found Nathalie, that is . . . when you discovered her in Deauville, and you knew she was dead, then I am sure you looked round a little, round this little apartment of hers.'

'That's right, of course I did. It's a sort of instinct with us old policemen.'

Thierry laughed politely.

'Not so old, I think. But, *dis-moi donc*, did you find anything a little unusual?'

'What sort of thing?'

'I'm not sure exactly. Some papers, perhaps. Legal papers, letters, diaries – I can't be sure. They might have been in a box.'

'What sort of box?'

'I don't know. Cardboard, perhaps. Maybe metal. Perhaps the police found it and gave it to the coroner?'

Nicholas shook his head.

'Really, I saw nothing of the sort. I was there when the police first searched the apartment.'

'And nothing came to light? They searched all corners?'

'Very thoroughly, as a matter of fact. Look, just what is it you're looking for?'

'*Mon cher Nicholas*, it's nothing, really, *je t'assure* . . . your dear wife was to send me some company papers, that is all. I thought perhaps they may have been with her in Deauville, that she may have been planning to visit Reims. But clearly I was mistaken. Forgive me. I'll leave you now, and we'll speak again when I return from London.'

A moment later, he was gone, his hand extended to shake that of Father Joubert. Nicholas watched him go, troubled, knowing what it was he'd been asking for. It helped him make up his mind.

Going to the conservatory, he found some of the younger crowd and a lighter atmosphere than that prevailing inside. Peter was there with his girlfriend Daisy, a petite blonde with big eyes and a bigger brain whom he'd met in his final year at journalism school. Daisy was something in computing and e-commerce, earned much more than Peter, and shared with him a keen enthusiasm for French cinema. Nicholas, unsure at first of someone so full of unnatural energy as she was, had quickly been bowled over by her, as everyone was.

Nicholas greeted them both, then drew Peter aside.

'Pete, I'd like to have a word with you. Do you mind?'

'About what?'

'Let's find somewhere away from all this. Look, the rain's off. We can talk in the garden.'

They stepped outside. Everything smelled damp. The

spring flowers, battered a couple of weeks earlier by terrible winds, looked bedraggled again.

'What is it, Dad? Is it about Mum?'

'In a way. Pete, what do you know about Morocco?'

'Dates. Hippies. Camels. The kasbah. Beau Geste. Or was that Algeria?'

'I'd like you to go there, Pete. I'd like you to investigate a story.'

'What about?'

Nicholas shook his head as though trying to dislodge some painful thought.

'That's just the thing. I don't know. I can point you in the right direction, but I can't take you there.'

'Take it easy, Dad. Tell me how this started. Tell me everything you know.'

5

Letter from Béatrice Le Tourneau
11 September 1936

To M. and Mme Bombois
Epernay

le 11 septembre 1936
Hotel El-Minzah
Tangier

Cher Papa, Chère Maman,

France is certainly far behind us now. When the sun came up this morning, it showed us a new world entirely, and the air was filled with the queer music of Mohammedans chanting. They pray a lot more than we do, several times a day, in fact, and it's strange to hear them start up their wailing when you're in the middle of lunch or something. I don't doubt a glass or two of Gérard's Krug for breakfast would do them all the world of good. Didn't you think the champagne at the wedding breakfast was the most delicious ever?

We're staying at the Minzah, they all say it's very much the place, and it does have the most wonderful gardens, altogether *à l'Espagnole*. Gérard says we shall spend three or four days here, before heading on to Fès.

I thought summer would be over, as it is back home, but instead it's extremely hot, and sometimes you catch your breath as though the air around you has caught fire. Gérard dislikes it: he says it aggravates his asthma, but I find it thrilling, since it makes me think of deserts and kasbahs and camels and that sort of thing.

We did see a camel yesterday, crossing the Grand Socco, which is the main square, though not what you or I would call a square, not a *place* in the French sense. The square is packed with fruit sellers, vegetable hawkers, acrobats, fire-eaters, mountebanks and tatterdemalions of every sort. We watch from a distance, of course, and Gérard sees to it that I do not come into contact with any of the lower classes, which is to say, most of the Moors. I call them Moors, but they are all sorts, really, blacks from the south, Berbers, true Arabs, and some like Indians.

And foreigners, too. There are all sorts of us; we stand out here in our white skins and tailored clothes. Plenty of French, of course, Spaniards from the Spanish Protectorate, the English, who think they still own Tangier, some Portuguese and Greeks, I believe. And I do think I spotted some Americans in the hotel this morning. My English is not so perfect that I can tell one accent from the other with any great ease, but I am sure the family we saw originated on the other side of the Atlantic. They certainly were not English. Filthy rich, though, like all these *Ricains* one meets abroad.

We saw a group of Germans buying souvenirs in the medina, strutting along in their black uniforms, looking as though they owned the place, as I expect they hope to one day. Of course, Tangier is an International Zone, which means they're more or less free to do as they please.

51

Gérard says that they have spies here, that they are looking for a foothold in North Africa. Well, I for one shall keep well out of their way. Though I must admit they do look very handsome and assured, and their blond hair stands out so sharply against the African sun.

I'll write again from Fès. Be good. And, by the way, the little medicine chest is already proving its worth: Gérard developed a sniffle on the boat, but I've got him back on form again. Marriage is heavenly, you should have told me sooner.

Embrassez Jérôme et Jean-Hugues pour moi, et donnez des bons baisers à ma chère Marie-Louise. N'oubliez pas de nous donner de vos nouvelles.

Je vous embrasse,
Votre fille,
Béatrice (Le Tourneau!)

From Peter Budgeon to Nicholas Budgeon
21 March 2002

> To Commander Nicholas Budgeon
> 17a Belbroughton Road
> Summertown
> Oxford

From:
Hotel El-Djenina
8 rue El Antaki
Tangier
21 March 2002

Hi Dad,

Daisy and I got here yesterday on the *Ibn Battuta*, a smelly old ferry that's been making the crossing from Algeciras since forever. It's even possible that Mum's parents crossed the Med on board the same barge. We got a great bargain on our flights to Algeciras, and saved enough to spend the night at the Regina Hotel, a classy joint with a view all the way out to sea. Still, that will have to be the last of our luxuries. Our budget's tight, since I haven't been able to get any advance for this trip. The problem is, I don't have a story yet, except that I'm travelling in my grandparents' footsteps across Morocco, in the hope of digging up some sort of dirt from back in World War II.

Actually, I've had a little more time to read through the papers you gave me. I've brought them with me, incidentally, or photocopies at least, so I can update myself whenever I come across evidence or fresh clues. To be honest, this sort of thing's much more up your street than mine. I call myself an investigative reporter, but really, I've never been trained properly on how to conduct an investigation. I should have listened to you more when I was a kid.

I haven't come to any conclusions yet, there just isn't enough to go on. But Mum must have had a reason for holding on to the box, and keeping it quiet from everyone. Speaking of which, I think that's what you should do too: I certainly wouldn't breathe a word about these papers to any of Mum's brothers or sisters, since they all have an emotional investment in my grandparents, and I think there may be things in here that could upset people. For one thing, it isn't quite clear to me which side Grandmother was on during the war. For another, she could have been involved in some dubious activities in the build-up to the American invasion.

I'll just follow the leads I've got, ask questions when I can, and see what comes to light. I may ring you and ask for advice from time to time. What else are fathers for, eh?

I was in a bookshop selling French and English books today, and got into conversation with the owner, a bright young man called Abdelhak. He's about my age, maybe a few years older, and he's been running his shop for about a year. The thing is, he speaks good English, so I've asked him if he might translate the Arabic documents that came in Mother's box. I can't pay him much, but he looks as though he has independent means, so I reckon using him is less exploitative. Once I've sorted out the details, maybe you can send the Arabic stuff out.

We'll get to the bottom of this before long.

One thing, though, and I hope you don't think I'm being intrusive or difficult, but it is important: how exactly did Mother die? I don't mean the details, but – well, was it an accident as the coroner said, or did she kill herself? I feel I have a right to know anyway, but I also think it's relevant to this enquiry. A lot of the things I've read are disturbing, and I wonder if they might not have pushed her over the edge, so to speak. Whatever there may have been between you and her that led to her leaving is your business, but the French solicitors say they had only sent the box to her a few days earlier, and I just wonder whether there's a connection.

Daisy sends her best wishes (she says she doesn't know you well enough yet to send her love, but I know she likes you). You should be nice to her anyway, she could very well be your daughter-in-law one day before long.

Bye for now,

Your not-very-dutiful and not-at-all-obedient son,

Peter

19 rue Victor Hugo
Ville Nouvelle
Fès
17 July 1937

Ma Très Chère Marie-Louise,

We received your sad letter yesterday and have been stunned ever since. Poor Robert, and at such an early age. We trust he will not suffer, and that his passing will be painless. But you, my dear sister, how can you bear to be left a widow when you had barely been six years married? And little André – what will he do without a father? It is all too much to contemplate . . .

I know it is far too early to make any suggestions regarding your future, but you must not hesitate to join us here for a time, if that would help ease the burden. I know we are far from settled, and that our move to Meknès has been postponed more times than we would have liked, but we are looking forward to our first harvest next year, and the chance to produce our first wines. We shall have our own label, of course. I pass idle hours designing it: Château Le Tourneau, Agourai, 1939 (and 1940 and 1950, and on and on). Agourai is heavenly, our little *vignoble* is a haven of tranquillity, and you and dear André could spend as long as you liked there, until you got over things. Of course, you have first to go through to the end, and then start over.

You must not be put off by the journey here. Modern conditions make it so much easier than it was even ten years ago. I often look back on that long train journey through France with great pleasure. It was like being reborn. I often wish I was back on board, travelling endlessly south. Gérard is away so often nowadays, getting things right on the farm.

I'm not without things to do in his absence, however. Above all, I've been trying to get to know our neighbours. We live in the New Town, of course, and everyone we know socially is a fellow *colon*. The Moroccans only venture into this area as servants, then go back to their hovels in the medina, or Old Fès. They are really quite simple people, and you have to treat them firmly or you won't get a day's work out of them.

I've ventured a short way into the Arab city, to see the little stalls where they sell all manner of goods. It's terribly colourful, but it stinks to heaven, and I really don't understand how some Frenchmen can choose to live there. I suppose it's a very bohemian thing to do, but I don't share their enthusiasm for the Moors and their culture, and I can't see myself putting up with so much deprivation just in order to participate in their barbaric way of life.

The wretched calls to prayer five times a day, then at the end of Ramadan tens of thousands of innocent sheep slaughtered, a massive spillage of blood in every street and back yard, and the noise of weddings travelling on the night, the women making their war whoops like Red Indians, constant noise, and the same women veiled like walking theatres, the men staring at you, thinking every European woman's a whore, dead dogs left out unburied for months, the constant heat in the summer, and the wretched, driving rain all winter through, their holy places closed to Christians, their faces closed, their hearts closed to us when all we want to do is bring them civilization, the French way of life, *chansons*, champagne, lingerie, *joie de vivre* . . .

Je t'embrasse bien affectueusement,
Ta soeur,
Béa

From Peter Budgeon to Nicholas Budgeon
2 April 2002

> Nick Budgeon
> 17a Belbroughton Road
> Oxford

Hotel Lamdaghri
rue Abasse El Massadi
Ville Nouvelle
Fez
2 April 2002

Lebas, ya Kommandar Budge!
Daisy and I are picking up the local lingo like nobody's business. Actually, we're still at the *salam, hamdulillah, minfadlik, barakullah fik* stage of things, which barely gets us by. Fortunately, almost everybody speaks tolerable French.

As you'll see from the address (small, cheap, has a little courtyard that gets the sun for ten minutes every day), we've moved on to Fez. What an incredible city! It's really three towns patched onto one another: the Old Town, which makes up the medina, where we've just been shopping; New Fez, which was built from 1276, but isn't as interesting as the old part; and this bit, the French town, where Grand-maman lived for a couple of years while Grand-père went back and forwards to set up their vineyard at Agourai.

While Daisy trawls through the souks, I've been ignoring the sights as far as I can and asking old men questions. I have to speak in French, of course, but I've only needed an interpreter once so far. There are still quite a few old *colons* out here, tough old birds who refused to leave after Independence back in the fifties. I found a firm of solicitors, a French firm that handles legal affairs for young *coopérants* from the French Foreign Aid Ministry. They're rather grandly called Coissac de Chavrebière et Fils, and, believe it or not, this is the third generation of the buggers. But what's more to the point, they think they may have papers relating to Agourai and Grandfather's business associates. They're planning to get back to me in a day or two, which probably means in six months' time . . .

From Gérard Le Tourneau to his father Thibould

Vignoble Le Tourneau-Bombois
Agourai
Près de Meknès
Le Maroc
26 January 1939

> M. Thibould Le Tourneau
> Négociant en Vins
> 41b rue du Champs de Mars
> Reims

Cher Papa,

I simply do not know how to reply to your letter. You know very well that I have never been of a military disposition, and even if I had been, I am confident there will not be another war in Europe. Monsieur Hitler seems an honourable enough man to me, and clever enough to secure Germany's security without resorting to open hostility with any of his neighbours or with the British Empire. He does have problems with the Jews, but that is an internal matter for the Germans to solve. In the long term, I think it not impossible he may turn against Stalin, but if he does that, surely he will have every civilized country on his side, we French included.

Things look very different from over here in the *outremer*, for we are certain the Germans will continue to respect our Protectorates. Even in the event of a war in Europe, however protracted, it is highly unlikely that it will spread far in our direction. If it does, I would, naturally, join up in the Coloniale, which requires French officers. Or I might go into the public service, in order to make use of my administrative skills. Above all, however, I must do everything to ensure the continuation of the vineyards outside Meknès, not for myself or even for the good name of Le Tourneau, but for my wife and the child she is about to bear.

I'm enclosing our monthly report, as usual. You'll find we've made considerable progress over the last quarter. No profits, of course, but I think we agreed it would be premature to expect any for at least another year.

Our main competitors now are Toulal and the Sidi Larbi *domaine*. Oued Ykem continues to prosper. Their reds and rosés are, I have to admit, quite good, but I'm less confident about the long-term sustainability of their grapes. Our reds are already superior, in my opinion, to those of all three, and I believe that only a little more judicious investment will see us exporting – dare I say it? – to the French mainland. Can you possibly let me have the name of that contact of yours in the Ministry of Agriculture? I don't feel we can rely very much on the Colonial Administration.

And, of course, Béatrice's sister Marie-Louise joins us in three weeks' time. She will come out alone apart from young André. Naturally, they will move in with us to begin with. It really is the proper thing to do.

Of course, we won't leave a stone unturned in finding a new husband for her. There are many men of the right age here. Most of them are adventurers come out to make their fortune (I met one recently who had heard there were no wine labels to be had in Arabic, and that a good trade might be had were he to print some; it fell to me to point out to him that the Arabs, except the Jews among them, do not drink wine. He was most disappointed, having brought a small printing press with him all the way from a backwater town in Normandy, expressly for this purpose). But there are others – military men, some bankers, merchants, senior civil servants. I'm sure we shall see her settled within the year.

Don't take this too badly, Father. A man can serve his country without donning a soldier's uniform or brandishing a rifle. I shall serve in my own way. But let us pray I am right, and that no war comes this way. Should that happen, I don't doubt it can be dealt with: it's obvious the Jews are at the root of all our misery. Deal with them, and you've dealt with the crisis.

Embrasse Maman pour moi. Je la souhaite un très joyeux anniversaire.

Ton fils,
Gérard

From Peter Budgeon to Nicholas Budgeon
15 April 2002

Nick Budgeon
c/o Déjà Vu Press
120 Broad Street
Oxford

Hotel Gallia
rue de la Recette
off rue de Bab Agnaou
Marrakech
15 April 2002

Dad,

In all honesty, I wish you were here. I don't much
like the turn things are taking. The people I meet talk
of Nazis, of broken promises, of betrayals, of death and
dishonour. Nothing is clear. It is as though I have a box
of photographs, all taken with a broken camera, some
fuzzed, some overexposed, some with whole areas missing,
some torn or rusted or diseased from too long standing in
damp. They are all old men and women, some French,
some Moroccan, some Berbers, and all have a tiny fraction
of some greater truth that I cannot begin to reassemble.
Nevertheless, I sense it at the bottom of the box, I know
for certain now it is there, desperate to be known.

Something happened here years ago, before you or
Mother were born. Certain events have left their impression on minds and hearts and places. My witnesses sometimes take me to a square or a fountain, and they point
and say, 'So-and-so died here; another was shot in this
spot; this is where my brother was arrested; I never saw
his face again.' They have their memories, and on every
corner the memories have monuments.

I was followed yesterday, I'm sure of it. You would
have known, it was hard to tell. Perhaps it was a tout,

a guide looking for a tourist to show round the medina, a hashish pusher, I don't know. He never let me see his face, wrapping himself up in a light blue jellaba and staying permanently in the shadows. I haven't seen him today. Not yet, at least.

On a less gloomy note, Daisy and I have had a lot of time between interviews to talk about where we're going, and – you've probably guessed what I'm going to say. We plan to marry soon after we get back. The full Monty, long veils (but not of the Moroccan sort, please), little bridesmaids and little boys in military uniform, and a huge bash down by the river. A late summer wedding, with any luck.

All the best to Uncle Tim,

Pete

Commander Budgeon – just a note from your daughter-in-law in waiting. Do what you can to persuade your son to get the first plane back to London (with my good self on board, of course). He's going off his head with this investigation, and I honestly think he'll go mad if he keeps at it much longer.

By the way, we're off to somewhere called Ouarzazate in the morning. On a bus packed with chickens and old ladies. Pete's excited. I'm not so sure. We'll write from there.

Daisy

From Marie-Louise Leroux (née Bombois) to the Bombois family
20 April 1940

Hotel La Mamounia
Ave. Bâb Jedîd
Marrakech

Famille Bombois
5 rue de la Fauvette
Epernay
Marne
France
20 April 1940

Bonjour, Bonjour, Bonjour,
My dears,

Another letter from El-Maghreb El-Aqsa, the Land of the Furthest West. And an exciting one. You will remember my telling you how very sociable I have found it here in Fès, and how amiable I have found the colonists who live here. Now, I realize this may sound strange, almost impossible to believe, but I assure you I am not writing with any intention of deceiving you. I have been courted, wooed, and finally made a proposition by a man some seven years my senior, in every way as different from my late husband as a tin helmet from a sponge. I have answered him Yes, and in a short space he will become my husband and little André's father. The child loves him as I do, and we fully expect to become the most loving family this country has seen.

I shall soon be Mme Guénaud. Vital, my darling husband-to-be, is a judge. He trained at the Sorbonne and later volunteered for work in the colonies. Until recently, he was *assesseur* attached to the military tribunal at Fès, but he has now been appointed *conseiller* to the main court of appeal in Marrakech. You cannot imagine a more intelligent, warm-hearted and lovable man. He assures me he has never sent a man to death whom he did not know for certain to be guilty.

You may think that something a little improper is taking place when you note the address from which I write, and recall that the man I love is already in residence here. But the truth is that dear Béatrice is with me, to be my chaperone until we're married. She's terribly jealous of Vital and the refined social circles I shall move in when I am Mme Guénaud.

We all fear for you so much. There is talk everywhere that the Boche will invade France. If they break through and come in through Alsace and the Ardennes, as we expect they will, Reims and Epernay will be directly in the line of their march on Paris. Can you not try to leave before Hitler makes his move? Come to Morocco for our wedding, and stay until the worst is over. You can live with us, or with Béatrice and Gérard at their farm or their town house. The main thing is to get well away.

Our Jewish friends tell us grim tales of what is being done to their brethren in Germany and Poland. The Nazis treat them like vermin, and we are told they intend to exterminate them. Already, they are rounding them up in camps for that purpose. We have plenty of Jews here. M. Guénaud tells me they are mostly good people, and very important to the economy. Well, at least we are all safe here in Morocco. If Monsieur Hitler conquers Europe, he'll hardly want to burden himself with another empire.

Bons baisers,
Marie-Louise

6

Oxford
20 May

Days. He had come to realize how intricate they were, to see how we miss the little twists and turns that take us from midnight to midnight. Nathalie's death instilled in him an appreciation of time's trickery. One minute he was young, in Oxford, catching sight of her for the first time, the next he was standing in a cold churchyard among an indifferent congregation, watching her coffin slide into oblivion. He'd seen it in the service, among the criminals and terrorists he hunted, young men growing old before his watchful eyes.

And all those days between: days wasted, days mysteriously lost, whole days without longing or gratitude or joy, days when even anger was not to be had. In middle age, Nicholas thought, you began to regret the mistakes of youth without enough days left in which to undo the wrongs. Or you started to make amends, only to find you were making things worse. He'd given up trying. Time, he knew, did not heal: it just took you further from the scene of the crime.

Without his bombers and gunmen, his hate-driven men of

the shadows, what was he really? he wondered. Not much of a policeman, not much of a man. A rank-climber, a back-slapper who'd sacrificed his wife to gain another day behind his desk, allowed love to wither while he tended another garden. And where was the fruit? A pension? A cupboard full of medals and awards that meant absolutely nothing to anyone outside Special Branch? A skilled technique in the interrogation of subjects?

He thought of what it was to wheedle the truth out of someone, to extract the truth without resorting to torture, or to torture the soul, for that was the essence of his handiwork, the ability to cut deep inside a man's heart, to lay his victims on some sort of spiritual dissecting table, and to find all those little mechanisms of the soul that would delude them into betraying their cause and their friends.

What would a pensioner do with an art like that? Hone it down the pub of a Saturday night? Interrogate his neighbours about their taste in garden gnomes? It was such a farce, he thought. He felt like a prefect out of school, who finds that the rules he has lived by, which he has imposed on other boys with a cane and lines, mean absolutely nothing to the butcher and the fishmonger on the high street.

To hell with all of it, he thought. He'd found a new career, the publishing firm was doing well and was capable of taking up his time and interest. Short of writing his memoirs – which the rules of confidentiality would never allow him to do – he could find no way of making use of his earlier talents on Broad Street.

He went into work early every morning, and left in the evening, sometimes very late. There were no distractions, other than in work. He seldom watched television, apart from the news or *Newsnight*, if he caught them. There were videos at the weekend, chosen without discrimination, coloured pictures to help the time pass more quickly. What books he read were purely for the purposes of keeping up with work, and when he put them down there were manuscripts waiting to be scrutinized. One had arrived a few days earlier from an agent in St John's Wood. He and Tim had already discussed the title with the agent, who was most enthusiastic, and now Nick was working through the first few chapters and finding them better than he'd thought they might be.

He read his horoscope diligently each day, believing not a word of it. His luck had run out long ago, and no amount of stargazing or feng shui or casting of Saxon runes could save him. On Saturdays, he went down to London and drank in the Duke of York with a few of his old friends, men still in the service, Duncan Todd and Percy Craven and some younger men. They made him feel welcome, but he knew it was early days, and that very soon they'd resent the old boy joining them like a ghost at a booze-up. They talked shop, and he followed along with most of it, made comments, even; but increasingly they'd mention names he did not recognize, or lapse into silence when something hush-hush came up. He was an outsider now, and he needed to find new drinking partners. God knew where he'd find them, he thought.

It was enough to recognize his dilemma, though. The next Saturday night, he stayed in Oxford and drank in the Eagle and Child with Tim. On the Sunday, he embarked on the task of sorting through Nathalie's things. He hadn't realized just how far she had stretched herself. Traces of her were discernible everywhere: a tiny lipstick stain on a Wedgwood jasperware cup that nothing could remove; a hairpin in the kitchen ashtray; the stack of cat food for which she alone had been responsible, and which was about finished. Her wardrobe – a long, built-in affair as big as a small room – was so packed with her he was forced outside to catch his breath. Her perfume – Guerlain's rare Metallica – hung on the air and was present on her clothes. Dresses, shoes, scarves, the outfits she wore at the health centre, hats for weddings and funerals, knick-knacks whose purpose he could only guess at, all stimulated memories. In one drawer, he came across a stash of expensive lingerie he'd bought for her years earlier, on a series of wedding anniversaries: a Malizia camisole and briefs from La Perla, G-strings, Y-strings, and little waspies from Agent Provocateur, slips from Jane Woolrich. For a policeman, he'd learned his lessons well. The silk and lace ran through his fingers like sand. The presents had continued for year after year, expected and welcomed on both sides. Then one year he'd bought her perfume instead, a huge bottle from Lalique, worth a king's ransom; and the following year something else, until the lingerie was a thing forgotten, and all that went with it, until they were sleeping in separate rooms.

He found more papers, some crisp and white, others yellowed, stashed away in forgotten corners, remnants of letters, bills, business cards in French and English. In a locked wooden box in the top drawer of her desk, he discovered a little notebook in which she had scribbled down random thoughts, stabs at English prose writing, and some poems in French and English. He looked through them and found to his surprise that his wife had kept secret from him a real talent. There was nothing about him, as far as he could tell. He put them away in his desk and considered suggesting to Tim that they publish them.

Another letter came from Peter. The boy was certainly on to something. He and Daisy had visited Ouarzazate and had started asking questions. So far, nothing definite had been uncovered, but Peter had a strong conviction that people were hiding something from him.

One day, a small parcel of papers arrived from Edinburgh. Marie-Josephine was returning a selection of diaries and letters that Peter had removed from the box. A note said that the rest were of little interest. Peter had made photocopies to take with him to Morocco. Nick started to look through them, then grew tired. He had a fresh set of photocopies made, and lodged the originals with his bank.

It was late spring now, but the weather continued wintry. No birds returned from Africa, no green shoots pushed their heads above the soil, the telephone continued silent. Perhaps they were all omens, Tim suggested. 'Omens of what?' Nicholas asked, to be greeted with a shrugging of shoulders. Nicholas was not an imaginative man, and certainly no believer in predictions; he treated it all as another shift in the weather, and made a mental note to pursue the series on climate change further.

He spent the morning of 20 May in the sports centre on Maltfield Road. Too many days alone had brought him face to face with his growing belly and long-inactive limbs, and now he tried to get to the gym at least once a day. One of the walls had been blocked for rock-climbing, and two weeks earlier he'd signed up for a course. It was harder than it looked. All that morning, he hauled himself up and down the wall, his nose millimetres away from raw brick, his feet barely finding purchase on the narrow wooden blocks that formed such a tortuous pattern.

Afterwards, aching in shoulders, back, wrists and ankles, he drove to Tesco and stocked up with a week's supply of every unhealthy food known to man. Bacon, sausages, cheese, pork pies, double cream – one after the other, they went into his trolley, all the killer foods that Nathalie had, once upon a time, magicked back onto the shelf again. It would all keep, he thought; he could freeze most of it, and bring it out again when Peter got home.

Worn out by climbing and pushing a heavy trolley round long, polished aisles, he decided to rent a video and spend the evening at home. He heated a pizza in the oven, one with a stuffed crust that added to the calories, and settled down to watch *The Blair Witch Project*. An hour or so later, he was fast asleep in front of the screen. The movie, which would not, in his opinion, have frightened a three-year-old, had run its course without him and the VCR had switched itself off. When he woke, it was to find the screen throbbing to the pulse of *Who Wants to Be a Millionaire?*

The doorbell rang, and he realized it was not the first or second ring. Finding the remote, he pointed it at the television, cutting Chris Tarrant off in mid-question.

Grouchy, still groggy from his early sleep, he went to the door and opened it. Duncan Todd was standing there, looking awkward. No, not so much awkward as mentally unprepared for whatever it was he'd come to say. Nick, coming back fast from sleep, sensed in his old colleague's posture that something was wrong.

'What's wrong?' he asked.

'Can I come in? This is . . . I'd rather not say this on the doorstep.'

More bad news, then. Nick wondered how fast his heart would break.

'Come on in. I'm sorry, everything's a mess. I get along all right, I make do, but I'm not much of a house-keeper.'

He pushed to one side the plate with scraps of cold pizza, and the glass still half-full of Stella.

'Sit down, Duncan, take that chair, I'll sit in this one.'

'Oh, right. Thanks. Comfortable, this.'

'You've been here before, Duncan, you know the deal. I'll fetch a Stella in a moment, if that's what you'd like.'

'Whatever you say. But I didn't come . . . this isn't a social visit, Nick.'

'Guessed that. You could never keep a secret, Dunkie. Worst man they could have sent to Special Branch. Still, other talents, old boy, bags of them. Just no good at keeping mum. It's in your face. In your eyes. In your fucking genes, for all I know. It's time now, time to face it. Tell me what it is.'

'There's no easy way for me to say it, Nick,' Duncan began. He was a red-haired man, and his freckled skin matched his hair colouring, giving him that propensity to blush when on the spot. 'It's bad news,' he said. 'The worst.'

'Nathalie? More about Nathalie, is that it? She didn't kill herself after all, is that what you've come to tell me?'

'Not Nathalie. Peter. He's been found dead.'

'Where? The last thing . . .'

'A cheap hotel in a place called Ouarzazate.'

Nicholas was suddenly confused.

'Not in . . . ?' Then he remembered. 'But he can't be in . . . what it was you said. He was there weeks ago. Then they left for the Sahara. He and Daisy, they went south to the desert. There must be some mistake. The Moroccan police, they can't be relied on.'

Duncan shook his head.

'I'm afraid there's been no mistake, Nick. It's Pete all right. They faxed a photograph. There was no mistake.'

'In this place, Ouar . . . ?'

'Ouarzazate. It's on the southern edge of the High Atlas. Nick, I have to tell you . . . Peter wasn't alone. His girlfriend Daisy was with him.'

'Yes, I know that. They went out there together. Is she all right? Is she still out there with him?'

'I'm sorry, Nick. She's dead too. Their bodies are still in Ouarzazate. We've got somebody onto it, a man from the consulate. They'll be taken care of.'

'But . . . how did it . . . how did all this happen? You say they're both dead?'

Duncan nodded.

'Jesus.'

'Nick, what I'm about to say will be disagreeable, but I don't know how to soften it. From the first report, it looks as though Pete killed her, then killed himself. That's the way it looks. From the first report.'

The pizza congealed on the plate, the beer grew flat and stale in the half-empty glass. A long way away, sand dunes crumbled in the vast Saharan ocean. The sky over the Haut Atlas was black with thunder. In Ouarzazate, two bodies lay side by side, uncared for, and a prey to mountain dreams.

In the Land of the
Furthest Occident

7

Ouarzazate
21 May

Late-flowering almond blossom grew everywhere like a white veil across the ochre façades of the little town. Their rich smell blended with other smells: spices from the tiny souk, the stink of camels, the musk-laden perfumes of the women as they walked in heavy veils through the dusty streets in search of air. Not far away, snow still lay on the peaks of the High Atlas, permitting skiing on the northern slopes. To the south, a gentle yellow heat haze betrayed the presence of the desert. Although dawn had finished hours before, the morning still felt young. In a sky easy with scattered clouds and a flat wash of blue and indigo, a crescent moon still hovered between the visible and the invisible, too pale to appear more than a ghost crossing above the roofs of the little town.

In a Western movie, Ouarzazate would have been a two-horse town on its way to becoming something classier. Clint Eastwood would have drifted in on a dusty horse, his clothes white from the road, his eyes dry and slanting. He'd have checked into the cheapest hotel, thrown his saddlebags on the bed, and strolled across the street to the saloon.

Instead, Nicholas Budgeon stepped out of a *petit taxi*, a green Renault Four that had seen better days. He stood outside the Hotel Azghor, red faced and disoriented. He'd lost no time in getting to Morocco. No sooner had Duncan gone, than he'd thrown a few clothes into an overnight bag, finally unearthed his passport, and slipped it into his jacket pocket.

He'd run from the house and driven at full speed down the M40 to Heathrow. Not once did he see a blue light flashing in his rear-view mirror. Word had gone out, and Nick knew that, for however long this took, he was back within the charmed circle in which he'd lived for so long.

From Heathrow, he flew to Charles de Gaulle, just in time to miss the 21.05 Air France scheduled flight to Casablanca that would have allowed him to catch a Royal Air Maroc flight all the way down to the new airport at Ouarzazate itself. The next flight out was at around seven the next morning. He had too much adrenaline rushing around his system to make such a long wait tolerable, but he couldn't afford to hire a private jet, not if he was going to have enough money kept back for what could turn into a long and expensive investigation.

Everywhere he encountered shrugged shoulders and bored expressions. It was getting late. Everyone was tired. He went for a coffee, probably the worst coffee Paris had on offer, and sipped it slowly, watching his baggage, watching the crowds thin. The high, curved ceiling filled with a thousand echoes. A group of men in fezzes passed him, and for a moment he thought they must be Moroccans flying back home; but they turned out to be Shriners from Wisconsin, headed for a charter flight that would take them to a convention in a sunny beachside resort. They all carried identical shoulder bags printed in white with the name of their convention paradise, but strain as he might, Nick could not make out the name. It did not appear to be Ouarzazate, which was hot, sunny, stuffed with palm trees, and a long drive from the Atlantic.

His coffee grew cold, and he pushed it away violently, letting it slop into the saucer and across the Formica-topped table. His son was dead, and he was stuck here in a steel-and-glass-wrapped no-man's-land that reminded him of a giant greenhouse. He realized that he still had not rung Marie-Josephine, that she knew nothing of her brother's death. Unfair if she woke tomorrow and opened the *Guardian* to find a column reporting the affair. It was a story worth running: he must have timed things well, getting away before the first reporter rang to question him.

He dragged his case to a telephone and used his Amex card to ring Edinburgh.

'Yeah?' A man's voice answered, terse and wary.

'Is Marie-Josephine there?'

'Who?' A Scottish voice, Nick guessed.

'Marie-Josephine. This is her father.'

'Ah've got a Mary, if that's who you want. There's no Joseph, though. Look, why dae you no ca' back in the mornin', eh? There'll be –'

The phone was snatched away from the Scot, and Marie-Josephine's voice came on the line.

'Yes, who is it?'

'It's me, love. I need to speak to you. Something's happened. Something bad . . .'

He was in tears when he got back to the table he'd made his own. The slick of spilt coffee was still there, but the cup and saucer were gone. He'd have given anything to be with her, and he now hesitated about heading on so precipitously to Ouarzazate. There were bound to be flights to Edinburgh or Glasgow in the morning; all he had to do was turn up with an impressive piece of plastic in his hand. She'd need comforting, and Nick doubted whether Oor Wullie would be up to the task.

He made his way towards the nearest Air France desk. As he did so, he caught sight of a group of around twenty Arab men and women moving purposefully in the opposite direction. It took only a moment for him to see that the women were wearing the distinctive square-cowled veil and *jellaba* typical of Morocco.

He caught one of the men before the group turned a corner and disappeared. Speaking in French, he outlined his predicament.

'*Nous allons à Ouarzazate en charter,*' the man answered while his friends and their womenfolk looked on. The women watched with that peculiar stare of the veiled. Their eyes, turned solemn by the desert, looked at him incuriously. He could make out little patterns of henna on the skin about their eyes.

Their charter flight had been booked through a Moroccan tour company, Voyages al-Maghreb. They'd booked their seats months ago, and the man didn't think there'd be any to spare, but he might find a last place, *insha' Allah*.

Nick thanked him and headed back to the Air France ticket desk, where he was redirected to the Servisair counter. The girl on duty there had been bred in the same school as her Air France colleague. No seats. No hope of a seat. No seats this side of Christmas. She did not even consult her computer. Nick asked her to do so, and she refused. He went a little way away and made a telephone call.

Five minutes later, the telephone on the Servisair desk rang. The girl picked it up lazily. Nick watched her, watched her pale skin go grey, saw her expression change. He'd used his influence very seldom as a policeman; now, he had favours to collect. The man on the other end of the receptionist's telephone was a senior official in the French Police Nationale.

When she finally put the phone back in its cradle, he walked up to her again, American Express card in hand. She looked at him with something akin to fear, and said nothing. Minutes later, he walked away holding a flight ticket to Ouarzazate. The plane left in three hours' time.

He'd been able to sleep in the departure lounge, and again on the flight, but he still felt terrible, neither entirely awake, nor fully asleep. But there was no time to waste. He had to get to the murder scene before it was further contaminated, and do all he could there to gather evidence and take control of the investigation if he could. He knew the local police would put up obstacles every inch of the way, but Duncan had promised to liaise with National Police Headquarters in Rabat, in order to put the whole thing on some sort of official footing. In real terms, he had no status here, but he hoped that a little nudging from friends in London combined with the fact that he was Peter's father would count for something.

He walked down to the town centre. It wasn't hard to find your way about. Ouarzazate was made up of three layers: a small core of original buildings and a kasbah, built or fallen into ruin over the years until the French took control. In 1928, the new masters of Morocco built a garrison there, together with some buildings to house the local administration. In the 1980s had come the large hotels to cater for the rising number of tourists heading either into the mountains or down into the desert. To help keep them all moving, Ouarzazate boasted no fewer than five petrol stations.

The police station was situated halfway along Mohammed V, the main thoroughfare. Its main function was to protect the tourists, mostly young backpackers, who poured into Ouarzazate every season and who formed the backbone of the region's economy. Naïve and trusting for the most part, they were at the mercy of hustlers and con artists, thieves and opportunists who sought to line their own pockets at the expense of American, British, French and Australian kids who seemed to them fabulously wealthy. The police did what they could to sort out disputes, but the disputes kept on coming as long as the planes landed and the coaches pulled in from Agadir and Marrakech.

The little *kumissariya* was home to a duet of tourist policemen, a bulbous-headed sergeant whose plastic badge gave his name as M'hamed Benkirane, and a lanky constable by the name of Fouad Mrabet.

They greeted him in English, and he replied in French. The sergeant looked embarrassed.

'*J'en suis désolé, monsieur, mais . . .*'

His voice fell away.

The constable, a boy with a long face and long, tapering fingers, who betrayed some deep inner incertitude by the constant rubbing of his thumb-pad against his fingertips, ventured to explain.

'We don't speak so good French,' he said. 'We are speaking Arabic, of course, but it is not so much we speak it here. Our job is to speak always English. I have studied in high school, Sergeant M'hamed has learned from when he has worked in New York.'

'You have to speak English?'

'Is most useful. We are tourist police. See – is here on my badge. Most tourists, they speaks English. American, Australian, even French, they all speaks English.'

Nick shrugged.

'That's fine by me. Since I don't speak Arabic of any kind, let's stick to English.'

He reached into his pocket and brought out his passport.

'You should have received either a fax or a telephone call by now, explaining the reason for my visit.'

They looked at him, then at one another, and simultaneously shook their heads.

'No fax, Mister – Budgeon,' said the sergeant. 'We have no fax here. I guess we're waiting for a fax machine, but it's been three years, and we still haven't seen one. This is Morocco, Mister Burgess, it pays to be patient here.'

'What about a telephone call? You do have a telephone?'

The constable nodded.

'It's very early, Mister Berger, maybe later, maybe someone will call later.'

'The name is Budgeon.' Nick stabbed a finger against his name on the passport.

'British?' the sergeant asked.

Nick nodded.

'God bless the Queen.'

'I'm sure she will.'

'They ever tell you your Queen is real great buddy with my King?'

'No, they didn't. Listen, I don't want to sound rude, but I'm here on important business. I have a telephone number here that you can call. It's in Rabat, at your national police headquarters. The man at this number will tell you who I am and why I'm here. Please ring it.'

Nick tore a sheet from his notebook and passed it over the counter. It was beginning to grow hot. A fan stood in one corner, either switched off or broken. Flies buzzed around the door or played across the *affiches* of various kinds that covered the whitewashed walls of the little room. From somewhere nearby came the sound of Arabic singing, the Iraqi Kazem Essaher relayed to Ouarzazate via the ubiquitous satellite dish. No fax machine, thought Nick, but enough television dishes for a small city.

Benkirane passed the sheet back to Nick.

'No need to call Rabat,' he said. 'Just tell us why you are here. We will decide if Rabat is needed. You tell us first your business.'

Nick hesitated. He'd wanted to be backed up here by a little authority, however spurious. But he didn't want to risk making his two policemen uncooperative. He'd been warned by an old Foreign Office friend before leaving that, once a Moroccan decides not to co-operate, you might as well abandon whatever it was you thought of doing.

'I've come about my son,' he said. 'I thought you might have recognized the name. He's Peter Budgeon, of course. The boy who's accused of killing his girlfriend and then himself. I've come to see his body. Arrange for both of their bodies to be repatriated. Taken home.'

A poster above the constable's head warned tourists that the penalties for buying and selling hashish or other drugs were severe, and would be imposed without exception.

The sergeant looked puzzled.

'Body? I am sorry, Monsieur Boujean, but I don't get what you're about. You say someone has killed your son?'

'No, my information is that he killed himself. After killing his girlfriend. They were staying in a cheap hotel.'

'Here? In Ouarzazate?'

'That's what I was told.'

'When was this?' asked the constable.

'I think, let me see, I think the day before yesterday.'

'Here in Ouarzazate?'

'Yes, of course in Ouarzazate. That's why I'm here.'

He could feel his temper rising. What was so difficult about this? They were policemen, weren't they? And even tourist policemen must deal in corpses from time to time.

The sergeant shook his head.

'Is some mistake. I'm so sorry. But you have been sent so far by mistake.'

'My sources . . . Listen, this information came from the highest level of the British police. I'm a retired police commander. My information is impeccable.'

But already he'd started to doubt it. Perhaps there'd been some ghastly mistake, after all. Maybe it wasn't Peter, maybe Peter and Daisy were down in the Sahara . . .

'You should ring to your home. Ring to London. Speak to someone there. Or maybe your embassy in Rabat. They will know.'

'But how can you be sure?'

The constable looked pityingly at him.

'There has been no killing here. No suicide. There are no bodies in Ouarzazate morgue. We have had no reports of deaths of foreigners from anywhere in this region. Believe me, this is mistake. Your son is not here.'

8

In Morocco, it is never difficult to find a guide. Every male citizen between the ages of four and ninety is an official guide, albeit in the overwhelming majority of cases self-appointed to that calling. They all claim to speak the most fluent English, French and Spanish, and by some miracle every one of them has a brother/cousin/uncle/nephew/distant relation who owns a carpet shop. The shop may be variously called 'Gallerie of Art', 'Antiquarians', or simply 'Artisanal Emporium', but once through the door the tourist will invariably find him or herself in a carpet workshop. Meanwhile, next door, there will be more tourists, equally eager to see the sights, and equally stymied in their efforts to do so by yet another self-appointed guide and his carpet-selling cousin.

When Nicholas left the Azghor, having telephoned Duncan Todd and learned that he'd gone off to Cheltenham for a workshop, his problem was not how to find a guide, but how to find one who could get him from A to B without trying to inveigle him into visiting Ouarzazate's world-famous art gallery and museum. 'It only take five minute, I guarantee you get private treatment. Or maybe you rather I introduce you my sister . . .'

They were hanging around everywhere: street urchins, schoolboys mysteriously absent from class, bored teenagers, their shoes and clothes dusty from a vigorous game of football, their minds and hands empty, young adults on the lookout for single Western women. How might he choose one from another? A winning smile? A flash of intelligence in the eyes? Poise? Grace? He shrugged mentally. Wherever he looked, he saw precious little sign of either poise or grace.

Once he left the immediate precincts of the hotel, he was fair game. They rounded on him like harpies, with ecstatic cries of 'Guide! Guide, monsieur!' and 'You want guide, Mister?' that punctuated the air like the high-pitched calls of bats. He tried his best to fend them off, but they had attached themselves to him now, and were oblivious of all but the hope of a handful of dirhams he might pay over at the end of the day. And for some, perhaps, the less realizable hope that they might be taken up by a rich foreigner, for sexual or other reasons, given a passport, and taken out of Morocco to begin a new life on a foreign shore.

On the edge of the group, several yards removed from the others, a young man of about twenty-five was watching, like an actor waiting in the wings for the cue that would call him on stage. He was dressed in a cotton jellaba, pure white and newly laundered, and he wore leather shoes rather than the all-too-familiar trainers. Nick sensed that he was either comfortably off or a gang leader. Pete had mentioned in one of his letters that the crime bosses here could be identified by their white jellabas and sunglasses.

Nick came to a quick decision. Shaking his head briskly at each of his new friends, he forged a way through the crowd until he broke through and reached the boy. It was only then, close up, that he realized the startling resemblance the young man held to Peter, and for a moment, he felt his mouth grow dry and his tongue falter. The boy reddened and turned away, swinging on one heel as he made to hurry down the street.

'*Mais non*,' Nick cried after him, embarrassed that he must have seemed no more than another middle-aged European homosexual in search of a young man's favours. North Africa had been the chosen venue for such encounters ever since André Gide found his Adonis at Biskra in 1893, and the old and weary still sought out young flesh in Moroccan lanes and byways.

The young man half turned. Nick spoke rapidly in French, choosing the language out of instinct.

'No,' he said, 'you misunderstand. I need to speak to you. I want a guide. Not for the sights, for business. Perhaps you know someone.'

The boy halted. Nick felt the other youths melt away from him. They were acknowledging something, he thought; but what?

'You want help?' asked the boy. His French was fluent, the accent that of any educated Frenchman.

Nick approached him.

'I need someone who can take me where I need to go.'

A flicker of a smile passed over the young man's lips.

'And where exactly do you need to go?'

'I'm not sure exactly. I don't even know what there is here. Is there some sort of municipality, a mayor's office, something like that?'

'Yes, of course. There is something like that.'

'And the mortuary. Is there one?'

The boy's eyes widened, and Nick could sense his interest increasing.

'Strictly speaking, no. We have no coroner. For that we have to go to Marrakech. But there is a clinic, and a little room attached. Sometimes bodies are left there, if there's some question over how they died. Are you looking for a body, then?'

Nick explained. The boy frowned when he came to tell him how he'd been treated by the police.

'They are tourist police,' the young man said. 'They are paid to look after you.'

'But I'm not a tourist. Perhaps they saw that I haven't come here to spend money.'

'You are a guest in my country. But perhaps they are right when they say there has been no body.'

'Perhaps. But I want to ask around. They're tourist police, after all. This is more than a dispute with some greedy taxi driver.'

'Well, we shall see. I'll show you round. It will be an honour.'

'Steady. We haven't agreed on a price yet.'

'Price?'

'For showing me round.'

The young man shook his head. Again Nick noticed that oblique resemblance to Peter.

'There is nothing to pay,' he said decisively. 'I am not a guide: not professional, not amateur. You are my guest.'

'You don't have a cousin who sells carpets, by any chance?'

Nick was growing more relaxed, but he still did not quite

trust this all-too-plausible youngster with his 'my country is yours, my home is yours' routine.

'As a matter of fact, I do,' said the young man, smiling. 'But his shop is in Marrakech, and he never sells to tourists.'

'I'll look him up one day. But you haven't introduced yourself.'

'My apologies. My name is Sidi Djamil el-Mokri. You may call me Djamil.'

Nick detected something of a formality in the way el-Mokri introduced himself, and decided to respond in like fashion.

'I'm Commander Nicholas Budgeon. Formerly of Special Branch.'

El-Mokri looked at him quizzically.

'Special Branch?'

'It's a division of the British police. For combating terrorism.'

The Moroccan's eyebrows rose a fraction.

'You may call me Djamil,' he repeated. 'And now, I think we should try to find the mayor.'

The mayor turned out to be Djamil's uncle. He lived on the edge of town, in a pink villa between the run-down zoo and the new golf course. The villa was newly built, but had been designed to imitate the architecture of the kasbahs that dominated the region. Its more modern features – plate glass, three satellite dishes, a swimming pool to one side – clashed garishly with the rest, but were, Djamil explained, proud expressions of his uncle's status.

His name was Si M'hamed Abdellatif el-Mokri, and he

was the biggest man Nick had ever set eyes upon. In height, he must have approached seven feet, while his girth would have made a New Zealand rugby player quail. He was not fat, but very broad and a little muscle-bound. Black eyes like tiny olives moved above an otherwise still face. He caught sight of Nick the moment he set foot inside the room.

Djamil had taken Nick in through the front door, which was left open at all times, so that citizens might have constant access to their mayor. The reception room in which he held his audiences lay towards the back of the house. They made their way there down a long corridor through which wafted the smells of cooking, spiceless *tajine* and couscous that had already been boiled to death.

The reception room was already full of supplicants. It seemed more like a sultan's *diwan* than a small-town mayor's parlour. The interior decoration might have won prizes in a dozen European cities: each of the four walls was covered by a mural, and each mural consisted of a blow-up of a photograph. One showed an alpine scene, the one beside it the Sydney Opera House, the one next to that a herd of wildebeest running across an African plain, and the last the Eiffel Tower festooned with light.

At the heart of this multicoloured lunacy sat Djamil's uncle M'hamed, a lifetime *National Geographic* subscriber who had never set foot outside Morocco in his sixty-five years. His attention diverted, first by his nephew's entrance, then by the sight of a stranger in his chambers, he fell silent. Djamil walked casually to the front and greeted his uncle, first by taking his hands in his own, then by pouring out a string of enquiries after his health.

'*Ya 'ammi, labas? Kif halek? Nta bi-khayr?*'

The older man returned his greetings more or less at random, while drawing his head down and kissing him on both cheeks.

'*Labas, barakallah fik.*' Then, in a lower voice, 'What the fuck is this? Can't you see I'm busy? Take your tourist friends to one of your posh hotels.' Then loudly once more, '*Ana bi-khayr, al-hamdu-l illah . . .*'

'*Ash khbarek?* He's a policeman from England, a commander, a very important man. Naturally, I brought him to see you.'

After a minute or so of this, Djamil stepped back, his posture more deferential than ever, and Si M'hamed made a brief, dismissive gesture towards his audience. No one complained. They filed out one by one, each turning to bid a formal farewell as he passed through the doorway.

They were left alone. A servant entered, and Si M'hamed ordered mint tea to be brought from the café next door. Djamil bent forward again.

'He speaks French,' he said. 'Speak in French, he will understand.'

'What is this about?'

'He will explain.'

'Wait until the tea is here.'

The mayor got to his feet and smiled lopsidedly at his new guest.

'*Je vous en prie,*' he said, gesturing to a group of armchairs on the other side of the room. Nick and Djamil followed him there.

There were no windows in the room, but a wheezy air-conditioning system kept the atmosphere fresh enough to breathe. Nick found it uncomfortable.

They went through all the available formalities. 'How long have you been in Morocco? Do you intend to stay long? Are you here on holiday or business?'

Nick's vague answers fell into a growing silence. Then the door opened, and the servant came in carrying a wide brass tray on which were set a large beaten silver teapot stuffed with fresh mint leaves, and several glass cups in silver holders. Some suspicious-looking cakes lay on a glass plate.

The tea was served, and Nick took his first hot sip of the sweet green tea that was prepared everywhere here. To his surprise, he found it pleasant, if oversweet. He reckoned there must be enough sugar in the pot to kill a small town of diabetics.

Quickly, he explained the situation to Djamil's uncle. The mayor frowned as he listened. When Nick's account of what had happened drew to a close, he nodded. In truth, he'd taken in very little of what had been said. That did not concern him, since he had known most of his life that exercising authority in Ouarzazate had very little to do with mental acuteness or wisdom, and was mainly a matter of knowing whose button to push, and when.

He clapped his hands, and his manservant reappeared. Si M'hamed whispered some instructions to him, and the little man scurried off to do his bidding.

'*Eh, bien,*' said the mayor, returning his gaze to Nick. 'Tell me about yourself. Have you come from Paris?'

It took about forty minutes for the servant to return. He'd been outside, and now appeared with seven local worthies in tow. The two hapless policemen whom Nick had already met were there, and five others whom he did not recognize, all wearing white jellabas, and handworked *babouches* on their feet.

Djamil introduced them to Nick: Moulay Ahmed Dukkali, prayer leader at the town's main mosque; Sidi Mohyi'd-Din Derkaoui, head of a local mystical fraternity; Ben-asser Layarbi, the postmaster; Dr Abdeslam Fasi, the doctor in charge of the local clinic; and Si Moussa Gharbaoui, headmaster of the secondary school. With the exception of the policemen, these made up most of the local notability. Nick noticed right away that everyone else deferred to the two religious figures, and that the mystic seemed to be treated as the superior of the prayer leader.

Si M'hamed explained the situation, then asked Nick to go through it all again in his own words. By now, he was growing tired of what was fast becoming a charade, the purpose of which he could not fathom. Each of his interlocutors questioned him in turn, rehearsing the facts of the matter again and again. Nick noticed that Derkaoui said nothing through all this, but went on looking at him, as if to penetrate some hidden barrier.

'If there had been either a murder or a suicide,' said the doctor, a man of about forty dressed in Western clothes, 'the bodies would certainly have been sent to me to carry out a postmortem. But the truth is, I haven't been required to perform an autopsy in almost a year. This is a quiet town, monsieur. People pass through. They come and go away again. Nobody stays for long.'

'What about the inhabitants?'

The doctor shrugged.

Beside him, the headmaster seemed to wriggle before offering an implausible answer.

'We do not murder one another, monsieur.'

Moulay Ahmed nodded and added his own observation.

'And we do not commit suicide. We are Muslims. We have no need for suicide or any other Western vices.'

They talked in this manner for about an hour, and by the time they had finished, Nick was pretty well convinced that there'd been a dreadful mistake, though just how dreadful he had no idea. But for three things. One was the way in which the holy man kept looking at him. It was not a particularly spiritual look, and while he felt the old man's eyes on him – for the marabout must have been eighty at least – he felt as though they were expecting him to leap up at any moment and attack them. The old man feared him, and as he watched the others closely, he saw that they all feared him. Could that be because his story was true, after all?

Secondly, he became aware after a time that Djamil, the young man who'd brought him here, was looking guilty. He would let his gaze fall on Nick for a few moments, then snatch it away furtively. As though he knew something. As though he knew the foreigner's story might be true.

It was the third thing that clinched it, however. The postmaster patiently explained that, over the past month or so, he had neither sent nor received letters in the name of Peter Budgeon or Peter Le Tourneau. Nick remembered how Peter sometimes liked to use his mother's maiden name. He'd written a number of articles, signing off with it as a nom de plume, and if he wanted to keep certain things confidential, he would revert to it. But how had the postmaster known that? Nick squeezed his memory, but he could not remember saying anything about the name Le Tourneau to anyone in the room.

In the end, he expressed himself puzzled but satisfied.

'It must have been a huge mistake,' he said. 'My source in London must have misunderstood, or perhaps he was misinformed. Perhaps my son's all right, perhaps another tourist died, someone in another town, a Frenchman, a Pole, an Australian. I'm so sorry to have given you all so much trouble.'

They all nodded and made understanding noises at the back of their throats. One by one, they got up and shook his hand, then filed out. Without them, the constant hum of the air-conditioning seemed to grow louder. He stood at last himself, and shook the mayor's enormous hand, and let his eyes fill with a semblance of sincerity. Yet he knew they had all lied to him, and he wondered what to do next.

Djamil took him back to his hotel. As Nick made to go inside, the young man turned back to him.

'They were lying. You know that, don't you?'

Nick nodded.

'Is there anything you can do?' he asked.

Djamil shrugged.

'Maybe. Maybe not. This is a small town. My family run most of it. Don't be deceived – you are not in London now. It can be very dangerous here, and you will not find anyone to help you. Give me a little time. Meet me tonight. Chez Dmitri. Seven o'clock.'

He hurried away and was soon lost to sight. Nick turned into the hotel. He had some phone calls to make.

9

Au Maroc, tout s'arrange . . . They all say that. Some even believe it. The reason they say it in the first place is precisely because nothing ever seems to come right under the hot Moroccan sun or the cold Moroccan rains.

It took over an hour for Nick to get through to London, and when he did it wasn't much better. Someone had installed the world's most vicious automated answering system on New Scotland Yard's switchboard. Like all such systems, it was inexorable: once you were in, there was no apparent way out. All the caller could do was to stab unhappily on key after key, hoping that each stroke would take him a step further into the three-dimensional web.

A stern woman's voice gave directions. 'For the National Crime Squad, press button nine, followed by the star key . . . for the Public Order Department, press seventeen, one seven, followed by the star key, twice . . . for the Royalty and Diplomatic Protection Department and the Special Escort Group, simply press zero . . . for the Specialist Operations Branch, press seven five and the star key now . . .'

He pressed desperately, knowing how long it would

take to get back to this point if he had to start from the beginning again.

'For the Organized Crime Group, press one; for SO19, press two . . . for Special Branch, press seven, now . . .'

He stabbed the button and waited for a dialling tone, but was instead told to key in the initials of the person he wished to speak to, using the alphanumeric keypad. 'DT,' he keyed, and a phone at the other end sprang into life.

A young woman answered, her voice unknown to Nick. She hadn't been there three weeks ago.

'Commander Todd's office? May I help you?'

'You can certainly help by making sure I don't get re-routed to Photographic and Graphics Services or Operation Bumblebee.'

'Are you ringing from Photographic Services, sir?'

'No, I'm ringing from bloody Africa. Can you put me through to Commander Todd this instant, please? It's urgent. Would you like me to spell that for you?'

'There's no call to be sarcastic, sir. I understand what you're saying. However, the Commander receives a lot of urgent calls throughout the day. If you could tell me what this is about –'

'This will be about your job any minute. Just put me through. Tell him it's Nick Budgeon.'

'And you're ringing from?'

Before Nick could shout at her again, someone else picked up the phone.

'Nick, is that you?'

'It was the last time I looked in a mirror.'

There was a click on the line.

'Miss Green, would you please ensure that Commander

Budgeon and I are not disturbed? This is a private call. Yes, Nick. What have you found?'

Nick explained. When he came to a close, a short pause followed. For a few moments, he feared he'd been cut off.

When Duncan spoke again, Nick knew straight away that he'd been right to call.

'Nick, I don't know what this call is costing you. I need to get some papers; it's important. I may need to fax them to you. Can I . . . ? Listen, tell me where you're ringing from, the number and everything, and I'll get back to you as soon as I've tracked this stuff down.'

'Duncan, is there a mistake? Did I get the place wrong?'

A short, pregnant silence.

'No,' said Duncan. 'You got nothing wrong. They're stitching you up, Nick. But I need the documents to prove it.'

Nick gave him the name and number of his hotel. They said goodbye, and Nick hung up.

Three hours later, Nick woke from a deep sleep. The light that indicated messages on his telephone was not illuminated. He picked up the receiver and tried to ring out, but found he could not even get a dialling tone.

Still yawning, he made his way down to reception, where they informed him that the telephone system was broken. Had there been any faxes? he asked.

The receptionist, a sporting type with impressive biceps, whose uniform looked as though it was strangling his upper body, shrugged.

'Non, m'sieur. Pas de fax. Rien n'est pas arrivé aujourd'hui.'

'The same problem?'

'*Oui, m'sieur.*'

'Do you know when it will be fixed?'

'Maybe today. Maybe tomorrow. Very hard to say.'

He shrugged again.

Nick took himself off to the post office on the aptly named rue de la Poste. There, a drab employee with dirty red hair told him that no foreign calls were going in or out.

'*Ghedda*,' the red-haired man repeated. '*Ghedda.*' Come back tomorrow, and all may be well. Or not.

The other hotels would not let him use their telephones, since he was not a guest. In the end, he gave up and went for a late lunch in the pizzeria at the Hanane Club hotel. The pizza owed more to Texas than Italy, but it was large and hot, and Nick had never considered himself an adventurer in international cuisine. He ate it slowly, both reassured and troubled by Duncan Todd's response. Was it just coincidence that all telephone communications between Ouarzazate and England seemed to have been cut off for the duration?

That evening he left the Azghor with twenty minutes to spare before his appointment with Djamil in Dmitri's. It was already dark, and although the streets were fairly well lit by rows of street lamps, it was impossible to throw off the sense of remoteness. It was a remoteness he'd known very seldom: in the Hebrides, once on the west coast of Ireland, and once in Canada. It was unmistakable – as though nothing of any meaning existed beyond the lights. If the lights were to be extinguished, he thought, all that meaninglessness would come rushing in to overwhelm him.

'Monsieur Budgeon?'

A figure detached itself from the shadows on the other side of the road.

'It's me, Djamil. If you're hungry, we can go to Dmitri's. Otherwise, I'd like to head on. I don't think we should be seen together in public.'

'What exactly is it you want to show me?'

'You will see. You need to be a little patient. It isn't far. Can you ride a motorbike?'

'It was one of the first things they taught us at police college. The answer is yes.'

'Mine is just round the corner.'

'Djamil, can I trust you? How do I know you aren't just planning to knock me on the head at the first opportunity and steal my wallet?'

'You don't know. You have to trust, is all. Here. I'll steer, you take the pillion seat. This won't take long.'

'Why are you doing this?'

'You don't know what I'm doing.'

'You appear to be helping me. Perhaps you hope I'll pay you well.'

Djamil made no reply.

Satisfied that Nick was seated securely behind him, Djamil kicked his bike into life. They headed down to Mohammed V, then west along the Marrakech road. The bike's engine sounded as though it hadn't been tuned in years. It cut through the night like a rusty knife tearing through black velvet. Neither man spoke: there would have been little point.

They passed through a long section of brightly lit houses, the villas of Ouarzazate's rich. The night air was warm against Nick's hands and cheeks. Djamil swerved from time to time to avoid a pothole or some object fallen from a lorry. There was little traffic in either direction. A handful of headlights swept towards them and passed quickly away, swallowed up for ever in the night.

They'd gone about three miles when Djamil slowed down and turned left onto a narrower road heading southwest. They'd scarcely been on it a few minutes before lights showed ahead.

'Tifeltout,' said Djamil, braking to a halt and switching off the engine. 'You have heard of it, naturally.'

'I'm afraid not. Remember, I'm just a policeman.'

'You speak very good French for a policeman.'

'That's for family reasons. Why have you brought me out here? I don't have any money on me. I'm not worth threatening or beating up.'

'You have to trust me, Commander. I haven't brought you here to do you any harm. If I'd wanted to do that, or have that done, believe me, it would have been very easy in Ouarzazate. As things stand, I am running the greater risk in bringing you here at all.'

He propped the motorcycle against a nearby wall and set off along the road on foot. Nick walked alongside him, sizing up Tifeltout.

'Tifeltout is just a little place,' said Djamil as they walked through the darkness. He'd brought a Maglite, and shone its beam ahead of them, picking out a surface laced with potholes. 'But it has the most beautiful kasbah in Morocco.'

'Kasbah? As in the phrase, "Take me to your kasbah"?'

'I'm sorry?'

'Old movies. The raven-haired beauty was supposed to say something like that to the sheikh of Araby. I'll explain it all later. In the meantime, I assume a kasbah is some sort of palace.'

'Not really. It might have a palace. The kasbah at Ouarzazate was built as a palace for the Glaoui family, but none of them ever lived there.'

'Glaoui?'

'They were great lords at one time. Most of southern Morocco was in their hands.'

'When was this?'

'When were the Glaoui pashas powerful? From the beginning of the twentieth century till about 1956. They supported the French too eagerly. By the time of Independence, it was too late for them to switch sides. They were severely punished for their mistakes. My grandfather was chamberlain to the last of them, and our family was brought down with theirs.'

He stood for a moment, contemplating the great half-ruin in front of him.

'But you don't need to know about the Glaouis or the Mokris. I want to tell you what a kasbah is. Because it is dark, you will not be able to make much sense of the one we're going to. It's like a giant fortress, with walls and battlements and towers, but inside it's very like a village or a little town. A whole tribe could take refuge behind the walls, close the doors, and defy their enemies.

'All the old kasbahs are in some state of ruin now. What use are mud walls and plaster battlements against modern artillery? No one can hide behind a wooden door to escape a tank.

'But you Westerners think they are romantic. You come here to make romantic films, *The Sheltering Sky* or *Lawrence of Arabia*. And tourists turn up every day in coaches, get down, take photographs, and leave again. My people try to make as much money from them as they can.

'Tifeltout is the loveliest of all the kasbahs, but most of it is still in ruins, and it has been closed to visitors for the last six months. That is why it was chosen.'

'Chosen?'

'As the *makan al-hadith*. The scene of the crime. Come inside. Let me show you.'

The torch beam showed a rock-littered slope with traces of old steps buried in the soil. Nick scrambled up and found himself at the threshhold of a brass-studded wooden door. Djamil joined him and pushed it open, and they went inside.

For some reason, the night seemed a little blacker here. Then Nick realized they had been passing through a roofed section. Suddenly, they came out into a narrow alley white-washed by moonlight. He looked up to see stars, and a grey mass of ramparts slanting in every direction. To his left, a light flickered, and he stiffened, thinking someone was out there in the dark, coming towards them.

'It's all right,' whispered Djamil. 'They're just poor people who live here in the ruins. There are whole families over there.'

'Did my son come here?' Nick asked. 'With Daisy?'

'Don't talk so loudly,' Djamil admonished him. 'Just follow me.'

He turned the torch on a long wall to the right, and they walked down the alley until Djamil stopped at an old wooden door that was sagging on broken hinges. With an effort he pushed it open and slipped inside, playing the torch over the entrance so that Nick could push his own way in.

They were inside the main kasbah building now, and followed a narrow, winding corridor for what seemed an age, then up rickety stairs that cracked and groaned as they climbed them, then down another corridor that took them through a series of rooms filled with mouldering furniture and cobwebs. Moonlight came at times through broken latticework, or through ventilation grilles high up near the moulded ceilings. Fine white plasterwork still gleamed like intricately carved bones above their heads, but a grey film of dust lay on everything else.

Nick glanced down at the floor.

'Stop,' he said.

'What's wrong?'

'The dust. Look. There are more footprints here than just yours and mine.'

'I know.'

'How's that?'

'I was down here a few nights ago. With some of my family.'

'What for?'

'Be patient.'

They walked on. Then Djamil shone his torch on a red door that bore Arabic writing all round its edge. He seemed to hesitate, then pushed the door open. It swung away from him. Without a word, he handed the torch to Nick.

'I'm sorry,' he said.

Nick took the torch and stepped inside the room. It was like the others he'd been through. Part of the window had been taken away or had fallen out, and a long moonbeam streamed inside. A table with old photographs. The tracks of desert mice. A silver teapot left over from a forgotten feast. And something in one corner. A heap of rags. Not rags. Nick crossed the room.

They had been stabbed to death, Daisy first, perhaps, then Pete. Their hands had been tied behind their backs, and someone had stabbed them like that, stabbed them and cut their throats. The blood had long dried on their faces and bodies.

He bent down and drew a strand of hair back from his son's forehead. Both bodies exuded a sickly sweet odour of decay. Had they been hidden here all along, or had someone transferred them today from somewhere cooler?

He kissed Peter on both cheeks, and straightened Daisy's hair a little, then stood unsteadily. His heart was beating fast. His hands were shaking, and his eyes had filled with tears. He did not hear Djamil approach him.

'We can't stay here any longer, Commander. They may come to check. There's nothing more you can do. We have to leave.'

He let the young man lead him from the room. At the door, he looked back.

'I mean to make them pay,' he said. His voice was pitiless. 'You understand that? Whoever they are, whatever their influence, I shall make them pay for what they did.'

Djamil looked at him.

'Then you have signed a warrant for your own death, Commander. This is Morocco. This kasbah, these mountains, the desert to the south of us, everything belongs to them. Come now, I will take you back to your hotel.'

10

They sped back through the empty night, through a sullen blackness that tempted Nick's thoughts to journey in a dozen bleak directions. He'd thought himself grief-stricken before this, but what he'd just seen had blotted out a world of befores.

All the way a single face stared at him, as though shining on Djamil's back. Not Peter's face, not Nathalie's, no one he knew personally. The face belonged to a twelve-year-old boy, Liam O hEadhra, a schoolboy from West Belfast, a small child for his age, as brilliant on the hurley pitch as in the classroom, where he'd excelled in mathematics.

Liam's father had been a prominent nationalist – hence the change of his surname O'Hara to its correct Irish spelling – and a councillor for a Sinn Fein-dominated ward. He'd never been a man of violence, though, and was regularly heard decrying both Sinn Fein and the Provisional IRA. It was only his hard work for the community and his staunch Republican ideals that saw him through from election to election.

One year, however, O hEadhra Senior misread the situation. He made a speech in which he attacked the IRA leadership and sneered at Sinn Fein's inability to force them to disarm. The next morning, his body was found beside a road near the airport, his brains spilled over the grass verge on which he lay.

British intelligence got a rare break before noon that day. The IRA planned to do away with O hEadhra's wife and only child. Nick was contacted, and that afternoon Liam was whisked out of school and onto a plane for Glasgow, along with his mother. Nick set them up with new identities in another part of the country. Liam's mother, a woman in her early thirties called Grainne, knew where a lot of bodies were buried, and with her husband gone, it was only a matter of time before she started talking.

The cover didn't work. Grainne and her child should never have been given fresh identities on the British mainland. Special Branch should have sent them to Australia or Canada, somewhere big enough and anonymous enough to swallow them whole. Liam's accent stuck out at his new school, Grainne's at the shops. They fell on the boy first, so she'd suffer the double shock, the double grief.

He must have been accosted on his way home from school, an aunt or uncle, cousin or old friend from Belfast, someone he'd recognize and trust long enough to be snatched away. He was found the following morning, in a back alley where the wheelie bins had been left standing for the lorries. Nick was notified immediately, and flown to the spot by helicopter. He remembered every moment of the flight, his cigarette dripping ash on the metal floor.

They'd seen to it that the boy suffered. One of them had written a full account of what they'd done, and posted it through Nick's door that morning, just before the alarm went up. He read it later, then emptied the contents of his stomach down the toilet bowl. The words made sense to him. He'd been there after all, he'd seen the child's injuries. Liam must have taken hours to die, must have pleaded for death long before they killed him. No part of him was left untouched. A sadist had done it, or a group of sadists: no normal human being could have invented such wounds or such abrasions.

It was all kept quiet, of course, not a word leaked out to the press, not even the boy's family ever learned what had become of him; it was as if the earth had swallowed him up. Nick had to sit through a secret inquest while a pathologist described each blow in excruciating detail.

It took him three years to track them down, and when he did he made sure they never saw the inside of a courtroom. No one blamed him; they all wanted to do the same. But it had been Nick's case, Nick's responsibility. He carried the scars for years, still carried them. Just one little boy, he said to himself in those first days; but if you'd seen what they'd done to him . . .

He made very sure of his targets before bringing anybody in. They had to be guilty; he wasn't going to have the lives of innocents on his hands. Three years' stalking, with revenge in his heart – a terrible feeling; he'd never wanted to feel it again. He'd sought help afterwards, just to straighten himself out, and until tonight he'd thought himself free of that evil.

In the end he'd used a small team of SAS assassins, three men so steeped in brutality they'd have killed their own mothers. There were four targets, three men and a woman, a slip of a girl called Bridie Twomey. She'd been seventeen when she'd done it. She was the boy's cousin, the bait that had made him lower his guard, but she'd stayed on that night, she'd taken part in the torture. Nick had been reminded of Myra Hindley. He'd heard those tapes, he knew what was on them, and a tape like them, an imaginary tape, often played in his head, with the cries and pleas of little Liam. He'd told the SAS team they could do what they liked. The targets had to know why they were being killed. When it was over, he just felt numb.

Now, holding on hard to Djamil, his knees pressed against the motorbike, he felt the old horror surface, and he knew he would not sleep easy until he'd brought them to book. It didn't matter who they were, how many noble ancestors they'd had. He'd hunt them down one by one, and this time he wouldn't leave the final job to someone else.

Djamil drew up at the Blue Fountains intersection, just below Nick's hotel. It was far from late, but Ouarzazate had already fallen asleep. Nick could hear a steady pulse of Rai music from the Hanane Club, where the wealthier tourists and the more presentable local youth planned to boogie together for most of the night. Otherwise, Ouarzazate might have been a ghost town.

'Go straight to your hotel,' Djamil whispered. 'Don't answer the door to anyone.'

'And you?'

'I am going home. I told my parents I have met a tourist who wants to see the Aït Ben Haddou kasbah by moonlight, and that I will be a little late. They know nothing of this other matter.'

'Thank you. Thank you for all you've done. You must let me pay you something . . .'

Djamil put his hand out.

'No, I want nothing. You will offend me if you ask again. You must get up early and take the first flight to Paris. Try to forget what you have seen here. It is better you forget. There is nothing you can do, believe me. This is not England, it is Morocco, and this is Ouarzazate. Your rules do not apply here.'

He turned and took hold of the handlebars of his motor-cycle. As he did so, someone called out from the shadows near Mohammed V.

'*Sssss! A Si Djamil! Fein ghadi?*'

Djamil hesitated. Behind him, another voice called, this time in English.

'*A Si Djamil!* You don' like to speak with your ol' frien's?'

'Who you' frien', Djamil? Maybe you like to introduce him?'

'*Qu'est-ce que vous faîtes ici, Monsieur Djamil?*'

'*Ash khbarek, ya habibi. Kulshi bekhir?*'

The taunting continued without a moment's abatement. They were all round them, their faces hidden, their voices mocking, questioning and teasing in a torrent of Arabic, French and English.

'Who are they?' asked Nick. The voices were coming closer, hemming them in. At first, they concentrated exclusively on Djamil, but after a minute or so, Nick found himself included in the calls. He understood none of the Arabic, but the French and English were unmistakable.

'*Ya Nasrani! Fein ghadi? Ash katdir?*'

'Where you been, Mister? You been with M'sieur Djamil, kissie-kissie? You go fuck him, Mister?'

'*Il est très joli, n'est-ce pas? Très mignon pou' vous, M'sieu le Commandant . . .*'

'Or maybe you been somewhere, eh? Been somewhere you shouldn't go?'

They were circling now, moving in slowly. Nick guessed they did not know whether he or Djamil was armed. It might be worth the risk suggesting that they were.

'Are you armed, Djamil?' he asked quietly.

'I'm sorry. Not even a knife.'

'Maybe you can tell them you have a gun.'

'That won't stop them.'

'Who are they? Are they the street kids I saw earlier?'

'Some. I don't recognize all the voices. Mostly, they work for my uncle, or for his brother, Si Osman. I think you should get on this bike and ride out of here as fast as you can. Don't stop. That road will take you to the airport. Buy a ticket and take the first plane out of Ouarzazate. Don't come back.'

'What will you do?'

'I'll stay here. I'll talk with them. It's not really me they want, it's you.'

'Get on the bike. We can both get out of here.'

Djamil laughed.

'You only have to wave your passport and off you go. Anywhere in the world. I don't even have a passport. I can go nowhere but Morocco, and there is nowhere to hide in Morocco. Believe me.'

Nick watched the figures creep out of the darkness. Some were armed, perhaps all of them. Knives mostly, blades that flashed in the moonlight. And heavy sticks that did not.

He straddled the motorbike, pleading with Djamil to sit

113

behind him. Then someone came running up and hit him on the shoulder with something very hard. He made up his mind. If Peter and Daisy were to be avenged, he had to get out of here in one piece.

He slammed the kick-start and gunned the bike forwards into the road, scattering his attackers. One went down under his front wheel, almost throwing Nick from the saddle; the others fell back. He circled, trying to come close to Djamil.

'Get on the pillion!' he shouted. 'I'll take you out of here.'

For answer he heard Djamil call sharply to the men round him, then cry out pitifully loud and clear as one moved in and knifed him between the ribs. Nick saw the flicker of lifted knives, heard Djamil call out in fear and pain as his assailants dealt their blows. His cries grew quieter with every blow, and at last he fell to the ground, silent. His killers stepped back, their hands red with blood.

'*Andak*!' shouted one, twisting his body round to look in Nick's direction. '*En-Nasrani*!'

Nick did not hesitate another second. He kicked the bike into life a second time and drove away on the first road he could find.

In the Land of War

11

The daily journal of Marie-Louise Guénaud
15 rue du Dr Madelaine (ancienne rue du Djenan Hartsi)
Ville Nouvelle, Marrakech

Friday, 5 July 1940
News has just reached us of the terrible bombardment at
Oran, and on the radio today it has been announced that
the French government at Vichy has broken off relations
with Britain in retaliation. When I heard about the attack
on Mers el-Kebir harbour, and the devastation caused by
the British fleet to our ships, I was distraught, for I was
sure my dear brother Achille's submarine, the *Surcouf*, was
lying up there. But Vital checked, and it seems the *Surcouf*
is in Portsmouth after all, and has been commandeered
by the English. We all thought the French fleet would be
immune from attack, because Hitler had made a point of
leaving the ships under the command of our leadership
at Vichy.

Knowing Achille is safe after all is a blessed relief, but
the rest is bad news, of course. Like it or not, we are now
as much a part of the conflict as our friends and relatives
in Europe. As my dear Shadeeya puts it, we are all living

in the Dar al-Harb, the House of War. If the British were willing to shell a French-controlled port in Algeria, which is so very close to us, what's to stop them hitting targets here in Morocco tomorrow? Vital says there's no good military reason for them to do that at the moment, but even he admits the situation could change at any moment. And it can't do any good if Pétain decides to enter the war again, this time against our old allies. I truly hope we stay out of the conflict now, or, if we do go back in, at least we should be on the right side. Not that one dares say anything like that round here. We may not be under the German boot exactly, but nobody wants to upset them.

One of our French neighbours, a M. Delavigne, a senior manager with the Société Marseillaise de Crédit, was picked up yesterday leaving their offices on the rue Bab Agnaou. No warning or anything, two men in trench coats just turned up, slapped handcuffs on him, and bundled him into the back of a van. Vital has heard that he was taken to one of the prisons next to the Conseil de Guerre, up in the Military Quarter. He's making further enquiries, so his family will at least know where he is and what he's likely to be charged with. He lived just two doors from us. There's a wife, Renée, and two lovely children, two little girls. I spent some time with them yesterday: they're all very worried. I said we'd do what we could to find out what this is all about. Everyone's so jittery ever since the German invasion. They say this sort of thing is quite normal in wartime, but when a perfectly harmless little man like M. Delavigne can be hauled off to prison without a charge, well . . . you start to worry for yourself, you start to wonder which of us is next.

Saturday, 6 July

It seems that our neighbour may not have been that innocent after all. From what Vital has been able to dig up, he's been implicated in some sort of British plot to blow up a French ship, the *Jean Bart*, which was being built in Casablanca. If it's true, it's high treason, and I don't think there's anything any of us can do to turn the thing round. I visited his wife and children, who are violently distressed, though they don't yet know the full gravity of the situation, and I just couldn't take it on myself to be the bearer of such evil tidings. And perhaps there has been a terrible mistake after all. Poor M. Delavigne was always such an inoffensive man, the last person you'd think was a spy. He came to Morocco seven years ago, before either of his little girls was born.

There's still no word from my family in Epernay, nor from Vital's parents in Amiens. They are all in the occupied zone, and we worry that they have been caught up in the fighting there. And, of course, there are all our friends, many of them officers with the French forces. It's like a nightmare. Of course, we know all about the Boche atrocities in Poland, Czechoslovakia, Belgium, and elsewhere, so we don't expect they will have been more considerate to us French. It's a nightmare, because it's impossible to get accurate news. Vital is trying to buy a radio receiver that will pick up the BBC. Of course, he says he wants it for the Italian and German Arabic services, but everybody knows its real purpose. Our houseboy Mansour has been able to get us some out-of-date issues of a magazine called *Parade*. The English publish it in Cairo, and it gives some news and a pin-up at the back, usually Rita Hayworth.

Monday, 8 July

A letter this morning from Béa. The postal service hasn't been much affected by events, and as far as we know there's no censorship of the mails, though I think it won't be long before the military act on that. Their big problem lies in deciding whether the Moroccans can be trusted or not. On the one hand, the Sultan did issue a decree calling on his people to co-operate with the French. On the other, the nationalists may take this as their opportunity to agitate for independence. Some of them are probably pro-German, because the Germans are promising all the Arabs independence once the war is over. But I've heard that others put their faith in the British. It's all so wretchedly complicated.

Béa says they are to come to visit us next week. I haven't seen my dear sister since the wedding, and we shall have a lot to talk about.

Apparently, Gérard has volunteered for a government post now that the reins of power have shifted. He's to leave the day-to-day running of the vineyards and winery to his manager, Duval, while he carries out his new functions. I do hope it doesn't make him more pompous than he is already.

There's been awful news of M. Delavigne. He's already been tried by a military tribunal, found guilty, and sentenced to death. I can't believe it. Even if he really is guilty – and we haven't heard any evidence – surely the proper punishment should be prison. Vital says that treachery in time of war must always be a capital offence, and I suppose he's right. But it still feels hard to think of that innocuous little man being marched to the guillotine tomorrow morning, for a crime he probably did not commit.

Tuesday, 9 July

Stayed with Mme Delavigne this morning. She had been denied permission to say goodbye to her husband at the prison, and when I called just before dawn, she was utterly distraught, as were her little girls. They, poor souls, had no proper understanding of what was happening. All they know is, they want their father back, and their mother to stop crying.

Ever since his arrest, I've been sending telegrams to all sorts of people. Of course, I don't have influential connections, either here or in the *métropole*, but I have contacted both their sets of parents, and some other friends and relatives I thought could be useful. If nothing else, I think it essential her family know what's going on, so they can come out here, or arrange for her and the girls to travel back to France. She's from Montpellier, which means she's free to come and go. Surprisingly, I've not yet had a single reply from anyone. You'd think they'd get back to me right away.

Found time this afternoon to write back to Béatrice. Of course they must stay with us, we have plenty of room, and they were very kind and patient when I stayed with them in Fès. My news will wait until they're here.

Wednesday, 10 July

A most unpleasant evening yesterday. I had just put André to bed and was reading to him from one of Marcel Aymé's wonderful stories, the *Contes du chat perché*, which André adores. I was about two pages into the tale when there was a knock at the door. Shadeeya had already gone home for the night, and Vital was in his study, working hard on a murder trial that is due to start tomorrow, so I went downstairs and answered the door just as the caller knocked a second time.

In fact, it turned out to be two callers, two policemen in trench coats. The older introduced himself as Inspector Lenéru, and asked if he and his companion might come in. From their expressions, I sensed that I had little choice in the matter.

'We should like to speak with your husband as well, if he is free, madame,' the inspector told me. He was polite, but terribly cold, and evidently not prepared to stand for any refusal on my part. I fetched Vital, and we all made our way to the living room. They would not remove their coats – which were, frankly, totally unnecessary in the heat – nor would they accept so much as a cup of coffee; and when I asked them to sit down, you might have thought I'd suggested they take off their clothes. All this time, my poor heart was fluttering like a frightened bird, for I couldn't think what Vital or I had done to merit such a visit.

The inspector came straight to the point. He was watched all the time by his younger companion, who remained silent throughout the interview, but who lent an air of menace to the proceedings, for he was very well built and powerful looking.

'We understand that you have been spending some time with your neighbour, Mme Delavigne. Is that true?'

I explained exactly what had happened. And said perhaps a little more than I should have on the subject of M. Delavigne's incarceration and execution, for I caught Vital looking more than once in my direction and frowning, as though to bring me to a halt.

In the end, I don't think it mattered. The policemen had come with an express purpose, which was to warn us off.

Vital was told that enquiries such as those he had made in Delavigne's regard were off limits in future.

'Delavigne is a known associate of dubious elements in the town. He has expressed overt sympathies for the anti-German and anti-French forces, and he has engaged in subversive activities. Now he has met his proper punishment. But he is not our concern. Your enquiries, Monsieur le Juge, were thought in certain circles to have been inappropriate for someone in your position.'

Vital broke in. I could see he was angry, yet cautious.

'Monsieur,' he said, 'I think there has been some misunderstanding. M. Delavigne was not a friend or relative of mine, simply a neighbour whom I was surprised to see arrested. When I made my enquiries, he had not been found guilty. I . . .'

'His guilt or innocence were not your concern. He was under police guard. You knew he would be given a fair trial. There was no need for you to intervene. And even less for your wife to send telegrams to all and sundry. Mme Delavigne and her children have been taken into police custody for their own protection.'

'Was this with their consent?' I asked. Like Vital, I was growing furious.

'Mme Delavigne is in no position to give or withhold consent. Her own role in this matter may yet be investigated. We understand her father is a Spanish national, and have, therefore, arranged for her and her children to be sent to the concentration camp at Argèles-sur-Mer.'

'Where on earth is that?' Vital asked.

'Just south of Perpignan, almost slap on the Spanish border. They have proper facilities there for people like the Delavignes. I should warn you that any attempt to make enquiries on their behalf will meet with

123

official disapproval. Do I make myself clear?'

They left shortly after that. Neither of us got a wink of sleep last night. Vital is in court this morning, with his murder trial. We have agreed it is both pointless and dangerous to involve ourselves further with poor Mme Delavigne, but I know that, deep down, neither of us thinks the authorities have behaved properly. We can only hope that conditions in their seaside camp are reasonable.

Vital tells me there is talk of opening internment camps here in Morocco.

12

Tuesday, 16 July

Béatrice and Gérard arrived late this morning. They set off yesterday, in fact, travelling by way of Meknès and Petitjean to Casablanca, where they spent the night. Then it was a straight journey south as far as Marrakech, and there we all were at the railway station, Vital, little André, and myself. We'd hired a couple of *calèches*, one for the baggage and one for ourselves, which proved rather a squeeze. Mansour rode home with the luggage, much to my sister's alarm.

'I don't know how you can trust the boy,' she screeched as he went off regally in the back of the luggage *calèche*. 'They're all thieves, Marie-Louise, you should know that.' She was dressed in a blue costume, and wore on her head a little feathered hat with a quarter veil.

'Nonsense,' I said. Being married to a judge has given me fresh confidence, and I refuse to let her and her tiny prejudices ride roughshod over me. 'I know nothing of the sort. The Moroccans are remarkably honest.'

'It's true, Madame Le Tourneau,' said Vital. 'We find very little thievery among the native population. Much more among the French. It's a distressing fact, but not one we can ignore. Of course, this may be a problem unique to Marrakech. Fès is your territory. I would not like to comment on it.'

Gérard said nothing, but I could see he was put out, and felt that our little excursion had got off to a bad start.

We told the coachman to give us the regular tour of the ramparts, and off we trotted, for all the world like tourists, though to judge by Gérard's and Béa's manner, they had seen it all before.

The driver turned his head and, picking Vital out as the most well disposed among us, tried to negotiate a good price for our little trip. Vital merely tapped his knuckles on the Tariff of Fares next to him. There were the prices for journeys within the Ville Nouvelle (reasonable), across to the medina (much more), and, finally, the grand *Tour des Remparts*, which is enough to pay for a week at the Mamounia!

We passed through part of the New Town and got lost briefly at a *rond-point*. My brother-in-law admired the great many French flags that have gone on display since the invasion. He appears to be a great Pétainist. I wonder if he has much insight at all.

The walls proved a great success. Their redness and their sheer scale impressed even these visitors from Fès. We have an itinerary worked out for tomorrow morning, taking in half the major sites. Of course, I know we shan't get nearly so far, least of all in this terrible heat. But we can start at the Café de France, so they may see a little of the Djemaa el-Fna, and if we go no further, we shall have had a pleasant time.

Wednesday, 17 July
Perhaps I was over-optimistic to anticipate a pleasant time today. Things didn't go quite according to plan. Actually, it all went wrong yesterday to start with. After we got

back from our little tour of the ramparts, a delicious lunch was waiting for us. It had been prepared for us by Shadeeya and her fifteen-year-old daughter, Hind. It was the finest meal I've eaten since coming to Morocco, but all my sister and her husband did throughout was to pick and shake their heads and turn up their noses. It seems they now employ a French housemaid who also cooks for them, preparing traditional food typical of the Ardennes and Marne.

They restrict themselves terribly, keeping themselves as far as possible to the French town, eating only in French-owned hotels and restaurants, making friends only with their fellow French or, more recently, some Germans they have fallen in with.

It took all my skills as a hostess to avoid an argument about the Germans and how, according to my sweet brother-in-law, we need to go out of our way to be kind to them. Vital won't have that, of course, nor will I. The Boche are bullies, and the Nazis are just the biggest bullies among them. But we've agreed not to speak of this while our guests are with us.

Yesterday evening was spent, as a result, in some very dull conversation about our separate lives in Fès and Marrakech. Gérard boasted for around an hour about his precious vineyards and new bottling plant. It is all wonderfully modern, of course, and he genuinely believes he can drag the Moroccans into the twentieth century with all this gadgetry. Vital spoke a little about life as a judge on the *cour de cassation*, but Gérard seemed little interested. We finally went to bed unsure of where exactly family ties had landed us.

Things went more smoothly at breakfast this morning, and today's lunch was much more *à la française,* so we seem to be better disposed to one another. It was only late last night that I realized I had not yet shared my good news with Béatrice, but there wasn't a moment all morning.

After lunch, we went to our separate rooms for a siesta. When I woke, it was already dark, and the air was filled with the scraping of crickets. Vital was still asleep beside me. For a moment, I was tempted to wake him slowly with some judicious kisses, but these little afternoon naps of his are inclined to turn into the deepest kind of sleep.

Instead, I got up and put on my robe, and went out to the garden to breathe what little air there was in the night. Some people say that what they love in Morocco are the ancient cities, skylines of minaret and palm; others say it is the people they find most fascinating, and a few say it is the desert. But for me it has always been the night sky, that great jewelled creature that rides silently across all our lives. I love to breathe the desert-scented air while gazing at those endless worlds so far away from me.

I was lost in such meditations when I heard a footstep behind me in the dark. It was Béatrice. Like me, she had woken and come to the garden. She asked if I was well and happy, and if I found my new husband agreeable.

'If it weren't for this wretched war,' I said, 'I'd find no fault in anything.'

'Not even in Gérard?'

'In Gérard?'

'Come, Marie-Louise. You know very well. He can be a little difficult at times.'

'Well, perhaps a little,' I said, lying through my teeth. 'But I don't dislike him. And I hope this visit will give us all an opportunity to get to know one another better.'

'Yes, I hope so too. Now, tell me, what is your news?'

So we sat down and brought one another up to date on all that had happened since we last met.

Thursday, 18 July

Last night over dinner, Vital questioned Gérard about his forthcoming government position. It did not seem an unreasonable topic to enliven the dinner table, especially given Gérard's excessive fondness for talking about himself. But he simply was not to be drawn. I tried to tease him about his reticence, but he just looked me down as though I were a mischievous child whose humour was out of place in adult company. All he would say was that he had been approached by someone from a ministry in Rabat, and that he had been called on to carry out work of national importance. All requests for further details were curtly dismissed, and I formed the impression that he now bitterly regretted his earlier enthusiasm in referring to the new post at all.

Before we all retired, I tried to approach Béa on the subject, not so much – and I did make this perfectly clear – with the hope of getting her to come clean, but just to express the hurt I felt at being treated by my own brother-in-law with such distrust. Vital, I said, is a judge, a senior member of the colonial judiciary, and, by virtue of that alone, a man of very real discretion. We were upstairs, in André's room, settling him down in bed, before going back down for our desserts. Béa acted very kindly, taking my hand, and assuring me that she would speak with her husband that very night.

'But you must remember,' she said, 'that it is wartime, that a sizeable part of our homeland has been conquered and remains under foreign control. At such a time, the government needs men and women to carry out tasks that must remain somewhat secret. But you can rest assured that Gérard is involved in nothing dishonourable. And, who knows, dear Vital may one day very soon receive a similar invitation.'

I kissed her, and made to start work on André's nightly reading. We have moved on from M. Aymé to a wonderful book by an English writer, Arthur Ransome, *Hirondelles et Amazones*. I bought my copy in Reims about six years ago, when the translation first appeared.

I had only gone a few lines when Béa caught sight of the front cover of the book. She lifted a hand and pushed it down.

'My dear,' she said, her voice unexpectedly tense, 'I think you should be taking greater care what you read to the child. Are you not aware that Ransome is an Englishman, and, what is worse, a Bolshevik?'

'Oh, but surely . . .' I couldn't think what any of this had to do with such a delightful story of children messing about in boats.

'Listen, Marie-Louise. This man lived in Russia after the revolution, he became great friends with Lenin and Trotsky, and he even married Trotsky's secretary. Can you imagine anything more shameless?'

'I . . . I really had never heard of any of this. But it can't make any difference . . .'

'My dear sister, we are in the middle of a war that will decide the fate of France, of the whole of Europe. It's no longer acceptable to be so ignorant about subversives like this Ransome. Surely you would not wish little André to be infected by his Bolshevism?'

'Well, no, of course not. But there's nothing remotely Bolshevik in these books.'

'If André likes the books, he will think well of the man, and when he grows older, he may find and read Ransome's books about Russia. Need I tell you what heartbreak that might bring?'

And so on for over half an hour. We have been allowed *Tin-Tin* while Béatrice scours the local bookshops for 'more suitable' reading. Mme de Ségur is being recommended, along with M. Berquin and the equally turgid M. Bouilly. Everything is to be fearfully moralistic and upright, not to say downright old fashioned. There was no point in arguing. I'll just let her go back to Fès, then we'll bring M. Ransome out again and go on as before. I'm sure his Russian wife was terribly beautiful.

Friday, 19 July

Something happened today to cause me yet more concern. We had just eaten breakfast when Gérard went off by himself. He just stood up and announced that he was off and would come back for lunch. This was a few minutes after eight o'clock. When pressed, he said he had to meet someone on the experimental farm, just past the racecourse. It was a strange thing, I thought, for a guest to do, but we humoured him, and he set off in a *petit taxi* with the *Guide Bleu* firmly stuffed inside his pocket. He speaks tolerable Arabic, and we had no fears that he would get seriously lost.

When he returned over three hours later, he had a satisfied smile on his face, as though he had come from the accomplishment of some great mission. Vital joined us for lunch, and I thought he looked anxious about something. He was withdrawn throughout the meal, but I could get him to say nothing before it was time for us all to set off for the Lycée Mangin, where we were to have tea *à l'anglaise* with M. Antheil, André's headmaster, and a great friend of Vital's.

The tea went well enough, but I was eager to know what had occasioned Vital's mood at lunch. On our return home, I managed to get him to myself, and no sooner were we alone than I asked him outright what was troubling him.

'It was nothing,' he said. 'Please forget about it. Honestly, I'd as soon not think about it.'

In the end, I persuaded him to tell me what it was, and he gave in on condition I should say nothing to either Béatrice or Gérard on the matter.

It seems that, when Vital left court this morning, he took his usual route home. That is to say, on leaving the Tribunal, he walked as far as Ave. Aristide Briant, then turned north to the rue Circulaire, and then home. As he was approaching the police station opposite the *Parc des Sports*, he saw a man whom he took to be Gérard coming down the steps, followed by another man. There are no other buildings in that stretch, but Vital slipped behind a palm tree and watched. He knew by instinct that something odd was going on, and he wasn't disappointed. The two men came down to the pavement, and Vital saw that Gérard's companion was none other than our old friend, Inspector Lenéru.

Monday, 22 July

Mass yesterday. I had not thought of Béatrice as particularly pious, but she took it all very seriously. Gérard introduced himself to the priest and had a short but earnest chat with him. For myself, I went through the motions, but my heart was not in it. Nothing was said in the sermon about the war, or about the atrocities still being committed by the Boche. And yet the Bishop of Utrecht has spoken

132

out this month. The church lacks consistency, and I need something more than that.

They leave tomorrow, thank God. Their bags are packed, their tickets are ready, and their hearts are already elsewhere. They go back by the way they came, through Rabat, and I believe they will spend a few days there while Gérard attends some interviews regarding his new post. Perhaps all is not as decided as he has made it seem.

Tuesday, 23 July
They left amiably enough. Béa promised to write often, I said I would write back. I felt quite well disposed towards Gérard as he prepared to go. He's rather a sad man, devoted to the family trade, with little imagination, and absolutely no sense of humour that I can detect.

I wrote the above at noon. Since then, my opinion has changed. Gérard is not quite what he seems, and if I had suspicions of him before this, I have deeper and darker ones now.

We went to the railway station with them, of course. It's hardly far. While we were gone, Shadeeya set about putting the guest room back in order. The beds are little *banquettes* that are usually kept against the wall, in the Moroccan fashion, and, since they are light, she and her daughter were able to carry out this task without difficulty.

When we came back, Shadeeya had finished in the room and was preparing lunch. She called to me from the kitchen.

'*Ya, madame! Kullshi bi-kheir?*'

I assured her that all was indeed well. I think she could

sense the relief in my voice. A moment later, she was in the living room beside me, holding out some objects in her hands.

'*Shuf, madame.* Your sister's husband, he has dropped some things beneath bed.'

I glanced at them. Mere baubles: a hairbrush, a shoe-horn, a few pages from an old newspaper.

'Keep them,' I said. 'It's not worth the postage to send them back.'

She looked pleased with her trophies. About to go, she handed the paper to me.

'*Peux pas, madame . . .*'

I took it from her, and she vanished back to her cooking. Glancing at the paper, I realized it was neither *L'Atlas* nor *Le Sud Marocain*, the two weeklies on which we have come to rely, but something rather different. I had never seen the journal in question before, but I knew very well what it was.

'Vital,' I called. 'Come here a moment.'

When he came, I handed the paper silently to him. I saw him raise his eyebrows when he realized what he was holding.

'Where did you get this?' he asked. There was an edge of anger to his voice that I had never heard before.

I told him where Shadeeya had found it.

'You know what it is?'

I nodded. It was an issue of *L'Action Française*, the notorious journal of Charles Maurras' banned movement of the same name. L'Action Française stands for everything Vital and I find abhorrent. They are right-wingers of the worst kind, royalists, bigots, anti-Semites. They profess to love France, but they are willing to work with Pétain and the Nazis.

134

I thought back to what Vital had seen that day outside the police station – Gérard in deep conversation with Lenéru. Slowly, they are making their little pacts and alliances, the worst in our society plotting an end to everything we hold good. We burned the paper in the stove, but we cannot get the smell of it out of our noses for anything.

20 November
I saw Dr Chomat this morning. It is, thank God, good news. Very good news. He says I'm about six weeks pregnant. We've calculated that my baby ought to be due early next July. I told Vital when he came back from work, and he's over the moon. I won't sleep tonight. I want to go up on the roof and shout about it.

In the Pavilion
of Lost Souls

13

Taddert
22 May

They hadn't come after him, he was fairly sure of that. Several times between Ouarzazate and Marrakech, he came off the road, extinguished his lights, and waited. Once, he found himself in a walnut grove, and another time behind the culvert of a bridge that stretched above a mountain stream. Almost nobody came up from the southeast. A couple of hard-pressed lorries outlined with fairy lights coughed past, and a small car, too slow by far to contain pursuers of any merit, wheezed by half an hour or so behind them.

He'd ignored Djamil's suggestion that he head straight for the airport. It was where they'd be expecting him over the next day or two.

The road took him high into the Atlas, twisting and looping like some sort of demented worm through cedar forest, up and up towards the Tizi N'Tichka pass. As he climbed, the flat heat of the foothills gave way to a bitter mountain cold. By the time he reached the summit, his headlights picked out wide expanses of snow, untouched as yet by the coming summer heat. Whichever way he looked, he was met by a bleak moonlit vista of rocks and scree. A sharp wind cut through the pass, howling, as though an army of djinn were rushing to do battle high in the mountains.

By the time he reached the pass, it was past midnight. His frequent halts, and the slow pace forced on him by the constant twisting of the road, meant he was only about half-way to his destination, and at the point of real exhaustion. From here on, the road would lead downhill, and he knew that, if he continued in the dark and on the verge of sleep, he risked a false manoeuvre that would lead to a crash, or perhaps precipitate him right off the road, to burst into flames hundreds of feet below.

He decided to stay where he was. He'd seen little cafés on the way up from Ouarzazate, but he had no way of knowing which, if any, were slept in overnight. His map, scanned in the glare of the headlight, showed a village called Taddert on the other side of the pass, and he reckoned this was what he wanted. But not yet. Taddert was an obvious place to stop, and he was sure at least one telephone call had been made there by his friends in Ouarzazate.

He found a group of *limonade* stalls, locked up until morning. Choosing the largest, he went round the back and found a padlock guarding the door to the large cupboard in which the owner kept his stock. Within minutes, he had prised the lock open with the help of a brake lever broken from the bike. It took a little longer to clear the shelves of their bottles of Coke, Pepsi, Sidi Harazem, and Oulmès. He knocked the cap off a Coke and drained it.

Pulling the shelves free, he crawled inside. It was narrow and uncomfortable, but it kept out the wind and some of the cold. He made to close the doors, then thought better of it, and settled down as best he could. Dawn was not far away.

To the east, a sun of cinnabar and fallow had risen some way above Mount Tistouit when its rays slipped inside Nick's box. He had slept, but not particularly well, and all his limbs felt cramped and painful. His head was muggy, and he could feel a headache developing somewhere deep down in his brain. He had a bottle of sickly sweet Cigogne for breakfast, and a Nutz bar that he found in a locked drawer. He dared not waste time putting away the shelves and bottles he'd taken out, and contented himself by leaving a bundle of dirhams that was probably large enough to start a small lemonade empire.

Barely refreshed, he went to the side of the road. On the west side, there was a steep drop that ended in forest five hundred feet or more below. He wheeled the motorbike to the side, manhandled it onto the railings, and, with a final nudge, sent it hurtling into space. The crash was muffled by the trees, then was followed by angry billows of red and bright yellow flame. The flames continued to burn for a little while, and Nick was worried that they might take hold more fiercely and cause a forest fire, which would bring firefighters and others to the spot. But before long the damp that had built up during that long, rain-filled spring was enough to extinguish the flames and leave them with nothing more to feed on. Nick walked away satisfied.

He kept on walking as far as Taddert, a small village

whose row of cramped and run-down cafés catered for a passing trade of lorry drivers and tourists. With light, business was beginning to pick up. The silence of the night was giving way to a perpetual grinding of heavy-duty gears, as the first trucks of the day came through, some heading up towards the pass, the rest cautiously working their way down. He caught sight of a tour bus carrying what looked like a load of middle-aged Mormon missionaries of both sexes. It was followed closely by a minibus stuffed with young backpackers on an adventure holiday trekking in the High Atlas, or so Nick guessed.

He found a cheap French restaurant called the Auberge Le Noyer. Going inside, he found that it had a terrace at the back, overlooking a mountain stream, and that it offered a civilized breakfast. He ordered a *café crème*, some croissants with jam, and an omelette. Strictly speaking, omelettes were reserved for lunch and dinner, but the café had had more than its fair share of starving British holidaymakers demanding eggs.

He had chosen his table carefully. From where he sat, he could see through to the front door. He did not expect anyone to come looking for him – they must think he was already in Marrakech, or perhaps somewhere more off the beaten track by now. But it paid to keep one's back covered – and he was looking out for more than trouble.

He was just finishing his omelette when a string of about ten teenagers filed into the restaurant. A waiter directed them to the rear, and moments later they burst onto the terrace, talking loudly, and started to rearrange the vacant chairs and tables. Behind them came two adults, a man of about thirty wearing a beret, and a woman a little younger, dressed in jeans and a tee shirt. And as beautiful as the whole of the High Atlas put together, Nick thought.

He ordered another coffee and started work on his croissants, and as he did so he listened. The teenagers were French. They had strong Normandy accents, but Nick had no trouble following them.

He was in a jam, and he knew it. Common sense told him he should be on the next plane out of Morocco, putting Ouarzazate, Djamil, and all the kasbahs in creation far behind him. He should not lift another finger, not ask another question, not once refer to Peter's death, pretend it had not happened, because if he didn't do all that, if he persisted in seeking some impossible kind of justice, they would come for him and kill him as surely as they had murdered Peter, Daisy and their own kinsman. Up until Djamil's murder, he'd thought that he might be safe, that his being an outsider conferred some sort of immunity on him. Nothing could do that.

He'd seen his son's dead face, and running seemed nothing more than a cheap betrayal. Anyone could run, he thought; but only he could start to put things right. They had to be put right; he did not question that.

He could go to the British consulate here, lodge a complaint, say he'd seen the two victims; but he knew how far that would get him. A suave man in a Savile Row suit and tie would explain that everything had to pass through the Moroccans, that anything else would be interference, and that, after all, we have trade agreements with Morocco. He'd been through it before, spent long afternoons in baroque offices, wasted his time with men who did not care.

Or he could go to the Moroccan authorities directly, and they would be polite, and promise an investigation, and see him to the door. Nothing would be done. In all honesty, they had even less reason to care.

So he sat smearing croissants with butter and jam, and sipping hot coffee, while he glanced out over a landscape of unsurpassable beauty and listened to a tangle of teenage voices rip the silence to shreds. At the table next to him, a foul-mouthed girl in a red tank top was hitting a good-looking boy on the shoulder.

'*Je m'en branle! Arrête de dire des conneries. Ça me branche, tu sais.*'

What turned her on, apparently, was something called acid jazz. They were all planning to spend a night in Paris in order to do some serious dancing at a club called La Loco.

When he tired of inspecting these teenage wonders, Nick found himself glancing at a table near the back, where the expedition leaders were tucking into bowls of coffee and brioche. It was the woman he was looking at, of course. He could hardly take his eyes off her, and worried that she would grow annoyed and tell him to stop. He could scarcely help himself: she was animated, nervous, humorous, utterly fascinating, and it was almost a pain to him to remove his eyes from her face or her hands as they wove invisible traceries in the air around her.

He could not tell her relationship to the man. They were of an age to be lovers, or married, but somehow Nick sensed they did not match. She would touch his sleeve or hand from time to time, in order to emphasize a point she was making, and sometimes she would make him laugh, and sometimes

144

she would drift away from him, to look across at her noisy charges, or out at the scene beyond her.

He left a small wad of dirhams beneath his saucer so as to be ready to make a move. Close on half an hour had passed when the man, who wore serious walking shoes and thick socks, got to his feet and called for silence. Time to get back on board the minibus, he said. Time to move on to Marrakech.

This was it. His lines rehearsed, Nick got up and crossed the floor. Not to the man – he sensed he would be rebuffed there – but to the woman. She looked round, surprised, as he approached her. It had to work first time, he told himself. He couldn't afford to be stuck here, visible and vulnerable, all day.

'*Mademoiselle? Peux-je parler avec vous un moment?*' He spoke in deliberately faltering French, an Englishman a bit out of his depth among all these Gallic schoolchildren. He assumed that she and her male companion were teachers from whichever school the children were from.

'*Mais . . . oui, bien sûr, mais dépêchez-vous, monsieur. Nous sommes un peu pressé.*'

'I'm sorry, I . . . Do you speak English?'

'English? Yes, it's my second language. Or maybe you don't think so.'

'You speak it very well. Much better than my French. I . . . The thing is, I'm in a bit of a jam.'

'*Confiture?*' She looked at him, as though he was trying to tell her he'd spilled jam on his clothes.

'What? Oh, no, not jam like that. Trouble. I'm in some difficulty. And I overheard your friend say you were going to Marrakech. Is that right?'

'Yes. We've been on the kasbah trail, and now we're going back to base.'

'Wonderful, look, I think you can help me. I've been –'

He broke off. A waiter had left the door to the terrace open and, looking through to the street entrance, he saw two men come in. One, judging by the way he walked, was the hitman. The second he recognized from the day before, from the meeting in the mayor's house.

He looked round, estimating his chances of making a getaway by heading out across the stream.

'What's wrong?' the Frenchwoman asked, taking in at once the alarmed expression that had crossed his face. A moment later, she looked round into the main room and caught sight of the men, who were carefully scanning the clientele.

'Those men?' she asked.

He nodded.

In an instant she had pushed him down onto the nearest chair, and then she was beside him, embracing him, putting her arms round him and taking his face down onto a spot somewhere between her shoulder and her breast. With one hand she began to stroke his neck, while she held his left hand in hers. Moments later, the two heavies from Ouarzazate came onto the terrace. The tables were mainly empty following the dispersal of the teenagers. The men made in their direction, but the woman looked up at them with such a withering look that they hesitated.

'*Quoi? Qu'est-ce que tu veux, eh?*'

The look and the direct challenge were too much for them. Hands out as though to fend her off, they turned on their heels and went back the way they had come.

'Stay like that,' she said. 'They may come back.'

But it was her colleague who arrived instead. He looked at her, open mouthed. She unwound her arms from Nick's shoulders.

'*Ah! Stéphane. Viens, viens.*' She turned to Nick. '*Puis-je vous présenter, Monsieur . . . ?*'

'Smith.'

'*Vraiment?*'

Nick gave what he suspected was a ghastly smile.

'More or less,' he said.

She turned to her friend.

'Stéphane, have the *casseurs* gone yet?' She described the two gangster types who'd just been in.

'I saw them get into a car. Were they bothering you?'

She shrugged, then turned to Nick.

'I'm glad I was of some help.'

'Please, I . . . It isn't that simple. I need a lift to Marrakech. I'm willing to pay, but I need to go in a group like yours, not in a taxi.'

She looked at him suspiciously. He didn't look dangerous, but up here in the back of beyond, who could tell?

'They were carrying guns, weren't they?'

He nodded.

'Do you want to tell me . . . ?'

'*Dépêche-toi . . .*' her companion broke in. He was getting anxious. They were already behind schedule, and their charges had connections to make.

'OK,' she said. 'There's a spare seat at the back. But the first sign of trouble and you're out. My first responsibility is to those kids. They may be creeps, they may have terrible taste in clothes, but their parents pay hard money to be free of them.'

The minibus was waiting, its windows lined with sullen faces. Nick's pursuers were nowhere to be seen.

As they pulled away, the woman walked back to where he was sitting.

'I think we should introduce ourselves properly, don't you?'

He nodded.

'Nick,' he said, holding out his hand and thinking how fresh her skin had smelled. She'd been wearing Lalique perfume. Now he noticed a small coral ring on her middle finger. Not engaged, then, or married, unless she kept it a secret.

'Commander Nicholas Budgeon.'

Her eyes widened. Suddenly, her English stranger had taken on an identity. The little game she'd been playing had become more serious.

She took his hand and shook it hard.

'Justine,' she said. 'Justine Buoy. Welcome on board the Marrakech Express!'

14

Marrakech

The police had set up a checkpoint about ten kilometres outside the city, just above the spot where the main P31 strikes the northeast-heading road to Tamelelt and forces a left-hand turn at the T-junction. As a lorry in front went through, leaving only a small Renault between the minibus and the checkpoint, Nick got his first glimpse of the men manning it. They wore the grey uniform of the Sûreté, and were armed with automatic pistols. He noticed that a couple of them had been placed at either side of the road, and that these men were carrying small sub-machine-guns. He had never guessed he could pose that sort of threat to society.

The teenagers were doing their best to crane through the windows in order to see better. Their spirits had picked up suddenly at the prospect of some sort of excitement, however short-lived. Justine walked down from the front, telling them to sit in their seats. When she reached the rear, she squeezed in next to Nick.

'They're looking for you?'

'Probably,' he said. 'I imagine the combined police forces of five continents are after me.'

'And what terrible thing makes you so popular with the boys in blue?'

'My guess is that I've committed murder. Late last night, probably. In Ouarzazate. And quite possibly two further murders a few nights ago, in a kasbah outside the town.'

She looked at him with her eyes wide open, hardly daring to take the conversation further.

'I don't understand. You are telling the truth? But surely not?'

He smiled ruefully and shook his head.

'That I killed all these people? Of course not. I've done nothing wrong, believe me. But our friends in the grey suits are looking for me nonetheless.'

'Then, why . . . ?' Even as she spoke, the answer formed itself clearly in her mind. 'Yes,' she said. 'I see. Or I think so. You swear to me you are innocent?'

Ahead of them, the Renault was pulling slowly through the gap. Their driver slipped into gear.

'I swear.'

The minibus moved down to the checkpoint, accompanied by a mixture of cheers and catcalls from the schoolchildren.

'Quickly,' said Justine, pointing down to a small space between the rear seats and those in front. 'Get down there. Don't move.'

'No, that's pointless. I can't let you take the risk.'

'You want to end up in a Moroccan jail? Do you have any idea what that would be like?'

'A pretty good idea, yes.'

'Well then, don't argue. Lie down and keep your mouth shut.'

She stood up.

'That applies to all of you,' she shouted. 'Anyone who opens his or her mouth will have to answer to me.'

A policeman knocked at the window opposite the driver and was allowed on board. He clutched a clipboard to which was fastened a black and white photograph. Justine came down to greet him.

'*La-bas, a sidi*,' she began. 'How can we help you?' She spoke in Arabic, without apparent strain.

The policeman held the clipboard out to her. She recognized Nick straight away.

'Have you seen this man?' he asked. He was diffident, for he seldom encountered a woman in a position of authority, however minor.

She pretended to study the photograph and to ponder on it for several seconds, then nodded.

'Yes,' she said. 'Yes, I have.'

'Recently?'

'Yes. This morning. Just as we were leaving Ouarzazate. I'm sure it was the same man.'

'You're certain?'

'Fairly certain. He passed us on the street. He has an interesting face. I noticed him.'

'In Ouarzazate?'

'Yes, that's what I said. Now, officer, unless you have further questions, I have to make sure these young people catch a plane. May we proceed?'

The policeman nodded.

'Thank you,' he said. 'You've been very helpful.'

As he stepped down from the bus, he was already reaching for his radio.

*　　*　　*

151

There was a short row between Justine and Stéphane, in the course of which he disparaged her brains, her professionalism and her common sense, and came close to throwing her off the bus.

'Do you realize how stupid that was?' he shouted. 'You could have had us all arrested. Can you imagine what the school would have said, what their parents would have said, if they'd picked up the telephone and it was the French consul trying to explain how their little darlings happened to be languishing in that stinking jail in the Gueliz?'

'No, I can't imagine. I'm sure they would have been delighted! *Va te faire foutre, eh! Pour qui me prends-tu?*'

Nick tried to intervene.

'Look, ah, Stéphane . . . I'm sorry. It's my fault, I should never have put you at risk, but I honestly didn't think the police would be involved.'

Stéphane turned on him, swearing and gesticulating.

'I want you off this bus,' he screamed. 'I want you off now, before the next checkpoint. Understand?'

Nick put his hands up, as though to ward off an attack. The woman tried to get between them, while the driver shouted at them in Arabic to shut up and sit down.

'Listen,' said Nick, 'just tell your driver to pull over. I'll get off and find my own way to Marrakech. I don't want to cause any more trouble.'

Agitated though he was, Stéphane got the message.

'OK,' he said, 'OK. *C'est cool. Pas de panique, eh?*'

He snapped his fingers and told the driver to pull over. They were in open country. A family of crested larks watched from a tumbled wall. The bus slowed and halted, almost hitting a horse-drawn cart driven by an old man. The doors opened with a hissing sound. Nick made his way to the door while the pupils applauded. Justine came to the door.

'Will you be all right?' she asked.

'You've done all you can. But if you find a chance, please ring this number and speak to this man.' He handed her a slip of paper carrying Duncan's name and telephone number. Slipping his hand into his trouser pocket, he brought out a heap of Moroccan cash, but she closed his fingers round it.

'I'll make the call,' she said. 'Don't worry. If you can make it to the Djemaa el-Fna, I can . . .'

'I don't understand . . .' Nick started, but before she could answer Stéphane ordered the driver to get going. Nick leapt off onto the verge, and the bus pulled away, rejoining the constant stream of traffic.

He looked round. There was nothing out here, not even a farm, as far as he could see. It was still around ten kilometres to walk, which would be tiring. The first police car to pass would pick him out, a European on foot without a backpack. Then he remembered the old man and the cart.

It proved to be the slowest journey of his life, but there had been no more checkpoints, and the old man had been more than content with the sum Nick had been able to scrape together. They reached Bab Rhemat gate, and parted there. The old man could drive no further, since the narrow lanes and streets of the ancient city were barely wide enough to let a laden donkey pass, let alone a farm cart piled high with turnips. Nick watched him go, his bent back and grizzled head his only protection against the sorrows of his world. Ahead, the city started. He took a deep breath and plunged in. Within moments he had left the twenty-first century behind. Everything seemed to be as it might have been at any moment between the twelfth century and today. He wasn't really sure of his centuries, but wherever his eye fell – on the cobbles beneath his feet, the steps of the little shops, the gates of hidden mosques – he sensed the past in all its guises slip like perfumed smoke about him.

His first problem, however, was not the past, but his dwindling supply of cash. In his wallet were enough credit and debit cards to buy him the best hotel rooms and the finest meals in the city, but he knew that it would be a fatal mistake to use them. If he wanted a place to stay, the hotel would want a passport, and the details would be passed on that same day to the police. He could probably eat, but he would never know whether or not the police had left his name to be added to a list of undesirables. And whatever way he chose to get out of here, he'd have to buy tickets or hire a car or pay a driver.

It might have been possible to get away with it if he'd been in a position to sleep and eat down-market; but no dosshouses would be likely to take American Express, and brochette stall owners would have about as much use for a Visa card as for a wad of Chechen banknotes. All the things that spelled security to the average tourist were lining up to kick him hard in the testicles.

Tourists go to Marrakech for a variety of reasons: some for cheap hashish and the company of like-minded people; some for gay sex; some in search of an old hippy trail blazed by Brian Jones and the Master Musicians of Jajouka;

others because they feel on the edge down here, so close to the desert, to Africa, to some barbaric god no church or cathedral could ever hold. Within seconds of entering the red city, Nick could sense it everywhere. It was spices on the hot air, and the sharp cries of vendors, tannery smells, and the constant jostling, black faces, brown faces, the white faces of tourists, the constant teasing of half-opened doors and lattice windows, from which the eyes of hidden women stared out, the children running between everyone's feet, the donkeys, a load tied in panniers on either side, driven through alleyways tight enough to squeeze lemons.

Others came because Marrakech – like its imperial cousins Fès and Meknès – sucked them down at once into its ancient life. Unlike those heritage sites back home, this was an honest-to-goodness living city, whose history-soaked walls harboured a life that would not have seemed very strange to a man or woman of the twelfth century.

That was what Nick started to feel now, the living city wrapping its stones about him, like a sudden eloquence taking him by the core. On either side, shopkeepers called to him, trying to entice him inside to cast an eye over their wares. Some wore jellabas, others Western shirts and trousers. He wanted nothing from any of them, however, and continued walking northwards, sticking to the main thoroughfare. He was hassled from time to time, as any tourist was, but as he sank further into the city, his distrait manner started to act as a sort of insect repellent, and the children and young men who'd been trying to sell him hash or a woman or a boy fell away from him.

He wasn't at all sure where he was headed, or how long it might be before he was spotted and brought down. He thought he stood a chance if he could only find a way to alter his appearance. A phone call to Duncan would sort everything out: funds could be transferred directly through a bank, an interview could be set up with a high-ranking diplomat in Rabat, and he could be on the first flight out tomorrow.

Or he could wind up dead. He'd made it this far only by luck. And Justine's help. She'd said something in what he imagined was Arabic, but been whisked away before getting a chance to explain. Had it been a name? A person's name, a place name? He continued walking, running possible strategies through his head. He had an instinct that suggested neither his pursuers nor the police would want to make their manhunt too public. There was a chance that hotels had not yet been circulated with his photograph. If that was so, he could book into a top hotel, say the Mamounia, or a small but pricey one like the Maison Arabe, and use his Amex card to secure enough cash to take him to Rabat and the British embassy. If.

Another, more practical possibility occurred to him. If he could find a public telephone that took cards, he could ring Duncan and set some wheels in motion. Before he'd left his room in Ouarzazate, he'd been reading his guidebook. In the practicalities section, there'd been a note to the effect that Marrakech boasted a much improved telephone system, and that the main cabins took all major credit cards. He would still be without money, but help would be on the way. Assuming, of course, that they didn't have a man watching each of Marrakech's two public telephone sites.

He pushed forward, letting himself be guided by the flow of the people around him. Gradually, he had a sense that movement was chiefly in the direction he was heading, but he still had almost no idea of where he'd started or where he might end up. He'd spent some minutes poring over the sketch maps of Marrakech in his guide, and he'd formed the impression that the city lay on a northwest axis. On the east lay the old walled city, the section he was now in: he remembered it as a spearhead, its point thrusting towards the northwest. To its west, and joined hard to it, was the Gueliz, a modern city founded in 1913 by the French, barely a year after their invasion of Morocco.

Suddenly, he remembered something else. Marrakech's chief tourist attraction was a square, a huge open-air space where acrobats and fire-eaters performed alongside snake charmers and monkey tamers. He was sure that one of the telephone units was in or near this square, outside a post office. Yet he could not for the life of him remember the name of the square, and would not risk asking. Instead, he kept on as before, sensing that all major streets must inevitably lead to somewhere as important as that.

And so they did. Glancing up, Nick caught sight of a large French-style enamelled sign which read, in Arabic and in Roman characters, Djemaa el-Fna. It was the right place, he was sure of it. Seeing it written down again, he was also sure that those were the words Justine had called out to him as the bus pulled away.

A young shopkeeper was watching him. His little shop sold stationery items, mostly pads and pencils for the use of schoolchildren. He smiled at Nick, inviting him in.

'Entrez, m'sieur, vous êtes bienvenu . . .'

Nick paused, then went up to the young man.

157

'Djemaa el-Fna?' he asked. '*Qu'est-ce que ça veut dire?* What does it mean?'

The shopkeeper looked at him through half-closed eyes, like a lizard that senses a fly just out of reach.

'It means "The Gathering of the Dead", *m'sieur*. Wait until this evening, then go and watch them. They will all be there, the dead who are alive, the living who are dead.'

Nick watched him warily, conscious of how readily this man would bring him to mind if someone asked. He nodded and started off in the direction shown by an arrow on the sign.

'*M'sieur*,' came the man's voice behind him.

Nick stopped.

'You are in danger, *m'sieu*', *n'est-ce pas?*'

Nick held his breath. He sensed that he had already been recognized, and that the shopkeeper would call his friends in order to claim whatever reward had been offered.

'Danger?' he asked, making ready to run, once an opening presented itself. 'What do you mean?'

'I mean that you must know your friends, *m'sieu*', and learn to recognize your enemies.'

Nick turned, but the man had disappeared. He ran to the door of the shop, but there was no one inside. Narrow alleyways, *derbs* and *zenqas*, ran off the main street in every direction. If the man had gone down one of those, Nick reasoned, he would never be able to find him again.

His heart beating, he set off towards the Gathering of the Dead.

15

Even now, with the sun's heavy hand sending all but the hardiest of tourists off to find shade, the square seethed with human life. Two sides were occupied by covered stalls, most of which were devoted to traditional clothing, long dresses in pastel shades of blue and pink and orange, skirts, embroidered kaftans, shirts. A little further in, lesser traders had set out their wares on tables – basket-sellers, barbers, tooth extractors waving unpleasant-looking devices and grinning at every passer-by.

Nick walked about slowly, his head pounding, his skin baking in the atrocious heat, his eyes screwed up against the light of a desert sky. Everyone here had something to sell. Women displayed country goods, oranges, dates, melons, herbs, string-tied bundles of fresh mint, bowls brimming over with spices of every colour and smell, eggs, live chickens in wooden cages, their necks waiting to be wrung.

He watched a woman as old as the desert preside over a low counter packed with medicinal substances: dried herbs and pickled roots, the skins of snakes and lizards, shrivelled frogs, fragments of bone, bottles filled with coloured liquids, or with the bodies of small insects swimming in oil. She would measure out her goods onto small brass scales, decanting, stirring, murmuring what might have been spells. Once she looked up, and her eye fell squarely on his, and he thought he saw her make a quick movement with her hands, five fingers gathered to ward off the evil eye. '*Khamsa fi aynek*,' she hissed, then turned back to her customer, rolling a heap of dried grasses into a paper bag. Nick felt vulnerable to her spells, or perhaps to her intent, and moved away. In a corner of the square, a band of Gnaoua musicians began to play with a pulsing beat that echoed the rhythms in his head.

It gradually became clear to him that there were few limits to what you might hope to buy or sell here. He found radios, alarm clocks, battery torches, even old batteries. Young men displayed 'designer' jeans made in Agadir or Casablanca, with names like 'Lovis', 'Wangler', or 'Calvis Kleim'. Another held out a wooden box bearing brand-new 'Cartier' watches, a snip at around 300 dirhams apiece. Next to him, an old man wearing a dirty red fez offered a range of spectacles, all at prices well below those asked in Gueliz by the French opticians. Stall after stall offered bootleg tapes and CDs. Their importunate owners played the latest hits in an effort to woo passers-by, while in their corner, dancers of the Gnaoua brotherhood turned inwards to their souls as they played and clapped and sang.

Nick felt dizzy and, without asking permission, sat down between a bearded man selling stringed instruments made from tortoise shells and a *naqqasha*, a woman who drew patterns of henna and *harqus* with a wooden pen on the backs and palms of women's hands. The sounds of the square passed over him in waves, his head throbbed with pain, his stomach was torn between hunger and nausea. He felt as though an invisible surgeon was rummaging through his belly, squeezing now this organ, now the one next to it, before pronouncing him dead.

He opened his eyes, and wished he'd kept his sunglasses in his pocket the night before, when he'd gone out to meet Djamil. A stern voice inside his head warned him that, if he didn't do something quickly, he really would pass out, only to wake late at night to find himself stripped to his underwear, shivering from cold in some back alley, without the resources to save himself. If the sun and hunger didn't do for him, the police would.

He remembered the boy selling Cartier watches, and reasoned to himself that, if it was possible to sell obvious fakes for – he worked it out – £30, surely it must be easy enough to sell the real thing for a little more.

On his wrist he wore an old Rolex, one of the few things his father had left him when he died. The watch had been bought as a present by Nick's mother, in 1948, when his father was finally demobbed. It was a Viceroy, with gold hands and a smart steel case, and Nick knew it was worth a great deal more than £30. However much he was offered, he would be selling it at a loss. He hated to lose it, but knew he had no choice. Reluctantly, he unfastened it from his swollen wrist, and laid it on the ground before him.

No one came at first, and he feared he would faint and lose the watch. A terrible thirst consumed him. His mouth was like sand, his lips were drier than a cured lizard skin. Inside, the hunger went on working at him. He knew that a man could survive a hunger fast for extraordinary lengths of time, shrinking and shrinking as his stomach inched its way towards collapse – but not if he was deprived of drink. Water sellers passed by, their polished jugs and cups clanking seductively against their elaborate costumes.

Once or twice a tourist or a native passer-by would bend and pick up his watch, then offer a derisory sum, as though it was another fake. He did not want much, but he needed cash for a cheap room, some more for a couple of meals, and a little over for emergencies. No one offered him that much, or even near. Each time, he cried out.

'Ce n'est pas truqué! Vous m'entendez? C'est du vrai de vrai. Un Rolex.'

They just laughed and tossed the watch down, and walked on to the next attraction. He wondered what they needed: a certificate of authenticity? A *dahir* from the king?

Slowly, the light began to fade from the sky. He'd been in the square for hours, and still his watch remained unsold, while he felt feverish and desperate for sleep. He was profoundly tempted to get to his feet and hand himself in to the first policeman he saw. Maybe he could convince the man arresting him that he was an old cop himself, that he deserved preferential treatment.

He determined to stay on if he could. Many of the stalls were being folded up as the day drew to a close. They'd be back in the morning with fresh eggs and squawking chickens, but Nick only had this one chance. He'd read that the square remained alive through the evening, that, in fact, it became even more animated after dark, with jugglers, acrobats, magicians, musicians, and bands of Sufis chanting hymns and beating drums. He decided he'd been making a mistake just sitting here like the other hawkers, and determined to get up and approach people directly, tourists like himself, English-speaking onlookers to whom he could explain the value of his watch, and why it was such a bargain.

'*Ça coûte combien?*'

A woman's voice, the French neither Moroccan nor tourist.

He shrugged.

'*Mais, dîtes-moi. C'est de l'authentique?*'

He nodded.

'*1948*,' he said. 'It belonged to my father.'

A little silence. She picked up the watch as though to try it on.

'*Et vous, monsieur?* Are you the real thing?'

He looked up, and the first things he recognized were her hands, he could not say why, then he noticed the little coral ring and remembered, through the fog in his brain.

She bent down now and held out the watch, taking his wrist and strapping it back on.

'I think this is worth a lot of money,' she said.

He nodded, frightened to find her here, as though the square was filling with memories. Opening his eyes more fully, he saw her face illumined by the light of a gas flame a performer had lit nearby.

'What happened?' she asked.

'Not sure, I . . . need to drink. Getting . . . dehydrated. Fever.'

She reached out a hand and touched his forehead. He was burning up.

'Looks like I'm bound to you,' she said. She took him beneath the elbow and helped him to his feet. He almost fell back again, but she drew him to herself. She was strong and would not let him fall. He staggered once, then let her take him across the square and out of the ghastly heat.

Slowly, the square below filled with light, as groups of performers jostled for attention, storytellers working the crowd as they had done for centuries, boxers on a little stage, and the Gnaoua swaying to the snap of iron castanets. It seemed to Nick as though he'd been spirited up here, far above the crowds, by some magician from the desert. But if he looked up from his plate, Justine was there watching him eat, as real as he might ever have hoped.

'You see, I . . .'

'Don't talk,' she said. 'Eat.'

He'd started with a thick *harira*, and was now working his way slowly through a plate of well-cooked lamb kebabs. He'd wanted salad with them, but she'd warned him against it, telling him all sorts of horror stories about friends who'd ended up in hospital or died as the result of an incautious salad.

'Why are you still here?' he asked.

'Why shouldn't I be?'

'I thought your school party was hurrying to catch a flight.'

'It was.'

'So, how come . . . ?'

'How come I'm here, and they're probably touching down at this very moment in Paris?'

'Well, yes. I know you fell out with your colleague, but . . .'

'Stéphane and I are business partners, though I think not

for very much longer. We run a small agency based here in Marrakech, L'Agence Scolaire. It's quite simple, really: we take small parties of French schoolchildren for a week or two at a time, show them Marrakech, take them to the Sahara, drag them up a couple of mountains, and pop them back on the first plane home. Which is what we were doing today when you came along.'

'I thought you were a teacher.'

She looked at him as if offended.

'Do I look like a teacher?'

He shrugged.

'I don't know very many teachers. What should they look like?'

She shrugged in turn.

'It depends – if they are French schoolteachers or British schoolteachers.'

He could not be sure if she was taking the rise out of him.

'I didn't know . . .'

'That there was a difference? But of course there is a difference. A Frenchwoman can seduce a man at half a kilometre; an Englishwoman thinks a kilometre is a sack of potatoes.' She grinned at her own joke, then grew serious again.

'Sorry,' she said. 'One day my sense of humour will get me into serious trouble.' She glanced at his left hand, at the gold wedding ring.

'You are offended,' she said. 'And I can understand why.' He finished the last brochette. 'You are married,' she went on. 'To a beautiful Englishwoman.'

He stopped her there, just with a look.

'You didn't offend me,' he said. 'It was funny, and close to the truth. As for me, yes, I was married,' he said. 'But that's over now.'

'I'm sorry. I shouldn't have . . .'

'No, that's all right. My wife wasn't English either. She was French. Her name was Nathalie.'

'She left you?'

'You might say that. Look, can we change the subject?'

'But of course. I'm so sorry. I become inquisitive. It's natural. How do you feel now?'

'I feel better for food and drink. In other respects, nothing has changed. I'm still on the run. I have no money, and no obvious means of getting any, I'm carrying a passport that identifies me as a man the police are interested in, and somewhere down there half the Moroccan mafia is prowling the night, looking for a man wearing my face. Tell me some bad news.'

'You're forgetting one thing.'

'Namely?'

'Me.'

'I was going to ask. Just what's bugging you here? You risk a beating, then arrest, and finally a load of trouble for concealing me from thugs and police, and now you're at it again. I'm not young, handsome, gifted, or rich. What's in this for you?'

She sipped from a cooling cup of coffee.

'Nothing,' she said. 'I just happen to think you're innocent. You're on my conscience. I know what a shitty place this country can be, I know what bastards the police can be, and I know that, if those bully boys up in the hills had taken their time, you would very likely be in a ditch now, or at the bottom of a very steep cliff.'

'I'm sorry,' he said. 'I should be grateful. What am I saying? I *am* grateful, you can't imagine just how grateful I am. You've saved my life three times in one day, and here I am, looking as if somebody had just told me I've got cancer.'

'Forget about being grateful. Gratitude won't get you out of this. I need to know I did the right thing back there, so start by telling me what happened. Once we're straight about that, we can start thinking about how to put things right.'

She was prettier than a treeful of monkeys, he thought. And, yes, he was sure she could seduce a man at any distance and in any weather. Stéphane would have been mollified ages ago, he surmised, mollified and seduced for the thousandth time. When she'd finished feeding and calming him, she'd wander back to whatever flat or house she shared with her business partner, and slip into his arms, telling him the fascinating story of the troubled Englishman and his messy, messy life.

'Before I start,' he said, 'don't you think we should do something about where I'm to stay tonight? And before that, I need to make a telephone call.'

'The post office telephones don't close till nine,' she said. 'In any case, you need to keep away from them. If you like, we'll find a private kiosk. They use satellite communications for international calls. If you can believe it.'

He looked down across the teeming square, at a spectacle that had remained unchanged since the Middle Ages, as though the café in which they sat was a time machine, and found it hard to accept that anything from the twenty-first century could be found among those dark alleys and crumbling gardens.

'If you say so,' he said.

'I do say so. There are even cyber cafés down there. You may find them useful as well. As for tonight, you're staying with me – and you can use my phone.'

'No, that's much too risky, you can't . . .'

'I choose what risks I run. You stay with me until you're safe, or until I throw you out. *D'accord?*'

'Well, yes, of course. I'm in no position to object, but what about Stéphane?'

'Stéphane? What's he got to do with this?'

'Won't he mind my moving in?'

She burst into peals of laughter. When she had recovered herself, she smiled at him.

'I'm sorry. I think you've got the wrong idea. Stéphane is my *business* partner. I live alone. Please don't think I do this all the time. My neighbours would probably stone me to death if I did. But we'll deal with that later. For the moment, I just want to hear this story of yours. From the beginning. I'll order more coffees, then you can start.'

16

It was late as they made their way back to her house. The city, Nick thought, had been built for night. Or perhaps night itself had been created for the city, as a perfect garment for it to wear. The desert warmth and the darkness reshaped everything below. High roofs and minarets soared into a clustering of stars, and moonlight and starlight came trickling down in a silver stream that patterned cobblestones and gateways, fountains and windows, the domes of *koubbas* and the stairs of mosques.

The further they moved from the tourist areas, where fashionable restaurants and souvenir shops beguiled passers-by until midnight or beyond, the more the red city returned to itself. Justine knew her way as though born there.

'Have you lived here long?' Nick asked. He wanted to break the thickening silence, to interrupt the steady rhythm of their footsteps against the uneven stones.

She laughed, and for the second time he was surprised by the quality of her laughter, as though she abandoned the cautions of adulthood for a few moments.

'Haven't you noticed?'

'What?'

'My French accent is almost as bad as yours.'

'Bad? It seems perfectly fine to me.'

'Ask a Frenchman. I was born here, in Marrakech. My father is a doctor. He came here as a *coopérant*, doing voluntary work for the French Foreign Aid Ministry, in the seventies and once his tour was finished, he got married and came straight back. We lived in the Gueliz, on a little street off Avenue Poincaré. My mother helped with all the young *coopérants*, finding them accommodation, showing them the sights, putting on dinner parties. She died three years ago, and my father decided to retire and go back to France with my younger brother, who has learning difficulties. I wanted to stay on here.

'I'm as much Moroccan as I am French, except that I'm a Christian and won't go out in a veil. I speak Arabic more fluently than French, I have more Moroccan friends than French . . . So, *voilà*, I saw my father and brother off at the airport, cried my eyes out the minute their backs were turned, and found myself a house in the medina. Which is precisely here. This is Derb el-Hajar.'

They were in a lane so narrow there was barely room for two to walk abreast. On either side, tall windowless walls pressed in on them. There were no lights anywhere, and everything had to be done by moonlight and starlight. She had stopped in front of a faded green door. A baby cried out somewhere. Much further away, a band was playing at somebody's wedding, using enormous speakers to make sure the sound reached every part of the city. It came to them across the sky like phantom music playing in a phantom city, another Marrakech hidden from the one they were in. She turned a key in the lock, and they were in.

He woke the next morning with the worst headache he'd ever known. Overall, he felt terrible. He remembered ringing Duncan Todd's home number and getting the answering machine. He'd left a short message, and asked Duncan to get back to him on this number.

He found the kitchen and breakfast room as much by sheer good luck as anything. She had left breakfast ready for him: croissants, brioches, freshly baked Moroccan bread, and dried fruit on the table; freshly squeezed orange juice, milk, butter and yoghurt in the fridge; and coffee ready to percolate.

There was a note to tell him she'd had to go into her office in order to sort things out with Stéphane. It was her plan, as she had told him the night before, to take some welcome time off work, and to ask a young Moroccan friend to take her place.

On a large piece of card propped against a vase she had scrawled a bolder message with a felt pen:

DON'T GO ON THE ROOF!!! DON'T SET FOOT IN THE GARDEN!!!! STAY IN THE HOUSE AT ALL TIMES!! IF ANY-BODY COMES TO THE DOOR, DON'T ANSWER IT! IF THE PHONE RINGS, DON'T ANSWER IT UNLESS THE CALLER LEAVES A MESSAGE AND YOU KNOW THE VOICE.

There was a PS in biro underneath:

The Arabic for 'Go away!' is *sir fhalek*. Do not use this under any circumstances. The way through this is total silence. You'll find the ground coffee in the red jar next to the sink. You may, *faute de mieux*, use a razor from the bathroom cabinet. This is a woman's razor and can leave nasty cuts if you aren't careful. I have no aftershave. Do not touch the cat: he bites, and probably has rabies. J.

He was reaching for a croissant when the phone rang. It jangled four times before the answering machine cut in. He registered the dull click, and heard a man's voice come on, but he could make out nothing beyond that. He realized that it might be Duncan, so he got up and went off in search of the phone. Unaccustomed to the house, he discovered it just as the caller hung up. For a few moments, he felt chary about listening to what might be a call from Justine's lover – if she had one, which was very likely, he thought, and which made him intensely jealous for some reason – or someone she did business with. But he needed to speak to Duncan urgently; he could not afford to waste time for the sake of proprieties.

He switched the machine to play. Duncan's voice came back to him over a faint hum of interference.

'Nick, what the hell is going on? You don't say where you are, or who you're with, or anything. I'm at Heathrow. I've got a flight to Paris in ten minutes. I'll be too late for the ten-twenty to Casablanca, but there's a ten-to-three flight from Orly that gets into Marrakech at five past four your time. I'll assume the airport is out of bounds for you. Give me time to get to my hotel, and meet me there. Make it six o'clock to be on the safe side. I'm staying at the Pullman something-or-other. If you can't make it, try to leave a message. I'm taking unpaid leave to do this, Nick, so let's hope this isn't just another parking ticket.'

There was a beep, and the message ended. Nick wrote down the times and the name of the hotel, and wiped the tape. He transferred the paper to his back pocket and went back to the kitchen.

She returned late that morning, carrying a shopping bag stuffed with meat and vegetables.

Setting the bag down as she came in, she saw him standing in an archway facing her.

'You still here?' she asked.

'And just where did you think I might have gone in the thrilling world of Marrakech?'

'Make me a coffee, my feet are killing me.'

He told her to sit down, and made enough coffee to keep a cat awake. As if on cue, the cat came in, dropped a dead mouse in the middle of the floor, and waited to be congratulated. She hugged and stroked him.

'Do you have one?' she asked.

'A cat? No. We had one years ago, when the children were young. Jesus, I've just realized: I haven't told Marie-Josephine everything that's happened.'

'Take your time. Concentrate on yourself, on getting out of this. You're no use to Marie-Josephine dead.'

The coffee finished percolating. He got up and found two mugs.

'Anything from your friend yet?' she asked.

'Yes.'

He told her the gist of Duncan's message.

'We'll go there at five,' she said. 'The Pullman's in the Hivernage, in the south of the French city.'

'What do we do till then?'

173

'You make lunch for me. I feed the cat. I take a long bath. We eat lunch, but not, I regret to say, *al fresco*, since your presence here is a state secret, and I do not want my neighbours to catch sight of you in the courtyard, secluded though it is.'

'You don't think I was seen last night, do you?'

'I very much doubt it. But you will be seen if you go outside during the day. The roof is out of bounds in any case, since you're a man. It's a woman's province. They go up to the roofs to breathe and work and have a chat, and they like to remove their veils, maybe a bit more, and they would die of mortification if a man caught sight of them like that.'

'What about shopping? Didn't your greengrocer notice you'd bought more than usual?'

'I didn't go near him. I will this evening, just to buy in my day's shopping as usual. But for this I had to go to a supermarket in the Gueliz. See how I think of your safety.'

'Stocking up on provisions,' he said. 'It's a bit like the war.'

'You remember it?' Her eyebrows shot up.

'Of course not. Just how old do you think I am? My parents did, of course. They always had plenty of stories to tell. The Blitz. Rationing. My Uncle Ned, who fell down a drain while running from a doodlebug, and broke both legs and an arm. And Nathalie's parents, they had war memories, of course. Did I tell you that they spent the war in Marrakech? He was some sort of official during the Vichy period. He came out originally to set up a wine company. I believe it was already a thriving concern when the war started.'

'What sort of official was he, this . . . ?'

'Gérard. I'm not really sure. I expect they didn't like to talk about it much once the war was over. He and Nathalie's mother went back to France more or less on board the first plane. Nathalie hadn't been born then, of course.'

'A collaborationist, then?'

'Yes, probably. As you know, one doesn't ask. It's a very powerful family, one that would like to avoid embarrassments of that sort.'

'You didn't tell me your family had such close connections to Marrakech.'

He sighed. Last night he'd given her the bare facts of the situation and how he had come to be in Marrakech. But now he'd have to tell her a great deal more.

'Not my family, Nathalie's. It's really on account of that I'm here.'

He explained about the papers that had been found with Nathalie, and how Peter had come to Morocco in search of a story.

'Why do you think he was killed?' she asked when he came to an end.

He shrugged.

'It's what I'm here to find out. Obviously, he got in somebody's way, or asked too many questions in the wrong places. Or maybe he and Daisy just happened to be in the wrong place at the wrong time.'

'Could it be connected in some way to those papers? To your family?'

He nodded.

'It's possible. I just don't like . . .'

'If you could find those papers,' she said. 'Retrace his steps. Ask questions from the *right* people.'

'And hide from the police. And find my way about strange cities. Oh, and question some people in Arabic. I need a guide, but somehow I think the last one left and switched out the lights.'

'You think so?'

'I can't ask anyone to take me in tow as long as those apes from Ouarzazate are after me, and every police checkpoint has photos of me splashed all over it.'

She got to her feet and crossed to him, then bent and rumpled his hair.

'You're already in tow. I'm charging you my standard rate, plus a percentage of any treasure you find. And the usual local taxes, of course.'

'Of course. Who does the real work?'

'You do. Starting with lunch. Incidentally, the cat is called Napoléon.'

Nick glanced at the monster tabby on the floor beside him. He looked rather the worse for wear.

'He's been in a few battles, hasn't he?'

She looked puzzled, then laughed.

'No, not that Napoléon. His full name is Napoléon the Third. Sadly, cats do not have long lives round here. He's the third of his line. But he's a survivor. Aren't you, Napo?'

17

Before leaving for the hotel, they talked through every angle that had a bearing on Nick, his safety, and his ability to carry out what he now treated as an independent investigation into a double murder.

'The police photograph is a good likeness,' she said. 'Any idea where they could have got it from?'

He shook his head.

'Or maybe . . . my passport was at the hotel back there for a while. Could they . . . ?'

'Very likely, though the one I saw looked better than a passport shot. No matter, we've got to change your appearance. You speak good French, but no Arabic, so I've no choice but to make you a Frenchman. I bought some stuff while I was out: there's a little shop that sells party costumes and theatrical goods. It's for children mainly, but there are enough mad foreigners here to keep a couple of amateur theatrical groups going. So . . .'

With a flourish, she pulled out a plastic bag, from which she took all sorts of pots, brushes, and what closely resembled furnishing materials.

It took almost two hours, but by the time she'd finished

he looked distinctly Mediterranean. His hair was jet black, he sported a moustache, and his skin – his hands and face at least – was a smooth olive colour. He would never have passed for a Moroccan, but his appearance and his fluency in French together more or less guaranteed that no one would give him a second glance.

'What about clothes?' he asked. 'These are filthy.' He indicated the jacket and trousers he'd been wearing when his nightmare began.

'Don't worry, I bought some for you in the Gueliz. They're imports. Here, you can change in the bathroom. I don't know if they're to your taste, but . . .'

'They're perfect, but I must pay you. How much?'

'Forget it. You've got plenty of cards in that wallet.'

'Plenty of cards, but no papers. What if the police stop me and ask for an ID?'

She nodded.

'I'm working on that. I know someone who can help. He can get you a French passport in twenty-four hours, maybe less.'

'A fake?'

She sniffed.

'And risk being caught? This will be the real thing.'

'Stolen?'

'Undoubtedly. But in Ceuta or Mellila, not Morocco.'

Ceuta and Mellila were Spanish enclaves carved out of Moroccan territory on the northern coastline. Tourists went in and out like cuckoos on a clock. If passports were stolen, the loss had to be reported to the Spanish authorities, not the Moroccan.

'I drew some money from the bank, so you can have cash

on you at all times. Don't use it unless we get separated and you have to. And – here – this is my phone number. Better you memorize it and leave the paper here.'

He did so, and tore the paper up. Then, taking her pen and the pad she'd been writing on, he wrote down a name and number for her.

'This is my brother's number in Oxford. If anything happens to me and you can't get hold of Duncan, ring him.'

She tucked the slip into an address book sitting next to the telephone.

It was almost time to leave.

'What do you think?' he asked. 'Do I look safe enough to be let out on my own?'

She looked at him seriously, then burst into peals of laughter.

'Not with that moustache! I think I'd better trim it a bit more. You couldn't drink *harira* with it round your mouth. But the truth is, Monsieur Budgeon, that you don't get to go out alone. We go everywhere together. I'm your chaperone. I'm your way out of this.'

They set off for the hotel together. Justine had no car – it would have been useless within the medina, and for longer journeys she could always scrounge one from friends or hire one cheaply – so they walked to the Bab Doukkala gate and found a taxi to take them the rest of the way. At the hotel, she asked the driver to wait. He was one of several regulars who plied the Doukkala gate. Hers was a familiar face. He nodded and said he'd be there when they left.

* * *

Yes, Monsieur Todd had arrived, and yes, he was in his room. What name should the concierge give?

Nick was thrown. Duncan had not been warned to expect a French name.

Justine was there ahead of him, however.

'Say it is Monsieur Bouge and Madame Jean.'

'*Oui, madame. Bouge et Jean. Attendez, s'il vous plaît.*'

They watched as the concierge went through his routine, now waiting patiently for a reply, now speaking, now putting down the phone. All the time, Nick felt exposed and nervous. He had left the Middle Ages behind and found himself in a modern hotel, full of bright lights and polished tiles. Water sparkled in a fountain. Tourists in bright clothes came and went like visitors to an art gallery. Everywhere, sheets of glass reflected the lights, or mirrored passers-by, or simply exposed them to the public gaze.

'Monsieur Todd will see you now. Please go straight up. His room is number four hundred and nineteen. Have a nice day.'

They were halfway to the lift when someone called Justine's name. Nick froze. Justine turned and recognized friends who taught as *coopérants* at the nearby Cadi Ayyad University.

'You go on up,' she said. 'Your friend will be waiting for you.'

Nick did not hesitate. The lift doors opened, and he hastened inside.

'Jeanine! Victoire! How nice to see you.'

'Justine. Have we interrupted an important assignation?'

'A bit old for me, don't you think?'

'We've watched *Noce Blanche*, my dear. Age has never

180

been a barrier to men's passions, as you should know. You're very brave.'

'He's here on business.'

'Yes, of course he is. They're all on business. *Ma pauvre Justinette*, I'm afraid we have to go. Tonight's the big dinner with our Faculty Director. We hope to put him in a good mood. Our budget comes up for renewal tomorrow, of course. Now, you take care.'

'Call us,' said Victoire. Justine promised she would, and they headed off towards the restaurant.

When she turned back towards the lift, her heart fell six storeys. Walking nonchalantly ahead of her in the direction of the lifts were two Sûreté policemen. They were chatting together as they walked, but they didn't seem to be off-duty.

Room 419 was a little way along the corridor. Nick looked both ways. No one had seen him on the way up, and so far this floor was deserted. He went straight to the door and struck it with his knuckles. The door swung inwards a few inches. Duncan must have left it open for him to come in directly.

'Duncan? It's me, Nick. Thank God you made it. I'll just leave the door open, if you don't mind. I have a friend with me, someone I want you to meet.'

There was a short corridor ahead of him, leading to a half-open door. The room beyond was lit up. He pushed the door open wider and stepped inside.

Duncan was lying just beyond the door, his back to the ground, his eyes staring at the ceiling. There was no one else in the room, but a quick examination showed that

Duncan had been stabbed around twenty times with a sharp knife. The knife still protruded from his chest, while bloody wounds gaped all over his front, across his hands, and his neck.

Nick gaped at his dead friend in despair. Not only had this murder deprived him of his main lifeline back to safety, but he had no doubt that it was connected to the earlier killings, and that he would have to make solving it part of his now seemingly overwhelming enterprise. When he added it all together, he despaired of making progress: to find the identities of the killer or killers who had murdered Peter, Daisy, Djamil, and now Duncan; to clear his own name; and to bring everyone concerned to justice.

He started to get to his feet, but at that moment there was a sound of running feet from the entrance. He swore to himself, realizing it was more than likely that Duncan's killer or killers had been hanging around, waiting for him to arrive. Quickly, his eyes darted round the room in search of a weapon, but at that moment Justine appeared in the doorway.

'Justine . . . Thank God it's you. I found Duncan like this. He's still warm, his killers can't be far . . .'

Then he looked at her face. He thought he'd grown accustomed to its moods and changes, but he was not prepared for this. For a moment, he could not understand why she was looking at him like that, and then he looked down and understood why her eyes were filled with puzzlement, betrayal, and anger.

'No, Justine, it's not how it looks. I . . .'

But she'd already gone, running from him the way a

sheep, led to slaughter by its beloved shepherd, might try to flee.

He started to run after her, very nearly slipping on a pool of fresh blood. He dashed into the corridor and made for the door. As he reached it he crashed into someone coming from the opposite direction. He drew back, and as he did so recognized the uniform. He tried to twist and break away, but a second policeman arrived from nowhere and seized his arm.

'*Monsieur Budgeon? Vous êtes en état d'arrestation.*'

A little distance away, he heard the humming of the lift as it started its descent.

In the Spider's Habitation

18

Marrakech
The daily journal of Marie-Louise Guénaud

Friday, 20 June 1941
I feel so helpless. In spite of setbacks, the Germans are still forging ahead. Further trouble is brewing in the desert east of us, and it is likely the British will find themselves trapped in Egypt. Rommel's tanks are outside Tobruk, held off for the moment by a division of Australians, and our cinemas are full of his victories. It's only a matter of time before he moves on Cairo, everyone says so. The Arabs think it will be some sort of liberation for their cousins on the Nile. Little do they know.

The trouble is, we have no solid information. Nobody trusts the official press, we cannot always get the BBC (and I'm not sure how reliable even they are), and the French papers that are smuggled in from other parts of the empire are like gold dust; the authorities try to clamp down on them, and when you do find one it's months out of date. Anyway, the net result of all this is that gossip circulates everywhere and nobody really knows what to believe or do next.

We all pretend life is normal, and I know very well things are easier for us here in Morocco than in occupied France or any of the other countries the Boche have over-run; my dear André goes to school each day, Vital presides over his court with growing distaste, my sister rejoices in her little monkey of a baby, and I await mine with eager anticipation. André is growing jealous, but I tell him to play with his pretty cousin, so that perhaps he may come to think babies fine things after all. But she's not much of a baby, *la petite Hélène*, she scarcely whimpers, never cries, and is always limp, so there is not much fun in her for André.

Vital talks of giving up his job. He has had to adjudicate in some difficult matters recently. His greatest concern is for his Jewish friends. Before the war, he got to know many of the Jews in the Mellah, and some others from France who had taken up residence here in the Gueliz. They have, on the whole, been well treated in Morocco, and Vital thinks their community worthy of interest. Those I have met have invariably been polite and civilized, and I am not surprised by my husband's wish to know them better.

However, last October a law was passed to the effect that foreign nationals who are Jews are to be sent to what are now known as 'special camps'. They say these are not for Moroccan Jews, but there are rumours that they have been building a large number of them, and we've heard that all sorts of Jews are being sent to camps in Tunisia and Algeria. All the Algerian Jews have been stripped of their French nationality, which Vital says they were granted about seventy years ago. We have no idea what goes on in these camps, but we think it's some sort of forced labour.

And now, about three weeks ago, our government at

Vichy passed a new law calling for what they call the 'administrative arrest' – whatever that means – of all Jews whatsoever. French Jews, Arab Jews, it's all the same. This law is to be the new *Statut des Juifs*.

Sultan Mohammed does what he can to protect his own Jews, but he has no real power and can hardly be expected to resist indefinitely in these matters. He's been powerless to prevent the more petty regulations that restrict which trades and professions a Jew may take up, or where they may send their children to school, or that force them back into the old *mellahs*, turning them back into ghettos. Vital has seen numerous cases involving expropriation of money or property, loyal citizens forced to stand down from public office, and heaven knows what else. Of course, the way the Germans treat the Jews in Europe beggars belief.

Fedala
Saturday, 21 June
We've come to Fedala for a weekend, ourselves, Béatrice, Gérard, and the children. We see a lot of my sister and her mysterious husband ever since they moved to Marrakech. Of all the places he could have been posted to. And we still don't know exactly what he does. This isn't really the time of year for a seaside resort, but the weather is reasonably warm, and the sun shines as though to encourage us. Of course, everyone comes here in the season, and even now there are crowds strolling on the beach, or in the pleasure gardens. The sea air is bracing, and André can't get enough of the place: it's his first time at the seaside, he has been bought a bucket and spade, and there seems to be endless sand for him to dig in.

As for us adults, it's a real opportunity to get away from

189

our constant worries. Not that my sister and her husband seem to experience many of those. Oh, Béa worries enough about her precious Hélène, whether she's eating properly, should she be sleeping so long, are her bowel movements normal. I can see that she is a sickly child, but I honestly think her greatest problem is too much pampering. I don't mean by that, that children should not be pampered, but Béatrice has adopted the very worst habits, and I fear she will turn her little darling into something quite unpleasant, or possibly not that, but a most pitiable sort of human being.

But we have set aside our little (and big) differences for this weekend. Gérard drove us all here in his new car, a Peugeot model 402 which he had shipped out from Marseilles last month. My brother-in-law is showing signs of real influence, but I'm not sure where he's getting his money from. His vineyards can hardly be making that much profit, and I'm sure he invested almost everything in them. I'd guess he's receiving money from Reims, that's to say, from the occupied zone – and that means connections, very likely connections with the German authorities.

Fedala reminds me a little of Deauville, where we used to go as children. It has a casino, a golf course and a racecourse, and the beach is almost as long and as white. We are all staying at the Miramar, which is the best hotel and serves the best food. The hotel is only a short step from the casino, and Gérard has already won what he calls 'a small fortune' there, if he is to be believed. Béatrice tells me he has started to spend time at the casino in Marrakech, the one in the Hivernage. She does not say if he loses money or not. I hope, for her sake, that he does not.

Vital has no taste for gambling, thank heavens; indeed, I don't know if he has any vices at all. We see eye to eye in everything, and I could not be happier, were it not for this war. What I like most is to sit with him after he returns from work and has eaten, and talk about this and that. He is so well informed on almost every subject, and makes no difficulty about passing what he knows on to me. I feel a very different woman from the one who travelled out here to stay with my sister and her husband. More serious, able to look the world in the eye, or, at least, to see through its many veils.

Before coming here, we spent much of Friday night talking about a case that has recently come before Vital. It's an appeal – a rather desperate appeal, I have to say – on behalf of a young man, a Moroccan youth of twenty called Aziz. He's quite a bright boy, but he may not have chosen his friends well. He was taken on as an Arabic clerk for a Belgian company based in the medina and specializing in the export of high-quality dried fruit. Aziz dealt with their correspondence with native suppliers, and I understand he performed his duties well.

After last May's invasion, the Brussels firm of which this is just a foreign branch was taken over by a German enterprise, and things began to get quite difficult. Exports were being turned back even from French ports, and there was talk of shutting the Marrakech office down.

Then, about a month ago, M. Wouters and M. Brusselmans, the partners in charge of Morocco, who have lived in Marrakech for over ten years, were arrested on suspicion of communicating with a cell of Belgian resistance fighters, and passing on information about shipping passing through Moroccan ports. I really don't know if there is any substance to this, but the poor men have been sent under escort, first to Marseille, then to Brussels in order to be questioned by the Gestapo. Vital thinks they will face the death sentence. Of course, there will be no trial, the Gestapo will simply make its mind up. Whether they are guilty or not, of course, their execution will always serve as yet another whip with which to cow the populace.

Young Aziz has fallen foul of this. He is said to have masterminded communications between Moroccan workers in the ports and his Belgian bosses. His great mistake was to have made friends with some young Frenchmen who work for another import-export company in the same building, and who have shown themselves to be ardent supporters, not only of Pétain's despicable regime, but of Herr Hitler and his policies. They not only dropped Aziz at the first opportunity, but planted stories about his part in this supposed plot.

He's been found guilty and – I find this hard to believe – sentenced to death. But there are, thank God, certain complications that may yet save the poor boy's life. His parents died a few years ago, leaving the boy to live with his grandparents. But, since the boy is a Moroccan and a Muslim, there are certain difficulties. It would be difficult for the French authorities to put a Muslim to death, unless they obtained the permission of a religious judge, something they do not have and are unlikely to get in a situation like this. The native population do not consider this war any of their business, and there could be trouble if one of their number died on account of it.

There is to be a new hearing on Tuesday. Vital will not be the only judge sitting, and he knows he has to be extremely careful, especially since the Delavigne affair. He has spoken with the boy in the presence of his lawyers, and remains convinced of his innocence. Gérard and Béatrice know of it, of course, since it was Gérard who signed the papers for young Aziz's arrest, and who sent the Belgians off to their internment or death. They are, naturally, convinced that Aziz is as guilty as sin, and urge Vital to do his duty and reject the appeal.

'What if the boy is innocent?' Vital asked them this evening over dinner. There is a very good restaurant in the casino, and Gérard insisted on taking us all there. 'What if the evidence proves to my satisfaction that he had nothing to do with his bosses' little game?'

Gérard, whom I grow to detest more and more, just shrugged and said it made no material difference.

'What the hell do you mean?' Vital grew quite heated. 'What sort of court do you think I preside over? A court that wouldn't concern itself over sending a man to his death, innocent or not?'

'You're missing the point, my dear Vital. I'm sure it matters to the boy, and to you, and to something abstract called Justice, or whatever you like. But his death, if it comes to that, will serve *pour encourager les autres*. Like that man, what was his name – Delavigne – who was sent for the chop just before we moved here. In times like these, we need to be absolutely sure the blacks behave themselves. That means coming down hard on anyone we suspect of having truck with the enemy. They're not exempt, you know, not in wartime, in a state of emergency. Or perhaps you thought they were.'

'Gérard, your understanding of the average Moroccan is extremely limited. They really couldn't care about the blasted enemy. If the British move in here and replace us French, where will that leave them? Worse off than the Indians or the Egyptians, probably. Better the devil you know. But if you go around arresting them for no good reason, or sending them to camps, or executing them, don't act surprised if there's a rising one day that would make the hair stand up on top of your head.'

'A rising?' I noticed that Gérard was going slightly red. His fork fell to the plate. Outside, a fresh wind swept in from the Atlantic and battered our windows. 'Be careful what sentiments you give rein to in my presence, Vital. That could be taken as treachery in some places. I can assure you that anyone – and I mean anyone – found inciting the natives to revolt will answer to me directly.'

I broke in then, and changed the subject.

Sunday, 22 June

We all went for a long walk this morning, along the esplanade Miramar, which skirts the beach for some three kilometres. Last night's wind had gone down a little, but our hair was still swept about, and we didn't dare wear hats.

We worked up a healthy appetite for breakfast, then Gérard suggested we attend Mass together. The local church is no distance at all from where we're staying, so we put on our best clothes and headed forth. The priest, who goes by the name of Father Augustin Farrère, preached in a loud voice about God's vengeance, and suggested that this was about to be visited upon the British as a punishment for their desertion of the true faith in favour of Protestantism. He seemed an arrogant man, and not just on that account.

Confession was heard afterwards, but I did not make mine. In truth, I haven't confessed a single sin in eight years or so, though I suppose I've committed plenty. It gave me a sense of relief to get out of the church and feel the sea breeze against my skin, wet and salty, from somewhere far away. Dear God, why did the priest not preach to us about those poor young men at this very moment far out on the ocean, on destroyers or merchant ships, or on board submarines? I think it must be awful to set to sea in any of those, not knowing if you will return.

We left Gérard and Béatrice to their confessions, and went off alone, the two of us, hand in hand and thoroughly in love. Vital suggested slipping back to the hotel to make love. I was sorely tempted. There is nothing so wonderful as lovemaking in the afternoon. But we must consider André, and we don't suppose our dear relations can have that much to confess.

I dread Marrakech when we return tomorrow. How stifling it will be, how the walls hold the heat all day and let it out again throughout the night.

Marrakech
Monday, 23 June
The journey home was uneventful. Gérard was in a more relaxed and expansive mood than usual, and as he drove he shared some of his preoccupations. He believes that the best thing for the *patrie* at this stage in the war will be complete occupation by the Germans. He professes to be unsympathetic to Hitler and his general war aims, yet he speaks with admiration about the Reich and how it is policed. He's particularly keen on the concentration camps, and how they have been designed to give a short, sharp shock to their inmates, whom he calls criminals. I asked him how he could defend the deportation of loyal French men and women for no greater crime than patriotism, the roundup of French civilians, the murder of our innocent fellow countrymen. He just mumbled the same lame excuses and drove on whistling, as though he had not a care in the world.

195

When this war is over, and France returns to her rightful place in the world, what will we do with Gérard and his like? Or will Germany conquer everything, and evil finally triumph?

Tuesday, 24 June
Wretched, wretched day. Vital has just returned from court, and is quite depressed. Aziz's appeal came before the court today, and the initial presentation by the boy's lawyer gave reasonable grounds for supposing that the case against him would be dismissed. But when the prosecution lawyer stood up, he dropped a bombshell. Whatever Aziz's complicity or lack of it in the crime of which he was initially accused, it has now been revealed that he is guilty of helping a Jewish family to escape from Marrakech. They are Belgian Jews who have been here five years: the father is manager of the warehouse for the export company for which Aziz worked. The boy has a cousin who works on the docks at Casablanca, and together they dreamed up some scheme to get the Belgians from here by road to join a Brazilian merchant ship.

The worst bit is that it was our caring brother-in-law Gérard who exposed this shameful plot. This, it appears, is Gérard's main function. He is not a policeman in the true sense at all, but a secret policeman.

Wednesday, 25 June
I don't want this baby any longer. What sort of world would it be born into, after all? Talking about 'new life' just seems a wretched joke.

I sat in court today. Vital had a full day in his own court, but he wanted someone he could trust to attend Aziz's case in the courtroom next door.

The proceedings were brief and to the point. With two charges – and ones of such seeming seriousness – against him, the boy didn't stand a chance. He tried to explain his actions, but was made to sit down by the judge, an old man called Raclot, whom I have met once or twice at gatherings of the legal clan. Raclot listened instead to the summing up made by the state prosecutor, a sharp-tongued, vile individual called de la Nézière. He knows me too, and from time to time cast a glance at me, as though to question my right to be present there. I felt as though I was being made guilty by association.

The verdict was predictable. Aziz is sentenced to die. There is to be no appeal. His crime is high treason, and innocent though he is of any ill will towards France, they are intent on exacting the supreme penalty. The guillotine must be brought here from Casablanca, which should be a matter of some ten days. Aziz is to stay in the prison here until the machine arrives. On the following morning, he is to be taken out to the prison yard, and his head severed from his body. It is too cruel for words. Vital is to write to the central government in Vichy, but he knows their answer already.

19

Le bourreau prinst une corde, a laquelle tenoit actaché ung groux bloc, a tout une douloere tranchant, hantée dedans, venant d'amont entre deux pousteaulx, et tire ladite corde, en maniere que le bloc tranchant a celui gennevoys tumba antre le teste et les espaules, si que le teste s'en va d'ung couste et le corps tumbe de l'autre.*

Jean d'Auton, Histoire de Louis XII, 1615

Algiers, Algeria
Late June 1941
[IN CIPHERTEXT]

FAO IDAHO CONTROL AT G-2, US ARMY
HEADQUARTERS.

The naval attaché has permitted me to use their SIGABA M-134-C encryption machine. Machine was delivered courtesy of US Submarine *Pampanito* one week ago and

---

* The executioner takes a cord, to which a large block [of wood] has been attached, fitted with a sharp blade which is set in it, being brought up between two posts, he pulls on this cord so that the cutting block falls between the head and the shoulders of the victim ['a man from Genova'], with the result that the head topples in one direction, and the torso in the other.

is classified TOP SECRET even to the ambassador.

I met last night with three members of the Free French underground. Regular meetings are inadvisable: there are Gestapo spies everywhere, not to mention Italian agents from Mussolini's OVRA, and everyone's movements are noted by everybody else. My contacts used the following *noms de guerre*: Jacques Texcier, Raymond Déchelette, and Yves Hasquenoph, and they knew me as Bob Ballinger.

I am now more convinced than ever that, if the United States government does ever get round to declaring war, North Africa will be our back door to Berlin. My contacts assure me there is considerable support for the Resistance in Morocco, Tunisia and Algeria. This is true of the military too, and even the Foreign Legion. It seems that the Germans have been cramming the Legion with their own people, and that this has led to resentment and a split in the force. I recommend that we infiltrate some GIs into the Legion to get some first-hand information. Or maybe we have Americans serving there already.

The real problem is recruiting reliable people for the resistance work. The French won't trust the natives, which leaves only their fellow French. There is a lack of radios, they have absolutely no code transmitters, and they have only small stashes of guns and ammunition.

The Alliance network in France have placed an experienced soldier in charge of clandestine activities throughout North Africa. He is Commandant Léon Faye, and I believe he is sympathetic to working with the British. My contacts are not yet sure whether he will go along with US intervention here. I am trying to set up a meeting.

I think we may be concentrating too much on Algiers. Morocco has the Atlantic seaboard and can be brought into contact with West Africa. In the event of a landing,

I believe that is where we should be aiming.

My contacts say they cannot emphasize too strongly that the US should not seem to encourage any sort of independence movement for the Moroccans. This would alienate the colonists, who seek to retain the status quo after the war. Please make sure this is stressed to our various propaganda offices. If we don't work with the French and get their co-operation, in the event of our joining the war, we are doomed.

BALLINGER
4927BC8

15 rue du Dr Madelaine (ancienne rue du Djenan Hartsi)
Ville Nouvelle, Marrakech

Thursday, 26 June 1941

To M. Pétrus Loustaunau-Lacau
Procureur de la République
Vichy

Dear Pétrus,

I have chosen to write to you in private, at a time of personal disquiet, to ask for advice, and possibly for help. I enclose some papers relative to a case that has recently come before me, that of a young Moroccan boy who has been sentenced to death for what are, I believe, crimes he did not commit. He is, most certainly, guilty of a lesser offence (though I, for one, do not see how it can be an offence at all), that of helping some Belgian Jews slip out of Marrakech. However you interpret the law on this matter (the boy says he had understood the Sultan's assurances regarding Jews to refer to all members of that race living on Moroccan soil), it is clearly not a capital offence. Nor is there a shred of evidence which would connect the boy to the primary offence, that of treason.

I have written to the Department of Justice, even though an appeal in this matter has, strictly speaking, been denied. Aside from arguments of common humanity, my motive in writing these two letters is quite simple: at this time above all others, I consider it vital that we do all in our power to retain, if not the affection, then at least the allegiance of the Moroccan people. It doesn't look well when an Arab youth is sentenced to die for upholding his Sultan's decrees. More seriously, for Christians to execute a Muslim could be taken as an affront to their religion, and I don't have to tell you the possible consequences should that happen.

I hate to presume on our friendship, Pétrus. But you know I am a decent man, and a loyal Frenchman, no friend to treachery. I hate to see an innocent boy die just to satisfy some new-found taste for retribution. We conquered Morocco with good intentions, and we undertook the responsibility of succouring and protecting its people. There is a growing independence movement here and among the Arabs generally, and if we execute this boy, I feel sure they will make a martyr of him. Help me prevent that if you can.

Je vous prie d'accepter, Cher Pétrus, l'expression de mes salutations distinguées,
Vital

The daily journal of Marie-Louise Guénaud

Thursday, 26 June
I was allowed to visit Aziz in prison today, in the squalid *Quartier de Haute Surveillance*. Such inhumanity to lock a boy like that up in a cramped cell that feels more like an oven than anything. They let me in on 'humanitarian' grounds, because it appears that Aziz has no parents and

that the grandparents with whom he lives are incapable of making visits. Vital has heard that they are entirely dependent on him for rent and food, and that their landlord threatens to expel them if next month's money is not paid. That will be something else to look into.

They chained him for my visit, shackled him to the wall by his arms and legs, over-riding my protests with arguments about my personal safety. I asked to be taken somewhere, but this was met with a shake of the head and a grin from the jailer.

'How are you, Aziz?' I asked once they had left. He just looked back at me blankly. 'My name is Madame Guénaud. My husband is the judge who tried to help you yesterday.' He would not utter a word in reply. I tried out some of the very little Arabic I know, but he looked at me much as though I was a dog performing on two legs.

An idea struck me.

'Very well,' I said. 'I'll just try talking in my awful Arabic, and perhaps you'll correct me if I get something wrong.'

He showed no sign of having heard me, so I just went on, gabbling away as I do with our maid, telling him about the weather outside, what there was in the market, what news there was of the war. They'd allowed me fifteen minutes with him, with no guarantee of further time, so I knew it mattered very little what I said.

It was just as I heard footsteps in the corridor that something happened. I'd been talking about our maid Shadeeya, and had just mentioned how she'd knocked some glasses off the kitchen table this morning. *Tiyyeh el-kisan men et-tabla*, I said, giving a rather lively demonstration of poor Shadeeya's misfortune, and the look on her face when she saw what she'd done. I'd been there and seen it, and hadn't stopped laughing for ages. She'd been very put out, though relieved, not to say amazed, not to be punished for the incident.

As I was miming the whole thing, Aziz suddenly burst out laughing. His distant demeanour was gone in an instant. He laughed for a minute or two, then, as the key turned in the lock, he smiled at me.

'*Tiyyhet*,' he corrected me. 'Your maid she is a girl, not a man. You should not say *Tiyyeh*.'

Then they were in the cell with me.

'Thank you,' he said as they took me away. 'For coming to talk to me.'

'Don't worry,' I called. 'I'll be back.'

Well, I do mean to be back, even if it takes a visit to the Governor of the prison himself.

Shortly after I arrived back from the prison, the doorbell rang, and Shadeeya let Béatrice in. I had been expecting Béatrice, and had been surprised that she hadn't called before. She looked very hot, and seemed out of breath, as though she'd run the whole way from her house to ours.

'What is the meaning of this?' were her first words on entering the living room, where I had been resting from the heat.

'Of what?' I asked evenly, though I knew very well.

'You have been to the prison to visit that boy, that sneaking little degenerate. How could you do such a thing? To bring such disgrace on all our heads! A filthy little pimp-fuck of an Arab.'

'Béatrice,' I said, finding myself calmer than I had any reason to think I should be, 'if you cannot control your tongue and speak quietly and without using obscenities, I shall be obliged to have Shadeeya put you out of the house.'

'To have . . . ?! Listen to me, Miss Holier-than-Thou, you were always a disgrace, but now you've gone too far. To even think of such a thing, to go in person, you, a Christian woman, a French woman, a . . . a . . .'

Her tongue got itself in a knot, and I used the chance to butt in again.

'No, Béatrice, you will listen to me, and you will listen properly for once in your brainless life. I am visiting a child of God out of Christian charity, and I am astonished at your lack of thought or compassion or Christian spirit. You are welcome to come with me when you will: he needs friendly faces and kind smiles to see him through this terrible thing. If you must know, I also think he is innocent of the charges laid against him. It is up to you whether you think that or not. But do not deny me the right to attend a man in prison and under sentence of death, as our Lord commanded us to do. And now, Béatrice, I really think it is better that you go.'

And, with Shadeeya's help, I bustled her out. She had never known me stand up to her like that before, and the sheer shock of our confrontation was enough to render her speechless and powerless until she was well on her way. I went back to the living room and subsided in helpless bouts of laughter.

Vital came back from work this evening looking tired. After dinner, he told me there is a little news: the guillotine is already being made ready for transport.

20

The daily journal of Marie-Louise Guénaud

Monday, 30 June
Vital spoke to me over breakfast about how the execution will be done. He is sure it is something I should know, and I think, dear God, I think I know why.

What horrifies me most is the formality that surrounds it all, the sense of ceremony, even though it takes place shamefacedly, away from the public gaze, like a sordid liaison between a man and a woman, or two men.

I had always thought executions took place in public, but Vital says the law was changed a couple of years ago, when a decree was issued, confining the pitiful act to the prison yard. The public are not invited, only a group of state officials, all summoned to witness the death and set some sort of sanctimonious seal on it.

I was granted another meeting with Aziz this afternoon. The Governor has agreed, in view of my position and the fact that the boy has no one else who is permitted to visit him during these last days, to let me spend one hour each day with him until his final hours. He says he will let a priest attend him, should the boy show any sign of remorse and a wish to convert to the true Catholic faith. I suggested that a Muslim might be more appropriate, one of the heads of a Sufi brotherhood perhaps, since the natives set such store by them, or a prayer leader – I really don't know what would be appropriate. But he sneered at my suggestion anyway.

There will be no remorse, of course. The boy is innocent, at least in whatever lies between him and his God. He talked freely today, and I asked him about the Jewish family he helped. Had he not known it was illegal to help foreign Jews? I asked.

'You French will never understand,' he told me. 'It is always "French", "Moroccan", "German", "Belgian". None of these names mean anything to a Muslim. When I look at the world, I don't see it divided between nationalities as you do. For me and my friends, there are only Muslims, Jews, Christians, and pagans. Before the French came here, we never thought of Maroc as a separate country. It was just part of Dar al-Islam, the House of Islam. Now, it is Bayt al-'ankabut, the Spider's House . . .'

'We call it a web.'

'Yes. A few threads, nothing more. A mouse can destroy it in moments. You do not read the Koran, I think.'

I shook my head. 'Only a little bit. I have a French translation at home, but I find it difficult.'

'Yes, it is difficult, especially in Arabic, which has so many meanings for every word. But if you make an effort and read correctly, you will see that Jews and Christians are called "Peoples of the Book". This is because they possess books from God, the Torah and the Injil, the Gospel. Also, God calls them "Peoples of the *Dhimma*".'

He hesitated, trying to find the right word. I could not help him. Involuntarily, my eyes flickered about the cell. It was tiny, six feet by six, perhaps. Aziz was still shackled, tight against the wall. Sweat trickled down his face and appeared as a wet patch on his light jellaba. Insects ran everywhere: I had to fight down my disgust. The room looked as though it had never been cleaned. Was this a proper place in which to keep a condemned man? I asked myself.

'I think *dhimma* is maybe covenant. It is an agreement. In this case, the Jews are granted security from God. The Muslims are obliged to see they are not harmed, as long as they do not behave arrogantly and rebel against the Muslims. When my friends were threatened, I could not stand back and let them come to harm. It was my duty as a Muslim to protect them.'

Office of M. Henri Le Gentilhomme, Juge de l'Application des Peines, Marrakech

1 July 1941

Sirs,

At the request of M. Proudhon, the Procureur Général for this region, and under the terms of Article 26 of the Code Pénal, I am writing to inform those underlisted that they are hereby obliged to be present singularly and collectively at the execution of the traitor Aziz Larbi, the said execution to take place at daybreak on Tuesday the 8th of this month, in the Gueliz prison, Marrakech.

M. René Thivrier, presiding Judge of the Assizes
M. A. Desfourneaux of the Public Prosecutor's office,
  as designated by the Public Prosecutor, M. Proudhon

M. Albin Peytavin, a judge in the Tribunal for this district . . .

The daily journal of Marie-Louise Guénaud

2 July

He tells me more about himself each day. How quickly his shyness and anger have passed. But each hour is precious, there is no time to waste, and he has much to say. I listen and smile, as if there was all the time in the world. I was afraid he might want to talk more about his case, protest his innocence, demand that I make some sort of desolate appeal for him before Vital or his other judges. But, to my surprise, he has mentioned none of that. He seems to have accepted his fate. Yet, at times he lets slip some longing or other for the world he was part of until a month or so ago. I can't offer him anything to replace what they are preparing to take from him. So I put on a brave face, and ask about his family, and encourage him to talk about the happiest times in his life. Sadly, these seem to have been very few indeed.

When I got home, Vital told me that the guillotine is now complete, and will be delivered to Marrakech the day after tomorrow. This will leave sufficient time in which to put it through its paces.

Office of M. Henri Le Gentilhomme, Juge de l'Application des Peines, Marrakech

3 July 1941

Au Nom de la Loi

M. the Executioner of the High Works is hereby ordered to take possession of the individual named Aziz Larbi, condemned to the punishment of death by the Assizes

Court of Marrakech on 24 June 1941, and to proceed with his execution within the confines of the prison of Gueliz on 8 July at the legally established hour of daybreak.

The daily journal of Marie-Louise Guénaud

4 July

Each day now, I bring him a little decent food cooked by Shadeeya, light things like *harira*, and some hot mint tea from a nearby café, to wash it down. He is listless and quite without hope, yet he attacks his food with a hungry vigour that astonishes me, as though his body refuses to understand the end that it faces, that it will face in such a short space of days.

Vital continues to do all he can, and I don't doubt that, under normal circumstances, he would be able to get at least a stay of execution. Now, he has friends calling to whisper kindly warnings in his ears: 'Don't get involved', 'Think of the consequences', 'He's only an Arab', 'Let the Sultan deal with it, the boy's one of his own', 'We're at war, Vital, we don't have the luxury of going easy on traitors', 'Better safe than sorry', 'Watch it, or they'll think you're a member of the Resistance', 'Take care', 'Watch your back', 'You have a wife and child to look out for, and another on the way', 'You're letting the side down, and as for your wife . . .'

Aziz isn't a 'boy', of course, he's a grown man who had a life ahead of him. Today, he admitted to me that he had been introduced to a young woman, that they'd met on numerous occasions over the past year (strictly chaperoned, of course!), and that he had hoped to marry her. Her name is Nuriyya, and she is a teacher

209

in a *medrasa*, a little Arab school in the medina, where she instructs the girls in home economics and French.

Aziz spoke vividly of her, and left me with a strong impression of her personality. He wants to see her, and cannot understand why she has not come to visit him. He does not even have so much as a photograph of her to keep by him. I have promised to look into the matter.

From Antoine Solages, Executioner of the High Works, to M. le Juge de l'Application des Peines, Marrakech

4 July 1941

Monsieur le Juge,

I beg to report the safe delivery of the *bois de justice* from Casablanca port to the city of Marrakech, and from there to the Gueliz, where it now resides under the superintendency of M. Pilorges, my principal *valet*.

Specifically, M. Pilorges and I have taken delivery of the following:

One base of cruciform design, weighing 112 kilograms
One set of uprights 2.5 metres in height, wooden, with top-piece, fitted with brass grooves, iron tongues and gudgeons
One iron blade, to be resharpened
One *mouton*, plus two spare *moutons*
One *bascule*
Three sets of ropes
One set of shock absorbers, rubber
One *lunette*

The above will be assembled at the prison tomorrow, and the mechanism tested in readiness for the 8th.

Je vous prie d'agréer, cher Monsieur, l'assurance de
mes sentiments respectueux
  Antoine Solanges
  Bourreau d'État, Région Autonome de Marrakech

21

The daily journal of Marie-Louise Guénaud

5 July

He has begun to haunt my dreams, and with him the awful image of the guillotine. I am not in love with him, he has not affected me sexually in any way, but I feel a passion for him, and the thought of losing him so soon is unsupportable.

I managed to find Nuriyya at the *medrasa*, during her lunch break. She is a delightful girl, very pretty, yet as modest in her demeanour as any Muslim girl should be. I took to her at once, and we went for a walk together in the garden of the Bahia palace, which is only a short distance from the school.

The poor girl is in a dreadful state. It seems she goes to the prison every day and asks to be allowed to visit Aziz, saying he is her fiancé and demanding the right to see him. But, of course, she has no papers to prove any of this, so the guards send her away every time. Each day, when she turns up there (this is early in the morning, before school), she is sure she will be told he has been executed. I have assured her that he is still alive, and told her I will do my best to gain her entry. But I cannot give her any hope, for I know there is none.

I am to return to the school tomorrow, to take her to the prison. And I have told her Aziz would like to have a photograph. She says she will have one taken at one of the little booths on the Djemaa el-Fna. I've told her to go to the little one-armed man who, perhaps on account of his disability, is happy to oblige ladies who want a photograph without their veils.

To M. Vital Guénaud, Juge à la Cour de Cassation, Région
  de Marrakech
15 rue du Dr Madelaine (ancienne rue du Djenan Hartsi)
Ville Nouvelle, Marrakech

6 July 1941

My dear Vital,

Your most kind letter reached me this morning, and I am writing this reply now so that it can be taken the new Airmail service between Vichy and Rabat. Do you know, Vichy has been quite transformed by all these developments. Not many months ago, it was a sleepy little place, terribly provincial, with not very much going for it except the water. Now it feels like the hub of the universe, or the French universe at least! There's hardly room to accommodate all the government ministers who come in and out. But, of course, it's a terrible strain in some ways, and you're probably best out of it in your colonial haven. One hears such things of Fès and Marrakech, the palm trees, the mysterious kasbahs, the veiled yet slender young women. Let the British have Egypt, I say, and we'll hang on to Morocco!

Mind you, that's rather a risky thing to say, given that our German and Italian allies are making a sticking point of Egypt, and battling hard to get hold of it.

I don't think the war in that quarter will affect you, though.

You say nothing in your letter about the beautiful Mrs Guénaud. I say 'beautiful', because dear Loys showed me the most lovely photograph taken of you both at your wedding. She seems most charming, and a little bird (Loys, of course) has told me you are both expecting a happy event. I am delighted to hear it: to have reached your age, and not yet a father. Before you ask, Éloise is in fine form, and the boys are coming to the end of their careers at the Lycée. What the future will hold for them, who can say at a time like this?

I'm afraid there really is absolutely nothing I can do about your martyr. I understand your concern about possible civil unrest and so on, but frankly that's a matter for the soldiers up the hill in your Quartier Militaire. My sources tell me that the commandant there, Colonel Dusquesne, is a formidable old war horse, and that he'll clamp down on any unrest the second the new Abd el-Krim raises his banner. Leave it to him, Vital.

In fact, it will do you no good at all if I'm not wholly honest. Word has got back here about your special plead-ing for the boy, and no one – I really do mean no one – among the legal fraternity is minded to recommend you go any further with it. Stop while you're still in the clear. Quite frankly, these are not auspicious times in which to be making noble gestures, as any schoolboy could have told you. This country has just sustained the greatest and most shameful military defeat in its history, and the last thing any loyal Frenchman wants to do is taint himself and his family by even the most tenuous association with a traitor. There's no point in arguing that the boy is loyal to France. To begin with, there are very few Arabs who are, and even they, like Glaoui Pasha near you, are in it for what they can get out of it. For God's sake, Vital, use some common sense: the boy actually admits that he helped smuggle Jews out of French jurisdiction. That's treachery, however you play it, and it won't do you or your wife or your children the least good to be associated with it. I'm sorry to have gone on, but all that needed to be said. A kind father would have told you nothing else.

On a cheerier note, lots of changes are taking place here. You'd do well to come back. All the plum jobs that had gone to Jew-boys are suddenly vacant, and even the rawest recruit can get himself a very good post these days. You, as a senior lawyer, and very well liked by the right people, should be able to pull off something very rewarding. But you'll have to get yourself over here at top speed; these jobs won't just lie around indefinitely. Bad luck for the Jews, good news for the French.

Take care, and please follow my advice. And remember the Golden Rule for any lawyer: Never let yourself be guided by your heart. Use your head every time.

Amicalement,

Pétrus

The daily journal of Marie-Louise Guénaud

6 July

I brought Nuriyya to the prison today. She trembled all the way, and held onto my arm. She loves him, she says, and will kill herself if they go ahead with the execution. I have not yet told her it is set for two days' time.

I demanded to see the Governor, and used all my influence with him. He agreed that she could stay with him, but for no more than five minutes. She was grateful

215

for that, poor thing, and I took her to the cell, she weeping quietly all the way. The guards would not release him from his shackles, however much I pleaded with them, so Nuriyya had to go in to him like that, knowing he could not embrace her, would never hold her to him in this world. When she came out again, she was like a dead woman, and I never asked her what was said or done in those five minutes.

I took her back to the medina in a taxi. All the way she sat and stared dumbly through the window, but not once did I notice her give way to tears. Following her directions, I walked her home from the Aguenaou gate. She lives with her family in a tiny house at the end of a long, dark *derb*. Her mother opened the door and took her in, and as she did so Nuriyya fainted. She had to be carried in with my help and that of a sister. I was invited in to a scene of palpable distress. The marriage had been welcome on both sides, and this outcome had crushed her family as much as his. I spoke with her mother for a while, her younger sister interpreting. As best I could, I explained the situation, made sure they understood that no hope could be expected from any quarter. Her mother said that the Sultan had spoken with the Commissaire Résident Général, expressing concern that a Muslim was to be put to death in this manner, and that they awaited the outcome of this conversation. I asked how long ago this had been, and she said it had taken place about a week ago. I told the young girl that the execution had been set for the day after tomorrow, but asked her to say nothing to Nuriyya until some days after. She looked blankly at me, but I know she understood.

It was all I could bear, and I said so. The mother nodded and said she understood.

'Please come and see us again,' she said. 'After this is over. *Allah yahennik, Allah yahennik . . .*'

Her voice rang in my ears long afterwards. I could not go back to the prison then, nor for several hours. But equally I could not leave him without my visit, for he had very little time left, and I would only see him twice more. Some hours later, therefore, I made my way back to the prison. It is such a mean place, as though deliberately built to bring down the spirits of those confined there.

When I entered, I could see he was in low spirits.

'I wondered where you were,' he said.

'I had to take Nuriyya home,' I said. 'I spent time there with her mother and sister.'

'Najiyya. Yes, Najiyya will look after her.'

'What about your grandparents?' I asked. 'Is there someone who will look after them?'

'After I am gone?'

And so the floodgates opened. He told me about his grandparents, and his parents and their deaths, about brothers and sisters who had been scattered when they died, and taken in by relatives. He talked and talked and talked, and each time he mentioned a new name, I could see his longing to see them once again.

This evening, we were visited by Dr Monestier, Vital's oldest friend in Marrakech, and now, I believe, a great friend of mine. He works as a surgeon in the Hôpital Civil, a few streets away from the prison. Sometimes he calls on us uninvited (manners are so much less formal here), and will sit for hours with Vital, talking about the burning issues of the day. He is a source of information and wisdom, and I have grown to be very fond of him.

During his visit, he did nothing to embarrass me. In fact, I sensed approval, though I did not feel easy speaking about Aziz with anyone but Vital.

Before he left, however, I realized that there was something I wanted to ask him after all.

'Dr Monestier, if you don't mind, there's . . . I need to ask you something.'

I think he saw from my face the depth of my concern.

'But of course, Marie-Louise. Is this in my professional capacity? I thought you were happy with Dr Chomat. Isn't he giving you and your baby the attention you deserve?'

I shook my head.

'No, he's excellent. He says the baby is thriving, and he's making arrangements to be at the birth whatever happens.'

'Excellent. He's a good man. You're in safe hands. So, if it isn't your pregnancy, what's up?'

'You know about the young man I've been visiting in prison?'

He nodded, but said nothing. Vital was on the other side of the room. He stood up and came to me, bending to kiss my forehead.

'I think it's time I got to bed,' he said. 'I have a busy morning ahead of me. Don't let him keep you up too long, dear.'

I stood and returned his kiss. He glanced back at me from the door, a look of concern on his face, then left the doctor and myself alone.

'His name is Aziz. He is due to die on Tuesday at daybreak, and I no longer believe we can do anything to prevent it.'

'You think he's innocent?'

I thought my answer through, to see whether there was

the least shred of doubt in my mind, for I had no wish to deceive the good doctor.

'Yes,' I said. 'I am utterly convinced of it.'

'Very well, that's enough for me. What can I do?'

'He asked me something today, something I could not answer. I have been racking my brains ever since. He asked whether he will feel anything when the blade strikes his neck, and for how long he may remain conscious after his head has been struck off. My dear doctor, what can I tell him? I wish to tell him only the truth.'

'Why do you always call me "Doctor"?' he asked, a little smile on his lips. 'You should treat me as a friend. After all, you are a mother, you have been a widow, you are a devoted wife – and now you have become the most courageous woman I know. I have nothing but the most profound admiration for your visits to this boy. I doubt I would have the courage, I know that there are few among our fellow French who would be able to do so. But you asked me a question.

'The truth is that medical science has no exact answer. A certain Professor Soemmering once said that "if the air still circulated through the vocal organs, these heads would speak". Sadly for him, most of his colleagues thought him a damn fool for saying it, and I'm much inclined to be of their opinion.

'Nevertheless, it would be wrong of me to deceive you. Several of my profession have carried out experiments designed to determine the issue. In 1905, a certain Dr Beaurieux positioned himself to observe the fate of the head just severed from a criminal named Languille. He claims that there were spasmodic contractions for five or six seconds. Then the face relaxed and the eyelids closed.

'At this point, Beaurieux called Languille's name, and to

his horror the eyelids opened slowly and Languille looked directly at him. This lasted some seconds, then all was as before. He called the name a second time, and again the eyes opened and fixed him with a conscious stare. At the third call, there was no further movement. Something very like this was also observed by a certain Dr Pettigand.

'But none of this is very scientific. There is no bloodflow, the nerves leading to and from the brain have been severed in one stroke, what blood remains in the brain will have haemorrhaged. In short, my dear, the lights will have gone out. He need fear nothing. Tell him to imagine what it would be like to be hit hard on the head. Would he not lose consciousness at once, and in such a way that he would remember nothing later? At this moment, he does not need science, he needs reassurance. Give him that reassurance when you visit him tomorrow.'

22

I did my best. I said I had spoken with Dr Monestier, praised my friend's great learning, and suggested that he had some specialist knowledge of the matter. But Aziz, I could see, was not fully convinced, for he has a deep fear in him that he will see and hear everything after the blade falls.

'Will you not see the Angel of Death?' I asked, thinking to put my trivial knowledge of his religion to some use.

'That will happen in the grave,' he said. 'Two angels will come to question me and torment me. One is Monker, the other Naker. They will cause me to sit up, and they will examine me concerning my faith. But if I have no head, how will I answer them?'

I said I could arrange for a Mohammedan priest to attend him, but he shook his head, saying it was too late to change anything. Was there confession of sins among them? I asked, or absolution? He just moved his head from side to side and said it was enough to believe and to do good works.

He asked about the baby, and we made plans for it together, and debated whether it would turn out to be a boy or a girl. I said that, if it was a boy, I would call him Aziz, and, if a girl, Aziza, and he looked surprised and pleased.

Then, almost without our being aware of it, it was time

for me to go. I embraced him as best I could, and in moments we were both weeping. But suddenly he pulled up short, and made as best he could to push me away.

'What's wrong?' I asked. 'It will be too late tomorrow.'

But he looked at me, tears spread across his face, and made a final appeal.

'Be there,' he said. 'Tomorrow morning. At daybreak. I want you to be there.'

'But I'm not . . .'

'I have no one else to ask. Please don't leave me to face it alone. Say you will come.'

I thought hard before answering. Over these few days, I had made so many promises to him. Could I just turn my back on him now? The very thought of watching him undergo that barbaric treatment frightened me so badly I thought I might faint away. But I knew he needed bravery, not weakness. So I smiled and nodded and said I would be there. Then I turned and ran from the cell as though pursued by demons.

Tuesday, 8 July
The demons have not left me since then. Each hour, each minute they multiply. Gracious God, what is there to do?

Vital was disturbed to learn of Aziz's egregious request, and begged me not to go; but what could I do, how could I act otherwise? I had given my word, I had made a promise. In the end, Vital agreed, but remained unhappy about it.

I spent last night sleepless and troubled in spirit. Monestier brought me a draught, but I would not take it, for I knew I could be of no help to Aziz if I couldn't wake, or if I fell asleep in the prison courtyard. The absence of sleep made no difference to the demons. They circled about me all night, in different forms. A few times I fell asleep briefly, only to wake instantly out of the most horrid dreams I have ever known.

I rose early, well before daybreak, and made my way to the prison. This time, Vital came with me. Pierre Valois, one of the Tribunal judges, who was expected to attend the execution, had fallen ill at the last moment, leaving Vital the opportunity to put himself forward in his place, and to insist that I be present with him. So it was done. We were let into the prison through a side door, and marched down several stinking corridors until we came out again into the main yard. Here, about a dozen men, eight witnesses and some prison officers, were gathered round the great machine. All we could see was the little that was visible by the light of a few hand lanterns.

Slowly, the light came up, and when it was clear enough to see by, the warden joined us. He looked disapprovingly at me, but kept his peace. We could hear orders being given, and the sound of keys turning in locks. And finally the voice of the chief officer from nearby, speaking the time-honoured phrases:

'Your appeal has been rejected. *Soyez courageux.*'

Moments later, Aziz was brought out into the dim sunshine, blinking. I could see that he had not slept either, and that he had also been assailed by nightmares.

He looked at me. I was facing the guillotine directly so that there could be no mistake. He smiled a blunt smile, then they took him by the arms and strapped him upright to the wooden board of the *bascule*. Their quick movements ensured that he was made to endure as short a wait as possible. Once he was secure, they tilted the *bascule* until he was lying face down upon it. A further movement pushed the *bascule* and prisoner forward until his neck lay within the *lunette*, which was tightened round him. I felt my heart beat like a drum, and my hand fastened on Vital's with a vicelike intensity.

Next moment, the rope was released, and the blade, attached to the heavy *mouton*, whisked down with all its force, severing flesh and bone in a single, unobstructed action. I saw his head fall. One of the guards stepped forward and lifted it by the hair, setting it down on the severed neck, so that the witnesses could see with their own eyes that the deed had been done.

I do not know what demon then possessed me. I let go my grip on Vital's hand and stepped forward a few inches, then bent and spoke Aziz's name. Did I expect a response, or was I hoping to prove to my own satisfaction that the dead cannot see or hear us? I really cannot remember, for I was half in a trance, and my heart and brain would not let go of me, they were tugging and pulling so hard on me.

His eyes opened. The lids lifted slowly, and his pupils appeared, not dulled by a lack of consciousness, but sharp, almost alert. He looked full at me, and on his face I read the horror, and as I looked, I saw his lips move as though he was trying to say something. Then his eyes shut, and his lips were still, and I turned and did not call his name a second time.

To M. and Mme Bombois
5 rue de la Fauvette
Epernay

Saturday, 12 July 1941

My Dear Parents-in-Law,

I am writing with some very sad news concerning my dear wife, and your beloved daughter, Marie-Louise.

Forgive me if I do not enter into details now, or perhaps at all. What has happened has happened, and we must all make the best of it and support one another through it.

Yesterday, at 11 p.m., after several days' illness, my darling wife lost the child she had been carrying these several months, and to whose birth we had all been looking forward so eagerly. I fear that general strain, much of it occasioned by recent events, coupled with a particular anguish suffered by her in the past few weeks, was the cause of this tragedy. Her doctor, Monsieur Chomat, and my dear friend Docteur Monestier, two of the most honest and reliable men in town, are both agreed that it was external events that caused her loss, and not any illness or bodily weakness.

She is still in great mental torment, both for the baby and for a young man whom we knew, who was cruelly put to death a few days ago. The baby would have been called Aziz, a Moroccan name, and one I know she loved.

Rest assured that she has the very best medical attention, and that, with help and medicine, she will make a full recovery. She is young and I am healthy, and you must remain confident that you will be grandparents another time.

Forgive me if I do not write at length. There is much to see to, and the courts here are becoming busy, as I am sure they are with you. We think of you often in your tribulation, and we pray that the rigours of occupation never pass what is bearable for you. I have spoken with Marie-Louise in the last few minutes, and she asks me to write that she is over the worst and that she sends her fondest love to you both.

Béatrice has been to visit her several times, but not

Gérard who, I must be honest, does not much approve of us. I do what is possible to effect some sort of reconciliation, but Gérard has become quite a different person from the man I think you knew in France. These times are a trial for us all. But of one thing I know you can be sure: Marie-Louise is a daughter you can be proud of. She is brave, caring and wise. When it is time for her to do her duty, rest assured that she will not be found wanting.

Your fond son-in-law,

Vital

P.S. There is one other thing which I think should not be mentioned to Marie-Louise unless it proves unavoidable. It seems that the young man who died had a fiancée, a girl called Nuriyya, a beautiful name that means 'Illuminated' or something of the sort. Having discovered somehow the date of his execution, young Nuriyya was desperate to see Aziz one last time, but on each occasion when she turned up at the jail, she was turned away roughly. Yesterday morning, however, she arrived there well before anyone else, when it was still dark, and introduced herself to the guard on duty. This man, a ruffian who had joined the army merely to escape arrest in Paris, saw his chance, and persuaded Nuriyya that, if she permitted him to have his way with her, he would grant her request.

Believe me, for a girl of her religion and upbringing even to contemplate such a devil's bargain is hardly believable, but she was past all desperation and could not have cared less about her reputation. All that mattered to her was the chance to see her young man once more, and to tell him she loved him. So she let this scoundrel take her to the guardroom, strip her, and do what he wanted. This was bad enough, but the guard's colleagues arrived just then, ready to set the day's work in motion. Seeing the girl already naked and trembling, they too could think of nothing but their basest instincts. The rape continued.

And then one of the new arrivals, an unconscionable wretch named Lemaître, a brute with absolutely no moral sense, took it upon himself to drag the naked girl from the guardroom to the condemned cell, which lay only a few feet away. While one of his friends shook Aziz awake, Lemaître held the girl at the doorway, parading her charms before the poor boy, who saw his love naked for the first and last time, and was forced to recognize that her honour had been stripped from her as easily as her clothes. I cannot begin to guess what must have gone through that poor boy's head, but I know that he will have carried those thoughts with him to the guillotine, and died while they filled him with their poison.

The story, as you may guess, does not end there. Nuriyya's family, alerted to her absence and guessing where she had headed, arrived at the prison too late. She had already gone, a hooded figure slipping through the early morning shadows. From the prison, she must have made her way to Avenue Landais, and from there to the Avenue du Général Mangin. There, she turned right, heading on up past the État-Major, with Mangin Camp on the opposite side of the road. She left the road soon after that, arriving at the foot of Djebel Gueliz, the hill that overlooks the military quarter. It has fortifications along its top, but she climbed right up to these, a climb of some five hundred feet or more.

How long she hesitated, we shall never know, but her sad remains were spied not much later by a sentry scanning the area beneath the hill. She was buried the same day, following the custom, in the Mohammedan cemetery to the east of the old city. Marie-Louise does not know, and

I do not wish her to know for the present. In due course, I have no doubt she will ask after the girl, and then she will have to be told – but not the details. You may rest assured that I am doing all I can to have the miscreants court-martialled, but I regret that their punishment will prove lenient. And if you ask, should something not be done, my answer is that something shall be done.

In the Meditation Chambers
of Si Mahmoud Abou Chaib

23

She ran from the hotel, her eyes brimming with tears. He'd deceived her, right in front of her eyes, without shame, without feeling, rubbed her face in his latest killing, as good as laughed at her. Let the police arrest him, she thought; let them drag him off to prison and lock him up and throw away the key.

She dashed through the brightly lit foyer and out into the night. Blinking, she brought her hand up and brushed away the tears that were interfering with her vision. As she did so, she caught sight of two men standing facing the hotel. They glanced at her curiously, with the direct stare Moroccan men reserve for foreign women. She'd long ago lost her fear of that appraising look, long ago taught herself to walk the streets alone, fending off unwelcome scrutiny with a quick sneer or get-lost gesture. Now, she braced herself to do it again.

But the men had already taken their eyes off her and returned their gaze to the hotel entrance. They'd seemed to be laughing quietly together about something, and to be waiting for something else to happen.

The larger of the two leaned to one side to throw away a

cigarette butt. His face was illumined briefly by a lamp-post, and as Justine caught sight of it she recognized him. He was one of the two gangsters who'd come into the restaurant in Taddert. Her heart beating, she turned her head away, and took several steps in the opposite direction.

It was then that she realized her dreadful mistake. She should have known Nick wasn't Duncan Todd's killer – assuming it had been his London colleague on the floor. What possible motive could Nick have had in bringing his friend all the way to Marrakech just to stab him? Or to do it so publicly? Nick was already so deep in shit, he'd have to be insane to do something like that – and she was sure he was not in the least insane.

She guessed what must have happened: the two men who were now standing in front of her had gone up to Duncan Todd's room, killed him, and tipped off the police the moment they saw Nick enter the hotel. They must have seen through his disguise in some way, or perhaps she herself had given Nick away. She had seen the trap, but failed to recognize it for what it was; instead of helping, she'd abandoned him to his fate. But why were the hitmen still lounging about so casually outside the hotel? Probably they were just waiting to make sure Nick had really been arrested this time, after which they'd be in a car heading back to Ouarzazate.

There was a small bother at the door, and Justine turned to see the policemen coming through the main doors, dragging Nick, who was wearing handcuffs, between them. Behind them, a small crowd of hotel staff and confused guests choked the foyer. One glance at Nick told her he'd been beaten around the head. His new shirt was torn, and blood had dripped on it and on his trousers. A night in the cells, she thought, would leave him injured and ready to confess to anything.

Just then she remembered the taxi in which they'd come. She remembered asking the driver to wait for them. It was still sitting beneath a streetlight. Through the driver's open window, she could make out a steady stream of cigarette smoke, accompanied by a constant blast of Algerian Rai music sung by the ever-popular Cheb Zahouani.

There was no time for hesitation. She ran forward towards Nick and his keepers. The policemen were pulling him towards their patrol car. One of them – an immensely tall man with Berber features – had Nick with his left arm, while with his right he was trying to get through to someone on a mobile phone – headquarters, Justine guessed. The other – a short man who looked young enough to have just joined the force – held the prisoner tightly with his right arm while shouting incoherent abuse at him.

'Officers!' Justine shouted in Arabic as she ran up. 'For God's sake, do something. Those are the killers over there, I saw them do it, I saw them stab the Englishman upstairs! This one was just their accomplice. Come on, they'll get away!'

Both policemen looked totally confused. On her part, Justine was no clearer about what would happen next: all she'd hoped to achieve was some sort of distraction, some means of luring the policemen into dropping their guard for just a few seconds, long enough, perhaps, to get Nick away from them.

She'd scarcely reckoned with the two thugs from Ouarzazate. Seeing an unknown woman pointing at them and calling on the police, they did the wrong thing. One of them reached inside his jacket and drew out a pistol, while his companion started to run. The policemen just stood transfixed, like deer on an open road.

'*Dghiya! Dghiya!*' exclaimed Justine. 'Hurry up! You're losing him.'

The tall man made his mind up, whipped his gun from its holster, and set off in pursuit of the fleeing gangster. At the same moment, the other hitman raised his pistol, aimed at Nick, and fired. The shot hit its target hard, throwing Nick backwards to the ground, and pulling the shorter policeman back and down with him.

Justine screamed. She hadn't meant this to happen. She threw herself down beside Nick, raising his head, hoping against hope that he might somehow be unharmed. As she dropped, however, she slipped on a puddle of blood. He'd been hit in the thigh, and blood was already pouring from the large exit wound.

The policeman who'd been pulled down managed to struggle to his feet. He pulled his pistol free and fired off a sequence of three rounds at the gunman. The latter drew back, unhit, but shaken. The last thing he and his companion had expected was to be recognized and denounced to the police. Blindly firing off one more shot, he ran into the crowd that was gathering around the scene.

'Hurry!' Justine shouted. 'I'll look after your prisoner. He isn't going anywhere.'

The policeman hesitated, saw that Nick was down and bleeding, and made his decision. Two more prisoners would see him and his partner leap up the promotions ladder. Clutching his pistol, he ran off towards the spot where he had last seen the gunman.

'Quickly!' Justine hissed. 'Can you stand?'

Nick managed to nod. The pain in his leg was atrocious, and getting worse with every second. Someone had better get a tourniquet round his thigh quickly, he thought.

'Just stay conscious long enough to let me get you home. Now, hang on to me.'

She knew he was too heavy for her, but she tried anyhow. The cab was still waiting where she'd left it, and when the driver saw who she was and realized she was heading for him, instead of driving off at top speed, he opened his door and came running towards them. He took Nick from her. None of the people who'd stopped to gawp at the gunfight did anything to get in the way. They just watched as Justine and the driver pulled Nick across the road and bundled him into the back of the car. And they continued to stare as the cab took off with a squeal of tyres and a blast of its horn.

'To the hospital?' asked the driver.

'No, no, not the hospital. They'll be looking out for someone with a gunshot. Get us back to the Bab Doukkala. I'll take charge of him from there.'

'Let me help you.'

She shook her head. There were too many risks involved in letting the driver see where she lived. He could already give a good description of her, and she knew it wouldn't be long before a small army of armed police went swarming round her little *quartier*.

'I'm sorry,' she said to Nick, 'but I have to do this.'

Ignoring his cries of pain, she ripped off his trousers and tore off a long strip. Identifying the spots where the gunshot had entered his leg and left it again, she tied a tourniquet round his upper thigh and pulled it as tight as possible.

'Don't die on me,' she thought. 'I haven't given up everything just to have you die on me.'

He was crying out now in violent pain, and nothing she could do, from soft words to caresses, would make things better.

The bleeding grew less copious. Taking the rest of the fabric, she managed to bandage the thigh, placing Nick's sock on top of the wounds to make pressure pads. The taxi hurtled on, its headlights plucking palm trees out of the early evening darkness on both sides of the road.

It did not take long to reach their destination. The driver helped her haul Nick out of the car and over to the wall. Bystanders watched them with idle interest as they helped Nick sit down, his back against the ancient red stone.

'Here,' said Justine, thrusting all the money she had on her at the taxi driver.

'No, *Alalla*, I won't take anything.'

'Please – at least take something for the car. The back seat's ruined. It's covered in blood. You don't want the police to see it like that, do you?'

He saw the sense in what she was saying.

'Very well,' he said. 'But just a little.'

He peeled some notes off the top of the wad she was offering him, and she added several more, cramming them into his fist.

'What about the police?' she asked. 'What will you tell them if they come asking questions?'

He spat on the ground.

'I stay away from the Sûreté,' he said. 'And from the

traffic police. Don't worry, I will say nothing. I have not even been there tonight. I have been driving tourists to see the ramparts by night.'

They shook hands, and he went back to his car. She watched his tail-lights dwindle, then hurried back to Nick. He was still losing blood, and had lost consciousness.

Among those watching were several young men with mopeds. This was one of the places they came on a summer's evening to race one another along the straight roads of the Ville Nouvelle, or to watch out in the hope of snaring some single women tourists, a much talked-about dream that seldom came to pass.

She approached them, then spoke in a low voice, taking care to use Arabic. 'Listen,' she said, 'my friend here has been hurt. I need to get him to a doctor, but I don't want to take him to the Hôpital Civil. Do you understand?'

They grinned, and some nodded their heads.

'I need one of your mopeds, but I have very little money on me. If one of you will lend his moped, maybe another will come along behind. I'll pay you tomorrow. You can be sure of that.'

One of the youths, a teenager in a black leather jacket that might have made James Dean envious, stepped forward.

'Where do you want to go?' he asked.

'Do you know Dr Monestier?'

'I know where he lives,' said another boy in a white tee shirt.

'Follow me there,' she said. 'Now, can one of you help me get him on the pillion seat?'

24

'I've done what I can.'

The doctor threw down the needle and thread, and started to unpeel his rubber gloves.

'The bleeding should ease, but I want to give him a transfusion. He's lost a lot of blood.'

'Can't you . . . ?' Justine stared at Nick, where he lay, still unconscious, on the table.

'I have to obtain the blood first. This isn't a blood transfusion clinic, I just don't have the space to keep a supply of every type. I'll have to send Marcel to the Polyclinique in the morning. Frankly, I'd rather he was sent straight there, or to the Ibn Tofail.'

She shook her head.

'I'm sorry, Jules, but it's out of the question. I'll pay for anything you get from the Polyclinique, but I'm trusting you to handle the forms.'

'What makes you think I won't just go to the police and report the unexplained arrival of a patient with a serious gunshot wound?'

'The same thing that keeps you here, working in the

medina, when you could be up there in the Polyclinique du Sud, raking it in.'

He smiled. It gave her goosebumps every time, that smile. What's worse, the little doctor wasn't aware of his effect on women.

'And what exactly is that, do you think?'

'Cussedness. You like people more than money. And you never got married, so you have all this energy going spare. Is he in much danger?'

The doctor shrugged. It was the question everyone asked, and he'd found a million ways to skirt round it. But not with Justine. They'd known one another since she was a child, he'd treated her and helped bring her up. She called him cussed, when he knew very well that she could teach him all a man need ever know about the condition.

'Yes,' he said. 'If you insist on keeping him here or in your house. What will happen if I send him to the clinic?'

'The police will come looking for him. If they find him, they'll arrest him, and a few months from now we'll be waiting for them to hang him.'

'So, whatever you say, he is some sort of criminal?'

She shook her head.

'Now isn't the time to go into that. But, for the record, no, I don't think he's a criminal of any sort.'

She knew it was her heart speaking, nothing more – but far better her heart than any number of men with guns and bloodless ambitions.

He looked at her, then at the man on his table.

'He's been through a lot. I'll ask Marcel to get the blood now.'

He called his assistant, a young French medical *coopérant*, the latest in a long line of volunteers who'd queued up to spend a year working in the same clinic as the legendary Dr Monestier. Marcel was good looking, but evidently not concerned much about his appearance. His hair was tousled, his smart-but-casual jacket and trousers were creased, and there were bags under his bright grey eyes. Obviously, he wasn't in Marrakech on holiday.

His manner too proclaimed a certain seriousness of purpose, without the pomposity that might imply. The young doctor was self-effacing, even a little shy. As Dr Monestier gave him instructions, Justine could detect a look of respect on his face that made very clear the nature of their relationship. Marcel nodded, smiled nervously at Justine, and hared off into the night.

'Marcel shouldn't be long. I've told him to go to the Antaki Hospital. He can get there and back on foot.'

'What about the quality of the blood? If it's contaminated in some way . . .'

'Don't worry. It'll be fine. Trust me.'

'Once he's had the transfusion, I'd like to leave him here to sleep it off.'

'And after he sleeps it off? The police will come here, you know, Justine. There aren't many places a wounded man can go in Marrakech. To the Antaki, perhaps. More likely, given where the shooting took place, to the Ibn Tofail or the Avenzoar, or maybe the Polyclinique. Once they've covered those, they'll start knocking on doctors' doors. You didn't arrive here unobserved. What about your house?'

She shook her head.

'They'll come there as well. In the morning at the latest.'

'They can't get in without a warrant.'

'I didn't mean the police.'

Marcel returned with several litres of A-type blood. The drip stand had already been set up.

'Does he have a history of allergies?' Monestier asked.

'I really have no idea. I only met him yesterday.'

The doctor's eyebrows arched.

'And yet you say you're sure he's innocent?'

'Oh, I know that, there's no question of it. Allergies may take a little longer to figure out.'

'Well, we shall probably know in a few minutes if there's anything.'

Ten minutes later, Monestier smiled and drew the curtain round Nick's bed.

They left him sleeping, then took turns in the little bathroom. Monestier explained that there'd be patients arriving at the clinic in the morning, from seven o'clock onwards.

'I can't leave him where he is,' he said. 'Even if the police didn't come straight away, rumours would be bound to start.'

'How far can he be moved?'

'Not far. Don't think of a car journey. In any case, there are certain to be more roadblocks than before.'

She shook her head. Her old friend looked tired, she thought. She'd already asked more of him tonight than she had a right to.

'Just outside the ramparts,' she said. 'Do you think you can help me get him that far?'

The *zaouia* of Si Mahmoud Abou Chaib lies in a patch of deserted land outside the eastern walls of Marrakech, not far from the Bab Khemis. Built in the fifteenth century to house the gatherings of the Chaibiyya brotherhood of Sufi mystics, today it is a cluster of ruins open to the sky, all save the central mausoleum that was added to house the body of the order's founder. Si Mahmoud was at one time the best loved holy man in North Africa. His songs had been on everyone's lips, his prayers written on fine paper by the most skilled calligraphers.

'You've never been here before?' Justine asked. 'Not even as a child?'

'We were too afraid of the place as children. None of us ventured here.'

The doctor looked around him uneasily as childhood memories returned. Not long after his death, Si Mahmoud had been condemned as a heretic by a group of local theologians. Such strictures usually had little effect on religious brotherhoods that were accustomed to the condemnation of the orthodox, but in this case the decree of *takfir* had its impact.

The group's followers dwindled and in time died out. Men stopped singing the songs they had once loved. The jet-black ink was scratched off the smooth paper of Si Mahmoud's prayers, and new pens cut to trace new invocations. In time, the *zaouia* was abandoned. And before long men said Si Mahmoud was accursed, his tomb a breeding place for demons, his *zaouia* a home for ghosts. Only the bravest ventured there, or lovers desperate for seclusion.

They had borrowed a mule from a neighbour, and somehow they'd managed to get Nick onto its broad back. With Justine leading the way, they'd walked through echoing, deserted streets into which a large moon let down light like milk.

Monestier had tied to the mule a couple of foam-rubber mattresses that he'd taken from one of the *banquettes* in his living room. They found a dry space in an inner chamber of the *zaouia*, and put the mattresses down for Nick to sleep on.

'Take the mule back,' she said. 'I'll stay here with him. Send your boy with some food in the morning. Later, we can work out how best to do this.'

The doctor argued, but he found her adamant. He knew also that he could not let down his own patients, who would be queuing for him in the morning.

'Are you sure you'll be safe?' he asked.

'Don't tell me you're worried about some old ghosts,' she laughed.

'Not ghosts,' he said, 'but this isn't altogether a safe place. People have been attacked out here. A single woman – well, you're taking a risk. Don't forget, you'll have to be at home when the police call tomorrow.'

She nodded.

'Go now,' she said. 'I know how to look after myself. Once it's safe, we'll get him back to town.'

Standing at the *zaouia* entrance, she watched Monestier go, a dappled shadow in the moonlight walking back towards the high, crenellated walls of the city. The cold light changed the red stones to white as it fell steadily down. A little further off towards the east, the Issil River, shrunk by the summer sun, flowed white between soft banks.

She turned and went back to the little room in which Nick slept, and made a place for herself on the ground beside him. The morphine Monestier had injected into his bloodstream was still taking effect. She drew a blanket over his sleeping form, then lay down next to him. He cried out softly once, and then returned to sleep. She closed her eyes and tried to catch some sleep as well, but it would not come, and she did not try to force it.

And so her lonely vigil began. Was she here against her will, or by choice? She couldn't say. She had a sense of a malign Fate driving both Nick and her to this lair of owls and spiders, as though their presence in this one spot had been inevitable. At the same time, she was aware that she was still in control, and that she would find a way out of this mess for both of them.

25

He had become a swimmer in deep seas, his feet were like flippers, his hands clawed through the silent water, dragging, forever dragging him forward. Sometimes he felt heavy and breathless, his chest crushed by the pressure of the water on it, sometimes he was light and clear-headed, almost like a dragonfly tossed on violent waves. Then the currents from below would come and suck him down again, and he would lose whatever buoyancy he'd found, and be dragged down by the undertow again, to face the cold and silence and darkness, as though more than halfway to his death already.

On the second day, Monestier took him off the morphine altogether, providing him with regulated doses of milder painkillers. After this, Nick found himself waking more and more often, though never for more than a few minutes at a time.

'Let him sleep,' the doctor said. 'But tell me if it seems too deep, or if anything else appears out of the ordinary.'

The first time he woke properly, it was very late, and the sky far above him was black and alive with little stars. Just above his own level, he could make out a small light burning, a candle whose steady flame seemed for some reason to be located as far away as the furthest star.

Time passed, his head cleared a little and his eyes grew sharper, and he made out, just beyond the tiny yellow flame, larger movements, but indistinct. He closed his eyes for a little and almost slept again, but something prompted him to open them once more, and when he did he could see her, the candle held close to her face, bending over him. He could not remember who she was.

'It's all right,' she said, and for a moment or two he thought she was Nathalie, for she spoke in French. 'Go back to sleep. You're safe now. There's nothing to worry about.'

Had there been something to worry about? he wondered. He fancied there had been.

'Justine,' he said, knowing the name, but nothing more. 'Is she . . . ?'

'She's fine. I'm fine. Go back to sleep.'

He woke a few more times that night. The stars were there each time, their patterns changing as they shifted through the broad heavens.

Each time he looked, he saw her watching, and the darkness lost whatever terrors it might have had. He pretended he could see her face, look into her eyes, reach out and hold her hand. It was all an illusion, of course, but he knew she was there within reach, and that she was not Nathalie. Nathalie was in her grave, and the woman watching him was Justine, and he knew almost nothing about her.

He woke properly on the third day, just after first light. The sky was still purple, and tiny, barely perceptible stars wandered in it, then drowned as light rose from the east over palm trees and a small minaret.

'Welcome back,' she said. 'Are you hungry?'

'I'm ravenous,' he said. 'I can't remember when I last ate.'

'It's been a few days. I'm not very well equipped, but I've got some sardines in a tin, and Marcel will bring some bread later. You're not allowed to eat much straight away, but the doctor says you have to drink. It's hot out here during the day, and you mustn't dehydrate.'

'Who's Marcel?'

'Oh, he's the doctor's assistant. A *coopérant*.'

'I thought you had a boyfriend. The one on the bus.'

She laughed.

'Stéphane? Poor Stéphane, he's very disappointed in me. He says I play up too much, like Audrey Hepburn in *Breakfast at Tiffany's*. I've never seen *Breakfast at Tiffany's*, but I've heard it's very good. Have you seen it?'

He nodded. He almost said, 'When it came out,' but thought better of it.

'And does she? Does she play up?'

His leg was hurting badly, but he managed to smile.

'Oh, yes,' he said. 'Most terribly. She wasn't like that in real life, of course. She was terribly . . . she was a nice person. We don't seem to have many of those any more.'

'And elegant.'

'Oh, yes, very elegant. I expect you can be elegant when you want to be.'

She twisted her lips and lifted her nose slightly.

'But I'm French. We don't have to try. It's our natural state.' She hesitated. 'Is your wife very elegant?'

247

'Nathalie? She was lovely.'

'You always say "she was". As if she were . . .'

'That's exactly what she is. She committed suicide. I'm sorry, I think I misled you. But let's talk about this another time. My leg's killing me. Have you got something for the pain?'

Her face fell. She'd been so intent on talking that she hadn't noticed the little signals of distress. It wouldn't happen again, she told herself.

'I'm sorry, I should have given you this an hour ago. I just didn't want to wake you.'

She rummaged about in a small bag and produced a box of dihydrocodeine tablets.

'These are slow release,' she said, handing two tablets to him and pouring some water into a glass. 'They won't make you drowsy like the morphine.'

'I just want to dull the pain.' He was wincing visibly now.

She took his left hand in hers and held it tightly while he drank the tablets down. Some time passed in silence, but she did not let go. Then she felt him relax. All the colour had drained from his face, but she thought a little food would bring some of it back.

Marcel arrived carrying fresh round loaves, the first batch of the morning. He'd wrapped them in a cloth, and they were still warm. With them, he'd brought some Camembert, a locally made version of the cheese that was already going runny.

'Join us for breakfast,' Justine said, making room for the young man on the rug beside her.

'I can't stay long,' he said. 'Monsieur le Docteur wants me

back as quickly as possible. It's going to be a busy morning. When I left, there were already three AIDS cases waiting. Every week it gets worse, and there simply isn't enough money for the drugs. The old man's a saint, but there's only so much goodwill can do.'

'He's not so old,' Justine said. 'Around sixty, I'd guess. Nick here doesn't think that's too old, do you, Nick?'

'I wouldn't know. I'm only forty-five.'

She smiled and looked back at Marcel.

'Won't he agree to look for larger premises, bring in more *coopérants* like yourself?'

'He's frightened that either the Ministry of Co-operation or the government here will get hold of the clinic and take it out of his hands. He insists that he's the only one who knows what he's doing, and in a way he's right. His father taught him the ropes, he learned the rest himself.'

'That's all very well, but he mustn't let the whole thing go out of pride or stubbornness. He needs helpers, and he needs funds.'

Marcel finished off his slice of bread and sardine. Brushing away the crumbs from his lap, he stood.

'I really have to get back to the clinic. If he isn't too pressed, Monestier wants to see Nicholas before lunch, but we still have to be very careful. There are police all over the city.'

Marrakech was no place for a fugitive. Even inside the medina, barriers had been set up to slow down the steady stream of human traffic that pushed its way through the souks and across the little medieval squares, with their fountains built to provide water for the poor. Nick's photograph was the only substantial lead the police had, and wherever one went, it would be thrust under one's nose.

Justine had already been visited by the police, and had been able to take them through every room in her house without fear of discovery. She'd chatted with them, and assured them she'd do all in her power to track down the English murderer. But she knew it was only a matter of time before someone at the hotel – one of her friends, perhaps – linked her to Nick.

As Marcel walked away, Nick looked curiously at Justine.

'Justine, what did Marcel just say the doctor's name was?'

'The doctor? Monestier. Why?'

He watched Marcel's back as the young man walked quickly back towards the ramparts.

'Oh, nothing. Just a coincidence.'

'No, tell me. It's something to talk about.'

'It's just . . . Nathalie, my wife . . . shortly before she killed herself, she received a box of papers from an attorney in France. It was a mess of things: legal documents, letters, a journal, all things connected to her family. I don't know why they were sent, what prompted the lawyers to send them at that point. I only glanced through them, then I passed them on to Peter. I thought, maybe he could make a story out of them all. That's why he came to Morocco, that's what he was asking about when he was killed.'

'I see. But what has this to do with Dr Monestier?'

'Probably nothing, but I remember there were some references to a doctor here in Marrakech. I'm sure Monestier was the name, or something very like it. For a moment there, I thought it might be the same man. Then I realized my mistake. The letters and the journal all dated from before and during World War II. Any doctor working then would be a very old man by now, or dead and buried.'

She hesitated. The colour was coming back into his cheeks, but he still looked grey underneath. She reached forward and brushed a long strand of hair off his forehead.

'You may be right, all the same,' she said. 'My Dr Monestier is second-generation Marrakshi. His father was a doctor here before him. During the war.'

Monestier arrived in person, a little later than planned. His morning surgery had been a difficult one. Desperate mothers had started bringing children with AIDS to him. He'd given them some tablets and a little advice, and sent them off to watch their babies die. This wasn't why he'd started the clinic, and now it threatened to overwhelm him with its senselessness.

The police had been with him on the day following the shooting. They'd been to all the clinics, looking for a wounded man. Monestier had just shaken his head, showed them round the premises, and promised to look out for someone matching Nick's description.

'I need to know the truth,' he said as he finished taking Nick's blood pressure. 'From the beginning. Everything. I'm putting my clinic at risk, my life's work. The truth is the least I can expect.'

So Nick told his story all over again. Just the bare truth. No embellishments, no deviations. Monestier listened. And believed.

'And you think this is all connected to some papers your

wife received, some World War II papers connected to her family and which your son tried to mesh together into a single story. Frankly, I find that unlikely. The war is largely forgotten here. The French, but for a few of us, have long gone home. If there are memories, they are over in France, not here.'

'Nevertheless, I'm convinced the papers sparked Nathalie's death, and probably Peter's too.'

'Your family lived here during the war?'

Monestier watched as a stork took off from a tower midway along the walls. They'd have to take a risk tonight, and get the Englishman back to the city, he thought.

'Not mine, Nathalie's. Her mother and father. They went back to France after hostilities ended. He went back to the family business.'

'What was that?'

'Wine. Champagne, to be precise.'

'I see. What was their name?'

'Le Tourneau. It was Nathalie's maiden name. Her mother was a Bombois.'

'Le Tourneau? Here in Marrakech, you say?' The doctor suddenly looked very interested.

'Yes. He was, let me see, Gérard, and she was Béatrice.'

'Did they have any other family living here at the same time?'

'I . . . don't think so.'

'A sister, for example?'

'Of . . . ?'

'Of this Béatrice.'

'Nathalie never mentioned an aunt.'

'I see. Does the name Guénaud mean anything to you?'

'No, I don't think . . .' Then he remembered, he'd seen it on some of the papers.

'Yes, possibly, there were some people.'

'Vital and Marie-Louise Guénaud.'

'Yes, that could be right. The papers are still in Oxford. They can be checked.'

'Yes, I think they should be checked.'

'Who were they? Do you know?'

'The Guénauds? He was an appeal court judge. She was Béatrice Le Tourneau's sister. Something tells me you're right after all. Someone's been keeping the truth about the Guénauds secret since the war. And it seems they'll stop at nothing to stop the secret getting out.'

26

She knew by the fourth day that she loved him. Then, thinking back, she realized that there hadn't been a moment when she had not. Watching him come towards her in the little restaurant in Taddert, she'd already fallen for him, although she hadn't let herself admit it. Finding him later that day, crouched in the dust of the Djemaa el-Fna, clutching his one valuable possession in an open hand, she had fallen yet more deeply, and when he'd looked up helplessly and sighted her out of an ocean of despair, she'd loved him in every fibre of her being.

She was not, she reminded herself, a woman who gave her heart easily. In her short life, she'd had only two lasting relationships, one of two years' duration, the other of four. Both her lovers had had to woo her for months before she'd consented. It had hurt when each affair had ended, by her choice; but not too much. Now, watching him sleep, she knew how it would hurt this time if he left her, or if he died. This time she would not get over it.

He'd been asleep since shortly after breakfast. She'd brought a book to pass the time, a French translation of a novel by Paul Bowles, but she hadn't read a word. Instead, she'd sat watching his sleeping face, catching the different expressions that passed over it. Now, in a moment, his eyes flickered open and he was looking at her. He frowned with pain, and tried to raise himself to a sitting position.

Was it just pity? she wondered as she helped him. If he hadn't been in mortal danger, grieving for a dead wife and a murdered son, penniless, wounded, pursued by gangsters and police alike, would she even have looked at him? Perhaps not. Perhaps she would have thought him just another tourist, and passed on.

Yet she remembered that moment in the Taddert café, watching him approach her, when she'd known nothing of murders or police. She only had to close her eyes to bring it all back: the stillness, the meadow running away, the mountains in the distance, the teenagers all round her, chattering, and her own sensations, her sense that everything had stopped just to let him come to her.

Monestier wanted him brought back to the city as soon as possible, but the manhunt still continued. Justine had been visited twice now, the second time by plain-clothes detectives.

There'd been two of them, and she could see at once that they'd been watching bad French movies, *films noirs* about a tough underworld in which the police wore short black leather jackets and chain-smoked small cigarettes that they rolled in their own hands. They held out their IDs, but neither smiled. She could see them weighing her up; she'd gone through the procedure innumerable times at her doorway.

What they were thinking was: she can't possibly be here

alone, can she, where the hell's her maid anyway, how can her husband let her answer the front door like this?

'We'd like to talk to you.'

'About what?'

'About your movements.'

'Movements? What movements?'

'You were seen at the Pullman Hotel three nights ago. On the night of the shooting there.' This was put to her by the larger of the two. He looked like he worked out. He clenched and unclenched his hands, betraying his essential nervousness.

'I've already answered questions about this.'

'That doesn't matter. We need to know what you have to say about it.'

'You'd better come in.' She stood aside to make way for them. They looked at her as though suspecting some sudden double-cross, perhaps some attempt to compromise them.

'Is your husband at home?'

'I don't have a husband.'

'Well, I don't see how we can come in.' This from the big man's all-but-silent partner, a slim youth who looked as though he'd be more at ease with a knife than with his fists.

'You either come in or you leave. I'm not standing here at my own door to be questioned by a couple of cops. Now, which is it to be?'

She could see that their preference would have been to beat her up on the spot, teach her an important lesson about who was top dog round here. But they couldn't be sure of her: she could turn out to be top dog after all.

'A few minutes,' said the big man, 'then we have to go.'

In the living room she offered them drinks, a choice of alcohol or Coke. It wasn't hard to guess that two tough *mecs* like these would like to be seen drinking beer. But their fathers and brothers would beat them to a pulp if word got round. They ended up turning down both options.

She sat, but they preferred to stand. They towered over her, aware of their strength.

'You were seen at the Pullman Hotel. By Jeanine and Victoire Lamartine. They are friends of yours, I believe.'

'Yes, of course. I told the policeman who came here before that I'd seen them.'

'They say you were with a man.'

'Was I? Oh, no, that was a complete mistake. I was never with him. He was a Canadian, I think, and a bit lost. I was merely giving him directions. I think he went into the hotel immediately after. Didn't they tell you that?'

'Yes, they did. But if you weren't with this man, what were you doing at the hotel?'

She looked round the room, and suddenly it felt no longer hers. This had been her shelter, her refuge from a frequently hostile world, and now two sneering men in leather jackets had entered it to question her.

'I thought I'd explained that already. We may have a small party coming to do a walking tour of the Atlas foothills this autumn. I was there to consult the hotel management on terms.'

'The management say . . .'

'I turned up on spec. It was something I had to get out of the way before taking my holiday.'

'So why didn't you ask to speak to someone? The book-ings clerk, whoever.'

'Excuse me? Have you forgotten what happened? I think I did ask one of the staff to find the manager, but next thing it all started outside. Once everything was quiet I cleared off.'

'Why was that?'

'Shall I spell it out to you? I was alone, I felt vulnerable, I heard someone had just been shot outside, I was in no mood to hang around. I came straight back here. Just why the hell are you questioning me like this anyhow? Am I a suspect? Is that it? What do you suspect me of exactly?'

She'd caught them off balance. Up until now they'd held their cards close to their chests. Now she was forcing them to show their hand.

'No, you are not a suspect. Not at present. But we have to tie up loose ends. You were at the hotel, after all.'

'So were dozens of other people, hundreds maybe. Why pick on me?'

'You were alone. You had no one to act as an alibi.'

'Is it a crime to be single in Morocco? Do you think a woman should have a chaperone everywhere she goes?'

'We have a warrant to search your house.'

'Again?'

'Yes. I'm sorry. May we?'

They went through all the rooms, and again they found nothing to connect her to the missing Englishman. She asked them – smiling, winsome, intimate, speaking only French, not letting herself be drawn into any dangerous comparisons – she asked them if they had any leads.

'That's a police matter,' said the thin one. He had weathered skin, as though he spent most of his time outdoors.

'That's all very well, but the public have a right to know

what's going on. How can a woman, a single woman like myself, how can I sleep in my bed knowing there are gunmen on the loose? Is this New York suddenly? Why don't you do your job, instead of persecuting members of the public like me? Why don't you catch this Englishman? He can't be too hard to find. If he's killed before, he'll kill again. But instead you're wasting time here.'

It was a performance, but its thrusts went home. They were out of their depth with a woman like her, a single woman living alone in a society where that meant prostitution or worse. She was shameless, she was an assault on all they held sacred, an alien presence in the medina; but she'd kept her French nationality, and there was nothing they could do. She'd made it known that the French consul was a friend of hers (which he was) and that her parents had contacts galore back home.

She saw them out finally, exhausted by her pretence. Her whole life since the age of twelve or so had been spent warding off the unwelcome attentions of Moroccan men. Like Arabs everywhere, they had problems with sex. Marriage was generally late, but single women were simply unavailable to most men. They lived in a world where most women were still heavily veiled, but every day on the streets or beaches they saw Western women in various states of semi-undress, joking and laughing with men who were not close relations. They watched Hollywood films (suitably cut) in which beautiful women picked and chose their male partners, and went to bed with men to whom they weren't married.

There was a myth that, following World War II, European women, finding that most of the male population had been killed, set off in large numbers for Africa in order to sate their prodigious sexual appetites. Moroccan men believed that foreign women were freely available, so they made their clumsy approaches, their fumblings in the street, their staring, their tailing, only to be told what they could do with themselves. A man who approached a Moroccan girl the way they did foreigners would have been beaten up or worse.

When she was sure the policemen had left her *derb*, she made her way on foot to the ruined *zaouia*, where the mad Englishman lay waiting, fast asleep.

27

'Monestier really doesn't want you out here any longer,' she said.

'I quite like it out here. I have fresh air, I have your company, I have—'

'You're far too vulnerable. Sometimes there are wild dogs in this area. Just back that way are some scrapyards where all the city rubbish gets picked over by poor people. Some of them are a little crazy. Monestier thinks you could be at risk from them. Tourists sometimes pass near this *zaouia*. Shepherds come with their sheep or goats.'

'You said this place is considered cursed, that its reputation keeps people away.'

'That's perfectly true, and we've got away with it so far; but I wouldn't want to stake my life on it. There are plenty of young couples in Marrakech who have nowhere to meet or have sex. A ruin like this can be very attractive. Or a goat may stray in here. A goatboy may prefer to look for it in here than risk a bad beating when he goes back to camp. One day very soon, you'll be found. The police would be here in no time at all.'

'I could always ring you.'

She'd given him her mobile phone to use in case of trouble.

'Nick, this was never going to be more than a stop-gap. I'd like you to be more secure. The police have been over my house twice: they won't come again. Monestier would like to move you back tonight.'

'Can it be done safely?'

'We think so. It's for the best. You need to sleep in a proper bed, you need better hygiene for your wound. And I'd feel a lot better if I knew you were close at hand.'

'Do you worry about me?'

She stood up, as though to go to the entrance and look out. As he looked round, he saw her brush her eyes.

'I think of nothing else,' she said.

For the first time, he began to guess a little of her feelings.

As the night darkened, clouds drifted in from the mountains. There would be rain tomorrow or the next day, maybe even a full-out thunderstorm. Another reason for getting Nick indoors. He sat with Justine, watching the starlight play gently on the red stones of the city walls. Flecks of light danced on minarets and towers, palm trees waved their fronds softly in a mounting breeze. There was a bleating of sheep nearby, and a jangling of bells as the flock moved in the darkness. Dogs barked with deep voices that rang out harshly, now here, now there, as though they were marking out a vast, grey territory for themselves. Nick imagined them prowling, their padded feet silent on stone and earth, their yellow eyes catching what little light fell from the sky, their tongues hanging from between sharp teeth.

'They used to come here to sing to God,' Justine said. 'They had a gathering called the *hadra*. Properly speaking, that means "being in God's Presence". They would sit in a circle and begin to chant the names of God. That's called *dhikr*.'

'Which means?'

'Remembrance. The correct phrase is *dhikr Allah*, the remembering of God. They'd sit here with a few candles, and the dark night outside, and they'd sing God's praises, and slowly they'd be taken over by the whole experience, and fall into trances while they went on chanting and swaying, back and forwards, back and forwards, until their sheikh brought them back to earth. Then they'd go back to their homes again. It happened all over North Africa, all over Turkey, all over Central Asia . . . In a way, it's the real Islam. But I don't suppose you want a lecture about it from me.'

'No, it's interesting. Do they still have these *hadras*?'

'Yes, there are still plenty of orders. Not like before, of course, but quite a few.'

'Would they let us in?'

'To watch? I shouldn't think so. You must have found out by now that you can't even get into a mosque here.'

'Then I'll just have to sit here and imbibe the atmosphere.'

'In some *tarikas* they recited poetry. Very often the founder would leave behind a book of devotional hymns or poems. They were love poems, but with God as the Beloved. Some of the best known Arabic poetry is like this.'

'Do you know any?'

'What do you think? I was taught it at school, the way you were taught Shakespeare.'

He laughed. On the nearest part of the wall, starlight glistened on a stork's nest perched high on a battlemented tower.

'I couldn't get much further than "To be or not to be".'

'You English should be ashamed of yourselves. You have great poets, great playwrights, great novelists, but none of you can ever recite a line from any of them.'

'Recite a poem for me. One of these . . .'

'*Kasidas*. They're love poems. The Arab poets sang them in Spain, and from Spain the troubadours took them to France and beyond. It took Christians by surprise to learn that they could speak about the heart. And yet not a schoolchild in France or England today could name a single Arab poet.'

'You must know some by heart. Let me hear a line or two.'

She looked from the ruined entrance out on the stars and the crimson city, and the lines of a poem came directly to her, as though her own heart had fashioned them for tonight.

'This is part of a poem by an Egyptian poet, Ali Mahmud Taha. He died in 1949. He was only forty-eight. Listen.

'See where night falls about us. It is time, dearest, so
    let us go.
Love's bright angel summons us to his shining altar
While over here the darkness stirs the hymns of Sufis and
    their songs of love.

The joy of darkness penetrates the world, water and trees,
   clouds and their shadows on the sky.
Now let us dream, you and I, for tonight shall be our
   night of love.'

Her voice faltered and fell silent. He knew there were more verses, that the poet's vision stretched further into the darkness than he could imagine.

'He must have been standing somewhere just like this,' he said.

'By the Nile,' she answered, angry with herself for having blurted out what she most wanted to keep secret.

'There's a river not that many yards away. That could serve as our Nile.'

'There was moonlight.' She was frightened now, sensing her own need, wondering what he'd meant by 'our Nile'.

'We'll come back here when the moon's full again,' he said.

'I'd have thought you'd had enough of this place.'

'Yes, but not of this night.'

He sat beside her, his wounded leg stretched out straight in front of him. The night was filled with an orchestra of crickets.

'There's something like fifteen years between us,' she said at last. He was all she wanted, but she was desperate to push him away, fearing what might happen.

'Fifteen years is nothing,' he said, and his voice was suddenly overpainted with seriousness. 'It will pass like moments. I know nothing about poetry, but when I was younger, I spent about a week memorizing one poem that had taken my fancy. It's by Andrew Marvell. One day

I'll look for a complete copy and send it to you. But listen . . .

> 'Had we but world enough, and time,
> This coyness, Lady, were no crime.
> We would sit down and think which way
> To walk and pass our long love's day . . .
> But at my back I always hear
> Time's wingèd chariot hurrying near,
> And yonder all before us lie
> Deserts of vast eternity.'

She said nothing right away, but he could tell she was moved by Marvell's words.

'It's harder for me, Justine. I didn't ask for this either. I'm still in a state of grief. For Nathalie, for Peter. I have so many things to think of, so many worries. But I can't stop myself thinking about you. When you aren't here, I just lie and imagine you're beside me, when—'

'When I leave you here, I have to drag myself back home. This is crazy, isn't it?'

He fumbled in the darkness and found her hand. His fingers interlaced with hers.

'We have to get you out of the country,' she said. 'You must help us.'

'That's got nothing to do with what we were talking about.'

'Hasn't it?' Her voice was tired and tense. 'It's a condition.'

'A condition?'

'Of my loving you. I don't want you hurt again, or dead,

or locked up for life in solitary confinement. I don't want to love you and then find you bleeding on the pavement again. God, I thought I'd lost you.'

She was crying now, and turned, and he took her to him and gave her what comfort he could, and her tears subsided and dried.

'You can't make conditions like that,' he said. 'I tried it myself, but it didn't work. I'll love her, I said, if I find Peter's murderers, or if I get over Nathalie properly, or if I get out of this jam. Except that I did love you, and there was nothing I could do about it. None of those things would have made the slightest difference. I was just playing for time, so I wouldn't have to hurt you by saying I loved you. I don't want you to stop loving me, do you understand that?'

She nodded, her body heavy against his. She was so afraid.

'But the truth is, I have to track down these killers. I don't have any choice. I'm the only one with the ability or the commitment to do it. Between them, the hoods in Ouarzazate and the local police have muddled the case up so badly, they'll never get it straight again. Duncan would have been an enormous help, but now he's just become another part of the complication. On the other hand . . .'

Suddenly, she started laughing.

'What's wrong?' he asked, but she couldn't stop. She wasn't hysterical, but he had no idea what might have provoked the laughter.

Abruptly, she stopped.

'What is it?' he asked. 'What's wrong?'

'Nothing's wrong, you silly man. I'm laughing at us. Here we are, just having confessed that we love one another, and what are we doing? Most couples in our enviable position would be having a pretty solid snog by now. Or very likely they'd be well beyond the snogging stage and taking one another's clothes off. We, on the other hand, have been trying to find a way out of it, and are now talking about how to carry out a murder investigation. I don't know what turns you on, Nick, but I certainly do not get horny talking about the police.'

'You haven't told me what *does* turn you on.'

'Ah. You'll have to find that out for yourself. I take it that an ex-policeman like you knows something about women.'

She stopped, sensing a change in him.

'*The grave's a fine and private place,*' he quoted, looking round at the abandoned tomb. '*But none, I think, do there embrace.*'

Then he took her gently in his arms and kissed her, and her lips were like tiny fires. He drew back, then drew her in towards him again, and his lips found hers again.

Now let us sport us while we may . . .

28

The doctor and his assistant turned up shortly after midnight. Monestier was in no mood to leave Nick where he was.

'We have to take the risk,' he said. 'They've left us no choice. A child has gone missing, a little girl of four. The search for her has been widening since yesterday, and tomorrow they plan to sweep the whole of this sector. If you stay here, they'll be sure to flush you out. There'll be policemen, soldiers from the local barracks, locals lending a hand – you won't stand a chance.'

Monestier had hired a small private ambulance in which to drive Nick all the way round to the Bab Doukkala, where a wheelchair was waiting to take him to the clinic. From the clinic he'd be transferred later to Justine's house. The ambulance and wheelchair had been chosen to allay any doubts about Nick's identity as a patient. The falsified passport had arrived a day or two late, but it looked perfect: Nick was now Guy Malafosse, born 3 January 1957 in Lyon.

They set off slowly, without a flashing light. There was barely room in the little vehicle for all of them. Justine drove, with Marcel beside her, while Monestier remained behind with Nick, who had acquired a heavy plaster and a new medical chart saying 'fractured femur'. The plaster hurt quite a lot, but he preferred to take no more painkillers. The side effects from the dihydrocodeine had proved too unpleasant. The pain, however unpleasant, was a welcome price to pay not to suffer them any longer.

At the gate, Monestier and Marcel took Nick away in the wheelchair, while Justine parked the ambulance beside the bus station, from where it would be collected in the morning. The old gate was closed, as it was most days now, but she slipped back inside the city through the modern entrance that no one ever thought to close.

The doctor, his assistant and their charge had vanished by the time she got there. They'd go back to the clinic, while she took a roundabout way home. Torn between feelings of elation when she thought of Nick and his love for her, and the dread that every moment, every step, every scared glance into the shadows brought, she found herself disoriented even here, within the cobbled streets and pitch-dark alleys of her home. Everything seemed familiar and unfamiliar at the same time.

Although it was late, another wedding was under way. Justine had attended many such events, sitting for hours on uncomfortable *banquettes*, drinking sweet mint tea, stuffing herself with food when it came, sometimes returning home at three or four in the morning, exhausted. She always felt sorry for the brides, those painted and jewelled creatures, wrapped in silver brocade, veiled, lost, perched on their thrones throughout the celebrations.

She'd known about this one well in advance, and had,

indeed, been invited. Faneeda, the daughter of Abdelhake Choukri, a bookseller from whom Justine bought Arabic texts from time to time, was being married to her cousin, Abdelaziz. Guests would have started to leave from about an hour ago, and Justine and Monestier had calculated that being seen abroad at such an hour would attract little attention.

The music, which had consisted of popular Moroccan and Algerian songs until now, stopped for a few moments. Then, into the silence that had momentarily taken hold of the city, came something different. Justine stopped, and she knew that anyone awake, at home or in the street, would stop as well. The first strains of the introductory music to the most famous of Arab songs sobbed through the night air. Umm Kalthoum, the queen of singers, dead these twenty-five years and more, more alive than Elvis or Lennon, stepped onto the stage and began to sing the opening words of *al-Atlal*, Ibrahim Naji's renowned *qasida*.

'*Ya fu'adi . . .*' she sang. *Oh, my heart.*

Justine felt the familiar shiver pass down her spine. However often she heard this, it never ceased to harrow her innermost self.

'*Ya fu'adi . . .*' The voice trembled, filled with emotion, yet precisely controlled.

'*Ya fu'adi . . .*' The third repetition. You could sense the audience holding its breath. Then the diva's growing power as she completed the first half-line. '*La tas'il ayna 'l-hawa.*' Oh my heart, do not ask where desire has gone . . .

The wedding party let three full verses play, then the music faded away. Justine looked round her, as though

271

snatched out of a spell, and recognized the street in which she was standing. Her house was only a few streets away after all.

Then, as she had expected, a loud drumming erupted, and the *tzaghreet*, the loud ululation of women celebrating. They were bringing the bride out now, carrying her aloft all the way to the house of her groom. Until now he had never seen her face. Until now, he had never touched so much as her hand. She'd be taken to his bedroom now, and in some confused fashion they'd make love, each almost fully dressed. To make love naked was considered a shameful thing. God, thought Justine, how they must long to sin, these sad, wrapped-up models of family honour and religious propriety.

A little later, the groom would declare that his bride had been a virgin, and another procession would set off not long before dawn, returning to her parents' house with the glad news. At breakfast, a relative would carry the bride's underpants back to her mother, who would wash them, rejoicing in her daughter's virginity.

Justine shuddered. She couldn't imagine being trapped like that. Suddenly, she wanted to be with Nick, to be naked with him, to embrace him and make love to him without a queue of friends and relatives outside the bedroom door, interested in nothing more than a few teaspoons of blood.

The procession moved away from her. She continued on her way, meeting a few guests on their way home, faceless shadows turning in nameless, shifting lanes.

She saw him as she turned the corner, barely a shadow, a dark caress against the wall. There was a dim light some way past him, where steep steps went down to a subterranean cellar. He was watching her house, and she guessed he must have been there for some time.

'Who's there?' she asked, her voice little more than a whisper. But she thought she already knew.

He did not answer.

'I'll call the police,' she said. 'Or my neighbours. They'll know what to do with you.'

'I am the police,' he said, and she knew it was the smaller of her two policemen. 'In case anyone asks, my name is Laghzaoui. Did you understand that? Inspector Laghzaoui.'

'If you want to ask me any questions,' she said, 'you'll have to come back in the morning.'

'Where have you been?' he asked. 'It's late for a single woman to be in the streets.'

'Where the hell do you think I've been? Or haven't you noticed there's a wedding going on?'

'Is that where you've been?' he asked. 'Are you sure? Did anyone see you there?'

'It's none of your business where I spend my nights. Or has there been another shooting? Or maybe, maybe another shooting's planned, and you'd just like to know my whereabouts to be sure I'm counted in?'

He came to her, pulling himself away from the shadows. Suddenly, he was very close, closer than she liked, and far closer than any man normally dared approach a woman in this society. She could sense his hostility, his strength, his lust. He'd be thinking about the wedding, imagining the coming bedroom scene, mixing it up with a hundred images of sex drawn from cinema posters and magazines, whatever fuelled his desire. The words of the poem, sung with such aching passion, burned in her.

Ya fu'adi, la tas'il ayna 'l-hawa . . .

'I'm busy in the morning,' he said. 'I don't have time to come here to ask you questions. But there are questions I need to ask. Ask me inside. I won't stay long.'

'You won't stay at all. I'm tired, and I want to go to bed. You know I can't ask a single man into my house.'

'You're not a Muslim. Christian women are allowed to do as they please. Ask me inside. We can reach an agreement. I can tell you what you need to know. I won't stay long.'

She put a hand on his chest, very gently, so as not to antagonize him. He stiffened and grabbed her wrist.

'Don't push me around.'

A swirl of drumbeats echoed suddenly among the dead streets. Above them, women's quick voices quivered in the jerky notes of the ululation, as they might at a birth or death.

Ya fu'adi . . . ya fu'adi . . . ya fu'adi . . .

'Let go of my arm.'

'You won't put up a fight. Better inside than out here in the street, don't you think?'

She knew she could fight him off long enough to get inside. Or perhaps not; she had no idea of his true strength. But would it be worth it?

His left hand slipped inside the pocket of the light jacket he was wearing, and came out again clutching something small and metallic. There was a dull click, and now he was holding a knife in his hand, the blade at least six inches long, and the situation had changed. It was as if a third party had entered the *derb*. There was no question now of fighting him off. The knife put him firmly in control. He did not brandish it, but ran the blade gently over her breasts. She prayed he'd stop, for she knew she'd lose it if he did much more.

Suddenly, there was a sound of footsteps coming their way, a man's steps. A few moments later, a shadow appeared halfway along the *derb*. The policeman closed the knife but continued holding it close beside his thigh.

'What's going on there? Are you interfering with my sister?'

It was Marcel's voice, speaking French. She felt relief pass over her in waves.

The policeman stepped towards Marcel. The knife had awakened his aggression, which he was now steering towards this new arrival.

'Watch out, Marcel,' she called. 'He's got a knife.'

Marcel seemed not to care. He walked straight up to the policeman.

'Listen, we don't want trouble. Nor do you. Just leave, and we'll forget the whole thing.'

The policeman, brought back to reality by the possibility that his intended victim had a brother, was beginning to realize just how deep was the shit in which he'd put himself. In Muslim countries, male relatives have absolute rights over a woman's honour. The brother could kill his sister right here and now with impunity. For that matter, he could kill a potential rapist and not another word would be said.

'How do I know you're who you say you are? You could be her lover, her . . .'

'I told you, I'm her brother. I also have very powerful friends in the French embassy. Try to think what you're getting yourself into here, and then think again. We don't want trouble. The lady said she wants to be left alone. So I think you should be going.'

It hung in the balance for several moments. The policeman hardly seemed to know what to do. He'd never slept with a woman, not even a prostitute. He felt a desperate urge to frighten the brother off and get down to business with the woman, but uncertainty held him back. The consequences of a mistake could be dire. If he were tried as a rapist and found guilty, he'd be an outcast, a hollow man as good as dead. He spat once, then slunk off, giving Marcel the widest possible berth.

'Let's get inside,' said Marcel when the policeman had gone a few yards up the *derb*. Justine got out her keys. They jangled as she did so, and she saw her hand was shaking.

'He had a knife,' she said.

'I know. I saw it. Let's get you in.'

She handed him the keys, and he worked out which ones were for the heavy wooden door. Moments later, they were inside.

'Nick,' she said. 'Is he all right?'

'Yes, he and Monestier are fine. I came to check you'd got home all right. I'm glad I did.'

She pressed his hand and kissed him on the cheek. Then she led him on into the living room.

'I need a brandy,' she said. 'Join me?'

'Yes, just a quick one. Until you're feeling more yourself. Who was he, do you know?'

She started to tell him, then broke off suddenly and headed for the door. He heard her running in the passage-way outside, then listened as she threw up in the down-stairs toilet. When she came back, she was white.

'I'm sorry, but . . . he's a revolting little man. I wish I hadn't seen his knife.'

'Don't worry, he won't be back.'

She looked at him thoughtfully.

'Don't be so sure,' she said.

They wheeled Nick to Justine's house later that morning, just before first light. He could not stay in the clinic; too many people were in and out during the day, and the quarters where Monestier lived were too cramped now that Marcel was also staying there.

She directed them to carry him to the spare bedroom, where a bed had been made up for him. Marcel had found a pair of wonderful bright-green pyjamas for him in the Kissaria. Dressed in these, he was helped into bed. Within minutes, he was fast asleep.

'We won't stay,' said Monestier. 'We have an early start.'

'You always have an early start. You've been up all night. Won't you at least let me make you something for breakfast?'

Monestier shook his head.

'No, my dear. You need some sleep too. You've been badly shaken. Marcel told me about it. He and I are going to take turns to nap during the day. We'll be back this evening.'

'In the meantime,' said the younger man, 'take great

care. Don't answer the door unless it's to someone you know and can trust. If there's anything odd, just say you're ill.'

She let them go. Before closing the door behind them, she looked up, and through a gap between two walls she saw the sky, full of purple and golden light, and galaxies turning pale and going back to darkness. *Oh my heart*, she thought.

She pulled herself upstairs and went to the guest room and looked down at the man she loved, fast asleep and very like a child. Without waiting to remove her clothes, she found a space on the bed next to him, and lay there for a long while holding him, until she too fell asleep.

The doctors returned that evening as they had promised. Justine made a meal, her version of *tajine*, which her mother had taught her.

'Before you ask,' she said, 'the invalid is fine.'

'Not entirely,' protested Nick. 'I still can't walk properly, and I do have pain.'

'I'll see to that, don't worry.'

'But no more . . . di . . . hydro . . .'

'Don't worry, it was just a stop-gap anyway. I need to examine the leg first. Once I'm satisfied you've picked up no infections, I'll give you a shot of something milder. Marcel says he trained in some acupuncture techniques at med school. If you feel up to being punctured, he's willing to have a go.'

'I'd sooner be shot.'

Marcel smiled.

'I don't really think so. I'll try the needles if you're still in pain. They don't hurt, and they will give you relief.'

They sat down to eat, and as they did so, Monestier talked. He told them about Béatrice Le Tourneau and her sister Marie-Louise, about their husbands, Gérard and Vital, their children, and the time when Marie-Louise lost a child because she'd witnessed an execution.

'I don't have all the facts,' the doctor said. 'Just what my father told me. He left some papers behind, notebooks from those days. I'm trying to dig them out: then I may have more to tell you.'

'Do you know how it all ended? Did they all go back to France after the war?'

Monestier shook his head.

'I'm afraid my knowledge doesn't stretch to that. My father stayed on here, even after Independence. They never turned against him. He was out of touch with the old country, especially after my mother died. But I'll see what I can find. And maybe we can get those original papers from your brother, Nick.'

'I'll try, but I have to take care he doesn't come blundering in. And I'm desperately worried about my daughter.'

'You'll think of something to say. Now, I don't intend to have another late night. I'm going to stay here in case Nick needs my help. Marcel will take care of the clinic. As for you two lovebirds . . . I'd advise separate beds for tonight, and plenty of sleep.'

'How do you . . . ?' Justine looked at Monestier in astonishment.

'Did you really think no one would notice? You've been making eyes at one another for days. If you hadn't both worked it out for yourselves, I think Marcel and I would have told you. We even had a bet on how long, didn't we, Marcel?'

'Come on, doctor. In our profession, we don't gamble with people's lives.'

He smiled at Nick.

'We've talked about it, of course. About you two. And we've decided it's a good thing. Provided you both manage to stay alive.'

Marcel left. The *derb* swallowed him up, and in moments his footsteps faded into the stone. Justine closed the door and went back to the dining room, where Monestier was eying her drinks cabinet in search of a nightcap.

She found Nick in the living room.

'Do you think he's right?' she asked.

'Who? Monestier?'

'Yes. About single beds.'

'Oh, I'm sure he's perfectly right, but I'm not sure it would be for the best. What do you think?'

She came up and put her arms round him.

'I think it's a dreadful idea. You just need to watch your leg, that's all.'

'Marcel left without giving me the needles.'

'I shouldn't worry. He'll be back in the morning.'

'In that case, let's get these dishes cleared and –'

At that moment, someone knocked at the door. A hard knock, repeated five or six times.

'Upstairs,' Justine whispered. 'Quickly. Now.'

The knock came again, louder this time. Justine

went out to the entrance hall.

'Who is it?' she called, first in Arabic, then in French.

The knocking began again.

In the House
of El-Glaoui

29

Marrakech
1 July 1942

She had never felt so nervous in her life. A chance encounter at a reception, a short conversation, and here she was waiting on the terrace of the Mamounia Hotel for someone she didn't know, someone she had no reason to trust. She should have said no. It was obvious she wasn't cut out for this sort of thing. Her heart was beating too quickly, her pulses fluttered like baby birds, she had a headache behind her left eye, and her stomach swarmed with killer moths.

All the time she sat, she cast glances to left and right, certain that, at any moment, one of General Hauteville's anti-subversive patrols would pick her out from the crowd, arrest her, and throw her into a bottomless dungeon somewhere, despised and forgotten. She did not have to be reminded that the Hôtel de la Mamounia Transatlantique was, in effect, the headquarters of the German Commission. At a table behind her sat a band of doughty women dressed in poorly tailored costumes, all speaking in German. The wives, Marie-Louise supposed, oblivious of the beautiful *muqarna* patterns on the pillars around them, or the *zouaq* painting that ran along the wooden ceilings above their heads.

Two of the men were visible, standing a few yards away, one leaning against a pillar, the other holding a cup of coffee, both wearing black SS uniforms. Her skin crawled to watch them, knowing their reputation as she did. They had limited powers in Morocco, but General Noguès, the Résident-Général in Rabat, was virulently opposed to the Allies and wanted to make a good impression on his German visitors. Behind him stood the vast majority of French settlers, supporters of Pétain almost to a man. This didn't mean they loved the Germans, but it did mean courting their favours, spurning their enemies and, if it came to it, betraying those of their neighbours who posed any sort of threat to the German forces fighting in North Africa.

During her illness, which had gone on for months, and her grief at the loss of little Aziz, and her black days, the days when she looked on in horror as the execution scene replayed itself as vividly as the first time, she had felt her heart break and had almost given up the struggle. Without Vital, she would never have made it through. Even though physically recovered from the miscarriage, she stayed indoors and received few visitors. Béatrice would come most days, and Gérard later, when he'd got over his initial anger with his 'idiotic sister-in-law'; but she'd found their company hard to bear, and once she was strong enough she kept them at bay as far as was possible.

Month had succeeded month, and her two doctors had insisted on her going outside, once the rains were over and the weather was growing dry and warm again. Mrs

Monestier, an amiable soul who dressed in sensible shoes and was never seen outside without her straw hat and blue ribbon, took her for long walks in the Aguedal and Bahia gardens. For weeks she chattered on about nothing consequential, reminiscing about her childhood in Nice, or the happy days she'd enjoyed being courted by the diffident Dr Monestier, or talking about her child, a boy who, she hoped, would follow in his father's footsteps and become a great physician.

She never mentioned the war, or Pétain, or Hitler, or Rommel, or Cairo, or any of the other topics considered essential by the rest of society. For her own part, Marie-Louise had no desire to reawaken memories that could only hurt her, and so was drawn imperceptibly into the safe world of Mme Monestier.

Mme Monestier, however, was neither as safe nor as dull as she let Marie-Louise believe. If the younger woman had not been so weighed down by her grief, she would have noticed earlier that the doctor's wife had as sharp a brain as her husband, and was an acute observer of the Marrakech social scene.

Béatrice, thinking less of her sister than of her own standing in that scene, had inadvertently done Marie-Louise a great favour, although had she known to just what that favour would lead, she would have thought twice and three times. The story of Marie-Louise and the traitor Aziz, above all that last visit to the prison yard, had got around with predictable speed. The miscarriage proved to be Béatrice's blessing, giving her a plausible excuse for her sister's otherwise incomprehensible actions. There had been something wrong with the baby from the start, and this had

had an unfortunate effect on Marie-Louise's mental state. As for her current grief, it stemmed quite clearly from the loss of the child, and anyone who attributed it to any other cause would have the Tourneaus to deal with.

By the spring, this meant that Marie-Louise had been pretty well rehabilitated in the eyes of Marrakech's matrons. 'Don't mention babies to her,' they said in one another's company, 'or guillotines. Especially the latter. She finds that whole episode so humiliating.' 'Well, I should think so,' the more forward would declare, only to find themselves transfixed by Béatrice's stony stare. 'You should think nothing of the sort. Remember, it was all due to her hormones. The sick baby. This dreadful war.'

Her good fairies were in attendance. By the time the little orange pom-poms of mimosa began to give way to the coral tree and the pink calodendrum, Marie-Louise's reputation was spotless once more, and her name was no longer a byword for mixing with the natives.

Some months later, to mark the onset of summer, the Germans announced a dinner and dance to be held at the Mamounia at the end of June. This was not as easy an event to arrange as might have been thought. No one attached to the royal house could be invited, since the Sultan had refused to receive any members of the German delegation at any of his palaces. They'd experienced a similar rebuttal from T'hami Pasha El-Glaoui, effective ruler of southern Morocco, whose grand palace imposed itself on the medina. His refusal embraced – or should have embraced – his whole entourage of officials and hangers-on.

The Commission had to content itself with the loyal French. Noguès gladly agreed to come from Rabat, with as many of his staff as he could spare. D'Hauteville would attend, of course, along with Colonel Ribaud and others. The judiciary was invited, and other French officials of the right standing. There would be no Jews, whatever their position in society.

It had been Marie-Louise's first night out, and she had hated every moment of it. The same old social climbers were there, practically preening themselves on being entertained by their country's conqueror, some hangers-on from the international community in Tangier, and a bunch of Moroccans of the better class who were attached neither to the king nor to El-Glaoui.

She danced mainly with Vital. The German officers, watched by their beefy wives, did their best to take at least one turn with the more winsome or significant French-women, although they studiously avoided the Moroccan women. Not long before the dancing faltered to an end, Marie-Louise was approached by one of Vital's colleagues, Pierre Valois, the judge whose absence on that fateful day had allowed her to attend Aziz's last moments. She pushed the thought aside as he came up to her and asked her for the next dance.

As they turned through the floor, the judge talked of little of consequence. He was a fine dancer, and his careful steps led her round faultlessly, so that they glided among the other dancers almost unnoticed. It was just as the orchestra was playing the last bars of the waltz that he bent forward and whispered hurriedly in her ear.

'Here, tomorrow, on the terrace, three p.m. Don't be late.' Then he smiled, kissed her on both cheeks in the French fashion, and disappeared once more.

'I think Pierre has taken a liking to you,' said Vital as she sat down beside him. She remonstrated, he parried, and then they were standing as the dance came to a formal end. She said nothing to him of Valois's queer assignation.

She wouldn't have turned up, for there had never been the least hint of an attraction between her and Pierre, and she certainly had no plans to start an affair. Yet an instinct told her that the invitation was of a different sort entirely, and she had come to the Mamounia, either to find out the truth or, if it did turn out that Pierre was hoping to seduce her, to give him the biggest brush-off of his life.

One of the German officers detached himself from the pillar and made his way across to her. When he was about a yard from her table, he clicked his heels, bowed, and spoke.

'*Gnädige Frau.*'

'Yes?'

'I was concerned to see you on your own.' He spoke fluent French, no doubt the main reason for him being appointed to the Commission. 'I am Standartenführer Gustav von Hodenberg. I believe I saw you and your husband last night at the dance. May I be of any assistance to you?'

She felt herself panicking, forced herself to see that she was in no danger. He was only trying to help. Or perhaps he thought he stood a chance of getting to know her, imagined she had come here with the intention of picking up a man.

'Hello, Marie-Louise. I'm so sorry I'm late.'

A woman's voice behind her absolved her of any need to answer von Hodenberg. She looked round to see Jeanine Gimpel, a teacher at the French Lycée. They'd met a couple of times before, but could hardly claim to know one another.

'Jeanine, of course. How nice of you to come. You're scarcely late at all. This is ... Stand ... I'm sorry, you all have such long titles.' Marie-Louise smiled weakly at the German officer.

'Standartenführer,' he replied, smiling benignly. 'I think it is the same as your "colonel". Standartenführer Gustav von Hodenberg at your service, *gnädige Fräulein.*' He repeated the clicking motion and bowed to Jeanine. It was a surprise to find he was a full colonel, for he looked not much over thirty. In wartime, promotions could be rapid. Jeanine gave him the slightest of acknowledgements and told him she was a *Frau*, not a *Fräulein.* He was not offended. The French did it all the time.

'I see I was mistaken,' he said to Marie-Louise. 'My apologies.'

He returned to his pillar and his friend. Jeanine sat down.

'Don't bother explaining,' she said. 'They do it at the drop of a hat. They think they're being polite. And I think they're lonely, poor devils, and on the lookout for any romantic opportunity that presents itself. He knows your husband would encounter problems if he lodged a complaint.'

She took off her hat and placed it on the other side of the table.

'Shall we have some coffee? Or perhaps you prefer tea? And some of those little patisseries they do so well here.'

'I really don't come here very often. I've never had tea and cakes.'

'Well, it's nice to do things in the English fashion for a change, don't you think?'

Before Marie-Louise could reply, Jeanine had noticed a waiter and beckoned him over.

'Two *cafés crèmes*, two bottles of Jony, and some cakes. And be quick about it. I've no time for lazy Arabs.'

He bustled away. Jeanine took one look at Marie-Louise's face, and had to stop herself bursting into laughter.

'I've offended you. I'm sorry,' she said.

'No, no, it's none of my business.'

'Marie-Louise, that's something you're going to have to get used to. Speaking offensively to Moroccans. From today on, you become hard. You speak harshly. If a German officer approaches you, you are polite, even friendly.'

'But I don't understand any of this. I was told to be here at this time, that's all. I hardly know you; we can't consider ourselves friends.'

'Before you know it, we will be the very best of friends.'

'But what's it all about?'

'I think you know. I think you've guessed exactly what I am and why I'm here.'

Marie-Louise looked at her, her mouth wide open. Was this really happening?

'The Resistance,' she whispered. 'You belong to the Resistance.'

Jeanine nodded.

'We've been watching you for a long time, receiving reports from people you'd never guess, my dear. I think I should tell you that none of us has forgotten for a moment your very great courage.'

'Courage? But I've never . . .'

'Courage comes in more than one form. I don't think many of us could have done what you did for that poor boy, Aziz. That you stayed with him to the very end like that, and at such a cost to yourself . . .'

'There was nothing else I could do. If you'd seen him . . .'

'I can see it's upsetting you to talk about it. Let's talk about something else. Your first mission, for example.'

'But I haven't said I'll join. I can't just . . . I'd have to talk it over with Vital.'

Jeanine shook her head.

'It's better that you don't. Even where both halves of a married couple are members, we prefer that they belong to different cells, and that they never talk about each other's work.'

'You mean, Vital . . . ?'

'I can't tell you. The truth is, I don't know. But I do know he's sympathetic.'

At that moment, the waiter returned with the coffees, water and cakes. Jeanine dismissed him brusquely. She knew that word got round, who was pleasant, who was horrid. This was the ideal place to build a reputation.

'Marie-Louise,' said Jeanine as she arranged the cups and plates on the table, 'this isn't the sort of thing we can afford to let someone mull over. I need a commitment today. I won't pretend this is anything but dangerous, what I'm asking you to do. But it is important, and it's going to be a lot more important in the coming months.'

'Do you mean . . . an invasion . . . ?'

'Keep your voice down. I can't answer that, but we are reaching a critical point in the war. The main resistance work is in the *métropole*, but the truth is that the war in

Europe may be profoundly influenced by what happens in North Africa. Drink your coffee. I will need your answer before you leave.'

Marie-Louise's hand strayed towards her cup, then back again.

'No, it's all right,' she said. 'I've already made up my mind. Thank you for asking me. Count me in. We'll wipe the smiles off their faces.'

Jeanine looked at her and smiled.

'No second thoughts?'

Marie-Louise shook her head.

'You can't imagine how pleased everyone will be. Now, drink your coffee, then we'll go for a little walk. We've a lot to talk about.'

30

CODED CABLE M55XL896
ORIGIN: US Embassy
OSS Section
Tangier
27 July 1942

From CODENAME PATRIOT [Col. William Eddy, OSS Station Chief, North Africa] FAO CODENAME SUNRAY [Gen. Bill Donovan, OC OSS], TORCH HQ [Norfolk House, Piccadilly, London].

Your communication dated 25/7/42 concerning Operation Torch received. Anticipate further briefing once date for invasion has been set. This office will provide weekly updates on Morocco, including Spanish-held territories, throughout build-up to landings.

Held meeting yesterday at El-Minzah Hotel. Present the following: Commandant Léon Faye (Free French representative), Captain Beaufre (Moroccan armed forces), and the millionaire businessman Jacques Lemaigre-Dubreuil. Lemaigre says he knows several dissident officers capable of pulling off a coup, if that's what we decide. He has also insisted on having General Giraud as the French leader to replace Pétain, and since Roosevelt seems dead set against de Gaulle, that may be how we have to go. Lemaigre thinks General Darlan worth a second look, in spite of his anti-Allied stance. He's fond of the Brits, and he has enormous influence back in France.

The majority of French troops still seem to be loyal to Pétain. Bob Murphy and I can muster up something like 10,000 Arab irregulars here in Morocco. They won't make great troops, but they could prove valuable for diversionary tactics in the event of landings.

But we will need to act quickly. In Morocco, Laval has been acting under German orders, replacing pro-Allied, anti-German French officers with collaborationists. In Marrakech, the police are under the control of a French fascist called Le Tourneau, who is hand in glove with a group of Gestapo officers who were sent to the city a few months ago as 'observers'.

Overall, I guess that by now the Vichy police have arrested upwards of 300 French officers suspected of lending their support to various underground and dissident movements. Some have been executed. The rest remain in custody, and I'm told our Gestapo observers have been busy down in the dungeons helping these guys talk. French fascists are now taking over the key military posts in North Africa, and it is absolutely certain that they would oppose a landing and order their men to open fire on Allied troops. We may have missed the moment.

In the meantime, the Free French in Morocco need weapons and ammunition, if they're to be of any use to us at all. Be sure they get what they ask for. I will put in a separate request for arms to be distributed among my tribesmen.

28 July 1942
O/C Ordnance Depot Cairo

Please supply the bearer for air drop to Patriot Group, Morocco, with the following stores in accordance with 1st Army Orders.

Sten guns	1,000
9 m/m ammo	800,000
303 Rifles	500
303 S.A.A.	200,000
Mills grenades	2,000
No. 75 Hawkins grenades	2,000

Capt. J. Wellinghouse

From CODENAME SUNRAY, TORCH HQ, to CODE-NAME PATRIOT, OSS section, US Embassy, Tangier
29 July 1942

ABOVE TOP SECRET
FOR YOUR EYES ONLY
DESTROY WHEN READ

The situation in Morocco and Algeria is causing both CODENAME FORMER NAVAL PERSON [Winston Churchill] and CODENAME CASABLANCA [F.D. Roosevelt] second thoughts. They have committed themselves to Operation Torch, since it is vital for the future conduct of the war that we open a second front as soon as possible. But they will not issue orders for a full mobilization of troops without some certainty that Allied troops will not get further tangled up in North Africa. Last month's debacle in the Cauldron, followed by the loss of Tobruk, has shaken everyone. Not even the victory at El Alamein this month has reversed the British sense of vulnerability.

Churchill wants to be sure that any landings will be supported inland by irregulars. Algeria has been largely secured in that respect, but we are still nervous about Morocco, particularly in the light of your warnings about fascists taking over key military posts.

We understand that El-Glaoui, the Pasha of Marrakech and ruler of the southern half of Morocco, is unfavourable towards the Germans, and that he is possessed of considerable forces within that region, as well as influence elsewhere. I have spoken to CODENAME MONSIEUR LEGRAND [Gen Charles de Gaulle], and he has made it clear that support for Free French forces will, in the event of victory, be rewarded very well indeed.

You will have to send someone entirely trustworthy to meet with Glaoui in order to broach the subject. Later, I'd like to send one of our people from Headquarters in to deal with the detail. This is urgent. If you need money or supplies to help with the mission, just ask. This could prove to be one of the most important acts of the war. Pin this guy Glaoui down. If the sweet talk doesn't get him on our side, maybe a few well-placed threats will have their effect. I understand he's the type who understands tough talk. Stay out of his dungeons, though. They tell me nobody ever sees the light of day again once they get stuck in one of them.

Funkabwehr Ground Station
Amiens, France
29 July

The radio corporal gently moved the oblong *Frequenzent-stellung* control on his E52a 'Köln' receiver. A message was coming through on the London-Tangier circuit, addressed to the US embassy. Several minutes passed, during which the radiotelegraph transmission was captured by his equipment. Once it was done, he told his assistant to punch the message onto a teletype tape, and promptly forgot about it.

In the meantime, his assistant, a young Berliner called Hans Piepe who had been posted to Amiens only a few weeks earlier, dialled a number on the teletypewriter exchange and waited for a direct connection. Three minutes later, he had it: he knew he was lucky. There had been heavy signals traffic all day, but it was starting to die off. He fed his tape into a mechanical transmitter, and watched as it chugged its way through at around sixty words per minute.

In a room at the headquarters of Fremde Herre West, the western section of Germany's intelligence evaluation service, a page printer delivered Donovan's coded message into the hands of the Abwehr's finest cryptanalysts. The intercept was printed out in two versions, one original, and a carbon made on yellow teletype paper. The watch officer saw the message's priority rating at a glance and took it next door, where it could be processed on a reconstructed US SIGABA M-134-C machine.

31

'You'll have to be very careful with him, Marie-Louise. In his way, he's more powerful than the Sultan, more influential than the French Résident-Général. In this region, his word is law. He can have a man made destitute, or have him flogged or tortured or killed for the flimsiest of reasons, or for no reason at all. On the surface, he's dreadfully urbane: he speaks fluent French and some English, he spends a lot of time in Europe, and he's a scratch golfer with a plus-four handicap.

'But that's all just surface. Underneath, he's still pretty much the barbarian he started out as. I don't mean his table manners are bad. In fact, in matters of that sort he's positively refined. But with his own people he can be both cruel and ill willed. His armies have carried out more than one massacre in the past, and his dungeons are littered with old bones.'

'Isn't that just rumour?'

'Everything's rumour here, my dear. It's just a matter of sifting out the truth. In the case of the Pasha, the truth seems to be beyond what anyone might reasonably suppose possible.

'One thing you can be sure of: he's immensely wealthy, wealthier than the king. He can't be bribed. Either he will find the Allied offer attractive, or he will not. Don't doubt his courage, or that of his men. They'll fight the Germans if they have to, to the last man if necessary.'

Jeanine Gimpel wore a lightweight flowered dress that fell to just above her knees. Marie-Louise looked at her, as if for the first time. Her new friend seemed frail, a born schoolmarm, her hair tied back in a small bun, glasses on her nose, pale skin that she kept shaded from the sun as much as possible. There were lines around her eyes, as though she did not sleep well. Just as Marie-Louise sometimes struggled to sleep, while scenes from Aziz's execution played in a corner of her brain.

At Jeanine's suggestion, they'd come to swim at the little swimming pool behind the Casino. She'd chosen her time well: it was just after lunch, and the pool was almost deserted. They shared one of the women's changing cubicles: with no one else around, they could talk freely without drawing attention to themselves.

'We'd better start undressing,' said Jeanine, 'otherwise the attendant will wonder what we're up to.' She turned her back to Marie-Louise, who unbuttoned her dress for her. To Marie-Louise's surprise, the teacher wore lovely underwear, quite a contrast to her outer garments, which were unremarkable. And as she removed the rest of her clothes, it was clear that the bun and the glasses belied a slim but sensual body that would have surprised anyone who knew her – except her husband, of course.

'And don't forget his reputation as a man,' Jeanine continued.

'I've heard he's fond of women.' Marie-Louise turned for Jeanine to unfasten her dress.

'Fond? He had a harem of ninety-six concubines when his brother died, and he added fifty-four of his brother's to his own. Since then, I don't know how many more there have been. He has agents who go round the Berber villages, picking out girls to send on to his kasbah. They never see the light of day again. And agents in France. And he employs men to watch at the railway stations for European women travelling alone . . .'

'Surely not.' Marie-Louise's voice was half-smothered as she pulled her dress over her head. The thought of her utilitarian underwear caused her to flush. There was a sound of rustling silk as Jeanine let her slip fall to the floor.

'He likes women, my dear, and he has the money and power to indulge himself. If you meet him, he won't leap on you or anything, but he will look you up and down and consider whether to make advances or not. You're very pretty. Dare I say, his type? With the right make-up . . .'

'You're not suggesting . . . ?'

'Of course not. Now, let's see what you're like beneath those beastly things. I'm amazed your husband puts up with you.'

'Is that why you brought me here?'

'There's no need to worry. You're the wife of a French judge. Glaoui knows how far he can go, and when he has to step back. But the course of the war could depend on what he makes of you, how favourably he's disposed to you. I'm not asking you to sleep with him, but I won't let you near him if I don't think you'd be capable of seducing him if it came to it.'

'I'm sorry, but this is unspeakable. A man like that, a . . .'

There was a pause. Outside, some children shouted with glee as they splashed one another.

'A Moroccan? Is that what you were about to say, Marie-Louise? A native? A Muslim? A black? I thought you were above that. As a matter of fact, would it be that terrible? He's said to be a fascinating lover. He can satisfy a woman several times in one night. So I've heard.'

'But, I'm a married woman . . .'

'Me too. In name, anyway. My husband couldn't satisfy a chicken. But the way this war is going, we could all be widows soon. Every day, soldiers are giving their lives in order to beat the Hun. Our Resistance fighters are killed or captured and put into the hands of the Gestapo. And you worry about a night or two of passion with T'hami El-Glaoui?'

Tears streaming down her face, her voice small, the words swallowed, Marie-Louise made a last attempt to defend herself.

'But . . . I love my husband. We love each other so much.'

Jeanine reached out and drew Marie-Louise to her. For a moment it felt unutterably strange to be embraced by another woman, to feel her breasts against her own, her hands on her back, rubbing gently, soothing. Then she accepted the intimacy and clung to her friend without shame. When they drew apart, both women were wiping tears from their eyes.

Jeanine smiled crookedly.

'Take those awful knickers off. Hurry up. Good. Now, turn round. And again. OK, you'll do.'

'Meaning what exactly?'

'If he saw you naked like that, he'd ask you to marry him.'

Marie-Louise laughed nervously. She'd never talked about things like this before.

'How can you tell?'

'It's guesswork. You can never be sure with men. But you've got a good figure. If I were a man, I'd want to take you to bed.'

For a moment, Marie-Louise sensed another truth behind her friend's words. She'd stepped into another world, a world in which naked women embraced. It made her feel uncomfortable. She reached for her swimming costume.

'I think we should get in the pool,' she said.

Jeanine put her own costume on. As she did so, she looked up at Marie-Louise.

'I didn't mean to confuse you. My husband . . . We're very fond of one another. It's good for us to be married. But . . .'

'I'd rather not know. I don't disapprove, it's just . . .'

'No, of course not. Well, we still have some talking to do. The big question is whether or not to send you to his palace here in town, or to his *kasbah* at Telouet. And how to get you in without arousing suspicion.'

'Am I expected to go in alone?'

Jeanine shrugged.

'No, not initially at least. Don't worry, we'll come up with something.'

32

Telouet
10 August 1942

Her backside was sore from riding on the donkey and she feared for her new silk underwear, which might soon be rubbed to shreds. Yet nothing else but a donkey would do to find a way through this steep, rocky countryside. Marie-Louise shifted again, and for a few agreeable moments the pain in one side of her bottom eased, only to reappear in the side now rubbing against the donkey's back.

Up ahead, Denis Bailey was experiencing similar problems, but he'd ridden donkeys in Greece before coming here, and was a little hardened to life in the saddle. She watched him bounce up and down on his little mount, several paces behind their Berber guide. The guide spoke no Arabic, but made up for it by vigorous gestures and cries directed to the donkeys, who appeared to understand him perfectly.

Denis was a British intelligence captain who'd been flown in from Cairo a couple of days earlier. He was in his forties, lanky and slightly stooped, and the top of his face was furnished with a pair of wire-framed spectacles that caught the afternoon light from time to time as they climbed up through the mountains.

Marie-Louise had discovered quickly that he'd been something of a mistake. Someone had read on his papers that he was an Arabist. This turned out to be true, but for all the use he was going to be in Morocco, he might as well have spoken Tibetan. He'd done a degree in classical Arabic many years earlier, and had emerged able to read the Koran, some early poetry, and postage stamps. In Egypt he'd made himself proficient in the local dialect, a form of Arabic wholly different from the classical, but equally incomprehensible to a Moroccan.

Nonetheless, he carried with him papers in several languages that guaranteed the Allies' full co-operation with Glaoui Pasha should he agree to enter the war on their side. Money was promised, and gold bullion, along with guns and ammunition of every kind, and the knighthood Si T'hami had long coveted. More than that, Captain Bailey had been authorized to convey to the Glaoui that, in the event of an Allied victory, there would be many changes in the running of Morocco, and that it might prove necessary to depose the ruling Sultan and replace him with a more dependable king.

Marie-Louise would make the introduction and act as interpreter. The captain, who spoke a little French, was travelling as her husband. Vital, in the meantime, had been gently persuaded to spend a few days away in Casablanca.

They'd travelled by motorcar from Marrakech and along the road, not many years old, that crossed the Tizi N'Tichka pass. At Tadlest, the car had been abandoned in favour of the donkeys that the Pasha had arranged to wait for them.

A narrow track went upwards along the Tiz N'Telouet towards the kasbah. Even at the height of summer, the way was cold.

They turned and twisted along narrow paths that hung above a steep precipice, and however far they went, the peaks of the High Atlas soared ten thousand feet and more above them, snow-capped, abraded by high winds, plumes of soft white snow scarfing them against a tile-blue sky. The path crumbled as their donkeys led them ever upwards, feet slipping and then finding purchase again at every step.

Suddenly, their guide cried out. The next moment, Marie-Louise's donkey rounded a bend.

'*Kasbah Sidi El-Glaoui!*' shouted the old man. '*Kasbah Telouet!*'

There, far ahead of them, set against a backdrop of blue sky and shimmering mountain, stood a vision that took her breath away. Dar El-Glaoui, the House of Glaoui Pasha. She wasn't sure exactly what she'd expected. Perhaps something like the Glaouis' great palace in the city, or the family *kasbah* there. This was like neither, was like nothing she'd ever seen. Towers, curtain walls and crenellated roofs seemed to stretch right across her line of sight. She had heard he was building the greatest fortress and palace the world had ever known, but now she started to believe it. It was a cross between ancient Egyptian temples and the palaces of Lhasa, with a bit of the Bastille thrown in.

They continued for several hours. Telouet stood at six thousand feet, at a level mid-way between plain and mountain peak. Above this height, no vegetation grew. The flanks of the high mountains were devoid of greenery. But here, around the outer walls of the great castle, Marie-Louise could make out thickets of almond trees and, as she drew nearer, meadow flowers of every colour. Some palm trees – nothing as lush as those down on the plains all round Marrakech – were dotted singly or in pairs at irregular intervals.

The guide led them to an enormous gate some twenty feet or more high, and here they dismounted at last. In the sky above them hovered birds of prey, vultures, ravens, kites and hawks. Marie-Louise shivered, sure she was being eyed up by something with a sharp beak and predatory claws.

After much knocking, there was a sound of keys jangling on the other side of the door. A heavy key turned, then the gate swung open to reveal a tall Negro, the keeper of the gates. Around his neck he wore a silken band to which was attached a ring bearing dozens of keys. Telouet was kept secure. Only the birds of prey had unlimited access to its battlements.

They were ushered through into a broad forecourt whose tiled surface sloped gently downwards on one side to a curtain wall. High up, green roofs shimmered like grass swards, and the shadow of an eagle's wing sliced long and deep across the battlements. Further down, Marie-Louise made out rows of little windows mounted with filigree ironwork. Long familiar with these *moucharabiehs*, she sensed at once the presence of a hundred eyes. Unseen by any passing man, the women of the household could look out onto public places. Their arrival would not, she was sure, have gone unnoticed. These glimpses were all the poor creatures had of the outside world to which they'd once belonged. Marie-Louise shivered again, feeling herself swallowed up, with no way to return if the Glaoui decided not to release her.

They plunged right away into the kasbah itself. Their guide had vanished, handing over responsibility for El-Glaoui's guests to the black slave. Indoors was a dazzling mixture of bright light and deep gloom. Where there was opportunity, long slits had been cut into outward-facing walls, bringing shafts of light into rooms and corridors. Elsewhere, a mixture of oil lamps and open flames provided an uncertain glow.

They caught glimpses of hidden grandeur everywhere. Ceilings of finely carved stucco, lacquered wood, fine brocades and silk carpets from as far away as Persia, brass lamps, cages for a tribe of mechanical birds, pillars like polished glass, archways in the traditional horseshoe style, glass cupboards filled with valuable objects, vases ablaze with red roses, chairs inlaid with mother-of-pearl, tables flecked with gold, chandeliers awaiting the advent of electric light.

The slave conducted them ever more deeply inside the sprawling building, until they reached a suite of reception rooms. Here they were left, while the slave went off in search of someone. He did not speak a word to them, and they guessed he must be dumb. Where was their host?

About half an hour later, a sort of chamberlain arrived and introduced himself to them as Alla el-Mokri. He spoke excellent French, and invited them to make themselves comfortable.

'My Master cannot see you right away,' he said apologetically. He was an old man, and gave the impression of having been a retainer here all his life. 'Some complications have arisen. You must be patient. I will see that someone brings you coffee and something to eat. Later, you will dine with El-Glaoui. He knows you are here. Be comfortable. Ask if there is anything you need.'

The coffee came, and sweets. Lamps were lit, and late afternoon became early evening. They spoke from time to time, but given the restrictions on the sort of personal information one could divulge to the other, their conversations tended to dry up rather soon.

When mid-evening came, a young man ushered them to a private dining room, where the table had been laid for three. But dinner was served, and still the Glaoui made no appearance. They went on waiting with dying hopes. The plates were cleared away, and they were returned to the reception room for more coffee. None of the servants involved in this enterprise would reply to any of Marie-Louise's questions.

Just as they had agreed that it was time for bed, the door opened and a large man in a light jellaba entered the room. He held out his hand to Marie-Louise, took hers in his, and bent to kiss it. As he did so, he looked her full in the eyes, and she detected a flicker of amusement – one might almost have said, complicity – moving across his lips. Releasing her hand several moments later than was strictly proper, he straightened and reached for Denis's hand, which he shook perfunctorily.

'You must forgive me,' he said, indicating that they should return to their seats. 'Life in these *kasbahs* can be immensely troublesome. Strictly speaking, Telouet is the residence of one of my brother's and his wives, although it is my property. He is away at present on a tour of the other *kasbahs* controlled by him, and since I wanted a little time away from Marrakech, I am here in his place. Naturally, the moment the master's back is turned, everyone makes the chance to stir up mischief or demand an audience.'

'There's no need to apologize,' said Marie-Louise. 'We understand you are a very busy man. Greatness does not come without responsibilities.'

'Greatness is for God alone,' the Glaoui said, but she could see that he had been flattered by her remark.

She knew that an introductory approach had already been made to the Pasha while he was in Marrakech, but she had no way of knowing what had been discussed.

'Your Lordship, I wonder if you could tell me exactly what was suggested to you when you met with our colleague in Marrakech.'

'You don't waste time, miss. Or is it madame?'

'Madame,' she answered, blushing as she did so.

'My congratulations to your husband. He is a very fortunate man. But, you are right. We have no time for small talk. Let's get down to business.'

They talked at length, and it rapidly became clear that El-Glaoui knew what he was doing. He needed no advisers, for he had a finger on every small detail. He understood the risks he was running, and wanted to be assured of his reward should the venture succeed. On one thing only was he unclear, and that was the issue of why he should transfer his very genuine allegiance from Vichy France to a rump of rebels under the command of de Gaulle. He knew that Roosevelt had severe reservations about de Gaulle and the Free French, and this made him uneasy: were he to throw in his lot with the Gaullists, what guarantee would he have that, at the end of the war, they would even be in power? He might then have to deal with men who considered him a traitor, and that could mean the downfall of the Glaoui family and the destruction of all he had worked for.

They did what they could to reassure him, and pointed out that, whatever happened, the Vichy regime would not survive an Allied victory.

It was after midnight when their discussions came to an end. The Pasha offered to walk Denis to his rooms, and told Marie-Louise he would return for her shortly. As the two men stood, no one noticed a slight flicker as part of a curtain fell back into place, or heard the muffled footsteps of someone hurrying away.

33

He came back for her ten minutes later, smiling and suave, like the star of some Valentino movie. He sat down next to her and offered her a large whisky. He himself had not touched a drink all the time they'd been talking.

'They must have chosen you very carefully,' he said.

'I don't know what you . . .'

'They knew that a man wouldn't be enough, that it needed a woman to persuade me.'

'That's strange. I didn't think you cared much for the opinions of women.'

He laughed.

'Did you know that, with one or two exceptions, the women in my household are totally illiterate? They are ignorant creatures, even the most beautiful of them. In the end, they bore me. That's why I find European women so desirable. The ones I meet aren't just physically attractive. They tend to have brains, or character, which is frequently better. You, I suspect, have all three.'

'Well, I'm glad to have made such an impression on you. But I really didn't come here for that. The things we talked about are extremely serious. Stopping the Germans requires all our energies.'

'Believe me, I want to stop the Nazis as much as you do, maybe more. Look at my skin. Much of my blood is African. The Nazis would send me to one of their camps as a racial inferior. But surely we're free to use some of our energies for other things.'

'Such as?'

'Such as lovemaking. It's considered a great accomplishment among my people, and I think you French pride yourselves on your skills in the boudoir.'

'Monsieur el-Glaoui, this conversation has already gone too far. I told you earlier I am a married woman. My husband . . .'

'Yes?'

'Is an important man. He trusts me, but I don't think he'd like to hear you'd made passes at me.'

'Passes?' The Pasha laughed.

'Wasn't that a pass just now? All that talk of the boudoir?'

'But why should I not be interested in the boudoir, madame? I have more wives and concubines than Solomon. Most of my wives are not merely unintelligent but ugly, and I married them for political reasons. But others were chosen for their beauty. Faces like angels, breasts like small, ripe fruit, slender hips, rounded buttocks. Even at my age, I still feel like a young man every time I watch one of them undress. Believe me, I know a great deal about the boudoir. And I know, from the little we have talked, and the little I have seen of you, that I would consider it an honour if you decided to share my bed. You would not go unrewarded.'

'I'm not a prostitute, if that's what you're implying.'

'I wouldn't suggest it for a moment. But we're wasting time. I have to be up early in the morning.'

'If I say "no", will it influence your decision?'

'My political decisions are never influenced by my loins. My mind is already made up. I will start the uprising on whatever date you choose, provided I have received the money and arms by then.'

'You can be sure of it. I'm very flattered by your kind invitation, and I don't doubt that you could teach me a great deal about boudoir skills. But I have to refuse you. My husband is a good man who loves me. I love him as much in return. I could not go back to him with you on my conscience.'

'And I would not have it otherwise. Goodnight, madame. Sleep well. I'll send one of the serving girls to see you safely to your bedroom. We won't meet again.'

Late that night, a silent figure slipped through the main gate of Kasbah Telouet. No one saw him go as he descended the long trail through the Atlas foothills; no one was there to watch as he turned, early in the morning, onto the French-built road that would take him, many hours later, to Marrakech. Even if someone had noticed him, what would they have seen? A simple peasant riding a mule, no more.

[Translated from an Arabic original
SS Hauptamt Marrakech
11 August 1942]

To the Commander of the German Mission
Hotel Mamounia
Marrakech
11 August 1942

Dear Sir,

You will find enclosed a full transcript of a meeting held yesterday between H.E. T'hami El-Glaoui, Pasha of Marrakech, a member of the French Resistance, and a representative of the British forces in North Africa. It is self-explanatory.

As for myself, I am Head Chamberlain to El-Glaoui, and a man of some influence in my own right. It is on record that I have for many years been a supporter of His Excellency the Mufti of Jerusalem, Hajj Amin al-Husaini, may God grant him success. His support for the Reich and its war on the Jewish conspirators is well known to you.

In return for further information concerning my master and his doings, I make a simple request: that the money and arms due to be shipped to the Pasha be diverted by your own operatives and delivered to me at the Kasbah of Tifeltout, where my family currently reside. This will effectively put a stop to any uprising planned by El-Glaoui. In the event of an Allied landing, however, the arms and money will be available to me and my people to make raids on any invading forces seeking to cross the border between Morocco and Algeria.

The bearer of this letter will be happy to return a reply

to me. May God bless your efforts and reward them with
success. *Al-hamdu li'llah.*

Allal el-Mokri
Chamberlain to Glaoui Pasha

Typed note attached to the above, in German.

Please see that the attached letter reaches High Command
immediately. Make doubly sure it is not intercepted, and
that any replies are encoded at the highest level. We
recommend agreement to the suggestion contained in
the letter, as soon as direct contact has been made with
the writer.

SS Standartenführer von Hodenberg
Deputy Chief of the German Commission
Marrakech

In the Palace of
the Scorpion

34

The German Commission
Mamounia Hotel, Marrakech
3 November 1942

'Heil Hitler!'
  'Heil Hitler!'
Gérard let his arm drop to his side. On the wall behind him, a long red banner hung dead centre, a swastika prominent in the white circle at its heart. To his left, a portrait of Adolf Hitler scowled on the room's occupants. In front of him stood Standartenführer Gustav von Hodenberg. In addition to being Deputy Chief of the German Commission, von Hodenberg was the official liaison officer for the SS. He and Gérard had met many times before.

'Please, Gérard, sit down. Make yourself comfortable. It's always good to see you. How is your charming wife?'

Von Hodenberg's French reflected his upbringing and the years he had spent in business in Paris before the war. He was by far the most urbane of the Germans posted to Marrakech, and the best suited for relations with the French authorities. He regarded himself as a complete person, a man of distinction through birth, occupation, culture, resources and early membership in the Nazi party. Underneath his urbanity, he was a sly, greedy man, cruel, a torturer, and a cynic. With Gérard Le Tourneau's assiduous help, he had created a little warren of dungeons in which to probe anyone obtuse enough not to see which way the world was turning.

'She's very well, Herr Standartenführer. She sends her regards. And a little box of her *marrons glacés* – I've left it with your secretary.'

'Give her my thanks. I think she knows how much I appreciate her little offerings. And now, you said you had urgent business. Not more rumours, I hope?'

'Plenty of those,' Gérard said. It was almost common knowledge that the Allies would invade, but no one knew when or where.

'What do you have for me today?'

'Something special.'

'Which is?'

Gérard reached inside the little briefcase he brought with him on these visits, and brought out a photograph, a portrait of a woman. He handed it to the colonel.

'Mmm. An attractive woman. I've seen her once or twice at the hotel. I assume she is French.'

Gérard nodded.

'And who exactly is she?'

'She is the Free French operative who persuaded El-Glaoui to take Allied guns and money.'

A little silence followed as von Hodenberg let this information sink in.

'I see. You have proof of this, I'm sure?'

'More than enough.'

'Her name?'

'Marie-Louise Guénaud. Her husband is—'

'Yes, I know who her husband is. Is he mixed up in this in any way?'

'I believe so. Not with Glaoui, but in other ways.'

'Isn't she your sister-in-law?'

Gérard nodded. His face showed no emotion.

'You're comfortable with this?'

'Perfectly. I've long suspected her of leftist leanings. She's a bad influence on my nephew. I worry for the boy.'

'And your wife?'

'Yes?'

'Does she know her sister is a *résistante*? Have you told her?'

'I could not keep something like this a secret from her. She knows. And approves of the stance I am taking.'

'What do you suggest we do?'

'I have reason to believe she will receive a visit tomorrow. It will be no more than a messenger, a boy, perhaps, carrying a letter, or an oral message.'

'A message for whom?'

'For El-Glaoui. Telling him the moment for his uprising has come.'

'But surely . . .'

'The Allies think he has taken possession of his guns and gold.'

'And this message will confirm that Allied landings are due to take place?'

'I hope so, yes.'

'What do you want to do with your sister-in-law?'

323

'I would recommend her arrest and trial on a charge of treason. But if matters are moving so fast . . .'

'I understand. What about her husband?'

'The same, of course. I have documents for all this. My watchers know their business. To be frank, I'd prefer it if I were not directly involved. Tongues might wag. Some might suggest I was only working out some family vendetta. They must be made an example of.'

'Then I shall see to it. You've acted nobly, bringing all this to me. I shan't forget it. Now, let's look at all this in more detail. How should we go about things tomorrow?'

They talked for almost half an hour. Finally, Gérard stood, saluted the Standartenführer, and made for the door. As he reached it, the colonel's voice called him back.

'My dear Le Tourneau, I have been thinking. I wonder if I can be of some small help to you, to repay you for your forthrightness in coming to me with this intelligence. I think I should tell you the identity of the individual to whom we have been sending the Glaoui's gold. You may find it necessary to speak to him. After all, he is in receipt of materials that could be used to engineer a rebellion against the government. You may have to persuade him to part with some of it. Given the circumstances, you may have to enter into some sort of private arrangement with him. I think you understand me.'

'Yes, I think I do.'

'Then come here and let me tell you all I know.'

35

Marrakech
4 November 1942

Abd el-Krim hesitated before raising the glass of mint tea to his lips. He'd been on edge all morning, ever since hearing that his suit for Salima's hand had been unsuccessful. He blamed her father, who had his eyes set much higher, on a religious judge whose wife had died five months ago, and who was now inviting offers from parents with daughters to give away. The judge was sixty and Salima was fourteen, while Abd el-Krim was seventeen and a poor relation. He thought it a dreadful injustice if the old goat were to be the first to drink from what a friend of his had called 'the cup of Salima's beauty'. What they meant was . . . well, Abd el-Krim knew very well what they meant, although he went bright red if such thoughts entered his head uninvited.

Perhaps the French could help, he thought. Perhaps he could slip round to the Commissariat and explain the situation. They disapproved of arranged marriages, he knew that, frowned on too much attachment to traditional ways. Men like the judge were obstacles in their path, determined opponents of the Christians and their satanic plans. Maybe they'd send someone to have a word with the judge. Or maybe not.

The French who patrolled the streets of Marrakech today had little in common with the ones he'd known previously. They arrested people for very little reason, or no reason at all, they harassed the Jews in the Mellah, and rounded them up and sent them God knows where. Some said to Paris, some to Devil's Island, some to Germany.

He drained the rest of the sweet tea in a single swallow and set it back on the table. The taste lingered on his palate briefly, then faded. On the wall opposite, the light shimmered like gold, and the heat hung on the air, thick and oppressive, slightly sticky, like his tea. Although it was winter, down here, so close to the Sahara, the desert winds could turn the climate back to summer.

He'd come here before starting his walk. The tiny café was situated in the square outside the Ben Youssef mosque. If Abd el-Krim looked up directly, he could see the green-tiled dome of the mosque and its green-faced minaret. Its walls were draped with long, spinning strands of tailors' silk, yellow and red and blue against the prevailing green.

He'd wandered up to the square from the Suq al-Sarrajin, where he was employed as apprentice to his uncle Omar, who had given him the afternoon off to run his errand. His uncle was reputed to be the most skilful saddler in Marrakech, and Abd el-Krim knew he was fortunate to be learning the trade at his hands. Yet on days like today, when he found himself free from the endless stitching and working of stiff leather, free and with a few dirhams in his pocket, he wondered if there wasn't more to life than slaving for the rich.

Abd el-Krim had to admit that his uncle didn't work him very hard. For one thing, there was little work to come by these days. Since the war in Europe had started, the only tourists were either French or German, and even local riders thought twice about ordering all the leatherwork needed to deck out a horse for display in a fantasia. For another, Abd el-Krim liked to sneak away whenever he could. He could often be found here at the café, if he had enough money for a pot of tea.

This morning, the neighbourhood teacher Mustafa had paid him for carrying out his message and had given him extra money, urging him to have a *café simple* in the Café de France on the Djemaa el-Fna. Abd el-Krim had often thought how good it would be to have enough money to pay for a seat on the café's roof terrace, so that he could watch everything that went on in the famous square below, the way tourists did – but he'd slipped Moulay Mustafa's money into his bag, to join the few dirhams he'd already put aside for when he married.

The square sprang suddenly into life as the voice of the muezzin rolled out, staccato, from the minaret of Ben Youssef. Moments later, a second muezzin began his chant, calling all believers within earshot to prayer. A third followed, and one by one the mosques of the city were caught up in a complexity of weaving and interweaving voices.

He got to his feet as though stirred by the call to prayer, and as he did so he patted his jellaba, checking that the little parcel was still tied round his waist, under the garment. Just then a siren began to scream in the French city, its cry raucous and alien, yet curiously flat, as though it could not sustain its shrill urgency beyond the confines of the new town. Most days now there was trouble over there. News drifted back to the Arab town in worried murmurs, from café to café, from *hammam* to *hammam*. One day a shooting, the next a knifing, the day after that a woman thrown screaming from a fifth-floor window.

Dropping a couple of coins on the table, he straightened up. As he did so, he noticed Mbarak sitting at the other end of the small room, his eyes fixed on him. Mbarak lived in the Derb esh-Shems, an alley situated several hundred yards from the one in which Abd el-Krim and his family lived, all packed together into a few rooms.

Mbarak and he weren't friends: they had scarcely spoken to one another over the years. Every so often, they'd pass one another in the street, or catch a glimpse of each other on Fridays at the mosque. But Mbarak ran with a different pack from Abd el-Krim. He had friends with unsavoury reputations, men like Masoud the Butcher, and boys nearer his own age, although Abd el-Krim had never seen him in their company. At nineteen or so, Mbarak had no specific trade, but earned a hand-to-mouth living as a *dallal*, a broker who was willing to clinch a deal in anything from used clothes to tired girls and women. He was reputed to spend a lot of his time in the *quartier réservé*, where, it was said, he introduced tourists and men from out of town to the *madames* of certain houses.

Rumour had it that he also spent time in the Ville Nouvelle, that some of the French made him welcome there.

Thinking of the Ville Nouvelle made Abd el-Krim jump

into action. He thanked the café owner, who had come over to clear the little table. The man leaned forward, wiping a pool of spilled tea with a dirty cloth. Tilting his head a tiny fraction, and rolling his eyes, he drew Abd el-Krim's attention back to Mbarak.

'Be careful with that one,' he said quietly. 'He was in here earlier, asking about you. Just get yourself off, head on down to the Djemaa, lose yourself in the crowd. You don't want trouble with his sort.'

Abd el-Krim wanted to ask what the man meant by 'his sort', but he was already gone, fussing over a pile of fresh mint his boy had just brought in from the vegetable market. Abd el-Krim left the table, turning his back on Mbarak.

'*Allah yhennik,*' he called.

The owner looked round.

'*Thella firasik,*' he mouthed. 'Take care.'

He did as the café owner had suggested, slipping through the winding lanes and narrow streets that linked the main souks one with the other. Accustomed to passing the bulk of his waking time in this spider's web, today he felt somehow cut off from it all, from the noises, sights and smells that made up this world in miniature.

He imagined his mother sitting in their two-room apartment, where she spent most days sewing coloured threads onto white kaftans for a few pennies. She was Aït Ouaouzguite by origin, and her speciality was to embroider cream-coloured *haiks* with the bright threads of her people.

His father had been dead for three years now, and Abd el-Krim felt guilty that he still could not take his place as breadwinner for his mother and four sisters. Perhaps something would happen today, he thought, something more than just fetching a packet from the old town to the new.

He reached the Djemaa el-Fna and was plunged at once into its frantic activity. It would come even more alive this evening, of course, when the acrobats and magicians, the snake charmers and the monkeys would be joined by row upon row of food stalls, and the shrill music of the numerous dervish brotherhoods that jostled for the attention of passers-by.

He made a circuit of the square and left it once more, taking a short cut through the southwest corner, where a line of *calèches* were waiting for customers, their tired horses standing patiently, shaking their heads from time to time to dislodge the clouds of flies that hung about them. Heading north into the Shari Fatima Zohra, he walked at an even pace out of the old town, all the way down to the Bab Doukkala.

A police checkpoint had been installed here, guarded by peak-capped gendarmes, for whom Morocco was just one more tour of duty. They scrutinized him and asked to see his ID, then patted him to make sure he was not carrying weapons. Their checks were so perfunctory that they missed the thin packet, as he had known they would. He was just another lazy good-for-nothing, something half a step up from a Jew or a dog. They let him go. As he walked away, he noticed two men on the other side of the street, dressed in trench coats, observing everyone who came in or went out by the Doukkala Gate.

He walked across the Place el-Mourabetine, leaving the cemetery for lepers on his left as he entered the Boulevard de Safi. Here he looked round, but no one seemed to be watching or following him. He had no idea what was in the packet he carried, nor did he know the identity of the man he was to give it to. He had a name – M. Vert – and a brief description – thirty, pale skin, blond hair, small beard – and reckoned that was all he needed, that and the address to which he was to take the packet. His cover story was that M. Vert had asked for his services to water his garden. It was as plausible as it needed to be.

No Moroccan would be seen in these streets on his own business. Everything in sight had been put there for the French: schools for the education of their children, the post office to take their letters and let them make telephone calls back to the mainland, a cinema to entertain them, cafés where they could sip wine and drink Parisian-style coffee, or smoke Gauloises cigarettes, or feast on ham and other unclean foods. Abd el-Krim despised them, just as he despised the Germans and the British and the Jews, all non-Muslims, all infidels. Let them destroy one another, he thought, and the Muslims will regain their independence.

From time to time he sensed French eyes on him. The nervous ones thought every Moroccan was out to knife them, or throw a bomb into their exclusive clubs. To others, he was simply invisible: if asked ten minutes from now whether a native had passed, they would shake their heads and shrug their shoulders, and say, '*Non, je pense pas. Pourquoi?*'

Here in the Ville Nouvelle, he was a camel out of the desert. Back beyond the ramparts, he could merge with his surroundings, become part of the background in seconds, or assert his individuality moments later. Here, he was nothing, but back there he could become anything. He could win Salima's hand and live with her, and start a family. On one occasion he'd seen her face. That had been during a visit to her mother's house, when she'd let her veil fall, whether by accident or deliberately he could not guess. He'd thought her beautiful, having few female faces to compare hers with, and the image of her that he treasured was made up of that glimpse and a series of movie posters from the Gueliz.

Following a mental map which he'd learned by heart on Moulay Mustafa's instructions, he made his way through a maze of unfamiliar side streets. Moulay Mustafa ran a little Koran school in the street where Abd el-Krim lived. His pupils liked him, and in recent years he'd started teaching them more than the rote recitation of the book: a little mathematics, some proper Arabic, some geography. He'd encouraged Abd el-Krim to come along, said he would teach him for no payment; but his uncle Omar had snorted at the suggestion, and told Abd el-Krim that a saddler needed none of those skills, just nimble fingers, strong hands, and a good eye.

Nonetheless, Abd el-Krim fancied he wanted more than that. It wasn't that he was ashamed of his trade, or the mean circumstances under which he lived: he understood that God considered all men equal, and that Fate had placed him in this position in life and none other. He knew that rebellion was the most heinous of sins in the eyes of God, and that it was not for the likes of himself, unlettered and ignorant, to question the whys and wherefores of the world.

Yet sometimes he would look up from his stitching

and see a Frenchwoman pass, unveiled, her features fine and arrogant, all her attention focused on some item of craftsmanship that had taken its maker days or weeks to create, and for which she intended to pay next to nothing. Or her husband, a Frenchman in a white suit and dark glasses, letting his hand rest nonchalantly on her waist, all the while unconcerned that any passing man might look at her and desire her. At such moments, Abd el-Krim would find himself wishing he were rich or French or anything but a poor saddler's apprentice who would never wear a white suit, or touch a woman in public, or ride in a motorcar with leather seats and chrome lights.

A car just like the one he'd imagined swept past him, its white bonnet and panels highly polished. None of the several passengers looked round: he wasn't worth a second glance. They were only interested in real curiosities, such as the Tuareg men with their camels and heavy veils, or Soussi-speaking Berbers from the Draa Valley, or blacks from beyond the southern desert – anything with an Arabian Nights flavour, that hinted of jewelled turbans or harem girls paraded for a mad Sultan's delight.

36

He almost missed the street name, a small blue-and-white plaque placed high up on a wall: rue du Dr Madelaine. He couldn't read it, of course, but Moulay Mustafa had written it out for him in clear letters, and instructed him in what to look for. Now, he took the paper from his pocket and compared it with the name on the wall. They seemed to match.

A *taxi-baby* went past, its three wheels and tiny interior presenting a total contrast to the vehicle that had just swept by. A young Moroccan woman sat in the back, her face veiled: the maid or cook for the folk preceding her.

It was no trouble to find number 15, the house with blue paint and heaps of bougainvillea. A wall surrounded the little villa, and a wrought-iron gate in the middle allowed Abd el-Krim a glimpse into the formal garden that lay between it and the front door. He tried the gate, but it was locked and he could find no way to open it.

He made to go round the side. As he did so, the *taxi-baby* went past again, empty this time, and travelling in the opposite direction. The little street was deserted. All the men were out at work, in government offices or with the police or military. He realized that it wouldn't do to be caught here like this, sneaking round the back of a French *colon*'s house. He'd be picked up by the gendarmes, arrested as a thief, tossed into the back of a police jeep, and sent to jail by the police court on rue Ibn Hanbal. He'd better hurry.

The rear was overlooked by other houses, and Abd el-Krim imagined a thin-faced French housewife gazing idly through an upstairs window and catching sight of him. She'd have a telephone, a device of which Abd el-Krim had often heard, but which he'd never seen. It was said that every French house had a long speaking tube that went all the way to the *commissariat de police*.

The rear gate opened at a push, and Abd el-Krim went inside. He found himself in a larger garden, a well-tended garden whose flowers and plants had just been watered. The sun was slowly burning the water off the leaves and petals again, but for the moment everything felt cool and moist, and Abd el-Krim breathed in deeply, taking secret pleasure in the fragrance of white jasmine and honeysuckle.

He was tempted to linger. It was the first time he'd ever set foot in a private garden, although he'd caught glimpses of some in the old city, fountains bordered by red and blue and yellow flowers for which he had no name, trees heavy with plums and medlars, graceful bamboos shaking in the slightest of breezes.

The back door opened, and a plump woman in Moroccan dress, but unveiled, came to the door. She must be the housekeeper, he thought.

'*La-bas.*'

He returned her greeting.

'*La-bas, al-hamdu li'llah.*'

'Are you looking for someone?'

He nodded.

'For M'sieu Vert,' he said.

'Is that all?'

'I have a packet for him.'

She stretched her hand out. He noticed she had oily skin, and a large wart on her forehead.

'I'll take it to him.'

He shook his head.

'I was told to put it in his hands directly.'

She seemed to be weighing him up, deciding whether he could be trusted or not.

'Very well, then,' she said. 'Come inside.'

She led him through a large kitchen, then along a corridor that brought them to an open door behind which music was being played. Abd el-Krim had heard Western music a few times, but never quite like this. It was piano music, skilfully played: he recognized the instrument, but the tune meant nothing to him.

The housekeeper ushered him into the room ahead of her.

'Madame . . .' she started.

The music stopped in mid-flow.

Abd el-Krim looked across the room, and his heart stopped when he caught sight of the Frenchwoman, face unveiled, dressed in tight-fitting garments, her hair combed straight on either side of her face. She had spun round on some sort of stool, and she was smiling nervously at him.

'*Al-salam alaykum!*' said Marie-Louise. 'You have come from our mutual friend.'

'*Oui, Madame.* Mou –'

She put her finger to her lips, and he almost thought she winked at him. She looked like all other Frenchwomen to him, yet her smile was warm, and he sensed something more than mere politeness in her welcome.

'Have you brought something for me?' she asked. Her Arabic was far from perfect, but he had never before heard a foreigner speak his language with such a degree of fluency.

He hesitated. He had not expected to find himself with a woman. It was embarrassing.

'My package is for M'sieu Vert. A blond man.'

The woman smiled.

'I'm afraid M. Vert is not here today. He was summoned to an urgent meeting in Fès. But I'm his deputy. You can give the package to me.'

He hesitated, then made up his mind. Something about her convinced him that he could trust her. But he still hesitated.

'I . . . it's under my jellaba . . .'

'And you don't know how to get it out again?' Her smile grew broader.

He nodded.

'I understand. Look, Latifa will show you to a small bathroom where you can remove your jellaba in private. Don't take long. Your packet is urgent.'

He took less than two minutes, returning with the little packet wrapped up neatly in swathes of brown paper.

She asked if he was thirsty. He nodded.

'Latifa will bring you a lemonade. You've no need to worry, it isn't alcoholic.'

Latifa went out to the kitchen. Abd el-Krim wondered if that was her real name.

The Frenchwoman held her hand out, and he gave her the packet. She was not smiling now. This was serious business. He wondered if it had something to do with the war they were fighting in France.

She retired to a little desk set against an alcove, and tore the package open. From it, she took some papers, which she began to read. Latifa returned with a tall glass containing coloured water and ice. He began to drink. He wanted to gulp the delicious concoction down in a few swallows, but given his surroundings, he took small sips instead. The Frenchwoman had put on little tortoiseshell glasses that she wore perched on the end of her pretty nose. Abd el-Krim wondered how old she was: twenty, thirty, thirty-five? She wore a dark blue silk scarf round her neck, fastened with a simple silver brooch.

When she had finished reading, she removed her glasses and laid them on top of the papers, rubbing the bridge of her nose where the spectacles had been resting. She did not speak to him, but once she looked his way and gave him a worried smile. Finally, she took some notepaper from a box on the desk, and a fountain pen from a drawer beneath it.

'I'd like you to take a letter back to our friend. I'll pay you, of course. Keep it under your jellaba, and take care.'

'You don't have to pay me,' he said, wondering what had come over him. Whatever she was involved in, it was no concern of his, no concern of any Muslim. But she had a white neck and pale blue eyes.

'Let me pay this time,' she said. 'I'll speak to our friend about the next. I take it you're willing to come again?'

Of course he was willing. How else was he to relive all this, the house, the garden, the ice-cold drink, the woman with a smile that left him helpless? He dreamed of bringing Salima here, with her father and mother, dreamed of showing her what friends he had, what circles he now moved in.

'Yes,' he said, his mouth and tongue still tingling from the lemon-flavoured drink.

'You must be sure no one gets to know of your visits, except for the man who sent you here. Do you understand? You must not breathe a word to anyone: your uncle, your mother, your sisters, your friends. I'm telling you this because I cannot afford to have you make any mistakes.'

He looked at her, taking in her cleanness, her lack of physical flaws, her unlined face, and he thought Allah must have created her from different clay.

'What would happen if I made a mistake, if someone found out I'd come here?'

'Very likely you would be arrested. After that . . .' She shrugged her narrow shoulders.

'Would I be killed?'

Her eyes widened.

'It's very likely, yes.'

'And you?'

She scarcely hesitated.

'They would execute me, yes, most certainly.'

'I don't mind,' he said. 'They don't frighten me.' He didn't know who 'they' were, but he could not imagine anyone that frightening.

At that very moment, the sound of revving engines came

339

to them from the street outside – two or three large cars being driven very fast.

The woman was the first to react.

'We've got to get you out of here,' she said. He could sense the urgency in her voice, even though it contained not the least trace of panic.

There was a sound of squealing brakes, followed within seconds by car doors opening and slamming shut. Heavy feet sounded on the road, and Abd el-Krim could make out a French voice shouting orders.

'Quickly,' the woman said. 'Go back the way you came. Go as fast as you can – Latifa will show you the way.'

But it was already too late. The men outside had no intention of standing on ceremony. Someone kicked the front door open: three or four heavy kicks sent it crashing out of its lock and hinges, to fall to the floor with a loud bang.

Latifa dragged him bodily from the room, along the corridor and through the kitchen.

'Once you're through the garden,' she said, 'go right almost to the roundabout, then right again and keep on until you come to a church, l'Église des Saints-Martyrs. Go inside; no one will notice you. Find a place to hide until dark, then make your way back to the medina.'

'But . . .'

'No questions.' They were at the door now. 'Save yourself. Run.'

'But the Madame.'

'She can take care of herself. Now go!'

She pushed him out and closed the door. He ran down the garden, no longer beautiful, and opened the gate.

They were already waiting for him. Three French policemen, and a fourth man in a leather coat too heavy for the
weather. A foreigner, and not French. Abd el-Krim had seen
them from time to time before, always on the edge of things.
He'd heard a name whispered in the souks: Gestapo.

37

They took their time with her. At first because they really wanted to find out what and who she knew, but in the end for no other reason than because they wanted to hurt her, to get some sort of revenge for her refusal to talk.

On several occasions, they walked Marie-Louise down the corridor, to the cell in which they were keeping her husband. Vital had been treated even more badly than his wife, and each time she saw him they said they'd spare him if she talked. But she wouldn't talk, so they let her watch while they destroyed Vital before her eyes. It had grown unreal by then, but she was never allowed to lose consciousness for more than a few seconds.

She tried to buy them off with inconsequential things, the location of code books, a small arms dump in the Rif, a listing of code names. This was not what they were after, however, and she was well aware of it. Marie-Louise knew the date of the coming landings, the invasion that would place North Africa in Allied hands. Everyone expected an assault, but no one knew when. Except those in the know, and they included Marie-Louise Guénaud.

Vital knew of Operation Torch, but he had never been made privy to the date of the landings. Each time they brought her to him, Marie-Louise came closer to blurting out what she knew. Perhaps, if there had been a real hope of saving him, or at least of diminishing in some way the suffering he was going through, she might have bent. Oh, how she would have bent. But betraying the operation would have cost thousands, perhaps tens of thousands of lives, and protracted the war and all the suffering it brought, and protected the concentration camps about which she heard so many rumours – and all for nothing.

Their captors weren't going to smile and thank them, weren't going to bring in doctors and nurses to bind up their wounds or replace their missing teeth or mend their fractures. They'd do what they'd planned to do all along, and take them out and shoot them in the nearest yard. Handing over the dates wasn't going to change anything, so she forced herself to blot out the pain as best she could, and ignore the shouting that went on day and night, and not mind the light that never went out, and kiss dear Vital in her thoughts every time they brought her to him.

She was interrogated by three French examiners, but much of the time a fourth man was there, the German Gestapo agent. On the first day, they stripped her naked and shaved her hair, her head hair and her pubic hair, and they placed her on a large chair, a little like one of those electric chairs they used in America to execute people.

At first, the assaults had been mainly verbal, but after

about a day her interrogators had started to administer slaps, then blows to the back of her head, or her breasts or belly. When they'd punched her a bit, they'd made her stand, shouting all the time like madmen, as though they were trying to exorcize some demons out of her, to drag her soul out screaming by their relentless cries and exhortations.

'You know the dates! Tell us! Tell us what you know, and you can go free! Come on, you bitch, out with it, it's just a couple of dates, it won't hurt you, you'll feel better when you've given it up, we'll let you see your husband again. You haven't committed a serious crime, you haven't killed anyone, you haven't betrayed the state. We'll go easy on you, we'll see to it you have light sentences, both of you, you can get back together again after the war. Just tell us the fucking dates! Just pretend we aren't here, just whisper them to the thin air, and you'll be in your husband's arms again.'

When they'd exhausted all that for the time being, they began to torture her in earnest. First, they brought a large machine with dials and buttons, and placed it on a low table next to her. There were wires that dangled from the machine. Two of these were equipped with electrodes. The electrodes were attached to her nipples, and one of the gentlemen questioning her would press a button for a second or ten seconds or thirty seconds before putting his next question. That was how it went, but she never talked, even though she passed out from the pain at twenty seconds or so.

She thought for a long time that nothing could be worse than that, but she was mistaken. There was something much, much worse. The electric box had a third wire, on the end of which was a long metal device. Two women were brought in, Frenchwomen with hard faces and cold hands, and they held her legs wide apart while the German violated her, using the metal cylinder. Then someone would switch on the machine.

They did not try to question her while the current was surging through her. There would have been no point. In that state she couldn't think or feel properly. Everything went into the pain until every nerve end, every cell, every memory became pain. She was aware of her own voice screaming – they didn't gag her, Vital was only a door or two away, her cries carried to him effortlessly – and then came blackness, a blissful nothingness from which she would be slapped awake within seconds.

'It will not happen again if you tell us the dates. Think of your husband. Think of your child.'

She never stopped thinking of them. They'd told her that André was with her sister Béatrice, that Béatrice would keep him by order of the local court, that she would never see him again unless she told them the dates.

It wasn't just the dates, however. She knew more than that. She knew the beaches on which landings would be made, on the west coast, she knew the disposal of battle groups, the identities of the battleships. It had all been for Glaoui Pasha, so he would be in time to co-ordinate his moves with those of the Allies. Now, all that would be for nothing; but the landings would go ahead, the Germans would be driven from North Africa, and the long fight back for Europe would begin. That was why she had to scream and say nothing.

Several times each day she saw a man who did not take part in the proceedings, but who stood by the door of her cell and watched. On the second day, she realized who it was: her brother-in-law Gérard come to see her brought down to size. He never spoke to her, never joined in the questioning, never made himself known to her, but he watched intently, even while they were torturing her.

'*Écoute, Yankee Robert arrive, Robert arrive.*'

The words kept running through her head: in a few days, the BBC would broadcast them, alerting every patriot group in North Africa to make ready for the first wave of Allied troops. All she had to do was give them the message, and she could rest.

'Port Lyautey, Fedala, Safi.'

The names of the entry points were constantly on the tip of her tongue, and she knew how simple it would be to blurt them out, after which she could have peace.

'8 November.' The date lay curled on her tongue, two little words with which she might purchase some sleep.

Marrakech
Sunday, 8 November

'Wake up, Marie-Louise. Wake up.'

She shot out of sleep like a lost child running to its mother, only to find that her mother was the wicked witch she'd been running from all along. She was still in the large chair, the lights in the ceiling were still blazing, and she still ached in every portion of her body. A man's hand was on her shoulder, heavy, shaking her awake. How long had she been asleep?

'Snap out of it, Marie-Louise. You've been out of it long enough.'

She looked round. Gérard was standing beside her. He looked very stern.

'Gérard. What are you doing here?'

'That doesn't concern you. Now, I want you to take hold of my arm and get yourself out of the chair. Do you think you can do that?'

'But . . .' Her mind cleared as much as it was going to. 'What day is it?'

'Saturday.'

'Are you sure?'

'Well, of course I'm sure.'

She made a quick calculation. One day to go. If all went according to plan, the landings would begin tomorrow morning.

She just prayed that one of the back-up measures had gone into action. Or that the so-called M. Vert had managed to get hold of the message after all, and somehow transmit it to El-Glaoui.

'Where am I, Gérard? What is this place?'

He helped her out of the chair. She tottered, and he took most of her weight.

'No matter. We're leaving now. We're going for a short journey.'

'Gérard, where is Vital?'

'You'll see him where we're going. He's gone ahead.'

'What about my little André? Is he all right?'

347

'The boy is with your sister. It's better he stays with her. You've been declared unfit to look after him.'

'Unfit? But I'm his mother. Béatrice doesn't love him like I do. She can't possibly . . .'

'It's too late to argue. There's no time. Come along.'

And he half-dragged, half-supported her out of the cell and into the short corridor she'd been in whenever she was taken to visit Vital.

Outside the building, a black Renault was waiting for them in a little courtyard. Gérard pushed her inside, onto the rear seat, and got in after her. A policeman appeared from inside the building and got into the driving seat.

They drove out of the courtyard and onto the street. Marie-Louise recognized right away where she was, at the police station behind the church, only a street or two from her own home. Moments later, they passed the top of her street.

The rue Circulaire took them east, then north past the Muslim cemetery, and Marie-Louise guessed they were headed towards the prison, a little further up. As they drove, they were passed again and again by jeeps and heavy lorries, grey military vehicles that thundered into the distance, driving urgently, as though needed at some battle.

'You're sure this is Saturday?' she asked.

Gérard smiled at her grimly. He would not give her the satisfaction of knowing D-day had arrived, that Allied troops had landed, and that battles were raging to the west as General Noguès fought to retain control. It was the same picture in Tunisia and Algeria. The tide was turning, and Gérard was getting ready to turn with it.

He just had some unfinished business to deal with, then his uniform would go in the nearest bin and he would transform himself once again into the grape farmer he had always been.

'Why would it be anything else?' he asked. Up ahead, the prison was coming into sight. More lorries passed them, their rears crammed with the faces of *tirailleurs*, Moroccan troops on whose loyalty the authorities were suddenly dependent.

They turned into the prison, and Gérard hurried her out of the car and in through a door she recognized from her visits to Aziz. She smelled the familiar stench of fear and loneliness. Gérard hurried her along a corridor, then into a passage between two rows of cells. Men sat or stood on either side, damned into blank-eyed submission, their faces turned to her, her degradation visible in their expressions.

They passed the cell in which Aziz had been kept, the condemned cell, and she knew all at once where they were taking her.

Gérard tugged open a door, and pushed her through. Suddenly, she found herself outside, in a drab little yard. She'd been here before, on the other side. Vital, his hands bound behind his back, his white shirt stained with blood, his collar wide open, stood a few yards away.

The guillotine seemed like the only steadfast thing in a world gone crazy. Its tall side-struts seemed to go up for ever into the blue sky, as if it was the world tree, the linchpole of the universe.

Vital grew aware of the new arrivals, and turned to face her. They had beaten him badly. His entire face was nothing but a mat of bruises, blue, black and yellow, and his eyes were tiny red coals in swollen sockets. He managed a smile, and his lips formed the words '*Je t'aime*'. The next moment, the executioner stepped behind him and led him to the *bascule*, where he and his assistant strapped him tightly.

Just then, Marie-Louise noticed a movement somewhere on the other side of the guillotine, and realized that there was a witness to the proceedings after all. Béatrice was sitting on a little stool, her cheeks white, her eyes fixed on Vital. All it would have taken to complete the picture would have been knitting needles and a hat with a cockade. Yet, when Marie-Louise looked more closely, she could see in her sister's eyes not the hatred she might have expected, but fear.

There wasn't even time to offer up a prayer. The *bascule* was run down and forward, Vital's neck was clamped in the *lunette*, an order was given, and the heavy blade came down with a crash. Béatrice shuddered and turned her eyes away.

It took about five minutes to remove Vital's head and body. Marie-Louise had no tears left. Then, just as the executioner came for her, she heard bells. She knew them at once. They'd been familiar to her from Sunday to Sunday throughout all her time in Marrakech: the bells of Saints-Martyrs church, calling the French to Mass. It was Sunday after all, she thought in triumph, and she'd kept her promise. The Allies had landed.

'Sunday, the eighth of November,' she said, smiling at Gérard as she was pulled past. 'May you and my sister live for ever in hell.'

The rest took only seconds. The last thing she saw was a pool of blood on the spot where Vital's head had fallen.

In the Heart
of the Sands

38

Marrakech

Monestier opened the door, in order to leave the others time in which to do something about Nick. The knocking could only mean the police were outside, and the doctor was not surprised to see the small policeman, Laghzaoui, standing in front of him. He recognized him from Justine's description, and he could tell from the way he swayed slightly that he had managed to make himself drunk. The chances were that he wasn't used to drink, perhaps he'd never been drunk in his life before.

'I want the woman,' he said in Arabic.

'She isn't here.'

'I saw her go in. She was with her brother. If it was her brother.'

'That was last night. She told me about you. I think you want to be very careful. You could get reported. Marcel is here, if you'd like to speak to him.'

'Who's Marcel?'

'Her brother. I told you, she's not here.'

'I have a warrant.'

'Warrant? What for?'

'To search the house. She's hiding the Englishman here, we're sure of it. You have to let me in.'

Without waiting, he pushed past Monestier into the courtyard. The doctor ran after him, wishing he knew exactly what was going on inside.

Laghzaoui reached the inner doorway, which lay open, revealing the interior of the house.

'I'll do a deal,' he said, turning his head and catching Monestier with his glance. He wasn't too intoxicated, the doctor reckoned, but that only made him more dangerous.

'Deal?'

'Give me half an hour with the woman, twenty minutes, as long as it takes, and the Englishman can go fuck himself for all I care.'

'There's no Englishman here,' said Monestier.

'Fuck you. Who are you, anyway? I've not seen you before.'

'I'm Dr Monestier. I run the free clinic. Everybody knows me here. Don't take liberties with me. Don't try to bribe or threaten me. Your job's on the line. Believe me.'

'Stop talking so hard. I'm going inside. Don't try to stop me.'

At that moment, Justine came down the stairs and walked towards them.

'Inspector,' she said. 'How delightful to see you. I can see you've been imbibing. Won't you come in and have another? I have some very fine whisky: I'm sure a man like you will appreciate it.'

Laghzaoui wasn't at all sure what to do. The room into which he was bidden swayed uncomfortably. Somehow, it was worse being inside. The heat of the day had gathered itself in the room, and not even the large fan that turned in one corner made much impact.

The policeman went up to the fan and tried to cool himself by standing in front of it. He was sobering fast, now that he had tested his nerve by forcing his way in.

'The Inspector says he has a warrant to search this house,' said Monestier to Justine.

'Really. And just what would you be looking for, Inspector?'

'I've told the doctor. He lied: he said you weren't here. Lying to the police is an offence. I could have him arrested, I could have you arrested as an accomplice. But I've already told the doc—'

'It would be so much better if you sat down.'

'I don't want to sit down.'

'Not even for a drink?'

'I'll drink with you. I told the doc. I said, I think we can do a deal. The Englishman's nothing to me. A nice arrest, that's all, if it came to it. But nothing more. You, on the other hand, I like. I don't know what you charge your usual clients, but your friend's freedom should be worth as much. I can put in a report saying I've searched the house, that the Englishman isn't here.'

She steered him to a long divan. His knees wobbled slightly as he sat.

'You think I'm a prostitute? That I sell myself for money?'

'Don't you? Why else would you be living on your own like this, hanging about in hotels with foreigners, wearing clothes like that?'

'In Europe, all this would be considered normal.'

'We aren't in Europe.'

'We're not that far away. Consider this a European house. You can have a drink here. No one will mind. Dr Monestier is a wonderful barman.' She smiled conspiratorially at the doctor. 'Aren't you, Doctor?'

Monestier, who had never made a cocktail in his life, nodded his head obediently.

'His cocktails are famous,' Justine went on. 'Tell me, have you ever had a margarita?'

Laghzaoui shook his head bemusedly.

'Then the doctor will make one for you.'

She looked at Monestier.

'Doctor, take what you need from the cupboard, and make up your potion in the kitchen. Ask Marcel if he can help you.'

Monestier, catching her drift at last, nodded and left the room.

With his departure, Justine sat down facing her visitor. She was shaking all over, yet managed to conceal it. What if he got violent again?

'I still think I'm offering a fair deal,' Laghzaoui muttered.

'And what's that, exactly?'

'I get to sleep with you, and in return your English friend is free to go home.'

'Free to leave Morocco?'

He shook his head.

'I can't do anything about that. They're looking for him at the airports. I can't interfere.'

'Do you know anyone who can?'

He thought for a few moments.

'You'd have to go high up,' he said. 'A lot higher than the likes of me. Chief Inspector Knidiri, he might do. But you'd have to offer him a lot. More than what I've just asked you for. He can always get women, all the women he wants, a man in his position. But he'll demand money, a great deal of money. If you have enough to pay him with, your friend can walk through any airport he chooses and fly home.'

'I don't think I have that sort of money. And although I'm sure my sexual prowess is second to none, I don't suppose I'm all that much a match for the dear Chief Inspector's harem. In any case, I've already told you, I'm not a prostitute, so that leaves me rather without resources, don't you think?'

Just then, the door opened and Marcel appeared, carrying a tray. On the tray stood a large cocktail glass filled with bright pink liquid. The young doctor smiled nervously as he handed it to Laghzaoui.

'This is my brother, Marcel,' said Justine. 'You met him last night.'

The policeman nodded. He had not forgotten Marcel.

In all likelihood, the drink tasted terrible. Marcel had concocted it ad hoc from the bottles Monestier had brought in from the drinks cabinet. He had added copious but not – he hoped – fatal quantities of the sleeping draught from Nick's bedside table.

Laghzaoui, determined not to lose face in front of these sophisticated Europeans, and eager to prove to the woman that he was as much a man as any she knew, sipped hard at his drink.

'It packs some punch, eh?' said Justine.

The policeman nodded in full agreement.

'They say it goes down best if you take it in one long swallow. You'll get the full effect that way.'

Laghzaoui hesitated, but was embarrassed to admit to inexperience. Taking a slow breath, he put the glass to his lips and swallowed the contents down. The immediate effect was that he felt as if he'd gone on fire. The taste was bad enough, but the sensations in his throat and chest were something he'd never experienced in his life. Did Europeans really enjoy this stuff?

She sat beside him, smiling, encouraging, watching closely. There'd been enough alcohol in the glass to have an effect on anyone not used to it. He looked round, shook his head a few times, and tried to paw her. She pushed his hands away gently, but they came back again each time, albeit increasingly uncoordinated and slow.

It took several minutes, but in the end he went under and fell sprawled on the divan.

Marcel, who'd been standing just outside the doorway, came back in and crossed to the policeman. He took his pulse, looked into his eyes, and pronounced him unconscious.

'What do we do now?' asked Justine. 'I can't just keep him here.'

Monestier appeared in the doorway.

'Let Marcel and myself take care of that. I'll hire a 4-by-4, and Marcel will drive him south, into the Sahara. He'll take a day or two to recover from his final dose of Marcel's knockout drops. It's very likely he'll wake with no memory of this evening's escapade. If he does remember, he may be too embarrassed to mention it to anyone.'

'You can't just leave him in the desert.'

Monestier shrugged.

'Why not? He'd have raped you, and God knows what else. But Marcel won't just abandon him. I have influence in the deep south, across the Mauretanian border.'

'I didn't think anybody lived down there. Except . . .' She looked at him, astonishment in her eyes.

'I spent a lot of time there many years ago. I still go down once or twice a year. They know me. They trust me. If I ask them for a favour, they'll provide it. They'll keep Monsieur Laghzaoui for as long as I ask them to. For the rest of his life, if need be.'

'As a slave?'

'Yes, of course, that's their way. They'll treat him as a slave. Life will be harsh for him, just as it's harsh for them. But they don't use cruelty. He'll come to no lasting harm. It may even do him good.'

'What about Nick?' she asked. 'Those people from the hotel will still be looking for him.'

Monestier nodded.

'Yes, I know. But let's take care of this first. We'll sort Nick out tomorrow.'

39

Marcel left with his charge early the following morning. A radio broadcast said winds were gathering in the Sahara, and sand had started to lift into plumes along the Erg Chech and throughout Tiris Zemmour, as far north as the 'Ain Ben Tili spring.

Nick lay in bed, listening to the flies buzz. A *harmattan* was coming, Justine said, and with it the red sand of the desert. Marrakech seemed still, its sounds muted, its people subdued.

'Is it safe for Marcel to be going into the desert with this starting?' he asked Monestier, who had come to dress his wounds.

The doctor grinned.

'Of course it is. He'll have done his business and be back here before the *harmattan* sets in.'

'You can be sure of that?'

'Not sure. The desert always holds surprises. But I'm pretty sure.'

'And how long before Laghzaoui makes his escape?'

Monestier used a long strip of plaster to hold the bandage in place.

'There,' he said. 'You'll be walking properly in a day or two, or I shall want to know why.'

'I asked how long it will be before the policeman makes a run for it.'

'Oh, you needn't worry about that. He won't escape. A man like that, he's been brought up on tales of the deep desert and the nomads who rule in it. He'll know that running away is suicide. He'll stay there till this is all over and you're safely home. Then we'll see about bringing him back. But if I decide to leave him there, provided I pay my dues, he'll stay there for the rest of his life. If I thought he was likely to prove a continuing threat to Justine, he wouldn't come out. But I think a year or so with the Blue Men should cure him of any thoughts in that direction.'

'Blue Men?'

'They dress in indigo clothes, and the men wear veils, not the women. They're close relations of the Tuareg. Perhaps they are Tuareg. No one really knows.'

'You say they're nomads?'

'Semi-nomads now. The ones I visit live in a town called Khufra. Most of it is buried beneath the sand. They still prefer to travel by camel. They are Muslims, but worship other gods as well. Don't worry, Laghzaoui will be safe with them.'

Monestier went away, and Justine came up from the kitchen, where she'd been preparing lunch.

'We could make love,' she said. 'Or I could punch your sore leg.'

'Before lunch?'

'I'd heard about you English. Strictly bedtime, strictly

intercourse, strictly five minutes. The man comes if he's able, in about half a minute, the woman – what is it?'

'Lies back and thinks of England. Not much fun in that now, though. Railway disasters. Foot and mouth disease. The royal family. The Millennium Dome.'

'Did your wife lie back and think of England?'

'My wife was French.'

'She can't have been if you don't know about the pre-*déjeuner*.'

'I was never home for lunch. We had the children at week-ends. Not even the French can do anything about that.'

'Most couples form little circles and rotate the children, Saturdays and Sundays. There are also nannies, babysitters and hotels. Nor should you forget early afternoons, late afternoons, early evenings . . . Nicholas, there are no chil-dren and no policemen, one of our doctors is on his way to the desert, the other is out there saving the sick. I can be rough and shake your leg about a lot, or I can be gentle and give you a blow job that will be the envy of all Marrakech. Which is it to be?'

'Can you give me the choices again?'

'You say your son brought photocopies of this material to Morocco?'

Monestier had come to look in on Nick before start-ing his evening clinic. Nick had demanded to be allowed downstairs, where there would be room for him to walk about, but the doctor had vetoed it. The stairs between the house's two storeys were narrow and twisting, as befitted a building of its antiquity, and Monestier feared an accident were Nick to risk climbing down before he was ready.

Instead, they'd started to talk about what could be done in the next few days.

'Yes. It was in one of his letters.'

'Which means the originals are . . . where?'

'In my house in Oxford. Peter made copies of what looked like the most important ones, and left all the originals behind.'

'Can't we get them out?' asked Justine. 'There must be more. We have to know why Pete and Daisy went to Ouarzazate.'

'It may not be in the papers,' Nick said. 'He'd been asking questions from Tangier onwards. The papers will have taken him only so far. Someone may have told him about Ouarzazate.'

'Well, we don't know that,' said Monestier. 'And, if necessary, we can always try to track down some of the people he spoke to.'

'Can your brother get into your house?' asked Justine. She sat on the edge of the bed, holding his hand. The afternoon had turned out better than she could have imagined.

'Yes. I think it's time we made a phone call.'

Justine wrote down the number he gave her and took it downstairs.

'Hello?'

'Is this Tim Budgeon?'

'Yes. Who's this?'

'I'm a friend of your brother's. He asked me to call you.'

'Why, what's wrong? Why can't he come to the phone himself?'

'He had a little accident a few days ago. It's nothing, just a small fracture; but it means he can't get to this phone.'

'I'm coming out. Where is he? He's still in Morocco? That's where you're calling from, isn't it?'

'Yes, but I can't say where.'

'Something's wrong, isn't it?'

'Yes, something's wrong.'

'Then I'm coming out.'

'Mr Budgeon, please listen to me. You must not try to travel to Morocco under any circumstances. Trust me. Your brother is safe with me.'

'What about Peter? What happened to him and Daisy? Did Nick find out anything?'

'They ran into trouble. Your brother and I are trying to sort things out, but we need your help.'

'Help?'

'Have you got a key to Nick's house?'

'Of course. I've been in most days – looking after his blessed plants. By the way, you haven't told me your name?'

'Justine. Believe me, your brother is safe with me. Now, here's what I want you to do . . .'

40

There was more than one border here, but to the nomads they meant nothing. Algeria, Mauretania, Morocco, the Western Sahara all blended into one expanse of shattered stone and varicoloured sand. They knew the names of sand seas, of the great dunes, and the snow-capped mountains that reared up from time to time amidst the sand. They could plot a route from one oasis to the next, from a half-hidden well to one even more well concealed by the shifting sands.

Marcel had been taught to think like them. By ignoring the main tourist trails that took bored foreigners in search of a day's or a week's adventure in difficult conditions but without real danger, he was able to cross into Mauretania and start travelling south in search of his Blue Men.

He caught sight of the first traces towards late afternoon. Laghzaoui was showing signs of struggling out of his sleep. Marcel considered giving him a further dose of the drug, but decided against it. Instead, he tied the policeman up firmly in the rear of the 4-by-4. As he prepared to drive off, he noticed a small black flag fluttering in the growing wind.

It would have been placed there to mark a stone well. He restarted the engine and drove on.

Half an hour later, a figure appeared on the crest of a dune. He was dressed in blue, and a long *litham* was wound about the bottom half of his face, leaving only his eyes visible. Marcel parked and climbed up to him. The Tuareg remained still, watching him come. Beside him, a camel was crouching, its head turned away from the wind, as still as its master, its eyes, like his, fixed on Marcel.

The man recognized him. Marcel had treated an abscess in his leg the year before.

They spoke in broken Arabic, the Tuareg's coloured by Algerian dialect and his native Tamachek tongue.

'My name is Ajeder,' he said. 'I know you. You fixed my leg last year.'

'Yes, I remember. How is the leg?'

'Good. I have no problem walking or sitting on the camel.'

'I'm pleased to hear it. Dr Monestier has sent me to take a look at everyone who is sick. And I have a favour to ask.'

The small town was all but buried in sand. Underneath, the sand was of various colours, blue, purple and green, but on top it was a uniform shade of ochre. The small mud houses, joined together by roofed-over passages, seemed like the shells of some great desert animals that had burrowed their way beneath the surface in search of coolness or darkness or just to die.

The Blue Men had made this their home, but from time to time the men would go out to travel among the dunes. Some ventured north into Morocco as far as Marrakech, to trade or to let their women dance the *guedra* for rich tourists, others headed south or east to a different Africa, to meet with other Tuareg.

The women, their faces unveiled, smiled at him, and little children scampered about his feet. Laghzaoui, who had come almost fully awake, dragged himself along behind him, prodded from time to time by Ajeder, who carried a long staff as though designed for the purpose.

They were taken directly to the house of the headman, an elderly Tuareg called Awinagh, who was the town's spiritual and temporal leader. Not for the first time, Marcel was taken by surprise by the bright blue eyes that shone out above the old man's tightly wrapped veil.

He too remembered Marcel, who made his greetings with the obsequiousness required in approaching a man of his rank, lowering his eyes and adopting the posture of a servant. They talked while tea was brought, then drank while speaking of the ailments that had befallen members of the group in the past year.

The problem with Laghzaoui was settled in a few moments: interfering officials were a perpetual source of irritation to the freewheeling Tuareg. Awinagh would have done almost anything for Monestier: he had known his father before him, and remembered him with affection. The policeman was led away to begin his year in slavery. He would be kept as part of Awinagh's household, never beaten or mistreated, fed the same food as his master's family, given the same clothes to wear, spoken to with kindness. But for a year he would be kept away from mischief.

'There will be a caravan twelve months from now,' the old man said. 'The men will travel as far as Marrakech and give him his manumission. When their trade is done, they will vanish back into the sands.'

'I thought the caravans were a thing of the past.'

The *immeghar* nodded.

'For long centuries we ruled the sands. Two or three times a year, our caravans would bring treasures from the south, ostrich feathers and ivory and precious woods and gold, luxuries for the cities of the north. And our riders would return with salt, great blocks of salt that they had bought measure for measure with gold. And then your people came with your great ships and your railways and your roads, and the caravans dwindled year by year. I am the last to have seen the great ones go by, a thousand camels and more. Now a few dozen travel the sands with what little we can find to trade. In my sons' time it will end, and the Blue Men will no longer walk the great desert from end to end. Some will be forced to learn Arabic, and others will be made to remove the veil, and our stories will die out.'

Marcel said nothing. No apologies would bring back the caravans.

'Will Dr Monestier come this year?'

'I hope so. At present, he is much preoccupied.'

'What is happening up there?'

'In Morocco, or in Marrakech?'

'Marrakech.'

Using the simplest of terms, Marcel told him what he could. The story seemed strangely remote from where he was sitting. Out here in the desert, a man could run for miles and miles and, if he knew where he was going, evade capture for years if necessary. Or find himself inexplicably lost between one blink of the eye and the next, and wander in diminishing circles to die in the blood tints of the setting sun.

When he came to the story of Marie-Louise and Vital, the *sheikh* stiffened as though Marcel had paraded old ghosts in front of his half-veiled eyes. The Frenchman continued to tell his tale, aware that the old man now watched him with feverish interest. When he came to the end, he explained that something was still missing, that the final act had been played out in darkness somewhere, and that he knew nothing more.

'I knew them,' Awinagh said, a blunt statement of fact.

'You mean they travelled down here?'

The *immeghar* shook his head.

'No, but I used to go up beyond the sands, to Marrakech. That is where I met this Dr Monestier's father, and it was he who introduced me to them on one occasion. I remember they were extremely interested in the desert, and I wondered at the time if that was on account of the war the French were fighting. I never understood that war, like all the wars of the *Nasranis*. They tell me millions of men and women died in it. I find it hard to believe that there are so many people in the world, let alone that so many could die and still leave the world populated.'

'Do you know which year this was? The year you met them?'

'We don't watch the years like you *Nasranis*. We are concerned only with the seasons, and with the coming and going of generations. I am sorry the young couple died. They seemed good people. What will the Englishman do now?'

Marcel explained that he would probably look for some way to go back to Ouarzazate, that Nick was certain the solution to the mystery of Pete's death lay there and nowhere else.

As he said all this, Awinagh's posture changed. Suddenly, the old man got to his feet. He took a few paces towards Marcel and placed his hands on his shoulders, dragging him to his feet.

'Whatever happens,' he shouted, 'you must prevent this man from going to Ouarzazate. He doesn't know what's there. Hurry, you must leave now. You must drive back to Marrakech at once!'

Marcel did not know what to do. The sun had gone down, and the desert would be enveloped in darkness. He could hear the crying of the wind as it built up outside. Already, clouds of sand would have covered the sky, blotting out the moon and stars, and blotting out the faintest traces of his track.

'Hurry,' said the old man. 'You must hurry. Before it's too late.'

41

The next day, Monestier brought guns. He didn't say where he'd found them, and neither Nick nor Justine embarrassed him by asking. Nick, who'd handled enough small arms in his life, checked the pistols over.

'I'm impressed,' he said. 'Whoever lent or sold these to you knew his business.'

The little armoury consisted of two Heckler & Koch MP-15s, a Browning Hi-Power that looked as though it had come fresh from its packaging, and a backup in the form of a wartime-era Luger. There was enough ammunition to serve the needs of an army brigade.

'What are these for?' asked Nick.

'We're going to Ouarzazate,' said the doctor. 'There's no point in messing about, they'll just run us ragged. We confront Pete's killers with the facts, we apply some pressure, and we clear your name.'

'You make it sound simple,' said Justine. She was playing with the Browning, delighted by the feel of it, the smoothness of its action. It was the first gun she had ever held.

Nick took it from her gently.

'You should never play with a loaded gun,' he said.

'But surely . . .'

'You should be able to tell from the weight. The magazine is still in the handle, and the safety is set on "fire". Like this.'

He lifted the pistol in a single action, took aim at an old pot in the courtyard, and fired. The explosion rippled through the little house, and carried out into the alleyways beyond.

He put the gun down and turned to Monestier.

'Thanks for the guns. I hope we won't have to use them, but in a situation like this, you never know. Out of curiosity, where did the Luger come from?'

'The Luger is mine. My father gave it to me: it was something he picked up during the war, or maybe afterwards.'

'Really? There must have been an awful lot of guns circulating here after the Desert War.'

'Most of it went to Egypt, I think. But some trickled this way.'

'And your father . . . what happened to him after the war?'

'Oh, he stayed on here in Marrakech. He never reopened his clinic. It remained shut until I opened it again in 1964, after I finished my medical studies at Montpelier.'

'Was your father still alive then?'

'Yes, he . . . What am I saying? He'd been dead a few years by then. He left the clinic to me in his will. Now, what do we do about Ouarzazate?'

'I have an idea,' said Nick. He turned to Justine.

'Justine, how good is your Arabic?'

'You mean my Moroccan Arabic?'

'Is there a difference?'

'Of course there is, you silly man. I'll tell you about it sometime. What is it you want to do? Speak or write?'

'Speak. I want you to make a phone call.'

'In that case, Moroccan. Which I speak better than French. Who do you want me to speak to?'

'To Si M'hamed Abdellatif el-Mokri. He's the mayor of Ouarzazate. I think it was he who tried to have me killed when I was there.'

'And you want to phone him?' Justine seemed perplexed.

'Can you suggest anyone else?'

Outside, the desert was changing shape. Dunes were flattened or thrown up, landmarks were obliterated and created.

Inside, the Tuareg huddled in their mud and pisé dwellings. They had heard the wind before, had long ago accustomed themselves to it. But they feared it all the same, they feared the changes it would bring to their world.

In the *immeghar*'s house, the old man filled the smoky room with memories. A group of his best warriors had gathered about him. They spoke in Tamachek now, and Marcel was left to gnaw at his worries and wish the wind would die down.

Against the rear wall, the men had piled their weapons. Old rifles, for the most part, hand-me-downs from fathers and uncles, ex-service rifles from the Desert War, pistols from every era of French rule, revolvers liberated from the Foreign Legion – all of them polished, cared for, and as deadly as they had ever been.

The wind howled. The Tuareg talked. In the morning, the sun would rise, and perhaps the wind would die down.

*   *   *

Later that day, the fax in Justine's study started pushing out paper. Most of it was junk. Some of it was golden. They passed the sheets from hand to hand, reading silently, or at times aloud, picking out the most important passages, gradually slotting this fact or that into the framework they had already built for whatever had happened all those years ago.

When they came to an end, each of them remained seated, lost in thought. Monestier, who had such immediate ties to that past, sat for a long time, visibly distressed.

'I think it's time for that phone call,' Nick said to Justine. 'I think we're ready to go to Ouarzazate. You know what to say?'

'Just what you told me.'

'When you've finished, I'd like to make a call of my own, if you don't mind.'

'To your brother?'

He shook his head.

'Let's just say it's to an old friend.'

42

The rendezvous was set for noon, on top of the Mansour Eddahbi Dam, a barrage across the Draa river valley, about ten miles from Ouarzazate. It was deliberately chosen because it provided an exposed location that could be approached by road from either side.

As they prepared to leave, Nick turned to Justine.

'How do you know he'll take the bait? Or that he won't just send some heavies down there to wait for whoever turns up?'

'I spelled it out to him, Nick. If there's the slightest funny business, he goes down first. Funny business includes not turning up on time. It also covers heavies and my not returning to Marrakech for any reason.'

'He knows what we want him to do?'

'No. He doesn't know who I am, but I've told him enough to make him take me seriously. He'll be listening to what I have to say. But I want him in the dark for the next few hours. I want him worried and ready to do a deal.'

The journey to Ouarzazate went without incident. Monestier had hired the ambulance again, and Nick was made to lie in the back, his hands and face bandaged, breathing (or so it seemed) through tubes inserted in his nostrils. There had been two police checkpoints, one on the outskirts of the city, the other where the road turned up into the Tizi N'Tichka pass. On each occasion, Monestier had produced documents indicating that his patient, M'Barek Bekkaï, was being taken home to Ouarzazate to die. Justine sat in the back, dressed in a nurse's uniform, and gave menacing glances that warned the police from interfering with a badly burned and dying man.

They arrived with plenty of time to spare. The morning sun hung like a pale orange in a stark blue sky. The sandstorm had come and gone, leaving an ochre hue on everything but the water in the lake below the barrage. Even the palm trees had a faint golden sheen, and the surfaces of roads, and the white domes of the palm-fringed *marabouts* that stood out in the landscape like strange ships from other planets. Relieved to find the world returned to itself, a host of birds sang, dippers and lanners and spotted sandgrouse. A flock of trumpeter finches lifted from a palm grove and skimmed across the lake, where a lone osprey was wetting its wings in celebration of a day without sand or wind. Monestier and Nick had come armed with binoculars, both as cover (birdwatchers were common here) and as a means of scouting the surrounding territory.

The top of the dam formed a narrow walkway with the risk of a steep fall on either side, down into the Draa river to the south, or the head of the reservoir to the north. Monestier and Nick climbed out of the ambulance and went in search of cover from which to watch both ends of the dam. Meanwhile, Justine found a small palm grove in which to park the ambulance, and changed out of her nurse's dress.

The sandstorms had sent most tourists scuttling northwards. The lake and river were devoid of sightseers, and the golf club, whose greens stood out incongruously against the barren landscape, was hardly occupied. Boys with what looked like vacuum cleaners were busy hoovering the fairways, in order to bring the course back to its carefully maintained condition of perfect greenness. Birds perched on the flags at each hole. A lone golfer, accompanied by a caddy on a slow-moving cart, worked his way from green to green.

Si M'hamed turned up five minutes early. He drove in from the Ouarzazate direction in a Mercedes. He was the only occupant. Getting out of the car, he looked round in all directions, saw no one, and shrugged. He then made his way to the centre of the dam. Even at some distance, he still appeared a large man, the sort of man who could swipe an adversary clean off the dam, to fall, already unconscious, into the waters below.

The arrangement was that Justine would start negotiations, while Nick and Monestier continued to look out for any backup the mayor might have ordered to follow him.

She emerged from cover, blinking in the sunshine. El-Mokri really did seem to have come alone. But then, she reflected, she had spelled out for him very clearly the consequences of any kind of double-cross.

'Monsieur el-Mokri?' She reached out a hand towards him, but he did not reciprocate.

'I trust you've fulfilled the conditions I set for this meeting,' she continued.

'Perfectly. Can you tell me exactly what this is all about?'

'In a few minutes, we'll be joined by two of my companions. They may be able to answer some of your questions. The bottom line is that we know about the money and arms your father diverted to Ouarzazate during the world war.'

El-Mokri looked at her in amazement, then burst out laughing.

'That money belonged to him. He had every right to keep it where he could be sure it was safe. What else was he going to do? Give it to the Germans? Hand it over to the Sultan, perhaps? Watch the bastard spend it on helping Jews make themselves rich at our expense? Even if you do know all about this – and I very much doubt it – what can you do? Who can you tell?'

'The people who lost the money in the first place: the British and the Americans. It was a lot of money. And nobody likes to be cheated.'

'You do realize that, even if any money were handed over – which it won't be – your friends in high places won't pay you a single *sou* for your help. I can reward you better than that. Or I can make sure you never see Marrakech again, or your little house in Derb el-Hajar.'

'How do you . . . ?'

'Did you think you were playing cat and mouse with me? That all you had to do was turn up here and threaten me, and that I'd pay you whatever it is you want? You should have found out more about me before you set all this in motion. I'm a powerful man. An influential man.'

Hearing footsteps behind him, he turned. Nick was about ten yards away.

'What does he say?' asked Nick.

'That he's an influential man.'

Nick nodded, then drew a gun from his pocket, one of the Heckler & Kochs.

'Listen to me,' he said, switching the conversation to French. 'My name is Nicholas Budgeon. We've met before, not very long ago. You swore to me then that nothing bad had happened to my son Peter and his girlfriend Daisy while they were in Ouarzazate.'

'Yes, yes, I know all this. I gave you my answer then. I'm surprised you have the impertinence to come back, and in such a shameful manner.'

'That night,' Nick went on, as though no one had spoken, 'I was taken to the Kasbah Tifeltout, where I was shown their bodies. Someone had stabbed them to death. I didn't know why then, but I think I know why now. And I hold you personally responsible.'

'Give it up, policeman. You offend me, before God you do. *La'anakallah.*'

'He just asked God to curse you.'

Monestier had arrived from the other end. He glanced down at the water on both sides of them.

'Dizzying, isn't it? A person could slip, fall over and drown. So it's best nobody makes a sudden movement.'

'I was asking Mr el-Mokri about Peter. I don't think he knew I was shown the bodies.'

'Oh, I'm not so sure. I told him – didn't I, M'hamed?'

As he spoke, the doctor defied his own warning and stepped forward suddenly, putting his arm round Justine's

381

neck, drawing his pistol from his pocket and putting it to her temple.

Nick made to run at him, but el-Mokri blocked his way.

The doctor spoke again. 'It's best you just hand your gun over to our friend. We have a little journey to make, and I don't want trouble.'

'I don't understand.'

'If there's time, I'll tell you the rest. For the moment, hand the gun over before he pushes you off the edge. I'd shoot you both here and toss you into the water, but you'd just bob up to the surface in a week or two.'

Broken by this unimagined betrayal, Nick handed the gun to the mayor. El-Mokri took it, pointed it at Nick's head, and nodded towards the western end of the dam.

As they reached the bank, a long black car appeared from nowhere. Two doors opened. The windows were heavily tinted. They got inside, the doors slammed shut, and the car described a tight circle before heading back towards Ouarzazate.

43

In Marrakech, Laghzaoui's unhappy colleague came to knock on Justine's front door. The people of the *derb* heard the banging, and turned a deaf ear to it. They didn't know who he was, or what he had come for; and although every last one of them was desperately curious to know what had been going on at the Frenchwoman's house, they also knew that it would be improper of them to ask. Their children played up and down the alleyway, and stray dogs investigated it for scraps. The policeman gave up in the end and walked away, wondering what the hell had become of his number two.

Inside the house, Napoléon settled down for a nap, after filling his belly from the bowl Justine had set out for him in the living room. He licked his paws and smoothed down his fur, then rolled himself into a suitably groomed ball.

As he did so, there came the sound of a telephone ringing. It rang four times, then stopped. Moments later, something clicked and the fax began to squeeze out the first of half a dozen sheets, the last pages of Nathalie Budgeon's document box, six sheets that had lain hidden until now in a drawer in Peter Budgeon's desk. One by one, they slid onto a tray, where they remained, waiting for someone to pick them up and read them. Tim Budgeon had added a seventh sheet, on which he had scribbled the following note:

Nick,
   This is why Nathalie killed herself. Not for all that went before, not for Gérard's and Béatrice's betrayal, dreadful as it was, not for the terror of Marie-Louise's unspeakable fate, but for this. Ring me, for God's sake. Surely this can't still be going on.
   Tim

They had plenty of petrol, but nowhere to drive to. Their food would last another five or six days, longer if they were frugal. Marcel wondered if aeroplanes ever ventured across this tract, but there hadn't been one all day. In order to conserve fuel, they'd been obliged to shut the engine off, which meant there was no air-conditioning. The Tuaregs had brought sheets from which to make a tent, and now they all sat inside, waiting for the sun to go down.

After much deliberation, it had been decided that speed was the most important thing, and Marcel had agreed to drive straight back to Marrakech, bringing with him three armed Tuareg. It had all seemed very simple at first. The Tuareg knew the desert, and how to shift in it and find directions, while Marcel's jeep provided them with a method of transport considerably faster than their camels. Together, they'd be able to make the journey safely, and in good time.

They didn't set out until the storm had died down enough to make travel feasible. Visibility was good, even if light winds were still causing fine drifting of the top sands. Only a couple of hours later did Marcel realize what this meant: the tracks he'd imagined leaving behind the jeep just weren't there: every trace of their passage had been obliterated by the gentle wind. Wherever they had come to, it was, as his Arab friends would have said, the Qalb el-Badiyya, the very heart of the desert.

At first it hadn't seemed that important, but as time passed and they did not enter the region of scrub and stone that would have led back to southern Morocco, Marcel began to worry. What was worse, it soon became apparent that his Tuareg companions were as nonplussed as he was. None of them had ever travelled by wheeled vehicle before. Deprived of the slow trot of their camels, by which they were accustomed to measuring the road, they could not work out where they were. The sandstorm had changed the landscape so completely that they could not use landmarks or simple visual signs as a means of confirming their position. They were hopelessly lost. And out there on the horizon, they could see the dark clouds of another storm rolling its way slowly towards them.

44

The mass of Tifeltout, shorn of darkness, rose gradually out of the countryside in which it was situated, a cross between some fabled city of the half-desert and a construction of Sauron, Tolkien's Dark Lord. Crenellated towers clawed at the stars by night and the sun by day, and their high points snatched at the ochre sand that drifted past on the wind. Below the crenellations, dark windows masked by iron grilles wore a curtain of whitewash on each edge. Tall wooden doorways studded with heavy nails and protected by outsized locks promised entry to some remarkable subterranean world.

To Nick, all this meant nothing. Tifeltout was his son's tomb, and the tomb of a beautiful young woman who might soon have been his daughter-in-law. Even at a distance, it smelled of death and decay. Parts of the vast structure had fallen into ruin, others had been well preserved, but the overall feel was of a lightless dungeon whose rooms and passages must be occupied by djinn and ghosts.

They were hauled inside, then pushed and prodded by el-Mokri's bodyguards. Two more henchmen, both of whom Nick recognized from his visit to the mayor's house, joined them as they came through the door. El-Mokri himself fell behind with Monestier. The two men talked in lowered voices as they walked through corridor after corridor, sending spiders scuttling, small birds flying in desperation for the roof, and awakening little colonies of mouse-tailed bats, five or six at a time, startling them into a mad winged scamper along the ceilings.

They took a different route from the one along which Djamil had led Nick on his previous visit here. There was no point in asking where they were headed: Nick just assumed it would be to somewhere suitable for their execution and burial – a pit, perhaps, where they could be lined up, shot, and covered over with quicklime and earth.

It was not a pit. They came to a door about six foot high, a wooden door studded with large brass nails and locked with no fewer than four heavy-duty padlocks. While his men took care of their prisoners, el-Mokri went to the door and opened the locks with four large keys. He placed the locks to one side and returned the keys to his pocket, then stood back while one of the escort party put his shoulder to the door and pushed it inwards. He went inside for about a minute, and they could see lights building inside the room as he went from lamp to lamp, lighting and brightening them.

Once enough lights were burning, el-Mokri went in, followed by Monestier, Nick and Justine. They scarcely noticed their bearded chaperons file in after them. Their eyes were caught and dazzled by a sight beyond their dreams. Nick and Justine stared open-eyed at it all. Standing behind them now, el-Mokri told them what he'd told no one outside his family before.

'My father,' he began, 'was Allal el-Mokri, Chamberlain to Si T'hami El-Glaoui. In 1942, he was seventy years old by the sun, much more by the moon, and he had served the Glaoui family all his life. I was five. I remember being presented to Glaoui Pasha in that year, before the invasions. We spoke a little, then he sent me in to amuse his wives. I did not know then who he was precisely, but in my child's eyes, he was the Sultan of all Morocco, perhaps the Caliph of all Islam, like Omar or Haroun al-Rashid.

'My father was the Glaouis' most faithful servant. When he was a young man, he was sent to serve them under Hajj Mohammed Tibibt. Not long after that, Hajj Mohammed became *Caid* of Telouet and began the task of building its kasbah into the vast edifice it became. Then his son Madani El-F'ki, and after him his brother T'hami – Glaoui Pasha. All this time, my father had been a faithful servant, and had seen his sons go from oasis to oasis, kasbah to kasbah, to serve T'hami's brothers and allies, and he'd watched his daughters married off with fine dowries. He had grandchildren and great-grandchildren, and with them his cares had multiplied.

'My father worried because, all his life, times had never been very stable. The French had brought some peace and some order to the country, but until recently they'd barely penetrated the lands of the south. He worried because his master, T'hami, had given himself so very closely to the French cause. Beneath the surface, ignored by T'hami, or despised by him, some sort of movement for Moroccan independence was taking hold of ordinary people.'

The mayor saw that they were listening to him attentively enough, in an attempt to understand; but all the time they were looking at the sight before them, as if unable to drag their eyes away. He'd experienced the same thing as a young man, when his father had first brought him to this room and shown him its contents.

'Now, my father had concluded some time earlier that he needed something to fall back on, some money, or some land, and he reckoned he now had what he needed. He was not a fool, however: if none of the promised shipments reached T'hami or his agents, an enquiry would be made and the subterfuge revealed. So he gave instructions to ensure that a portion of the crates and boxes destined for Telouet actually reached Telouet. And he added crates and boxes of his own devising to take the place of those he diverted to Tifeltout.

'No one came to check. Everyone was too occupied with building up an invasion force, a force big enough to drive the Germans and the Vichy French out of North Africa. The money and the supplies came, and before long this room was packed with riches enough for a king. But my father didn't stop there.'

He paused, and they looked at the room's riches in silence. Gold bullion, bars of silver, boxes stuffed with gold dinars, guns, bazookas, flame-throwers, machine-guns, bowls brimming with diamonds, emeralds, rubies, splashes of shadow out of which paintings struggled to return to daylight, Picassos and Modiglianis and Klimts, old French promissory notes scattered in profusion, maps drawn in 1942, English–Arabic phrasebooks ... The list went on and on, the stores went as high as the ceiling and as far back as the rear of the room. Aladdin's cave: but who was the genie, and where was the lamp?

'I think,' el-Mokri went on, 'your friend Dr Monestier should go on from here.'

Monestier, conscious of the cold looks directed at him by Nick and Justine, hesitated before speaking. At last he found some courage and continued the narrative.

'Allal el-Mokri was a friend of my late father's. My father used to treat Glaoui Pasha and his family when they were in Marrakech, and Allal, as Head Chamberlain, was included in this group. Since he was often in Marrakech to look after the palace in Glaoui's absence, and since he had a number of ailments that required ongoing treatment, he came to know my father quite well.

'Shortly before the Allied landings, a number of people, some German, some French, had expressed their concerns to my father. They were worried about what might happen to them if they had to remain in Morocco, and either wanted passage out of the country or somewhere to hide until the worst was over and they could take up new identities. My father wanted to help, and one day, when he was attending Allal el-Mokri, he asked his assistance. El-Mokri saw his chance at once: if these poor people – we'd call them traitors or war criminals now, I suppose – could put up enough money, they'd be free to start new lives at Ouarzazate: here in Tifeltout to start with, then in the town itself.

'My father had an additional motive for doing what he did. My mother had come under suspicion of involvement with the Resistance, and he knew they would come to arrest her any day. When he made the offer of a rat-line to one of his German patients, SS Standartenführer von Hodenberg, he made it part of the deal that my mother be spared.'

'And did nothing to prevent the death of a woman like Marie-Louise Guénaud,' Nick said angrily.

'There was nothing he could have done about that, believe me. Gérard Le Tourneau had decided she and her husband should die. By the time my father knew she was to be arrested, it was already too late.

'Over the next few months, dozens of wanted men and women made their way down this rat-line to safety. Von Hodenberg knew how to divert large amounts of German money, and before long Tifeltout had vast riches, just as you see. After the war, some of the wealth was invested in the United States, and it still brings in a steady income. Some of the refugees went back to Germany and France, but there were warrants out for the arrest of the others, so they stayed and brought their families here, or set up families. Most of that generation are dead now, of course, but their children live on here.

'My father never had to leave Marrakech. He was never suspected of involvement in anything untoward. His main justification for what he did was that he was free to take whatever funds he needed in order to establish his free clinic for the poor of Marrakech. You've benefited from its facilities, you know what good it does. It's why I stayed on there myself, to continue his life's work, to make amends. It's why I brought you here today. I can't let that work be destroyed, not for anyone. And it's why all this has to stop here. Your investigation, anyone else's investigation.'

'My son . . .' Nick began.

'Your son came here snooping around, asking too many questions,' el-Mokri broke in. 'He had to die. Don't ask for justice. If Germany had won the war, there might have been some justice in the world. But they were beaten, and the British and French and Jews were in control again. At least this wealth gives us a chance of fighting back, of wiping the smirk off all your faces.'

There was a movement at the door. A young man had entered, blond-haired and pale-skinned. Nick was surprised when he spoke to el-Mokri in fluent Arabic.

'Everything's ready, sir. He doesn't want to wait in case the weather gets worse.'

Justine whispered a quick translation to Nick.

'You've seen all I brought you here to see,' said the mayor. 'Now it's time to put all this foolishness to an end. If you know any prayers, you'd be best to start saying them now.'

45

They were led, as before, down winding corridors devoid of all but a grey aquarium light. Monestier went ahead with el-Mokri. The light step that Nick had previously admired in the doctor had vanished, to be replaced by a half-shuffle and an air of weariness that aged him by a decade or more. Nick took Justine's hand and leaned across and kissed her. As he drew back, he whispered for her alone to hear.

'Don't give up hope. If they keep us long enough before shooting us . . .'

She returned his kiss.

'They won't keep us lying about in some dungeon.'

'All we need is a little more time. Believe me.'

'What have you got up your sleeve?'

'There's nothing up my sleeve. But . . .'

Just then they came to a narrow door. The blond man, whose name turned out to be Hamid, addressed the locks fervently with a long brass key. All open, he pulled back on the door's single leaf, and it was as though he had opened a furnace, for the heat and light of the sun came streaming into their faces and on down the long corridor that had led them here.

They came out onto a dusty courtyard scoured white by constant exposure to the summer sun. Heat bounced back in ripples from its beaten surface, and the light was reflected directly into their eyes. They were joined by their escorts and by el-Mokri and Monestier.

Then Justine turned, and she knew they were finished. Not many yards away, there stood a tall object with familiar features, a guillotine, its polished blade dancing in a hundred shafts of light.

'No!' Monestier's voice was shrill in the all-encompassing silence. 'This wasn't what we agreed! You said they'd be sent on their way once things quietened down.'

El-Mokri did not answer. At the far end of the courtyard, at a spot no one could see into on account of the sun, something moved, fluttered, and moved again. A voice rang out, weak but audible, speaking in good French tinged with a foreign accent. German, perhaps, thought Justine.

'Whatever he may have said to you, you can be sure he was lying through his little yellow teeth. Did you really think we would let the Englishman go free, that we could set him loose to start his interfering all over again? Or the woman? You did your duty, Dr Monestier, and you will have your reward as usual; but be very careful whom you speak to and what you say from now on.'

Monestier stood like a child who has been rebuked by a feared yet respected teacher. Nick strained his eyes to look in the direction from which the voice had come, and some moments later he made out a shuffling form coming towards him. An old man moving with sticks, wisps of white hair on a shrunken skull, a face like a corpse's, eyes bright with life. Nick scarcely noticed these things. What he noticed was the SS uniform, a little shabby now, a few sizes too big for its wearer's diminished frame. At a leap, he guessed who the old man was.

They waited while the SS man made his slow progress towards them. His leather-shod feet grated on the coarse desert sand that blanketed the courtyard. He stopped once for breath. Nick reckoned he must be ninety or more. Finally, he stopped about a yard away from Nick.

'I think you know my name already, Commander. Word gets around, doesn't it? SS Standartenführer Gustav von Hodenberg at your service. And yours, mademoiselle. This won't take long: I've no wish to torture you.'

'Let the woman go. She's not involved in this. All she tried to do was get me out of the country. She won't tell anyone about this. Monestier can vouch for her. You can trust her.'

Von Hodenberg hesitated, looking Justine up and down. The days were long gone when the sight of a beautiful young woman would fill him with pleasure. Monestier had told them of the relationship that had developed between the Englishman and Mademoiselle Buoy.

'I leave it up to you,' the German said. 'One of you must stay and face the consequences; the other will be free to go once the execution has taken place.'

Nick and Justine exchanged glances. It was clear what they had to do.

'Neither of us will leave,' Justine said. 'Just get on with what you mean to do.'

'Very well.' Von Hodenberg nodded to el-Mokri. 'Tell your men to go ahead.'

More gunmen joined them. Two of them tied Nick's and Justine's hands behind their backs.

'I'm sorry I got you into all this,' Nick said. Justine's was one death he did not know how to face. 'If I hadn't . . .'

She smiled at him.

'If you hadn't asked for my help up there at Taddert, I'd never have got to know you, never have fallen in love with you. I can think of better endings, but I don't regret a thing.'

Their guards marched them towards the guillotine. The mechanism had already been tested. The blade hung at the top of its frame, its trajectory simple and fatal.

One of the guards grabbed Nick and a second strapped him to the *bascule*. As he did so, a sound echoed across the valley. Nick recognized it straight away: a helicopter engine, followed by another. Military choppers, by the strength of the sound, and coming this way at speed. His heart leaped to his throat.

The night before, Nick had summoned up old favours, every one he could think of. What it boiled down to was the chance – the faintest chance – of a rescue mission by a UK Special Forces unit headed by an SAS colonel with whom Nick had frequently liaised on anti-terrorist business. Logistics apart, it had been a long shot.

'Hurry!' Von Hodenberg's voice rang out and was at once swept away by the growing roar of heavy rotors. The guard next to Nick turned the *bascule* and sent him forward so that his head was ready to be clamped in the jaws of the guillotine. Now it only remained to pull the lever that released the blade.

'Nooooo!' A long scream came from Justine's lips. 'Don't you see it's too late? Better for you to let him live!'

But her words were muffled by the choppers that were moving overhead already, blotting out the sunshine and filling the courtyard with shadow.

Monestier ran forward and started a desperate struggle to pull Nick's body out of the machine. His body stretched forward over Nick's, as though in an attempt to protect it. Behind him el-Mokri gestured to his man, and the blade slipped from its moorings and dropped with tremendous speed, striking the doctor across the shoulders and cutting half through his torso. Beneath him, Nick was showered in blood.

Some of the guards began shooting upwards, trying to hit the figures rappelling down cords suspended from the first chopper. A split-second response came from the body of the helicopter, accurate assault rifle fire that picked el-Mokri's bodyguards off one by one. By the time the commandos were on the ground, only el-Mokri and von Hodenberg were still standing. Justine ran to the guillotine, screaming for help.

Within moments, Nick was being released from his predicament. Justine, also freed from her bonds, grabbed him, soaked in blood as he was, and clung to him, and kissed him. All the strength had gone out of him, as though it was his own blood that had been poured out on the courtyard floor, and he felt free of all emotion, free of regret and need and fear. He found her mouth and kissed her through a film of Monestier's blood. His breath found its way into her, and her breath went through him, and they were all one or the other needed.

It took half an hour for the assault force to take control of the kasbah. Nick and Justine were helped to some living quarters, where they could wash off some of the blood.

Soon after that, Nick's colonel turned up.

'Well, Nick, it looks as if we turned up just in time. You do look a dreadful mess.'

'You're forgetting your manners, Ronnie. This young lady is Mademoiselle Justine Buoy. Justine, this is Colonel Ronnie Manning, one of Britain's finest. I take it you've found the treasure chamber, Ronnie?'

'If it isn't the treasure chamber, I don't like to think what else is in store. God, Nick, you certainly pick them.'

'This one picked me, Ron. I never . . . Ron, do me another favour. Find my boy. Find Peter and his fiancée. I want to bring them home. Can you do that?'

'We'll drop everything else. I'm sorry, I should have had the lads onto it before.'

'Your lads have done more than enough for me. But I'm not going home without Peter.'

They found a lot of bodies, and young men who looked like old men in dungeons that had been built by the Glaouis. Pete and Daisy were still wearing the clothes they'd been stabbed in, and still had their personal effects. It took several hours of digging, but they found them in the end. The embassy, still in a tizz after hearing what had gone on, was left with little choice but to make arrangements to bring its citizens home with honour and dignity. Later, when the ambassador visited Tifeltout and was shown the extent of what had been stolen from the Allied powers, the embassy abandoned its protests.

Nick was back in England by then, and Justine with him.

They attended two funerals, and Nick made a completion of sorts. He still felt a great emptiness where Pete had been, but when he thought of death he gripped Justine's waiting hand and made contact with the living world again.

Si M'hamed el-Mokri was in prison in Marrakech, awaiting trial on a mountain of charges. His treasury gone, his influence washed away, his followers scattered, he had no friends in high places and a tribe of enemies camped at his gates.

Meanwhile, in a somewhat cleaner cell in Berlin, an old man with little but memories sat at a desk, scratching from day to day the justifications for his crimes. He was not expected to live long enough to be tried. All around him in his whitewashed cell, the shades of his victims circled and sang, and during the long hours of night he saw them come to him, as pitiless as he had been with them.

'Where will we live?'

'What? Live? Here in Oxford, of course.'

'I have a home in Marrakech.'

He pulled her to his side of the sofa.

'You can sell it, and come here to live. In this house. It's a lovely city. You just have to ignore the students.'

'I don't want to live here.'

'You like the house, don't you?'

'Of course I do.'

'And you think the city's magical, don't you?'

'Of course.'

'Well, then . . .'

'Nick, if you weren't in it, Oxford would be vile. This

house would be ordinary. I stay here because I want to stay with you.'

'Well, then . . .'

'But you're taking advantage.'

He put his fingers on her lips.

'Of course I am. But I have an even better idea. How about spending six months of the year in Oxford, and six in Marrakech? Would that do?'

'Could we afford to do that? My business over there is pretty well finished.'

'You mean, it was finished. I had a letter this morning, from France.'

'From?'

'Reims. Nathalie's family over there are shitting themselves. They made so many efforts to stop the truth getting out about Gérard and Béatrice, and now I'm in a position to destroy their little game for ever. But it seems there was a substantial legacy which should have been paid to Marie-Louise, and they are suddenly of the opinion that it should go to me, in memory of Nathalie and Peter. I see absolutely no reason why we should let them off the hook. How would you like to be a director of Déjà Vu Tours Limited?'

'How would you like to take all my clothes off and take me to bed?'

'You haven't been listening to a word, have you?'

'No.'